Carmen Reid is the author of the bestselling novels *Three in a Bed, Did the Earth Move?, How Was it For You?* and *Up All Night.*

After working as a journalist in London she moved to Glasgow, Scotland where she looks after one husband, two children, a puppy, three goldfish and writes almost all the rest of the time.

For more information on Carmen Reid and her books, visit her website at www.carmenreid.com

Also by Carmen Reid

THREE IN A BED
DID THE EARTH MOVE?
HOW WAS IT FOR YOU?
UP ALL NIGHT

and published by Corgi Books

THE PERSONAL SHOPPER

Carmen Reid

CORGI BOOKS

TRANSWORLD PUBLISHERS
61–63 Uxbridge Road, London W5 5SA
a division of The Random House Group Ltd
www.booksattransworld.co.uk

THE PERSONAL SHOPPER
A CORGI BOOK: 9780552154819

First publication in Great Britain
Corgi edition published 2007

Addresses for Random House Group Ltd companies outside the UK
can be found at: www.randomhouse.co.uk
The Random House Group Ltd Reg. No. 954009

The Random House Group Ltd makes every effort to ensure
that the papers used in its books are made from trees that have
been legally sourced from well-managed and credibly certified
forests. Our paper procurement policy can be found at:
www.randomhouse.co.uk/paper.htm

Typeset in 11/14pt Palatino by
Kestrel Data, Exeter, Devon
Printed in the UK by
CPI Cox & Wyman, Reading, RG1 8EX

4 6 8 10 9 7 5

This one's for
Diana
and my mum

Chapter One

The first of Svetlana's new outfits for spring:

Dress in vibrant purple, green and white (Pucci)
Wide green suede belt (Pucci)
Purple boots with rapier heels (Manolo)
White cashmere coat (MaxMara)
Green handbag (Chloé)
Total est. cost: £2,800

'Sexy, but ladylike'

Annie Valentine, senior personal shopper at the five floors of London retail heaven, called The Store (because less is oh-so-much-much-more), watched Svetlana Wisneski emerge from behind the fuchsia velvet curtain of the changing room. The silk jersey dress clung to the curves of the billionaire's wife and, in three-inch heels, she towered like a blonde superhuman.

The effect was breathtaking, but Annie, who always exceeded her monthly commission targets and almost always scooped the 10 per cent bonus for highest overall sales figures, immediately read the slightly dissatisfied look on her VIP client's high-cheekboned, high-maintenance face.

'Not working for you, darlin'?' Annie asked. 'Not channelling spring, lambs frolicking, Easter bonnets or April in Paris?'

Svetlana shook her head gravely.

'Never mind . . . have no fear . . . we will find it for you here . . .' Annie singsonged, flicking at speed through a rail packed with sensational dresses – Chloé, Missoni, Temperley, Gucci, Versace – many so new in they were not yet out of their plastic wrappers. She pulled out another stunning day dress and offered: 'Mmmm . . . how about Pucci? This could be delicious.'

'We trrrry,' came Svetlana's deep-voiced reply.

No-one left Annie's two hours of personal attention in anything less than the perfect outfit – more usually perfect outfits – blowing three, four, even five times as much as they'd planned to spend because her advice, delivered in a down-to-earth, no-nonsense, London-born-and-bred accent, was so persuasively excellent.

Annie shopped for her customers, for her friends and for herself with the ruthless zeal of a Wall Street stockbroker on her last day of probation.

Nothing was too much trouble for this gold standard professional: she scoured every glossy, white, down-lit corner of The Store for the exactly right item and she knew every department's designer collections right down to its 'diffusion' thongs.

'*Just for you, mind!*' this bustling, tireless, working wonder could track down a coat direct from the atelier, charm grumpy Italian boot-makers into parting with the last size 41 available in that style. She could even, in a wardrobe emergency, cut a deal with the tiny Brighton boutique which had the only other one of *those* dresses in a size 12.

This afternoon's client, statuesque Svetlana, was a cherished customer. Married to the richest pot-bellied, lumpy-looking Russian in London, Svetlana was one of a select handful of shoppers entitled to a free limousine ride home with the boot full of purchases.

Today, early in February, the everlasting winter sales were almost over and the bright new Spring collections were finally breaking through in shades of palest lemon, baby pink, green, green and more green, ultraviolet and sky blue. Svetlana was in to shop for the new season as early as possible because she liked to be first and to have the pick of the new.

For close to an hour, Annie had walked this elite customer and her dumpy personal assistant Olga round every one of The Store's glittering floors. They'd begun in the dazzling cosmetics hall where assistants had brought out compacts and testers and sample sizes, trilling the delights of spring's 'fresh new palette'.

While Svetlana had let herself be lavishly made up and manicured, Olga had scathingly pronounced the shimmery nude polish 'almost invisible' and 'far too expensive'.

'She works for him,' Svetlana had whispered in explanation to Annie when Olga was out of earshot.

'Who?' Annie had asked, suspecting the answer.

'Potato-face,' came Svetlana's low voice as she examined her Ocean Spray eyelids and Blossom no. 5 lips in the magnifying mirror. 'He thinks I spend too much money and *she* is spying on me.'

'No!' Annie assured her, although, much to her continued disappointment, she knew nothing of life as a trophy wife, whereas Svetlana was on her third and most wealthy husband. She'd traded up spouses the way other women trade up houses. It was obvious to Annie that if she wanted advice on finding a rich husband (and boy, could she do with one, her eye-watering credit card bills had come in this morning), this was the woman to ask. Surely it was just a matter of the right question at the right moment to get the conversation started?

Up the glass escalators they'd sailed, into white-marble-floored designer heaven where clothes were hung and lit as preciously as works of art . . . and cost as much too.

Should a customer be so foolish as to display any shock at the astronomical price tags, the best sales staff would gush: 'But it's such a unique piece. Fabulous quality. You'll wear it for years.' The condescending ones would cock an eyebrow and ask: 'Oh? Too expensive for Madam?' in a way that made Annie want to shriek: As if *you* could afford it!

But then the girls here did buy the clothes. They used their staff discount, maxed their plastic and shared cramped studio flats to wear McQueen and Jimmy Choo on their nights out. It made no sense but was unmistakably glamorous.

Once Svetlana had toured the new collections of the designers she regularly chose – Yves Saint Laurent and Givenchy for dressing up, Donna Karan for casual –

Annie had tried to entice her into some different, more colourful, directions: Missoni, Pucci, Matthew Williamson.

The billionaire's wife had looked mournfully through the rails: 'No, no . . . well . . . maybe . . . I don't know if Igor will like it,' she'd declared. 'He likes sexy but lady-like, always ladylike.' As if, over the two years they'd shopped together, Annie hadn't realized. 'Sexy but lady-like' was Svetlana's mantra.

Annie was not usually a fan of the lazy, indulgent and spoiled wealthy wives she regularly dressed, but she was beginning to understand that Svetlana was an exception. Svetlana's marriage was her career.

She hosted bi-weekly dinners and monthly cocktail parties, she attended endless business receptions, made charming small talk for hours, always looked impeccably elegant, and all for the benefit of Igor and his empire. Svetlana had staff to organize: cooks, housekeepers, cleaners and maids. She had five houses in three countries to furnish, refurbish and decorate. Clearly, it was a demanding, full-time job being Mrs Igor Wisneski. But as she'd confided to Annie – when Olga was once again out of earshot – she was approaching 35, and in need of all the help she could get to maintain her position. Although Svetlana was tall, naturally ice blonde and breathtaking, not to mention the mother of the gas baron's two sons and heirs, despite an extremely skilful mid-section facelift and perky breast enhancement, her place as drop dead gorgeous status wife was never taken for granted.

Annie knew the former Miss Ukraine was working tirelessly to maintain the interest of Potato-face, enduring a gruelling daily workout with a martial arts expert, fortnightly colonics and all manner of other invasive beauty injections and treatments.

She'd once pointed out the faint creases on her cheeks as 'blow job lines' with a telling roll of the eyes.

Now she stood before Annie, with a far more satisfied expression because she could see she was a knockout in the tight, belted Pucci.

Hand on slinky hip, Svetlana considered herself studiously in the three-way mirrors before finally announcing: 'I like it,' which in her serious, thoughtful manner was the highest accolade she gave. 'I don't know why I'm ever unsure about your ideas, Ahnnah' – she'd never got the hang of 'Annie' – 'You are always, always correct.'

'You need a pale coat for that dress,' Annie assured her. 'I have a white cashmere, knee-length, beautiful cut. I'll have it brought up along with a new Chloé – only in this morning – to hang off your arm.' She winked at Svetlana who, just like Annie, could never resist a soft, dreamy leather bag, jangling with gold links, buckles and the latest 'must have' logo. Fortunately, unlike Annie, Svetlana never baulked at a four-figure price tag.

'Erm . . . sorry to interrupt.' Paula, the other personal shopper on today, put her head round the curtain which separated Annie's section from hers.

Annie shook her head and raised her eyebrows: 'Urgent?' she asked.

'Your bid's been exceeded on the vintage Miss Selfridge . . .' Paula began.

Although she had primed Paula to keep an eye on the items she was bidding for on the internet today, this news wasn't important enough to justify abandoning Svetlana just as she turned her mind to new handbags.

'Thanks, but don't worry about it,' Annie instructed, and with a swish of 18 inches of genuine Asian hair extension, painstakingly braided into hundreds of tiny plaits each with a bead sewn at the end, Paula was gone.

Svetlana had firmly decided on three evening gowns, five day dresses, two trouser suits, a coat, four pairs of shoes and two handbags. She was debating the Manolo boots, a ball dress and 'something to cheer Olga up' when Paula appeared at the curtain again.

'Help!' she mouthed at Annie, who gave a little sigh. She suspected this was about Paula's next client. Paula wasn't exactly bad at her job, she was just young (24), inexperienced, and so obsessed with fashion that she couldn't translate what was hot into what would really suit and work for someone.

She would quite happily stuff a chunky 54-year-old barrister into Juicy Couture and studded gold mules because 'Wow, that is so now! So happening!'

Usually Annie tried to make sure Paula's clients were of the rake-thin, fashion police variety who wanted to be talked through combining a baby doll with a tulip skirt, gaucho belt and cork wedges by an expert, but this afternoon Annie had Svetlana, so Paula had to look after Martha Cooper, a new client.

'Can you excuse me for just a few minutes?' Annie asked Svetlana, who was turning from side to side in front of the mirror trying to decide whether the handbag in her left hand was a better match with the coat than the handbag in her right hand.

'Of courrrrse.'

'Definitely the green,' Annie pronounced and turned to follow Paula into the cream-carpeted reception area.

There she saw Martha, a very tall, slouchy late thirties, who had turned up for her consultation in the universal uniform of very busy stay-at-home mum: washed-out jeans, washed-out T-shirt, washed-out face, long hair with four inches of root, green gym shoes and Martha's own personal touch, a truly diabolical grey parka. No wonder Paula had panicked.

For a second, it struck Annie that such a lack of care about appearance, fashion and what people thought of you was almost enviable. Then she imagined how she would look without heels, red lipstick, foundation and a full head of blond highlights . . . and the moment passed.

'Hi, Martha, I'm Annie Valentine, lovely to meet you.' Annie held out a hand and treated Martha to her most reassuring smile. 'Have you been looking around?'

'Er . . . yes . . . And now I'm even more worried,' came Martha's reply.

Annie was used to dressing all kinds of women: WAGs, rich wives, wealthy daughters, business high-flyers, fashion mavens and of course, women who'd clearly lost their way somewhere along the line. But she hadn't had such a bad case in her suite for some time. Poor Martha, she'd wandered the floors, clocked the price tags, made no sense at all of the more complicated garments and now here she was, faced with one of the most glamorous shop assistants she'd ever encountered: Paula, as lithe and elegant as a young Naomi Campbell, complete with nutcracker buns and ultraviolet talons. Although Annie was a little more real looking, she

14

was still extremely groomed and elegant: a shimmering (originally mouse-brown) blonde, expertly made up with perfect brows, French manicure and light tan, tastefully dressed, high-heeled and utterly convincing in her role of persuading endless women and occasional men to part with extraordinary amounts of money in an effort to look more stylish and attractive.

Martha was probably now convinced she did not belong here, but in an episode of *What Not To Wear*.

'You are going to have such fun with us today,' Annie told her with a genuinely kind smile but still keeping hold of Martha's hand, so that she couldn't bolt.

In fact, Annie loved clients like Martha. You had to start slowly with the most sober clothes The Store had to offer, but these clients were always the most grateful and the most enduringly loyal because Annie helped them to work out all the things a woman needed to know about her look – ideally by 20, but definitely by 30.

By 30, according to Annie, every woman should have put in the hours in the fitting room to work out the colours, the shapes and the cuts that flattered. Round neck or V? Knee-length or longer? High waistbands or low? Shades of red and orange or blues and purples?

By 30, every woman should also have grasped the power of one great accessory and have the fundamentals of a personal style in place.

Great dressers also understood the importance of trademark items, such as Princess Diana's blue blazer; Mrs Thatcher's pussycat bow; Posh's bustier; Liz Hurley's white jeans.

These were the secrets, the dressing lessons, which Annie could reveal.

'Great height,' Annie told Martha straight away.

'Pros and cons . . .' was Martha's reply. 'Sleeves . . .' She made a chopping motion close to her elbow. 'Dress waistbands come in under my armpits,' she gestured.

'Don't worry, we'll work with it. Follow me into my boudoir.' She finally let go of Martha's hand, trusting her to follow.

In the airy, opaque-windowed room at the heart of the Personal Shopping area, Annie and Martha sat down together on the fuchsia velvet sofa for a preliminary chat, while Paula hovered close by.

'So, how old are your children?' Annie wondered, not needing to ask if Martha had any.

'Oh . . . Six, five and just turned two.'

'You must be busy,' Annie sympathized.

'I must be insane!' was Martha's response.

'And are you going back to work?' was Annie's next question as this was usually the reason harassed toddler mothers appeared in her suite in a panic.

'Yes . . . first job in seven years. Three days a week in Personnel . . . nothing from Life Before Children fits . . . and I've no idea what people wear in offices any more. It seems to be all cardigans, sparkly skirts and high heels.' Martha ended her explanation with a plaintive: 'Help!'

'OK. Well . . .' Annie was almost rubbing her hands. This was going to be easy – not to mention a joy to put right. Martha was tall, still a size 12-ish and with the right clothes and a bit of care and attention, she would scrub up nicely. She wouldn't recognize herself.

'Paula is your guide for today, so' – Annie shot Paula her 'pay attention' look – 'she is going to help you buy *not* a trouser suit. No, no! Sooo over! But trousers which fit and flatter. I'd recommend grey, straight legs – not too narrow, not too wide – then a short, *toning*, but not matching, bang-up-to-date, swingy jacket with a single button. OK?

You need to find day shoes that fit well and that you love in a colour to go with the suit. Now, Martha, you are not allowed brown or black and I'm not even going to mention navy. I'm sorry, those are my rules!' but she winked at Martha, so it wasn't too bossy. 'Go for gold, green, purple, red, orange, yellow . . . Something lovely. Who needs black?

So, once you have the shoes,' she went on, 'you're to find three knockout tops which go with the trousers, jacket and the footwear. Three is the minimum. No slacking, we make you work here. Then, your final mission for today, should you choose to accept, is to find a colourful skirt that goes with all three tops, the shoes and the short jacket. OK? Got me?'

Martha and Paula nodded obediently.

'This way, I promise you'll be beautifully dressed for the office every single day. Obviously if you want to look at raincoats, umbrellas, boots, cardigans . . . or *make-up*,' there was a noticeable stress on this final item, 'Paula can advise, but get the basics in place first. You can always come back to us. In fact we'd love you to come back. We're a bit like the dentist, we like you in for regular check-ups.

Now . . . just one last thing, darlin', then I really have to shoot back to my other client, how are you planning to . . . er . . . style your hair for work?' Annie had considered the question carefully and had decided this was the most tactful way to frame: *For God's sake, woman, get a decent cut and colour!*

'Style my hair? Style . . .' Martha repeated the word slowly as if it was foreign to her, 'my hair?'

Annie nodded encouragingly, but wasn't expecting the confession that followed.

Martha gave a deep sigh then blurted out: 'All I'd like is to be free of headlice just long enough to remember to make an appointment and actually get to the hair-dresser's.'

'Oh! Oh no!' Annie, who'd once had to deal with an 'outbreak' on her son's head, at least had some sym-pathy, but Paula had taken several steps backwards and now looked as if she wanted to run screaming from the room.

'Oh, I'm clear at the moment,' Martha added quickly, sensing The Store's personal shopping staff weren't as used to talk of headlice as her mother and toddler group.

'I'd forgotten about headlice,' Annie said, trying to resist the urge to scratch her head at the thought. 'My children are older now. So . . . well . . . better get the haircut as soon as you can, before they pop up again. Right!' Annie had to get back to Svetlana, no doubt about it. 'Off you go, you two. And make sure I get a look at the finished result!'

'Now what?!' Annie wanted to know when, twenty minutes later, Paula was back in her section again. 'I can't do your job for you!' she hissed, losing patience.

'Donna! In your office,' Paula said huffily.

'What!' This was not good news. Annie tried to see

as little of her witch of a boss as possible, but there were several days in every month, carefully recorded in Annie's diary, when Donna was a hormonal madwoman who had to be avoided at all costs.

'She's logged on to your computer!' Paula warned.

No doubt about it, Annie would have to go, and just as she'd finally begun to hit Svetlana for some priceless new husband advice.

'I am so, so sorry,' Annie told the Russians. 'There's a tiny problem I have to sort out.'

'No matter,' Svetlana assured her. 'We are finished here. Everything is decided. We get ready to go now.'

'OK, I'll see you in a minute,' Annie said as she rushed out of the changing room towards the windowless matchbox of an office which housed her desk, files, company computer and, most importantly, personal laptop, which right now was plugged into The Store's internet connection and up and running on her eBay homepage.

Personal shopping at The Store was Annie's day job. Around it, she crammed in private home makeovers via her Dress to Express service, then there was the Annie V Trading Station on eBay which did great business selling designer items: BNWT (brand new with tags), new, nearly new, secondhand and vintage. Where did Annie source these items? Her own staff-discounted wardrobe, The Store's sale rail, the bargain bins of other shops, junk shops, charity shops, other eBay auctions and sites. Annie had a saleswoman's eye for a great bargain and a profitable resale.

Personally, she never bought anything at full price: not a haircut (her hairdresser came to all her sale pre-previews), not a bottle of shampoo (bulk buy on the internet), not a tin of beans (she knew what was on offer at every supermarket and cash and carry within a 20-mile radius of her home), not a car (secondhand, Christmas Eve, fantastic deal). And she was generous with her knowledge: family and friends all benefited from her bargains. Everyone who knew her well had a cupboard at home stuffed with tinned tomatoes, disposable barbecues, Christmas cards, jumbo boxes of nude hold-ups . . . and all manner of other goods, which she'd secured for them at knockdown rates.

'Donna! Hi there!' Annie did a passable impersonation of a friendly greeting. 'Sorry, we've both got clients in at the moment, but can I help you with anything?'

Donna, who'd been Retail Manager, Women's Fashion, for five months now, did not take her short 'squoval' orange nails from the keyboard. She carried on typing, eyes in narrow black Prada frames, fixed to the screen in front of her.

Despite the charming floral Issa dress wrapped round her lithe body, Donna, with her long dark hair scraped back from her face, still looked ready for the kill.

'Annie V's Trading Station,' she snarled. 'My goodness, what a lot of items I recognize here. Isn't that one of our latest Mulberry bags? And look, it's about to be sold for a hundred and fifty pounds more than its RRP.'

'It's come from a client who's fed up with it already,' Annie explained. 'You know how fickle some of them are. Look, this is all totally above board, Donna, I can even show you my Trading Station tax returns.'

'Of course, I'm sure it is. There's just one slight problem, Annie.' Donna turned to glare at her now, her

Botoxed brow doing its best to scrunch into a stern warning, while Annie tried not to wonder yet again why Donna didn't wax the noticeable moustache from her upper lip. Was it a lesbian thing?

'You're doing this at work,' Donna snapped. 'And you've already had two verbal warnings from me about this.'

'Verbal warnings?' Was snakewoman trying to insinuate that previous conversations about Annie's internet activity counted as official warnings?

'We've had several *discussions* about this, yes,' Annie agreed, wishing some ball-breaking lawyer, maybe one of those slick American ones from the TV, was by her side. 'And I've explained to you that I am not doing this at work. My computer is on, open at the web-page. When I have the odd moment, you know, tea break . . . nipping out for lunch . . . I have a quick look. I'm not causing my work a problem in any way whatsoever. Why don't you look over my sales figures for this month, Donna?' Annie dared her. 'Complain to me if there's a problem there.'

'It's not just about sales figures,' Donna countered. 'You're setting other members of staff a bad example. So I'm giving you this.' She picked up a white envelope and handed it to Annie. 'It's a written warning, so we're both clear.'

'What!!!'

The devious, scheming cow!

It had been obvious to Annie from Donna's first week that she was the kind of manager who actually felt threatened by a really good member of staff, rather than supported. But much as she suspected Donna would love to be rid of her, so she could rule the roost without the slightest opposition, Annie had always thought her awe-inspiring sales power would protect her. Now, holding a written warning in her hand, she wasn't so sure.

'And what about Paula?' Donna launched straight into a new line of attack. 'She's not pulling her weight. You have another month to train her up properly for this job or we'll have to find someone else.'

Considering Paula had been chosen for the position by Donna, and Donna alone, this was somewhat unfair, but Annie had come to expect nothing less from her.

The mobile beside the computer began to ring. Annie had two mobiles and as this was her business phone, her heart sank as Donna snatched it up and barked: 'Hello?' into the receiver.

'Yes . . . aha . . . oh really? . . . Well, that's very interesting . . . No. I'll get her to call you back.' Donna clicked off the phone and glared at Annie: 'That was your estate agent. He wants to talk to you about a "very exciting new investment opportunity". I suggest you call him back when you've read your warning and finished for the day.' There was no mistaking the withering look which came with this.

Just then, Svetlana appeared at the office door. 'Ahnnah, we are ready to leave,' she said, demanding immediate attention. 'Could you arrange for everything to be taken to the back door? Olga and I will go and meet the car.'

Annie kissed Svetlana and then Olga four times, the Russian way, and thanked them profusely for their visit. She was thanked profusely in return.

Svetlana, as if noticing Donna for the first time, asked her: 'Are you Ahnnah's boss?'

When Donna gave a curt nod in reply, Svetlana enthused: 'She is wonderful. The best stylist in London. Rrrreally. Be nice to her, because if she ever leaves The Store, I will leave with her.'

Donna's expression darkened, but she did her best to force a smile.

Then, in a small, carefree gesture of thanks, Svetlana handed last season's Chloé handbag to Annie with the words: 'I don't want it any more. You have it. For your business. I am very admiring of your enterprise.'

'No, no, darlin', I really couldn't . . .' Annie began.

'Yes, of courrrrrse,' Svetlana insisted, 'and there's something inside for you. Special information, Ahnnah, because it is time for you to find New Husband. It's not good to be alone for long time.'

Before Annie could even say thank you, Svetlana had swept out of the suite towards her packed limousine and her luxury life in Mayfair.

The look of genuine pain on Donna's face was a joy to behold, but it didn't stop her from snapping: 'What a walking cliché that woman is.'

Chapter Two

Becca Wolstonecroft at Parents' Evening:

Grey T-shirt (M&S)
Pink fleece (M&S)
Grey (formerly black) chinos (Gap)
Grey (formerly white) underwear (M&S)
Short black socks (husband's)
In misguided attempt to disguise the above:
Cream fake fur coat (Xmas gift six years ago)
Total est. cost: £220

'Good God! How much?!!'

Shortly before closing time, Annie left The Store with two luxurious handbags over one shoulder: her own pumpkin-coloured Chloé which now held Svetlana's, slipped into a protective cloth inside. She hadn't decided yet whether she was going to keep it or sell it.

On her other shoulder was an enormous tote bag filled with the day's other treasures: three Tupperware boxes crammed with leftovers from the staff canteen for supper, eight bottles of Clarins facial oil (out of date), twelve (last season's) Estée Lauder lipsticks, one pair of (damaged) men's trousers, bought at a snip. She'd fix them herself and sell BNWT.

Donna's warning letter, which told her she faced dismissal for any further 'irregular activities', had been read then scrunched up in fury. It was now buried underneath all the other items because Annie was doing her best not to think about life without her job at The Store. She was her family's sole provider. Yes, she worked very hard to supplement her main income, but if Donna pushed her off the tightrope, there was no safety net.

Her personal mobile began to ring in a rap version of the *Star Wars* theme, because her nine-year-old son, Owen, had doctored it again. On the line was her 14-nearly-15-year-old daughter Lana (what you get at 35 if you think babies are soooo cute when you're 20 and madly in love).

'Hi, Lana,' Annie answered, 'you're reminding me, aren't you? But I haven't forgotten, honest. I'm out on the dot and I will be sitting down with your form teacher at seven fifteen p.m. Honest, honest, cross my heart and hope to die. I will not be late,' Annie assured her daughter, 'promise.'

'And you're to get me out of the charity thing, OK?' Lana was using her whiny voice. 'Speak to Owen's teacher about that.'

'I'll think about it,' Annie told her, not promising anything further.

She trotted briskly, on two-and-a-half-inch heels, towards the underground station, passing the kind of fashion mistakes that made her want to stop people on the street: 'Darlin', skinny jeans? Tucked into boots? That can make Kate Moss look a bit porky. On you, it's the Tamworth Two: a pair of pigs fighting to break free.'

'A furry gilet, babes??? Three years after all the other ones were rounded up and shot?'

Annie was heading for Highgate, one of the nicest and oldest parts of north London, where she lived at last. Hundreds of years ago, Highgate had begun life as a hamlet and there were still flagstone pavements and listed Georgian houses with lumpy glass windows and sagging oak beams. Although it was now bisected by a main road permanently clogged with nose-to-tail traffic, Highgate still felt (ah! She could hear the estate agent's pitch) 'villagey'. The high street had real shops as well as a Tesco Metro, banks and estate agents. People moved there, fell in love with the place and tended to stay, making it slightly more neighbourly than many other parts of London.

Annie had always wanted to live in Highgate, despite the outrageous prices, and she'd achieved the cramped three-bedroomed flat she shared with her two children through her personal property development programme.

It was testament to her unflagging energy, not to mention her dislike of settling down or staying still, that she'd moved home eight times in the past ten years. Always buying the run-down, junky places no-one else wanted and using cheap tradesmen, her own basic, but tireless, DIY skills and, above all, her unerringly great taste to turn in a profit and move on to something just a little bit better and a little bit closer to her dream destination.

Rotten carpets, mouldy bathrooms, dodgy roofs, rattling windows, rodent infestations, dry rot: none of these things could frighten Annie any longer, she'd lived through them all and come out the other side with equity.

In her current flat, she'd just had a fabulous (heavily discounted) limestone bathroom installed complete with rolltop bath and steam sauna shower; now she was preparing to sell for maximum profit in the spring and move on to the next doer-upper, even though she'd be really sorry to say goodbye to the shower. Well . . . in fact, she'd be really sorry to say goodbye to this flat, for many reasons, and she suspected it was going to be hard to convince the children it was a good idea . . . but, like it or not, she needed the money.

Heels clacking on the pavement, she headed from Highgate underground station, not in the direction of her home, but towards St Vincent's, the excellent, although totally exclusive and smug, private day school her two children attended.

Sending her children to St Vincent's at a cost of over £2,000 a month was what kept Annie focused and motivated through her long days of wheeling, dealing, advising and selling. She'd been brought up, the oldest of three girls, in a much less inviting corner of London by a single, non-stop-working mother who had sent her girls to the local primary and then the local comprehensive until one by one they'd hit the critical age of 14. Then, chiropodist (although she preferred 'podiatrist') Fern had used her overtime, her savings and their natural intelligence to secure them places at the extraordinarily upmarket Francis Holland School for Girls to 'get their exams' and 'a bit of polish'.

For Annie, Francis Holland had been the Promised Land, the Holy Grail: a fantasy school for the rich and glamorous which, in a slightly limited way, she'd been allowed to join. Yes, she'd suffered a degree of taunting for living in the wrong part of town and having an accent more gravel than cut glass. But mainly she'd attracted a big friend and fan base because she was street smart, savvy and cool and because she knew so many, many boys.

Annie had left four years later with several defining attributes: the qualifications necessary for art school (not medical school, much to Fern's disappointment), the firm conviction that if she ever had children they'd go to a school like that from day one, no matter what the cost, and finally, perhaps most importantly, she'd learned that even if you didn't fit in, you had to be yourself, because people responded so much better to down-to-earth reality than to nervous, put-on airs and graces.

'Ah, Mrs Valentine, lovely to see you. And how are we doing?'

The headmaster, Mr Ketteringham-Smith, ramrod straight and severely smart in his light grey meet-the-parents suit, was greeting at the main door in person with a charming-verging-on-the-smarming smile.

'Top form, headmaster,' she assured him with her best smile. 'And how about you? You're looking fit.'

'Oh, well . . . am I?' He was flustered by the compliment.

'Definitely, you look like you've been coaching the First XV single-handed.' This, admittedly, was going a tad far, but at least Lana was not around to be humiliated to death by her mother flirting with the head.

'Well . . . erm . . . like to keep my hand in, now and again,' came his reply.

She restrained herself from the cheeky answer to this because although there were many, many interesting men to be found wandering the corridors of St Vincent's on a parents' evening, slightly balding Mr Ketteringham-Smith was not one of them.

Annie, perhaps understandably, had a thing about dads. Well, first of all, she'd never had much of one. Who had Fern chosen to give her heart to? Fern had picked a cargo ship captain. What an obvious mistake! Cargo ship captain? The warning was in the title. Mick Mitchell was always away. Not just at work, an hour's commute away, but on the other side of the world away: places like Hong Kong and Rio de Janeiro. The brief times he was home, he still liked to be captain, which infuriated Fern, who was used to doing everything for herself and by herself when she was without him. But it was the all-too-regular medical evidence (requiring hefty doses of antibiotics) of the other women in the other ports that finally sank his boat.

Owen and Lana's dad, Roddy Valentine – mischievous and funny, a Celtic blue-black-haired heart-throb – had been so much better at family life at first. But then he was an actor, away a lot, and despite his assurances Annie had not been able to stop herself from wondering about the possibility of other women. However, nothing had prepared her for the abrupt and shocking end to her marriage. The total and irrevocable breakdown and break-up. The full stop. Overnight, Roddy had become history and she'd had to deal with it, somehow get over it, use every ounce of strength to pick herself and her two devastated children up and carry on.

How had this happened? It was a story that she didn't like to tell. It was a story that somewhere in her head she didn't really believe. She still didn't like to hear his name unexpectedly, as it made her jump. Although Roddy had left over two and a half years ago now, she still woke up most mornings and looked across the bed for her handsome husband, momentarily convinced that it had all been a terrible dream.

A schoolboy handed her an information sheet and she scanned it over, checking the order of events and the rooms she should be heading towards.

An hour and a half had been allocated for form teacher talks, then it was into the hall for the head-master's speech and the performances. Would anyone notice if she skipped the main event?

'Annie! Hello! How are you?' Becca Wolstonecroft was bounding over, a plump, curly-blond-haired, friendly face, mother of four. Either fabulously rich sending four kids here, or fabulously broke, Annie hadn't yet figured out which.

'You're looking wonderful – as usual,' Becca said, kissing her on the cheek.

'Oh that's sweet of you,' was Annie's response. 'Maybe you need new glasses, babes.'

'No, no. Now that's it, Annie, I'm going to have to get you to make me over one of these days. Look at me!'

Becca tipped her chin down and gestured with her arms. 'I look like a bloody Lab.'

Annie choked back the laugh this deserved. Not just because it was funny, but because, yes, blond knee-length fake fur wasn't perhaps the best look for Becca's short, stocky physique.

'Don't be silly,' Annie insisted. 'It's cuddly and . . . so . . .' she struggled . . . 'warm.'

'Oh yes well, a warm, cuddly Lab then!' Becca exclaimed.

'Right, OK. Do you do anything on a Tuesday evening?' Annie asked.

'No,' she said hesitantly.

'Next Tuesday evening, then.'

'Hmmm?' Becca sounded confused.

Annie had already whipped her pink mock croc Filofax out of her handbag – she didn't hold with electronic diaries, having crashed too many of them in the past. She also didn't hold with handing out her business card and expecting people to call: they never did, you had to get them to commit while you had them by the short and curlies. She never left a St Vincent's event without netting at least one new client.

'Next Tuesday evening,' Annie began. 'Me in your wardrobe sorting you out, telling you what to keep and what to bin. Explaining in detail, with pictures, what and where you need to buy to make sure you always look amazing from now on.'

Becca was looking very doubtful: 'Erm . . . well . . . What do you charge?'

'Probably just a bit more than the value of your current outfit,' Annie teased.

'And what do you think that is?' Becca looked down at her furry coat.

'Hmmm . . . all in, including the M&S shoes . . . two hundred and twenty pounds?' came the guess.

'Good God! *How much!?*' Becca seemed genuinely horrified.

'It'll be mates' rates,' Annie assured her. 'We'll be all done for less than a trolley dash round the M&S food hall.'

'Well, er . . .'

'Look, I'll pencil you in. What's your telephone number and I'll phone to confirm a few days before?'

'OK, great.' Becca brightened up, obviously under the delusion that when the call came, she'd be able to play for time. But Annie happily scribbled the number down knowing perfectly well that on the phone, she would win.

'C'mon.' Becca dived for a change of subject. 'I want to get Eric's teacher out of the way first. Shall we go up to Godzilla's room together?'

'Don't,' Annie warned her. 'I'll probably shake her by the hand and call her that.'

Lana's, and therefore Eric's, current form teacher was the school battleaxe: the kind of dragon who roared just for the sake of roaring and enjoyed sending children scurrying away in fear.

'Eric!' Becca called to her husband, Eric senior, a red-faced man stuffed into a pinstriped suit. 'This way. Let's get started.'

Upstairs in the corridors and in the classrooms, parents were milling, looking at the artwork on the walls (*'Gosh, Jessamy's showing so much talent, look at the brush* strokes. *We should take her to Florence for the summer holidays. She should be inspired by the masters'*); leafing through jotters and textbooks (*'Isaac's just brilliant at maths . . . look at this, he hasn't set a foot wrong. The Kumon classes after school were worth every penny'*); waiting for their turn to speak to the form teachers (*'George already thinks she's Oxbridge material . . . that's right, she's ten in April . . . but she already reads Dickens. Oh? Henry's on to James Joyce?'*)

At St Vincent's, parents were very, very interested in how their children were doing and never missed the opportunity for a progress report.

'Jill!' Annie tapped the shoulder of one of the mothers, who had recently become a client of hers. 'Look at you! Lovely.' She smiled, appreciating Jill from head to toe, taking in the caramel mac they'd bought together, the gorgeous velvet scarf tied just so, and the confident Bobbi Brown glow on Jill's face.

Smiling back, Jill said: 'Thank you,' just as Annie had taught her: *'Thank you is enough, no more "oh this old thing?" or "I just threw this on" or "I ran backwards through a bush on my way over here" . . . or whatever else you used to say in response to compliments.'*

After several minutes of chat, Jill pointed surreptitiously and whispered to Annie: 'There's Tor! Tor Fleming. She's been completely shafted in the divorce: Richard's keeping the house, he gets joint custody of Angela with all the plum holiday weeks and Tor doesn't even get an allowance. Totally shafted. I think she's going to fall apart. Look at her. No-one needs you more than her, Annie.'

Annie followed the discreetly pointed finger to the

mother of one of Lana's classmates. Poor Tor. Her bare, exhausted face hovered above a shapeless pale blue anorak and beneath a scruffy mid-brown bob with a tragic grey parting. Worst of all, Richard – tall, handsome and commanding, expensive navy blue overcoat, smart golfing umbrella to hand – was several steps ahead of her, scrutinizing a painting on the wall with too much interest. They'd obviously decided to put Angela first and come to this evening together.

Annie bustled forward, straight past Richard with an effusive 'Tor! How are you? I haven't seen you for ages, you've got to come round . . .'

Soon enough, it was Annie's turn to pull up the chair opposite Lana's form teacher, the feared fifty-something, super-strict Miss Gordanza.

After a curt hello, Miss Gordanza turned to the three pages of typed notes she had on her desk about Lana – and term was only in its first half.

'Well, Mrs Valentine, there were certainly some difficulties with Lana in the run-up to Christmas,' Miss Gordanza began, adjusting purple cat's-eye spectacles on her over-powdered, pointed nose.

'Difficulties' was putting it mildly. Lana and her gang of friends had egged each other on to play a series of increasingly daring and dodgy pranks throughout the Christmas term: raw fish hidden in classrooms over a holiday weekend and then the spectacular treacle-based sabotage of the school orchestra's brass instruments. The Christmas concert had come to a very sticky end.

An MI5-scale investigation had followed involving the headmaster, various teachers, Lana, five of her friends and all relevant parents. The girls had been punished and had left for the holidays in disgrace. Back at school in January, a clever penance had been devised: Lana and the others involved were now in charge of the school's charity fund-raising group, although Lana was still trying to weasel out.

'She's enjoying school a lot more,' Annie was telling Miss Gordanza. 'She promised me a fresh new start this term and she seems to be keeping to that. She's really into her GCSE course . . .' she heard herself gushing a lot more enthusiastically than Lana might have.

'I'll be keeping a close eye on her,' Miss Gordanza said as Annie fixated on the harsh fuchsia lipstick on the teacher's thin lips. It was the kind of pink tide line that wouldn't have dared to rub off, even at night. Probably Miss Gordanza woke up every morning to that same little pink pinched mouth.

'Yes, so will I,' Annie assured Godzilla, focusing on her gold locket, because the teacher was wearing the national dress of fifty-something battleaxes: a navy skirt with knife-pleats and a pale acrylic turtleneck, stretched tight over the ample bosom to create a little trampoline for the locket. She probably wasn't going to agree to a makeover though, was she?

'There are . . . I mean . . . Lana is bound to have issues because of her father's . . . ah . . . situation,' Miss Gordanza went on awkwardly. 'But I'm sure they're not beyond the control of this school.'

'Yes well . . .' Annie told her gently, 'I'm sure we all have issues, Miss Godzil— zanza.' She thought she'd saved herself.

'So many people call me that, I'm considering a name

change,' the teacher added testily, without looking up again from the typed sheet.

'Sorry.' Annie suddenly felt mortified and about ten years old. 'Sorry. I didn't mean to—'

'No matter. Shall we turn to Lana's subject choices?'

Owen's new form teacher, back in the Junior School, was the head of music, Mr Leon. He was a recent addition to the school staff and already very popular. Not just with the pupils, it seemed. Certain mothers had a tell-tale twinkle and had even been seen to blush in his presence. But Annie, who'd met him several times now, failed to see the attraction. To her, Mr Leon was undoubtedly nice and a terribly committed teacher, but he was just a little too English-eccentric-stroke-tramp for her to see why anyone would be interested.

Waiting in the corridor for her turn to speak to him, Annie could overhear the anxious parents ahead of her: 'Marcus is astonishingly bright,' the mother was informing Mr Leon. 'We want to make sure he's being stretched.'

'Well, unfortunately we don't keep a rack on the premises any more, Mrs Gillingham, but I'll see what other ideas I can come up with,' Mr Leon replied, provoking at first silence, then a confused titter from Mr and Mrs Gillingham.

When her turn arrived, Annie went in to find Mr Leon seated on the corner of his desk, humming cheerfully.

'Mrs Valentine! Come on in. All child torture suggestions gratefully received.'

He unfolded his arms, stood up, tried to sweep a hand through his hair but got stuck in the tangle, so pulled out and waved at the two chairs set out for parents beside his own. St Vincent's parents tended to come in pairs, it occurred to Annie with a pang.

'What about the violin?' Mr Leon asked, sitting down and crossing his arms again. It made him look strained and uncomfortable in the clothes he'd chosen for this evening in an effort to be smart. Not a big effort, it had to be said. Tonight he'd taken the eccentric tramp look and run with it: worn-out cords paired, unhappily, with clumpy brown hiking boots and a tight tweed jacket so hairy, she wondered when it was going to bark.

His top shirt button was undone and his tie had been pulled into a tiny scrunched knot, at odds with his broad shoulders, tanned face and spectacular mop of hair. He looked like he'd come down a mountain and stepped into the first clothes to hand. There was a funny smell wafting about him as well: damp, slightly smoky, even boggy.

'What *about* the violin?' Annie repeated, wondering if she'd missed the start of this conversation.

'We should get Owen playing the violin. He's doing brilliantly with the piano. He can play just about every instrument he picks up in my class, he's nine, great age to start, very good ear, really very good. Plus,' he rushed on, 'we're desperate for new violins coming up through the ranks. Three will be leaving at the end of this year.'

She had to assume he was talking about members of the school orchestra.

'Mr Leon—' she began.

'Ed,' he interrupted. 'Please call me Ed.'

He turned away and fumbled in his pockets, catching

a violent sneeze just in time with his crumpled cotton handkerchief.

'Well, bless you, Ed. Where did you catch that cold?'

'Fifth form orienteering in Snowdonia, just got back.' He blew his nose vigorously. 'Brilliant time.'

'Bit cold for camping, wasn't it?' She understood the damp boggy smell now.

'The kids were in the youth hostel, but it wasn't any problem for me, I've got Arctic kit.'

'Right. Well . . .' *Sleeping outdoors in February?! See? Mad, eccentric tramp.* 'Believe me, Ed, there is no way that either of us is going to persuade Owen to take up the violin. No way! You may not have been able to discuss this fully with him' – this was her way of gently introducing Owen's acute and, at times, crippling shyness – 'but I can assure you the super-cool-skateboarding, science-kit-blasting rapper boy that I know won't want to play something as poncy and nerdy as the violin.'

'I play the violin,' Ed told her.

'Oh . . . well . . .'

'It's not just about concertos,' he assured her. 'Although they are lovely. There's folk music, Irish jigs, even rock 'n' roll.'

'No, I don't think he'll go for it and I don't want to force him.'

'I just think of the violin as such a personal voice, a way to express—' Ed began.

But Annie gently reminded him: 'Owen has a perfectly good voice of his own. He uses it beautifully at home and when he's really comfortable with people. It's our job, everyone's job, to help him feel just as comfortable at school.'

'I totally agree,' Ed said quickly, 'but he's very good at music and we should be encouraging that. All creative outlets are a good thing for children. Did you know that Owen speaks about five words a day to me, which is great progress and I'm trying, just as gently as I can, to increase that. What about guitar then?' He suggested. 'Guitars are cool.'

'I suppose so,' she said carefully, worried she was going to agree to something by mistake.

'Well, that's it then,' Ed said enthusiastically. 'Guitar lessons!'

See.

She worried about shy Owen having to cope with one-to-one lessons from a stranger. 'I don't know if he'd want to have . . .'

'I'd be happy to give him guitar lessons,' Ed cut in. 'At home, even, if that would make him feel more comfortable. Don't you think that would be a good idea? Seeing me, his class teacher, in a much more normal, less threatening setting? It might really help him to relax at school.'

'Erm, well . . .' Annie was reluctant. Aside from what Owen might think of this, she didn't know if she wanted this big hairy man in her home, clumping about in hiking boots, wafting bog.

'Ask him what he thinks,' Ed urged her, 'then I'll give you a call to discuss when might be a good time. Let me take your number.' He clapped the pockets of his jacket but couldn't find pen, paper or anything useful. He began to look on his desk as Annie took out her mobile and prepared to commit his number direct to its memory, never mind chasing round the room for bits of paper.

Once numbers had been exchanged, Ed sat down again and asked: 'Right, so, and my favourite member of the Syrup Six is coming on nicely, isn't she?'

Annie had no idea what he was talking about.

'There weren't enough for a Treacle Ten, so ever since the sabotaged concert I've thought of them as the Syrup Six . . . Lana,' he explained.

'Oh, Lana! Yes, she's fine. But she's really not enjoying the fund-raising thing,' Annie began.

Why Ed Leon was the teacher in charge of fund-raising remained a mystery to Annie. He obviously couldn't even raise enough funds for new trousers.

'No?' he lifted an eyebrow. 'Well, she'll have to stick with it. This was her punishment and anyway, I think it's good for her to get involved with the school again, she was starting to tune out on us.'

'Yes . . . hmm . . . well, you could be right.'

'I've had an idea for the fund-raising which might make it more interesting for her,' he added. 'We might try and run a charity auction website. The Syrup Six will have to track down all sorts of things to flog off and there'll be a little group competition to see who can raise the most money. She'd enjoy that, wouldn't she?'

Annie couldn't help smiling. As Lana was already a budding eBay trader, this would be right up her street. 'She'll love it. But keep a sharp eye on her. She's likely to get naughty just as soon as she gets bored. Keep making it very hard and very interesting or watch out.'

'Will do. Now, how would Thursdays suit you for guitar lessons?' Ed wasn't going to let the subject drop.

'I'll have to see what Owen thinks first.'

'Oh yes, fair enough. Now, I suppose we should talk about his school work too – shouldn't we?'

'Mrs Valentine?'

With a start, Annie felt the tap on her shoulder. She was only ten feet or so from a little-known side exit, sure she'd made a clean getaway from the concert. But now it appeared she'd been rumbled.

Turning, she saw the tall, lean figure of the school bursar behind her.

'Oh, hello, Mr Cartledge, I was just . . . I'm afraid I have to leave early. Such a shame.' She tapped at her wristwatch (Cartier – eBay, third-hand, possibly fenced) for emphasis.

'Just a very quick word, Mrs Valentine, I was hoping to catch you.' He lowered his voice. 'Well, in a nut-shell . . .'

With a lurch, Annie knew what was coming next.

'Your cheque for this term's school fees has bounced, Mrs Valentine,' Mr Cartledge informed her.

She'd taken a risk buying the limestone bathroom and steam sauna shower so soon after Christmas. Looked like she was going to have to sell up sooner than expected.

'You do take credit cards, don't you?' Annie asked, thinking through the credit card juggle she would have to do. She knew perfectly well that five of her cards were dangerously close to their limits, but there was the sixth, emergency use only card. It might give her just a little bit of leeway.

'We make a one per cent charge for credit card payments,' Mr Cartledge said.

'Never mind, I think that's what I'll do, just this once!' She tried to sound as cheerful as she could.

'No . . . erm . . . problem, is there?'

'No, no,' Annie insisted. 'Just . . . cash flow . . . a funds-clearing situation,' she fibbed.

She'd put it on the emergency only card and just – well – just work harder. Make some extra sales in the day, find a few more home consultations, sell some more stuff on the website. It wasn't as if she hadn't juggled overdrafts and debts about like this before.

For most of the time Annie had been managing on her own, it felt fine. Most of the time she could cope. But there were moments when she hated it, resented it, felt she couldn't stand it for even one more day.

At times like this, she was certain that having anyone, any partner at all, would be better than being alone. A back-up, a supporter, that was all she was asking for, he didn't need to pay the mortgage (although OK, a small contribution would be useful), even if he was just someone to go home to, someone to give the kind of neck rub Roddy had been so good at. Someone who could soothingly remind her, just as Roddy would have done: 'Hey, it's only money. They print more of it every day.'

Once she was outside, Annie squeezed her eyes shut and then wiped carefully beneath her lower lashes. Only someone looking very, very closely would have seen the slightest of smudges there.

Unzipping her handbag, she delved about inside for two small pieces of chewing gum. She popped them into her mouth and crunched down. Sometimes just a little minty blast at the back of the mouth could fend off that choky, tearful feeling completely.

She tied the belt of her raincoat tightly around her, pulled up the collars, then straightened her shoulders and held up her head. A stiff, shiny Valentino trench-coat, even secondhand via the internet, was so useful for keeping all sorts of troubles at bay.

OK, she resolved, she'd put Svetlana's handbag up for auction tonight and maybe she'd look into the intriguing information the billionaire's wife had left inside.

Chapter Three

Dress-down Dinah:

Swirly blue and green above-the-knee dress (Topshop)
Dark straight jeans (Topshop)
Soft leather rubber-tread boots (Camper)
Green necklace, green sparkly hairclips (Claire's Accessories)
Pea green leather knee-length coat (Oxfam)
Total est. cost: £185

'So, ask me where I got my coat?'

'It could be worse,' Annie's younger sister Dinah told her as they surveyed a slimy, slightly mildewed shower curtain dangling by two hooks from a flimsy rail above a bath, possibly last cleaned in the 1990s.

'It could,' Annie agreed loudly. 'If there was a large black, plague-carrying rat sitting on the kitchen floor, for instance, that would be worse.'

'Shhh!' Dinah urged. It was just like her to worry about what the estate agent and inhabitants of this sink might overhear. Annie couldn't care less. This was the 'exclusive investment opportunity' she'd got out of bed early on a Sunday to view? What a joke.

She was exploring the possibility of swapping her beautiful, fully renovated home for both a doer-upper and a little buy-to-let, but if this was the quality of the doer-upper she could afford: forget it.

This was a gloomy basement prison, inhabited by three, probably more New Zealand travellers who clearly had better things to do than keep house. Every available surface was covered with their clobber: wet towels, un-emptied ashtrays, clothes and empty beer cans. In the sitting room, five curry takeaway boxes were sitting like pre-schoolers in an expectant semicircle round the TV.

'I don't think they've been watching *House Doctor*,' Dinah whispered to her.

'Their landlord must be insane trying to sell it while they're still all here.'

'As you can see,' the estate agent continued, 'the lounge could benefit from a little freshening up, but there's a lot of potential.'

Ha! Yes, with some effort, the room could be transformed from a filthy, north-facing gloomy dungeon with a view of a wall, to a clean, nicely painted north-facing gloomy dungeon with a view of a wall. On the plus side, the little kitchen faced south, was almost sunny on a good day and even had a minuscule strip of lawn outside it. But the deciding factor was the bedrooms: two little cubicles carved from one room with the ruthless use of plasterboard.

Each had a small double bed buried beneath a tumble

of more clothes, towels and stuff. The rooms smelled of damp, pants and cheesy trainers.

'It could look just so completely different all white, Annie,' said Dinah in her usual, touchingly positive way.

The estate agent was nodding agreement.

Were they joking?

In the kitchen, one of the tenants was making a fried egg sandwich, standing bravely beneath a flapping poly-styrene tile that was threatening to throw itself off the ceiling at any moment.

'What do you think of the flat?' Dinah asked him.

'Great!' came his brief reply. 'Obviously we don't want anyone to buy it right now!'

Annie caught herself staring at his bare bronzed pecs a moment too long. She couldn't think when she'd last been so close to tanned nipples. This really was a small kitchen.

'Shall we go and take a look outside then?' Dinah asked.

'Oh . . . yeah.' Annie tore her eyes from the pecs.

Out in the tiny garden, surrounded by tall walls on every side, Dinah's three-year-old daughter Billie skipped in a circle, oblivious to the disappointingly poor quality of the real estate around her. Her straight shoulder-length hair, the same light brown as Mummy's, bounced on her shoulders and she sang something under her breath.

She came to a stop before her beloved Aunty Annie (the adoration was mutual), made an attempt at crossing her chubby arms and asked, 'You can still be a fisher lady if you're a princess, can't you?'

'Yes, definitely.' Annie didn't know what a fisher lady

46

was, but she wasn't capable of denying this soft round face, bright eyes and perfect pink mouth anything at all. No-one else was either, which was probably something of a problem for Billie's long-term development, but no need to worry about that yet.

'Well, I'm going to be a princess fisher lady when I grow up, then.'

'What does a princess fisher lady do, babes?' Annie bent down to make sure she didn't miss a thing.

'Well . . .' Billie began, putting her hands on her hips and leaning forward in a theatrically conspiratorial kind of way, probably copied directly from her nursery school teacher, 'it's a princess, so she wears a pink dress and eats pink cakes all the time, but she also fishes, you know, with a fishing rod.'

'And that's what you're going to be when you grow up?'

'Yes.'

'Perfect. Now, I think we should go to my house and eat croissants. How does that sound?'

'Yesssss!' Billie began to skip in her circle again.

'So, ask me where I got my coat?' Dinah challenged Annie on the walk back to her flat.

'That's no use!' Annie laughed. 'Now I know you got it in Cancer Research or the PDSA. What did you pay?' she followed up immediately.

'Oxfam, thirty pounds,' came Dinah's completely honest reply.

'Could have got it for you for less,' Annie told her, but this wasn't true today, it was just a knee-jerk reaction, something she always liked to say to Dinah when they were talking about shopping.

'Could not!' Dinah retorted huffily.

Annie and her sister Dinah – three years younger – had always understood each other almost perfectly. They weren't alike. They appreciated each other's differences and clicked. Always had done, ever since Annie had worked out how to scramble – carefully, without stamping on the baby's head – into Dinah's cot in the morning to make her giggle.

Although Dinah spent far less on clothes than Annie, she still maintained a lively, edgy style all her own and never shied away from a fashion challenge: tank top and Bermudas? Mini kilt and woolly tights? Sweater dress and kinky boots? Bubble coat? Dinah was game.

There was still an element of competitive dressing between them, left over from the days when they stole tops from each other's wardrobes, fought to wear the same skirt to the same party, and cried when new dresses got ruined.

'How's Bryan?' Annie asked next, aware that she'd been with Dinah for almost an hour and not enquired once after her brother-in-law. But then it was a badly kept secret between the sisters that although Annie was crazy about Billie and couldn't imagine life without weekly get-togethers with Dinah, she wasn't quite so smitten with Bryan.

'He's fine.' Dinah sprang open one of her glittery green clips, readjusted it in her perky bob and smiled. 'Still waiting to hear about that project, over in Hammersmith.'

'Nothing else in the pipeline?'

'Oh loads, he's pitching for work all the time, but you know how competitive it is.'

One of life's true romantics, Dinah, in Annie's opinion. She was dreamy and sweet and softly pretty: pale skin, rosy cheeks, dark brown hair. After an unexpectedly druggie youth and many disastrous relationships, she'd finally found Bryan. A 'soul mate' (supposedly) just as kind and gentle as she was. Bryan was an architect, who only ever seemed to secure work on the smallest of projects like rearranging kitchen units, and as Dinah was an *occasional* children's book illustrator, they lived in a tiny flat, not far from Annie's, but still a million miles from Highgate, in a state they liked to describe as 'impoverished bliss'. It drove Annie slightly wild. She was always nagging them to be more proactive and ambitious . . . not that it made the slightest difference.

Annie would ask things like: 'But don't you want to do up the kitchen at some point?'

Dinah, oiling some ancient French casserole dish she'd bought at Brick Lane market for 20p, would answer, 'Oh, but at least this is a real wooden cupboard' (squeeeeeeak, cue cupboard door falling off hinge). 'Those MDF things get worn out so quickly. And this has character, I love to cook in here.' The fact that her kitchen was no bigger than most people's fridges didn't put her off either.

Or, 'Have you thought about where you're going to send Billie to school?' Annie, ever practical, would ask.

'Oh, her nursery's so *lovely* and most of her friends there are going to the local primary, so we'll probably send her there and . . . you know . . . see how it goes . . .' came Dinah's rose-tinted-spectacle reply.

'But you can't! It's a sink! It came bottom of the entire league table!'

'Did it?' Genuine surprise, followed by, 'But apparently they've got a *lovely* new head.'

Annie, preoccupied with earning enough money for her family, couldn't help suggesting moneymaking schemes for Dinah and Bryan: 'If Dinah had a job just three days a week even . . .' 'If you put together a website, Bryan, showcased your best ideas . . .' 'Dinah, have you tried contacting other publishers?' 'Have you tried advertising in property magazines, Bryan?'

But she suspected Dinah and Bryan quite liked things the way they were: they liked not having to work too hard, they liked being at home with each other and their precious little girl.

For Billie, however, Annie had great hopes. Billie was aiming high with her plans to become a princess, and she was already displaying the ferocious negotiating skills of a Washington lawyer.

'Just four more mouthfuls, darling,' Dinah would beg.

Billie would shake her head.

'Well, let's say three then, so long as they're big ones?'

Vigorous shake of head, lips glued together.

'Two?'

'NO!!' would come the roar.

'Just one tiny-winy little bit more then? Just for Mummy?'

'N-O spells NO!'

Billie had a shiny pink moneybox in which Annie encouraged her to store all the pound coins she slipped her. It wasn't going to be enough to pay for St Vincent's, though.

'Aunty Annie,' Billie piped up now, 'is it true that

Lana and Owen's daddy lives on a hill with other ladies?'

Startled by this question, Annie turned to look at Dinah for some guidance on how to reply.

Dinah just shrugged her shoulders and looked as if she was trying not to laugh.

'Well, er . . .' Annie began, but to her relief, Billie had already moved on.

'Mummy?' she asked next. 'You know the pink fish we eat . . . is that a real fish? The same as the ones you catch? Do we eat *real* fish?'

'I'm leaving that answer to you,' Annie smiled, suddenly recalling Owen's devoutly vegetarian phase, aged four.

Back at Annie's flat, there was an overwhelming smell of nail polish. Lana and her friends Greta and Suzie were giving each other lavish, diamanté-studded manicures and trying to eat toast at the same time with the wet talons.

Annie made the girls and Billie sit down at the kitchen table where she spread butter and jam and cut toast into manageable pieces for the manicurists, while Dinah went in search of Owen, who was in his room reading and hiding from the teen excitement in the kitchen.

Annie's children had managed to jumble up their parents' looks and features so thoroughly that they looked very like both their mother and father, but completely unlike each other.

Lana had Roddy's thick, straight black hair, blue eyes and pale skin, as well as Annie's fine mouth, nose and long limbs. Owen had Roddy's face but coloured with

Annie's brown eyes, rumpled mousy hair and a tawnier skin. Although he might one day fill out to be muscular and sturdy like his dad, at the moment Owen was a lanky, slouchy, skinny boy.

'Ask him to come through, will you?' Annie had said to Dinah. 'At least for a croissant.'

Owen eventually sloped in, blushed deepest pink at the sight of Lana's two teen invaders and picked a chair as far away from them as he could.

Greta and Suzie, being two of Lana's closest friends, knew not to speak to Owen or even look in his direction, which was easy enough as he was far too young to be of any interest.

After a while, he would usually calm down and chip into conversations with a few words of his own, but direct questions from non-family members were too stressful. When Annie brought his croissant over on a plate, she didn't say anything to cajole him into talking, but just massaged his slight shoulders for a few minutes, hoping to help him relax.

Sunday mornings were a constant problem in the Valentine household. There had once been lavish Sunday brunches with the most astonishing, home-made, thick and fluffy pancakes.

To Annie, it wasn't so long ago that brunch had never begun before 9.30 a.m. because she and Roddy had always insisted on a Sunday morning lie-in after Saturday's weekly 'date night' when a rota of three babysitters took charge of Lana and Owen while their parents went out. Didn't matter where they went out, the important thing was being out and having time together: for dinner somewhere smart if they were feeling flush, to see friends or to the cinema, or even for fish and chips on a park bench if they were skint, Roddy whispering in her ear: 'Can we go home yet? I want to do filthy things with you.'

Back at home, the ideal end to the evening was to lock the bedroom door and get close in the way only people who've been happily together for a long time can: 'I know just what you want and I'm so going to make you wait . . . and then wait . . . and wait some more . . . before I finally give it to you.'

Roddy had never liked life to be boring and he certainly didn't like love to be boring, so an evening in with him came with premeditation . . . with blindfolds or honey or ice cubes, maybe silky scarves, music and always surprises.

She had loved him, through and through and inside out, every completely thoroughly explored square inch of him. From his soft white shoulders, to his solid buttocks to his quirky toes. No part of him had been untouched by her, unloved by her or out of bounds for her. They had once been completely and totally intimate.

'We'll always have each other,' he'd told her so many times.

The liar.

The rule for the children on Sunday mornings had once been 'Do Not Disturb' until 9 a.m. at the very earliest.

Sunday brunch had once meant happy, sleepy parents in pyjamas and Roddy making pancakes with banana and maple syrup, or blueberries, or bacon and syrup, or even, not so successfully, Smarties.

The kitchen on Sundays had once been full of burning

butter smoke and sizzling fat, coffee fumes and the noise of Roddy's carefully selected seasonal tunes played loud, to sing along to. In winter, this meant crooning with Dean Martin about his marshmallow world; for summer, they'd learned all the words to things like the Itsy Bitsy Teeny Weeny Yellow Polka Dot Bikini song. When it was hot the pancakes had come with chilled straw-berries and even vanilla ice-cream.

For a while after Roddy had gone, Annie had tried to keep the Sunday morning pancake tradition going on her own. But she couldn't get it right. She burnt the butter and the pancakes came out black on the outside, raw in the middle. Or the batter went runny and they came out like crêpes. In desperation, she'd even tried pancake mixes, but the results were too sweet or too stodgy and provoked just as many tears as the bad home-cooked ones.

But then, when Dinah came round and made them wonderful pancakes, taking Roddy's big blackened cast iron frying pan down from the shelf, washing and re-greasing it carefully, Annie and her children under-stood that even perfect pancakes wouldn't work.

What was missing was all too obviously Roddy and his huge, sunny presence in their lives.

So Sundays were now a careful exercise in avoidance. There was a different routine going. Lana usually invited friends round, Owen and Annie often went out for a long, early morning walk, although more recently Annie had spent Sunday mornings viewing flats.

Today, Annie had brought back the new Sunday morning delicacy: butter croissants from the deli. She put them into the oven to warm, filling the room with a toasty comforting smell. There was lovely cherry jam and Lana's music on the stereo, pots of tea and the busy chatter of seven people in the kitchen. This way, Annie, Lana and Owen were able to not think about pancakes and 'Let it snow, let it snow, let it snow'.

Once the meal was over, Annie lured Dinah to the sitting room with the words: 'Follow me, I've got something very interesting to show you.'

The south-facing, windows-on-two-sides, third-floor sitting room was an Annie makeover triumph. She'd scraped, sanded and sealed the floorboards herself, she'd reclaimed the tiled fireplace inch by inch from the paint and plaster slapped over it. Now the room was a delicate shade of lemon-green with fresh yellow blinds (sale), luxurious green and lemon curtains (second-hand), a slouchy biscuit-coloured sofa (small ads) and all the little touches – antique mirror, sheepskin rugs, beautifully framed photographs – which ensured her flats always sold for a bomb.

Dinah snuggled, feet up, on the sofa and patted for Annie to sit down beside her.

'I have a new plan,' Annie told her, taking a seat.

'You always have a plan, Annie. Does this one involve going round another dodgy flat at nine thirty on a Sunday morning?'

'No, no, no,' Annie assured her. 'Although I'll have to find something else to move to. No, this plan is about giving up the Lonely Hearts columns.'

'Oh thank God!' was Dinah's reaction. 'I don't know how you've managed to keep putting yourself through all those blind dates. I know you tried very hard, Annie, but I didn't think it was ever going to work.'

Last summer, Annie had decided that the best cure for the aching loneliness her absent husband had left in her life was maybe not to pretend that everything was fine and she had been coping just perfectly on her own, but to find someone new.

She'd approached the project as she'd approach a shopping quest: she'd looked in all the places she could think of where available men were on offer and she'd tried out many, many different styles. Unfortunately finding a replacement partner was turning out to be much more difficult than finding a new pair of shoes.

Although she had spent almost every single Friday night for the past eight months on a date, Annie had to admit she was not making much progress.

She had been out with twenty-two men. She'd kept count. Eighteen of those men had been complete losers of the tragicomic variety: badly divorced, depressed, dumped, dysfunctional or defective – truly the very end-of-sale rail in the romance department.

Three had been a little more promising. Well . . . they'd been worth a second, even once a third date for closer inspection, but nothing had come of them. And then there had been the One Night Wonder.

Oscar, the man in a crumpled linen suit, incredibly good looking for the dating circuit, funny, attentive, utterly convincing and so persuasive that she had taken advantage of the children being away for the night and invited him home.

There was no hanging around waiting for Oscar to make a move, oh no. No sooner had she brought him in through the front door than he'd caught her wrist, spun her round and pulled her in close saying, 'We have to kiss, right now. It can't wait,' in a voice not unlike to Cary Grant's.

He was a fabulous kisser: moist, deliberate, practised, delicious and a great fit. He knew perfectly well she hadn't been this close to a man for too long and he was there to meet that need, no doubt about it.

His tongue moving against hers had felt breathtaking; she'd opened her mouth wider, twisted her tongue against his and wanted to eat him up, right there in the hallway.

Of course they'd gone to bed together. She'd expected to feel nervous, but instead found herself running up the stairs, not stopping to turn on the lights, and throwing herself on top of him.

Kissing her busily, he'd felt for the gap between her top and skirt, put cool fingers against the bare skin of her back, then moved them slowly to her stomach.

But still talking to her, joking, charming her all the way. *'Hello, I think I love you, what's your name again?'* he'd sung in a giggly whisper against her ear, running a finger teasingly round the rim of her belly button. Then two fingers had begun to walk from her knee upwards, taking the hem of her skirt with them.

'No, no,' she'd giggled back, pushing his hand away.

So the fingers had moved back to her belly button, circling round, playfully persuading.

When he kissed her, whenever their lips had brushed together, she'd felt an electrically charged tingle.

'You so want to. You do,' he'd told her, moving his hand slowly up her leg again, taking big wolfish bites and licks at her mouth and neck.

He'd smelled spicy, sweaty, grassy and delicious. She'd been unable to recall wanting anyone more, was ravenously hungry . . . starving.

'Nah ah, no,' she'd protested, but she'd been laughing and pushing closer, had begun to unbuckle and investigate him, both of them totally focused on each other.

His fingertips had moved . . . *just there, yesss* . . . softly, insistently against her as his tongue licked down her neck and his leg wrapped in behind hers.

It had got much more heated, deliciously desperate . . . frantically moving, probing fingers and mouths until they were naked and moving, sweating, gasping together, Annie determined to have him, make up for all the time she'd lost, cram in every sensation she'd been so deprived of.

Finally they'd fallen asleep in the not so small hours, they'd kept each other awake so long. He'd held her, whispered to her, been unbelievably tender and she had so, so fallen for him. But in the cool light of the morning, he'd already seemed detached – had to hurry off – left a number which when three days later she finally ventured to call turned out to be *wrong*!

'I'm emotionally scarred and vulnerable!' she'd shouted at the receiver once she'd hung up. 'It's against the rules to treat me like this! You total wanker!'

Her best friend, Connor, had christened Oscar the One Night Wonder and tried to make a joke of him ever afterwards, to ease Annie's pain as quickly as possible. Now, whenever she thought back to that little episode, she tried to remember just the very good bits (not so hard) and hey, Oscar had broken the ice, hadn't he?

He'd been the first person she'd ever slept with since her husband. Not that he deserved the honour.

Annie was now as expert at reading the Lonely Hearts as she was at the property ads.

'Successful businessman' meant 'runs corner shop', 'discreet fun' was always 'adultery', 'tall' equalled 'giant', for 'bubbly' read 'on horse-strength antidepressants'.

'You're going to meet your next Mr Right one of these days, you're going to bump smack bang into him when you're not even looking,' Dinah soothed her. 'You've just got to give yourself time to let it happen.'

Annie gave her a sympathetic look. Her sister was touchingly sweet and naïve in so many ways. Did she really think something this important could be left to chance? To fate? That she should rely on Mr Perfecto waltzing into The Store one day, setting eyes on her and declaring that she was the one?

In Annie's experience, men were nothing like that. Even when they were madly in love with you, they rarely did anything about it. They had to be seduced, cajoled, reassured: in short, hunted down.

Even securing Roddy, hardly one of life's shy and retiring types, had been hard work. Nineteen-year-old Annie, wildly in love, convinced this was the man for whom she was destined, had had to keep a constant track of his nightlife via a friend to make sure she turned up at all the right places, *accidentally*, looking as sensational as possible for the early nineties when everything came from Gap, was black or grey or plaid, and the highest heels were kitten. (See the first series of *Friends* for details and try to imagine: the

59

hair-straightener hadn't even been invented!) But the plaid miniskirts had worked and finally she had landed the prize. And there's nothing, nothing in the world as wonderful as the one you've longed for, dreamed of, ached over, suddenly turning all his dazzling attention on you. Full beam.

The very depressing thing about blind dating was that she'd not yet met anyone who even came close. Instead of bringing Annie a sexy new life full of glamorous, hot men and sizzling romance, the hopeless encounters made her miss Roddy and every moment of comfortable, intimate married life even more.

But never mind. New plan. Whenever her thoughts turned for too long to happy years in the marital bed, she shooed them away with deliberate reminders of Roddy's tatty tartan trouser bottoms and farts under the duvet.

When she met the next Mr Wonderful, he would definitely, definitely not fart under the duvet.

'Dinah, I haven't given up the chase, babes, I've just discovered a much, much better hunting ground,' Annie informed her sister. 'I've been trawling the bargain basements for a man, when I should be looking for a really class label.' With a flourish Annie brought out the glossy brochure she'd found inside Svetlana's cast-off handbag. 'One of the wealthiest wives in London gave this to me,' she explained, 'so it's got to be a very good idea.'

'Discerning Diners?' Dinah read aloud from the cover in a tone of disbelief: '*London's most exclusive dinner dating experience* . . . Oh Annie, I don't know . . .'

But Annie brushed her sister's reservations aside and eagerly spread out the profile pages of the 'dynamic, single, hand-selected guests' who would be coming to next week's five-course, five-star 'dining experience'. No more meeting crappy men in crappy bars. Annie was going in search of someone top of the range. This agency came with Svetlana's personal recommendation ('*I meet my second husband there*'). If Svetlana was now with a billionaire oil baron, surely Annie could manage a man with nice clothes and a six-figure salary.

'Isn't this going to be very expensive?' Dinah worried.

'That's the point!' Annie exclaimed. 'I could meet not just the man of my dreams, but the very wealthy man of my dreams.'

Dinah rolled her eyes. 'Annie, I think you may have watched Disney's *Cinderella* once too often during your formative years. This is the twenty-first century, rich men do not gallop in and solve all your emotional and financial problems. They come with problems of their own . . . and pre-nups and anyway . . . For goodness' sake, Annie! What you're telling me is you are now look-ing for a rich man.' There was no hiding the irritation in her voice. 'You know, not a nice man, or the right man, or someone you could fall in love with again, but Mr Moneybags.'

'No, no. Of course I want to fall in love again. I just think I should be looking for the right, really nice Mr Moneybags,' came Annie's reply, but when she saw the sceptical look on Dinah's face she added, 'Would it really hurt to look? The world's available men aren't divided into "Nice" and "Rich", you know. There's overlap, there are some great men who aren't short of a bob or two. Would that be so bad?'

'But the money issue is just going to colour your

61

judgement, Annie,' Dinah insisted. 'You'll pick a creep because he's loaded and supposedly going to solve all your problems.'

'Thanks for the vote of confidence, Dinah,' Annie snapped. 'That's really helpful.'

'Why do you have to do this anyway?' Dinah picked up the brochure and looked as if she was about to throw it across the room. 'You'll meet someone, when the time is right. Why are you trying to force it like this?'

'I need someone else. You have no idea. I want someone to be here for me, someone to share some of the pressure. I want to live somewhere nice—'

'You do live somewhere nice,' Dinah broke in.

'But I want to be able to afford to stay!' There. Annie hadn't meant to spell it out quite so clearly to her sister, because now Dinah would worry for her, but it had just come out.

'Oh Annie!' Anxiety was already crossing Dinah's face. 'There are other solutions. There are always other solutions.'

'I want someone . . .' Annie's voice was quieter now and she slumped back into the sofa. She wanted to try and explain it to her sister properly, but it was hard to do and besides, she didn't like to admit all this need. She liked everyone, even Dinah, to think she was all together and just perfectly fine.

'I want to find someone soon,' Annie went on, 'because I really, really want to get over Roddy and I think someone else would help. I mean, it's going to be three years soon. But I was with him for so long before, that three years feels like nothing. I think it's going to take another five before it even begins to feel less . . .

raw. And I'm thirty-five, I can't let all that time pass me by while I just wallow!'

Dinah's expression softened now, to one of great sympathy.

'And I'm so pissed off Roddy left us just after he'd landed the soap part!' Annie exclaimed. 'Just as things were about to get so good for us. A year into that job and we'd have been minted! Absolutely minted and all these problems wouldn't exist. I wouldn't have any of them. Not a single one. I wouldn't even need to work, I'd probably be swanning off to the hairdresser's and the tennis club every morning. Can't you understand how cheated I feel?'

'I know,' Dinah soothed, putting a hand on Annie's shoulder and wondering how many more times she would have to hear her sister make this furious speech, 'I know. It was very unfair. Really, really unfair. Of course you deserve someone else, someone new – just for you. I just worry about you. I want you to find someone great, Annie, and not settle for anything less. If you want to go to this dinner thing to have a look, well, you know . . . maybe you should go and I should just shut up.'

'Oh babes, I don't know what I'd do without you.' Annie sat up and wiped her eyes.

'No, don't be silly. What would I do without you? Come on, what have you got there? Details of your fellow Discerning Diners? Show!'

'Bet you I get a great date on my first dinner,' Annie challenged.

'Bet you don't.'

Chapter Four

Discerning Diner Annie:

Rose pink strappy cocktail dress (Monsoon sale)
Sequinned evening bag (Accessorize sale)
Purple suede Manolo heels (The Store's sale preview day)
Yellow cropped swing jacket (Valentino, eBay,
used but flawless)
Total est. cost £380

'I thought we were supposed to dress up!'

'Open the door!' Annie shouted to her children from her bedroom at the top of the stairs. 'That'll be Mr Leon.'

It was 6.45 p.m. and she was having a last minute fret about her hair. She'd decided not to scrape her blond locks into the usual slick ponytail for her first Discerning Diner dinner but to wear them loose. Now that the hair was falling down about her face in the artfully artless way caused by careful application of the tongs, she didn't know if she liked it.

She looked so different. Pretty . . . yes. Maybe too

pretty. Curly blond locks and a pink dress. Maybe it was too much. Despite over-exposure to *Cinderella*, she preferred herself all sharp and fashionably focused in darker shades with a sleek head.

But this was dating. High level, designer dating. And wasn't she always, always telling clients that they had to dress for the occasion?

She pressed her pink glossed lips together, slung her yolk-yellow Valentino over her shoulders and picked up her evening bag. Heels trip-trapping on the shiny oak stairs, she headed down to say hello to the music teacher.

Ed Leon with his hefty woollen overcoat and bright red guitar case was filling up the entire hallway as he chatted to Lana and Owen.

'Yeah, basic chords,' he was telling them. 'So easy once you've got the guitar tuned. But tuning the guitar, really tuning her up beautifully, that's the difficult bit, a real skill, no, an art, I'd say . . . Lana, why don't you join us?'

Ha! Good luck trying, Annie couldn't help thinking. Lana had moaned and scowled from the moment Annie had come through the front door about 'that geek Mr Leon' coming round.

'D'you know what he's called at school?' Lana had said.

'Do I want to know?' Annie had warned.

'Ed the Shed,' Owen had butted in. 'Because he smells a bit parky,' and when Annie had rattled with laughter, he'd added: 'You have to admit, it's funny.'

'We're going to do some chords,' Ed the Shed was telling Lana down in the hallway. 'We might break into a bit of 1980s retro guitar . . . hey, Owen? Have a little Michelle Shocked, Billy Bragg moment. C'mon, Lana, just listen in.'

'Who?' was Lana's response, but to Annie's surprise her daughter seemed to be showing some signs of interest.

Then Annie was at the bottom of the stairs where she caught Ed looking up at her and doing an obvious double-take at the heels, the hair and the dress, definitely the dress.

'Hello, Mr Leon, great of you to come.' She smiled a welcome. 'I'm leaving the three of you in peace and going out to a dinner party,' she explained over his insistent 'Please call me Ed'.

'OK, Ed,' was Owen's response. Immediately he turned bright pink, but he was smiling, obviously pleased with himself that he'd managed to say something so early into the tuition session.

'Owen!' Annie scolded, but gently, with an encouraging smile, 'I'm not sure Mr Leon meant—'

'Oh don't worry, it's fine,' Ed cut in, then gave a dramatic and unexpected sneeze.

'Bless you,' Annie and Lana chorused. Lana immediately picked up the box of tissues on the hallway table and offered them. She had a slight horror of nose issues, which might undo Ed's good work persuading her to join in with the lesson.

'Very kind,' Ed mumbled from behind a hastily snatched tissue.

'Into the sitting room,' Annie directed her children. 'Ed, can I have a tiny word?'

She came down the last of the stairs until she was

standing beside him and said in a low voice, 'We've not talked about payment for these lessons.'

'No, no . . .' He was waving his hand.

'But don't be silly,' she insisted. 'You've come over here, you're giving up your time to do this. You need to be paid.'

'Definitely not. I want to do this for Owen and . . . well . . . I do have the interests of the school orchestra at heart as well.' He held up a small brown violin case that Annie hadn't noticed before.

She looked at him for a moment: he had a kind face, slightly too kind. He was definitely the sort of dreamy, well-meaning twinky who would get himself into a situation where giving music lessons was *costing* him rather than making him some extra pocket money.

'Now look, Ed,' she told him a little firmly, 'I can understand if you don't want to be paid for the lessons, but I'm giving you something, OK? Don't bother saying no again,' she insisted when he began to shake his head. 'Are you a wine man or a beer drinker?' she asked, thinking that the ancient woolly overcoat suggested wine, but the guitar was definitely real ale.

'Emm . . .' Ed seemed unsure and slightly taken aback at the question. 'Well both, really – but red wine probably has the edge.'

'Well then, that's easy,' she told him. 'One lesson equals two bottles of red. Do we have a deal?' She held out her hand.

He offered his and they shook on it, his face creasing into a smile. 'If you insist,' he said.

'Yes, I bloody do . . . and don't be too impressed. They'll be cheap bottles. Come on in then,' she said and opened the sitting room door. Ed followed her into the room.

'Nice room,' was his enthusiastic response: 'So much space. Very nice,' he repeated and she suspected he now thought she was much wealthier than he'd expected, and there he was offering her children free music lessons. 'Bet you've got one of those terrifyingly high-tech kitchens as well.'

'Oh yeah,' she replied. 'It makes you dinner, then washes up and gives you a massage. Who needs a man?'

'Ha. Very good.' He nodded and began to take off his coat.

Annie took it from him, noting that he wasn't in his usual tweedy schoolwear, but in very well-worn jeans and an ancient dark blue Guernsey jumper, fraying at the cuffs. A desperately unironed shirt was peeking out at the collar and hem. This was obviously Ed doing casual. He looked like a refugee from a badly dressed war.

'So you're heading out?' he asked.

'Yes. Yeah. A party . . . dinner . . . thing.' She didn't want to be specific about the dating scene she was venturing into.

But Lana's acutely perceptive teen antenna flicked on and she didn't hesitate to inform Ed: 'Mum's going on another blind date.'

'Well, it's not quite like that . . . Lana!' Annie warned her daughter with a look, but no . . .

'What do you mean "not quite like that"?' came Lana's testy response. 'Forty single strangers are getting together for dinner tonight and you're going to be one of them.'

68

'Well! What can I say?' Annie forced a smile onto her face and gritted her teeth, forcing back the obvious *'Lana, babes, time of the month? Shall I get you a hot water bottle?'*

'There's a first time for everything,' she managed ii stead.

'Right,' said Ed. He looked astonished, which made Annie feel slightly ridiculous and irritated. 'Best of luck,' he added.

'I'll tell you how it goes,' she tried not to snap, giving Lana a pointed glare. 'Anyway, a friend of mine, Connor, will be round later on. He's babysitting because I don't like to leave them alone at night. Do I, babies?'

Owen made vomiting noises while Lana crossed her arms and scowled at her mother.

Annie climbed the hotel's thickly carpeted staircase with unbridled optimism. This was a classy place. Nothing cheesy about it. Well, OK, maybe booking the Anne Boleyn Function Room hadn't been the organizers' best decision: 'My second wife? Yes, she was beheaded, unfortunately. So sad. But there we are . . . that makes me single again.'

No more dates via the Lonely Hearts columns! Annie was triumphant. No more hasty glasses of wine downed while she made her excuses to the poor bewildered souls she kept encountering. No more internet dating! Her inbox would be free of the entirely deviant fantasies of Mr Perverted of Tampa Bay, Florida and pals.

Red carpet dinner dating. This was the way to go. Yes, it was expensive, at a moment in her financial life when she really couldn't afford it. But she was looking on it as an investment. Finding not just Mr Right, but Mr Wealthy-and-Right was going to be money so well spent. Anyway, this was a trial dinner. She'd only paid for the meal. The full subscription was due only if she signed up after tonight. Maybe she'd get lucky first time. She was feeling very lucky.

How Dinah had rolled her eyes as Annie had read to her from the brochure: 'A gourmet dining experience with forty hand-selected singles . . .'

'Look thorough the guest list,' Annie had urged her, handing over the profile pages studded with grainy printouts of passport-sized photos.

'There's a property developer, a Czech businessman, a computer entrepreneur, someone interesting from the West Country . . .' Annie had pointed out.

But Dinah had labelled each photo in her own way: 'Man who does DIY, Eastern European gangster, husband not over his wife who dated lesbians on the internet . . . mono-browed Welsh werewolf . . .'

'Stop it!' Annie had ticked her off. 'What about him then?' – she'd ringed one profile – 'Dominic runs a garden design consultancy. He loves French wine and Cuban music . . . Ooh!' Her eyebrows had perked up with interest. 'Half French. Now *he* is very, very promising.'

'Let's see the picture.' Dinah had peered at the page and grudgingly agreed that Dominic wasn't bad. In fact, really quite handsome: dark hair, nice jawline and smile . . .

'Why do you think he needs a dating agency?' she'd wondered.

'Maybe he's just so busy running his consultancy, he

can never find the time to meet anyone,' Annie mused. 'He *is* good looking, isn't he?'

Smoothing down her dress, pulling back her shoulders and setting what she hoped was a slightly mysterious smile on her face, Annie opened the Anne Boleyn room door and stepped inside.

At a reception table directly in front of her an over-enthusiastic girl with a stack of name badges was gushing: 'Hello and welcome to Discerning Diners.'

Name badges? Annie hadn't expected something as functional and conferencey as name badges, but far, far worse than that was the fact that everyone Annie could see milling around in the drinks area was dressed in regulation office clothes: the men were all in grey and navy suits, the women likewise. This was a sea of jackets, long-sleeved blouses and smart trousers with not one pretty dress to be seen anywhere, let alone a *strappy* one. She was going to look like a divorced and desperate housewife amidst all the high-flying, executive girls.

'So, what's your name?' the super-smiley blonde behind the desk wanted to know.

'It's Annie Valentine and . . . I thought we were supposed to dress up!' she added in dismay.

'We do ask everyone to make an effort, but I'm afraid so many people come straight from work, they don't have time. Can I take your jacket?'

'No . . . ummm . . . well . . .'

It was warm in the Anne Boleyn room, too warm for yellow wool gabardine with a satin lining, especially now that she was feeling the added heat of embarrassment.

She could either hover round the drinks reception

quietly sweating her jacket up and her make-up off, or she could be brave and breezy and take it off.

'Yes, I suppose so,' she relented, slipping off the Valentino and exposing slim shoulder straps, bare arms and a lot more cleavage than the event required.

'I'm going on to another party afterwards.' Suddenly the perfect excuse, not to mention fib, sprang to mind. She would tell everyone this. Oh and it meant she could leave early *if* – surely no chance of this – the evening was a horror.

'OK, Annie. Hi! Welcome! I'll take you over to Hillary, who's going to introduce you to everyone.'

With Hillary at her side, Annie was whisked through a blur of faces, smiles and introductions. She recognized some names from her list: the Czech turned out to be a rather meek-looking salesman; Idris was indeed a mono-browed Welshman, though probably not a werewolf; most disappointing of all was 'very, very, promising' Dominic, the garden designer, who was handsome, but came in at about five foot three. So, Annie, in heels, was a clear eight inches or so taller than him.

When they were ushered through to dinner, she felt a little disheartened to see that the name tag on the place next to hers was Dominic's.

A rather shy, bland man called Will was seated on her left opposite a pale, nondescript woman called Maisie. But some sort of salvation seemed to loom in the form of Lloyd, the greying but nonetheless debonair-looking fifty-something opposite her. When he smiled, introduced himself, shook hands over the table and complimented Annie on her 'ravishing' dress, she found that her will to live seemed to be returning.

But over the starter – spinach and nutmeg soup, which quiet man Will couldn't eat without splashing and slurping noisily – Annie discovered that Lucinda, the woman seated on Lloyd's left, was also very taken with him.

Within minutes, it also became clear that Lucinda was very, very chatty and was going to do most of the talking at the table, imagining that she was helping everyone to mingle by going round and asking all those excruciating personal questions Annie did not want to answer: *'Are you divorced?' 'How long have you been dating?' 'What do you do for a living?'*

As her turn to be asked approached, Annie made the mature decision to bolt for the loo.

When she came back, she felt she should leave off Lloyd and devote some attention to Dominic, so as not to be rude.

'The wine's nice, isn't it?' she asked him, remembering his interest from the profile pages.

'Not bad at all,' he replied, turning the bottle to read the label.

'I've taken the decision not to drink plonk any more,' she explained. 'Life's just too short.'

He held up the bottle and said, 'Indeed,' as he refilled her glass.

Was it her imagination or had he given a little wince? What had she done? Maybe it was her use of the word 'short'. He was obviously super-sensitive and she'd hurt his feelings. Subconsciously, she'd drawn attention to his height, or lack of it. Mental note not to use the word short again.

She asked him about his journey to the hotel and got an almost funny anecdote in reply.

Half French, Cuban-music-loving Dominic: it was obvious the French genes were strong, he was handsome in a dark and brooding kind of way, wore his shirt unbuttoned low and would have looked at home in a Parisian café puffing on a Gitane.

He should have been very promising date material. But eight inches ... eight inches was quite a gap to overcome. Even sitting down, his head was tilted up to meet her eye level, which whizzed Annie back in time to dancing with boys a whole head and neck shorter than her, making her feel like an overgrown freak.

'Your nephew's at St Vincent's!' she exclaimed, because they had just made this discovery. 'Small world.'

He gave the little wince again. Ooops.

As the first course had arrived, they began to talk about favourite foods; vegetables, to be precise.

'Aubergine in a tomato ragout,' he was telling her.

'Dwarf beans, steamed with butter, delicious,' Annie said.

Dwarf?? Why did she have to say dwarf? Wasn't 'beans' description enough?

Lloyd shot her a wink. Was he just being friendly or had he noticed her unfortunate choice of words? By the way, that was Lloyd, property developer, divorced, no children, large house in Wimbledon, hobbies: jazz and windsurfing – Lucinda had her uses.

'Have you been dinner dating long?' she asked Dominic, changing direction away from miniature food.

'A year or so,' he admitted.

'Met any interesting people?' She wondered if he'd had more luck than her.

'Lots. Lots of interesting people – but nothing serious.'

After a few moments of attempting to make chit-chat with taciturn Will, Annie turned back to Dominic as it was hard to wrestle Lloyd from Lucinda's focused attention for more than a moment or two.

'I love her, she's adorable . . .' Dominic was telling Maisie about his long-standing admiration for the French actress Audrey Tatou.

'Oh, I feel the same way about Billy Crystal,' Annie chipped in. 'Although he's obviously tiny.' It was out of her mouth before she could even think about it.

Dominic's smile was definitely too tight at the edges.

'So, tell me about your gardening work?' she asked, deciding any sort of apology would just make things worse.

This turned out to be a good question. Dominic was very enthusiastic about his job and talked with animation about the Modern Garden.

Annie and several other diners listened closely, chipping in with questions about their own little plots, wondering if he could offer a few tips. This was one of the many sad things about getting older, Roddy always used to joke; suddenly everyone's as interested in gardens and where to score the best bedding plants as they used to be in drugs. Bird-watching no longer meant checking out the hot chicks, but setting out feeding tables and encouraging the starlings. 'From big tits to blue tits: it's downhill all the way,' had been Roddy's take on it.

'It's not growing, it's just so . . . stumpy.' Aaargh! Wasn't there another word she could have used to describe a hedge that was failing to thrive? 'So totally, well, you know, not . . . bushy,' she managed.

'Stunted?' Lloyd offered, suppressing a smirk.

Annie had a sneaking suspicion that silent Will and Mousie Maisie were in fact smouldering with passion: they kept trying to take furtive glances at each other and blushing when they got caught. If only they could pluck up the courage to say slightly more than hello.

But just as she was wondering how to draw them into a conversation together, she heard Dominic tell Lucinda that he drove a mini-van. At this, she turned, caught Lloyd's eye and heard him give a snort of laughter which he quickly suppressed by drinking a mouthful of wine.

She smiled at him knowingly, feeling pleased that they had this secret communication going.

Fortunately Dominic didn't seem to notice . . . but it was talk of the midget gems that brought things to a head.

The conversation had moved on to favourite childhood sweets and out popped Annie's revelation: 'Midget gems.'

It wasn't a lie. Along with Caramac bars, these were her top nostalgia trip treats.

'Midget gems?' Dominic asked a touch coldly and with obvious disbelief. '*Midget* gems? I've never heard of those.'

'They were very tiny, multicoloured, iced biscuits,' she stumbled.

He didn't look convinced. Suddenly she wasn't so sure either. Maybe there was no such thing. Maybe they were 'Iced gems', but she was so busy trying not to commit height gaffes that the word 'midget' had perversely sprung to mind.

'Anyone else remember midget gems?' She looked round at the other diners, hoping someone would prove she hadn't lost her mind.

No. No-one could recall midget gems and put her out of her misery. Dominic glared at her and might have been about to say something but fortunately a little bell rang, which turned out to mean that the first course was finished and all the women had to stand up and move three places to their right. To Annie's relief, this put her in Lucinda's seat, right next to Lloyd. Unfortunately Dominic could still glare at her, but she'd try to ignore that.

Lloyd was a honey. He asked her about where she lived, he listened to her job description and property empire expansion plans with interest, he topped up her wine glass. He looked into her eyes and said in a low voice that he'd been coming to these dinners for over three months now and he'd met no-one as beautiful as her.

She asked where he'd got his tan and he muttered modestly about business in Argentina and how a trip to the Caribbean made February so much more bearable.

Annie felt a warm wave of happiness wash over her. A warm, sun-kissed Caribbean wave of happiness. Her luck was so, so in. He was lovely. Perfect. Her hands were itching to pick up her handbag, whisk out her mobile and commit his numbers to speed-dial.

'So you have children, do you?' he asked, picking up his wine glass to take a sip.

'A gorgeous fifteen-year-old, Lana, and then Owen, who's nine.'

'Fifteen?!' Lloyd was trying to restrain himself from a splutter.

'Well, she's my lovechild,' Annie explained, always pleased with the 'you look so much younger' effect that mentioning her 15-year-old daughter had on people. 'I had her when I was twenty.'

'You're thirty-five?!!' Lloyd asked. 'But you look so much younger!' Unfortunately, this sounded almost angry, unlike the usual compliment that revealing her age brought her. (Annie suspected it was her bright blond hair, use of first-class moisturizer – past-expiry-date Sisley – and the fact she found sunbathing boring which combined to give her a face that still looked late twenties, so long as she wasn't laughing. In photographs taken mid-cackle, she looked about a hundred.)

'Well, thank you,' she smiled at Lloyd, but he didn't look happy. 'What's the matter?' She decided it would be best to know.

'My cut-off point is thirty-three,' he said coldly.

'Thirty-three what?' she asked, not sure what he meant.

'Thirty-three years old,' he retorted. 'My ex-wife is thirty-four, so I'm going younger. *Much* younger.'

'Oh!' For a moment Annie was too taken aback to say anything. Then plenty of pithy responses came to mind like: 'You sad old goat', 'When are you booking yourself in for a full facelift?' or 'Is dating a teenager so much fun?'

But she reined them in and settled on a dignified 'Well, Lloyd, that's your loss. Women get so much more interesting in their thirties. Not to mention *expert*.' Unfortunately, she followed this with a snarled 'But why are you here when there are so many dodgy Thai agencies that could help you?'

There was nothing for it now. Having offended the man on her left and the man opposite, she had to concentrate on Will, the soup-slurping Mr Quiet.

'I think Maisie really likes you,' she told him, after a quick preliminary chat. 'You should get her number . . . get in touch with her. I think you'd both get along like a house on fire.'

Unfortunately this just made Will blush deeply and clam up completely. So now Annie had no-one to talk to. Time to execute plan A and claim she had to leave early to get to her 'other' fictional party.

With a quick glance round at everyone within earshot, she announced that she would have to leave and so sorry, etc etc.

Exiting the table head high in what she hoped was a dignified manner, she couldn't help taking a glance back to see if Lloyd had got up to follow her. Well, why not? Wasn't he desperate to know more about her? The dwarf-baiter? Even if she was 35!?

No! He wasn't even watching her go! His head was turned, he was deep in conversation with Lucinda, who – outrageously – had moved herself back into the chair Annie had just vacated.

But of course Hillary the hostess was chasing after her, catching up with her at the door.

'How did it go? You're looking so fabulous by the way,' she gushed. 'We will phone you tomorrow and ask if there's anyone you met tonight that you want to contact.'

'Thank you,' Annie managed, although she'd have

preferred a pithy, Pah, don't bother. What a bunch of losers!

She buttoned her jacket up, fled to the first pub she could find and gulped down a Bailey's while waiting for her minicab to turn up, more thoroughly humiliated than she could ever remember feeling after any school disco.

Chapter Five

Connor babysits:

Dark blue chunky cashmere rollneck (Armani)
Slouchy indigo jeans (Nudie)
White T-shirt (Paul Smith)
Pink and aqua socks (Paul Smith)
Tight boxers (Aussie Bum)
Suede bowling boots (Camper)
Total est. cost: £520

'Why does no-one want me?'

'Mizz Valentine, you been on a hot date?' the taxi driver greeted her with a grin. It was the same driver who'd taken her home from Dinah's house last Friday, Mr Abdul Nwocha and his not-so-trusty Nissan Bluebird. The week before she'd noticed an ominous rattle underneath the car, hinting at an exhaust close to exhaustion. It was still there.

But, like all the other drivers she knew at this cab firm, he was cheap but polite, friendly and waited outside your home until you were safely inside.

'How did it go?' he asked Annie once she was buckled into her seat.

'It was fine.' She offered him a smile. She wasn't even going to begin to describe the evening in its full glory. Yet another dating disaster, further proof, as if she needed it, that she was hopeless at this . . . that there was no-one good left out there . . . and that husbands were completely underrated. She squeezed away the tears of frustration that were threatening, balled up her hands and tried to concentrate on Mr Nwocha and his chat.

'Be seeing him again?' he asked, his dark face and shiny leather jacket gleaming in the oncoming head-lights, his tree-shaped air freshener swinging madly, sending blasts of throat-tightening fake pine as the car jolted on creaky suspension over the speed humps in the road. Each one threatened the exhaust with a death blow.

'No, somehow I don't think so.' She managed a smile. 'I don't think he was really in my Dream Date Top Ten . . . Busy night?' she asked, needing a change of subject.

'It will be, my friend.' He smiled and cranked up the tinny music coming from the radio.

Traffic, football and the weather filled the remaining minutes of the journey, then once Annie had paid and tipped him, despite his protests, and was getting out of the car, Mr Nwocha leaned over and patted her arm reassuringly: 'If you've no date for next week you can always give me a call.' A throaty giggle followed this, along with a wink.

'Thank you,' she smiled, 'I'm sure you'd be a very good date.' She winked back. 'Have a good night.'

'I'm a great cook,' he offered as she closed the cab door.

'Then you won't be alone for long,' she told him.

As she walked to her front door, her phone beeped with a text from Dinah.

DID I WIN THE BET? it read.

Annie wondered if Mr Nwocha's offer would count.

As she opened the door, she could hear the very, very welcome sound of Connor McCabe – the six-foot-three, dark-haired, devastatingly handsome actor that every woman deserved to have as a best friend – calling to her from the sitting room.

'Hello, sex bomb!' he greeted her as she stepped into the room. 'How did it go?'

Connor was sprawled right across her sofa, effortlessly gorgeous as always: hair in a messy Elvis-ish quiff – that was new – wearing rumpled jeans and a cuddly roll-neck. Two empty beer cans and a family pack of cheese and onion crisps were on the table beside him. He had the remote in one hand, a late night chat show on low volume on the telly.

'Snog!' he said, holding out his arms.

Annie leaned over and kissed him on the lips, feeling his arms hug her in tightly. He pulled her down onto the sofa on top of him.

'With or without tongues?' he joked, pecking at her lips again.

'I think without . . . what with the cheese and onion, but thanks for the offer,' Annie said, coming up for air. 'Nice to see you.'

She tucked her head against his chest and smelled, beneath the pungent crisp breath, comforting manly scents of shaving cream, beer and well-worn jumper.

'So, how did it go?' he wanted to know. 'Did you meet Mr Perfect?'

'Yeah right.' She rolled off and budged Connor over a bit so she was snugly sandwiched between the back of the sofa and his warm body. Ah, the comfort of a gay man. You could use their body for all the huggy, snugly stuff without risking any misunderstanding.

Then she gave him the story of the evening, blow by blow, leaving in as many stupid details and silly moments as she could.

When she'd finished, Connor wriggled a comforting arm around her.

'I do need to find someone,' she confided. 'I'm in danger of getting dodgy. I've realized I'm paying men to touch me.'

'What do you mean?!'

'My hairdresser's a man, my chiropractor, my dentist, my doctor . . . it's when I realized I was really quite enjoying my breast examination, that's when I suspected I'd turned into a dirty old woman.'

'Don't mess about, baby, book yourself in for that smear test now,' was Connor's advice.

She dug an elbow into his ribs.

'You need a hunky male personal trainer,' Connor suggested, 'or the suburban housewife's tried and tested: a tennis coach.'

'Ohh, I would . . . but not in the current economic climate.'

'Aha.'

'Anyway, how were the children?' she asked.

'They were fabulous,' he assured her. 'Lana's still awake in her room I think, listening to her iPod, Owen is probably playing the guitar under his covers to impress his music guru.'

'You met Ed?'

'Oh yes, I'm nearly as impressed with Edible Ed as your children are.'

'Ha. Edible Ed?' She wondered how anyone could find Ed remotely edible, unless they were a dust mite.

'C'mon,' Connor insisted. 'You've got to admit, he exudes a certain old school charm . . . but the "gaydar" says he's not one for the boys.'

'No . . . school rumour is he's something of a ladies' man, but I find it hard to believe. How's your love life anyway?'

'Oh, same old, same old,' Connor assured her. 'Absolutely nothing to report. Why does no-one want me?' He pulled a tragically sad face which earned him another dig in the ribs.

'So *The Manor*'s policeman remains "the most eligible bachelor in showbiz" then?' she teased. 'I dunno, Connor. You're gorgeous, you're on TV, you're loaded – maybe people are frightened by the curse of *Hello!* Maybe they don't want to wake up and find themselves being interviewed by *Grazia* magazine?'

'Oh very funny.'

She looked at his handsome chin. She'd inherited Connor. He'd been Roddy's best friend, but when Roddy exited stage left, he'd come over to her side.

Connor and Roddy had met on some low-budget film set in Romania. They'd been there for weeks, even

85

though they were bit parts, first and second prince on the right or something. They'd hatched a plan to leave their noble, badly paid film and theatre careers, which didn't seem to be going anywhere, and break into soaps: Roddy as a sexy baddie and Connor as handsome, hunky boy-next-door.

After extensive restyling by Annie, Roddy had emerged as crew-cut, leather-jacketed, slightly stubbly and wicked and had progressed from thug in *The Bill* to a bad, newly returned brother of somebody in *EastEnders*. Meanwhile, a scrubbed-clean, rosy-cheeked, knitwear-clad Connor had landed the starring role in the Sunday teatime-slot nostalgic series *The Manor*. On the back of this, stage roles in the West End came rolling in.

'How's work?' Annie asked.

'Oh daaaling, it's wonderful,' Connor said at first, then added grumpily: 'I'm never agreeing to go on stage again, it's bloody drudgery.'

'Ha! Bloody well paid drudgery,' she said and stroked his jumper knowingly. 'Eight-ply cashmere doesn't come cheap.'

'Give me telly any day. When are you coming to see me anyway?'

'Oh, well . . . very soon,' she assured him, secretly thinking that musicals, even those by Noël Coward, weren't really her thing.

'Now . . . Connor,' she began, since favours were being traded, 'my gorgeous one?' She linked fingers with him.

'Uh-oh,' he replied. 'This sounds as if it's going to be dangerous – expensive – or possibly both.'

'I've got a favour to ask. Actually, two favours.'

'You'll definitely have to grovel. Preferably on your knees.'

'How do you feel about camping? The tent kind?' she added quickly.

Connor pulled a face: 'I know everything about camping and nothing about tents.'

'There's this male-bonding, man-and-boy, orienteering event – men and their sons, or their nephews, or their friends' sons even.' She caught his eye, to make sure he understood. 'And Owen has showed me a leaflet for it, has been saying, about fifteen times a day: "Wouldn't that be really good fun? Doesn't that sound like a great place?" and so on. You know how much camping he used to do with Roddy . . . and I can't think of anyone else who could take him. And it's around the time of his birthday and—'

'I don't know anything about camping, Annie,' Connor moaned. 'And you can't camp, so even if you were male . . . you'll have to do something different. How about a spa weekend? I'd come on that.'

'I hope you're joking. Owen is going to be ten,' she reminded him.

'You're never too young to groom.'

Annie gave a sigh: 'OK, OK, I'll let you off camping. But now you have to say yes to my next request.'

'Hit me.'

'You know it's my mum's retirement party next month?'

'No! I don't think your mother's retirement was flagged up on my event horizon . . . but . . . so . . . would I be correct in thinking you're about to utter the oh-so-flattering words: "plus one"?'

'Connor?' Annie snuggled up against him. 'You could ask for favours in return for this.'

'Favours?' he wondered. 'You can't offer me sexual—'

'Material,' she clarified. 'It's worth at least two, maybe even three extra discount purchases from the Annie V Trading Station.'

'Oh, thanks a lot!' he said huffily, 'I want free designer knickers or I don't co-operate.'

'I may be able to arrange that,' she said, recalling a pyramid of Calvin Kleins on three for two at TK Maxx. Hopefully there wouldn't just be XXLs and XXSs left.

'Big family gathering for the retirement?' he wondered.

Annie nodded: 'I don't want to go on my own. I mean, obviously Lana and Owen are coming, but I want someone there just for me.'

He stroked her hair, then let a smile break over his impressive features. 'Will there be ageing aunties?' he asked.

'At least three. Maybe four.'

'Ooh, I do like a tipsy ageing aunty, that's my core fan base, you know . . . Wild drunken dancing?'

'Definitely. A live band apparently because it's a Scottish-themed ceilidh evening. In fact,' she sat up and grinned at him: she had just had one of her best ideas of the day, 'I'm going to hire you a kilt.'

'A kiltie?' Connor grinned back, revealing perfect – and laser-treated – teeth. 'Oh yes, Annie, yes! One of those black leather ones?'

'Whatever turns you on, darlin'.'

'A black leather kiltie with nothing underneath?' In a passable Sean Connery purr, he added: 'Moneypenny, how can I rrrefuse? And what will my delectable date for the evening be wearing?'

'Now that is a good question,' Annie replied.

Chapter Six

Paula on parade:

Genuine Asian hair extensions, braided (Blaxx salon)
Spray-on black Gucci dress (The Store's sale preview)
Fuchsia thong (Brick Lane market, three for £1)
A 'Hollywood' wax (Blaxx)
Orange and fuchsia striped false nails (Blaxx)
Orange suede Jimmy Choo stilettos (mates' rates
at Annie V's Trading Station)
Est. cost: £805

'What's on special offer at Asda?'

'Delia, girl, you're in early, aren't you?' On spotting the bustling, well-upholstered figure of the floor's cleaning lady, Annie had checked her watch and noted that it was still an hour and a half till closing time.

'I'm tidying out my cupboard,' Delia explained. Annie found this hard to understand, as Delia kept the neatest cleaning cupboard in the Western world. The frayed mops were carefully rinsed out, squeezed and hung to dry; the cloths were pegged up on their own little washing line and the bottles of industrial cleansers and polishes were always wiped down and lined up on the shelves with all the labels facing outwards.

'Then I'm planning a little shop for myself.' Delia's gleaming dark face split with a giggle which set her short shiny wig jiggling. 'No point working here if I can't spoil myself from time to time.'

Stepping close to Annie, she asked, 'I take it we're still OK with our little arrangement?'

'We certainly are,' Annie assured her, trying not to imagine what Donna would think of it.

On the very rare occasion when Delia bought something from The Store, Annie put it through the till under her name because she was entitled to a 20 per cent staff discount, whereas Delia, employed by a subcontracted cleaning company, was not. An injustice Annie was delighted to subvert. 'What are you buying?' she couldn't help asking.

'Oh, I'm going to enjoy myself looking for a while, then I'll come to you with my extravagances,' Delia chuckled and gave Annie's arm a squeeze, her chubby, dark brown hand adorned with five short, but beautifully lacquered plum fingernails.

'Trying anything on?'

'Oh no, you know me, Annie, I only shop for clothes at Harvey Nichols!' came Delia's reply with a hefty wink. 'Anyways, I couldn't get my big butt into anything you sell.'

'Yes you could,' Annie protested. 'Look, look, girl, just over here we have—'

But Delia cut her off: 'Stop your sales pitch right there,

you devil woman,' she said, waggling a fingertip. 'I'm not falling for it. I know just what I'm buying and first off, I'm walking my butt to lingerie.'

'Oooh!' Annie teased. 'Something fancy?'

Delia gave her great rattling, throaty, chest-clearing laugh at this. Now her gold hoop earrings were jangling. 'Oh yeah . . . I'm gonna make some lucky man's day,' she chuckled. 'See you later.'

Annie watched Delia walk off in the direction of the underwear department, still chuckling and swishing her substantial derrière from side to side just for Annie's benefit.

Delia had three jobs, four children and one cramped council flat on the very outer reaches of Isleworth. She had to take three buses to make it in for her 6 a.m. start every weekday morning. The bags under her eyes were like two broad sweeps of kohl, except they looked irremovable. Delia would have to be knocked out for a month to make any difference to those.

Considering her personal circumstances, she was allowed to be the most grouchy, bitchy, irritable person in the world – like many other members of the cleaning, not to mention sales staff – but Delia remained stubbornly happy and upbeat. Maybe there was inextinguishable Caribbean sunshine in her soul or maybe it was her devout Jehovah's Witness religion and the Power of Prayer.

Delia was always busy on Annie's behalf: 'I'm praying for you and yours, baby. Don't even try telling me not to.'

But Annie, almost as much as Delia, understood that when life handed you a bum deal you either had to get up, put on your face, pull back your shoulders and make the best of it, or else go under.

The phone in the Personal Shopping area began to ring, so Annie answered.

'Annie? Hi, it's Dale. You busy?'

'No-one in at the moment,' she told him.

'I'm going to send someone up to you, then. Check yourself over in the mirror, girlfriend.'

Click.

He hung up. No further information – although she suspected this might have something to do with her coffee break chit-chat about how she was on the lookout for a *very* wealthy husband and couldn't you boys down there in the menswear department do something to help me out, when you're not too busy chatting up the clients yourself, obviously.

Annie didn't trust Dale's judgement on a tie, let alone potential husband material, but nevertheless she redid her ponytail, applied a fresh dab of lip gloss, spritz of perfume and waited. Paula was busy on the shop floor, so for the moment she had the Personal Shopping suite to herself.

No sooner did she clap eyes on Mr Spencer Moore, as he was grandly introduced by Dale – weighed down by a selection of suits, shirts, jackets and ties – than her suspicions about the menswear assistant's judgement were confirmed.

Spencer was gay. Definitely. Why hadn't Dale been able to tell? Weren't the round red-rimmed glasses perched in the middle of his face clue enough?

'Mr Moore, hello, I'm Annie,' she gushed in the

direction of the new arrival. 'Come in, come on in. I'm here to help, so . . . Take the lovely big changing room on the right here. We'll hang everything up for you.

'He's gay!' she hissed at Dale as soon as she got the chance.

'Na-ah.' Dale shook his close-cropped head and raised his eyebrows at her teasingly: 'He's a divorced, straight man who dresses gay. I know. It's weird, he's an urban sub-species . . . a mutation possibly caused by his "designer" career. I thought he needed a woman's touch, plus, you might get a date out of it. He's loaded,' he added in a whisper, then: 'We split the commission, by the way.'

'Babes, if I get a date out of this, you can have all the commission,' she told him.

Dale, an only child, who'd wasted all Mummy's money on drama lessons, sashayed to the main door and blew her a goodbye kiss.

It turned out Spencer, late forties, fit and freshly divorced, obviously took the fashion section of the Sunday supplements far too seriously for a man of his age and status. Hence the confusing signals.

'Are you dating again, or is it too soon?' Annie asked, quickly defusing the rather bald question with: 'I'm just wondering if you'll need some more casual outfits.'

'Oh, definitely ready to date again,' Spencer confided as she paired a pale grey pinstriped suit with a pastel-coloured shirt and tie and urged him to try them on. Strangely, there was nothing more hetero than the right shade of pink.

'So we have to make a babe magnet of you,' she smiled.

'Er, well . . .'

She had to tone it down, she told herself. Clearly, he was a reserved kind of guy.

'Where do you live?' she asked him from the other side of the drawn curtain as he tried on the outfit she'd suggested.

'Kensington,' he told her. And didn't return the question, she noticed. Some customers always assumed that shop staff were so beneath them. It was up to her to put herself in a very different light.

'Oh lovely,' she told him, 'I was at school there. Francis Holland.' There, that would put him straight. Everyone had heard of Francis Holland, one of the smartest all-girl schools in London.

'Really?!' It was a little too surprised.

'Yes. I loved it. I discovered art there.' She didn't like the way that came out, now she was sounding posher than the Queen. 'Yeah, then did art school afterwards: theatre costume and design. I worked in films for a bit and now I'm a consultant here.' Consultant sounded great. Like she didn't work here all the time. Like she had another high-flying career elsewhere, away from The Store, which of course technically she did. There was Annie V's . . . the property business, on the verge of taking off . . . the home makeovers.

It seemed to do the trick. Spencer asked which art school she'd gone to and told her where he'd studied.

Then he pulled open the curtain, stepped out and asked: 'What do you think?' making eye contact now, appreciating that he was dealing with a high-calibre 'consultant'.

He looked good. The suit was a great cut but roomier and so a little more macho than the one he'd come in wearing. The pale pink suited his complexion. She couldn't get past those awful glasses though.

'Nice.' She stroked down the lapels, then made him turn around so she could run her hands over his shoulders and back, all in the name of smoothing out the suit obviously. 'Very nice. We'll put that on the "definitely maybe" rail and then I want you to try this on.'

She held out a cashmere blend Nicole Farhi. Super-hetero wear.

'This is real quality, Mr Moore.' She stroked the jacket to emphasize her point. 'I don't waste my money on anything inferior.'

He took the suit from her, meeting her eyes and brushing past her hand in the process, which she took to be an excellent sign. She pulled the curtain shut and grinned.

'"*Nowt as expensive as cheap*," as my dad used to say.' When Spencer made no response to this, she explained: 'Because cheap things wear out so quickly and have to be replaced.'

But then Paula breezed in and, not noticing the occupied cubicle, asked in a loud voice: 'Hey, Annie, what's on special offer at Asda this week?'

Annie pulled a face and pointed at the curtain.

'All right,' Paula said, much more quietly, 'but I've got loads of birthdays coming up, no money and I need to know where to get cheap presents.'

'Later!' Annie hissed.

Joy of joys, their boss Donna was now striding into the

suite looking as if she'd bitten on a bee: 'Paula! Annie's office, now!' she barked, acknowledging Annie only with a quick raise of the eyebrow.

'Yes, that will be fine, Donna,' Annie told her with mock politeness. 'Please make yourself at home in my office.'

Clearly a major telling-off was about to rain down on Paula's pretty, plaited head. The two personal shoppers exchanged sympathetic looks and Annie gave Paula a surreptitious wink.

Oblivious to the latest developments in in-store politics, Spencer pulled back the curtain to have his second outfit appraised.

'Hmm . . .' Annie smoothed down the jacket again, examined it from behind, but told him she wasn't as happy with this one. Together, they sorted through Dale's selections for the next possible ensemble.

Once Spencer was safely back behind the curtain, Annie decided that although she was trying to steer totally clear of Donna, she couldn't leave Paula in there to face the witch alone.

She tapped on the door of her office and opened it without waiting for a reply. 'Is everything OK in here?' she asked.

One glance at Paula's tear-stained face told her that it was not.

'Can I help with anything at all, Donna?' she went on. 'Would you like me to explain anything? I do oversee Paula after all.'

Donna spat out: 'We've had the suite's sales figures in for the month and Paula's are way down on January.'

'But February is always lower than January,' Annie

reminded her, trying to keep the indignation out of her voice.

'I'm aware of the general pattern of annual sales, thank you, Annie,' Donna snapped, 'but Paula's figures are much lower than they should be. There's a job on the shop floor open, so I'm pulling Paula out of here. People come to the Personal Shopping suite desperate to buy new clothes. If Paula can't sell to them, then who the hell can she sell to?'

Despite her written warning, Annie couldn't help mentioning 'the difficult new collections' in Paula's defence. What she would have loved to say was that if Donna hadn't gone to the trade shows right after she'd been dumped by her girlfriend, then maybe the collections wouldn't be quite so *difficult*. The sales team were now flat out trying to shift 'tulip' skirts (i.e. universally unflattering sacks) in shades of 'mushroom' and 'taupe' (otherwise known as hessian), not to mention cashmere trapeze tops in screaming orange and lime.

'Don't ever, ever complain about my collections!' Donna looked poised to gouge out an eye now. 'The Store is proud to showcase some of the most cutting-edge fashion in London . . . in Europe . . . in the world!'

Annie was bursting to say: I rest my case. But she had her own interests to look after, as well as Paula's.

She heard Spencer opening the changing room curtain, so knew she had to get back, but before she did Donna managed to issue another threat: 'And don't you dare abuse your staff discount, Annie Valentine, I'm keeping a very close eye on your transactions. If I find anyone has used it apart from you . . .'

Just because she couldn't find anything witchy to

say about Annie's sales she had to resort to this. Vicious cow.

Spencer was happily admiring himself in the mirror. 'This is fantastic! You're a genius!' he enthused, which cheered her up immediately. 'I'd never have thought of Romeo Gigli. I thought he was for girls.'

'Italian,' she told him. 'You can't go wrong with a good Italian. Mr Moore—' she began.

'Please, call me Spencer.' He straightened the heavy silk tie and admired his reflection in the mirror.

'OK, Spencer . . . we have to talk about your glasses.'

'Do we?'

'Yes we do.' Annie leaned in to tell him gently, as if breaking seriously bad news, 'I'm sorry, this may come as a terrible shock, but those are gay glasses.'

'Oh? The glasses? The glasses are gay?' He sounded completely taken aback.

'Yup. Definitely,' she assured him. 'Your shoes too. Too pointed and with top-stitching. I'd even say the belt as well. Women pick up on these things and you are giving off a gay vibe. Which is obviously great . . . if you're gay. But you're not. Right?'

'Well, no.'

'You need something smaller, maybe with a silver frame . . .' She reached up to take off his glasses and stared quite unapologetically at his face. Not bad, she was thinking, *in need of some general upgrading but some excellent period features.*

'You'd look very handsome with contacts,' she told him. 'We definitely need a moss green tie for you. With those distracting red frames, I hadn't noticed your eyes were green. We need to find you ties in exactly the same shade. But don't wear them with the pink shirt . . . obviously.'

Spencer had the decency to blush slightly. He was really quite nice; she was warming to him by the moment and wondering how she could arrange an out-of-store meeting . . . or at the very least a follow-up shopping session.

'Try on the Paul Smith,' she told him. 'I'll go in search of ties.'

As she stepped out of the suite, she ran right into Delia.

'Annie, I'm back . . . laden down!' An even happier Delia was carrying one of The Store's pink rubber shopping baskets and waving a shiny, gold-lettered bag from the cosmetics department: 'Oh, I've been pampered,' she confided, 'let me tell you!'

She held open the bag to show Annie the array of mini pots, sachets and trial sizes the girls in Cosmetics had no doubt been charmed into handing over to her.

'OK, here's my basket.'

Annie ushered her to a till well away from the shopping suite. Donna would be out of there like an angry wasp any moment and Annie didn't want to be caught doing anything Donna could sting her for. But there was no question of letting Delia down.

Annie tapped her code into the computer and rang up Delia's treats: four pairs of Sloggi super-comfort thongs, size 22, Chanel's No. 5 bath soap and a Mac nail varnish in brightest orange.

All good choices. Every woman, no matter how hard pressed, needed box-new, comfortable thongs in the knicker drawer, a perfectly indulgent bar of soap and a flash of designer colour, even if it was just on the nails.

Delia picked up the soap and sniffed it deeply: 'I love this. Absolutely love it. And I get to smell like Nicole Kidman,' she cackled. 'In a big bag please, Annie.' Delia winked at her. 'Today I'm a customer at The Store, not just the cleaner.'

Delia was just bustling out of sight when Donna stormed out, looking for her next assassination victim. Annie should really spike Donna's mineral water with Valium, she thought. For everyone's benefit.

Donna spotted her at the till and for one long, eerie moment stared straight at her. But then she carried on.

With a selection of ties in her hand, Annie headed back to the suite, taking a moment to pep-talk Paula, before she returned to Spencer.

'C'mon, girl,' she said and passed Paula a tissue. 'Don't let the Queen of Spleen get you down. Do a stint on the sales floor and then I'll wangle you back in here again. Honest. You just need practice. More experience with the customers. Donna forgets how long I've been doing this for. C'mon.' Annie worried about the proximity of Paula's nails to her tearful eyes. 'We're supposed to go out tonight, aren't we?' Annie reminded her. 'So, get changed. Glad rags on. Touch up the face. I'll be with you in' – she checked her watch – 'twenty or so.'

Spencer was tiring of trying new things on. Men's shopping tolerance was so tragically low, she'd noted before. It was time to close the deal with him . . . on all fronts.

Two suits, four shirts, two green ties (he must have liked the eye compliments), a pale suede blazer –

dangerously expensive but he went for it when she told him (*fairly* truthfully) how very like Pierce Brosnan he looked in it – two T-shirts and six pairs of new boxers, because 'You never know,' she'd winked at him cheekily.

'I've never, ever bought this much all at once before.' He looked concerned at the packed rail they'd amassed.

'You look great in everything,' she assured him. 'You're going to love wearing these clothes, you're going to get total value for money from them and wear them to bits. You've got to start going out straight away. This week! Tonight!' Was that hint enough?

But nothing came, so she prompted: 'What's your idea of a good night out?'

He thought for a moment before telling her: 'You know what I like? A really well-made gin and tonic in a great bar. Somewhere with atmosphere, not too noisy, not too quiet. Somewhere . . .'

'Classy,' she finished his sentence.

'I can't stand cocktails and girlie drinks, happy hour all that sort of thing,' he added.

'No, no. Me neither,' she nodded and fibbed out-rageously, 'Cocktails? Oh no . . .' but these words just served to summon up Paula, in a spray-on black dress and neon heels, and her high-volume question: 'Annie, are you ready yet?! We're going to miss happy hour at Freddy's and we're sharing a jug of margaritas after the day I've had.'

Classy. Oh yes.

'Theatre? I bet you like the theatre?' Annie made one last attempt at somehow connecting with Spencer, as she rang up his purchases.

'Oh, yes. I'm going to the Noël Coward thing that's just opened, what's it called again?'

Sunshine was breaking through the clouds.

'*After the Ball*? When are you going?' Annie could barely contain her grin.

'Thursday night, I think.'

'No! Really,' she gushed. 'My friend is in one of the lead roles and that's the night he's invited me along. He says Thursday night is the real theatre buff's night.' She was making this up as she went along. Every word. Well, OK, apart from Connor being the lead.

'Really!' Spencer didn't sound quite as pleased as she'd hoped.

'I might see you there then, in your fabulous new clothes.'

'Well, yes . . . That would be nice . . .'

'And contact lenses,' she advised. 'Either a small metal rim or contacts. Definitely.'

'Right . . . er . . .'

It was hard to judge from so few words whether Spencer was pleased at this turn of events, or worried that he now had a stalker on his hands.

Chapter Seven

Megan's outfit for her ex-husband's wedding:

Missoni dress (The Store)
Manolo boots (The Store)
Gucci bag (Gucci)
Philip Treacy hat (The Store)
3.5-carat emerald engagement ring (Ex-husband)
Cartier diamond watch (Ex-husband)
Asprey gold and diamond bracelet (Ex-husband)
Est. cost £220,000

'I want to look everything his cheap little girlfriend is not.'

'Nooooooooooooo!' shrieked Taylor. She yanked the four-figure silky, frothy Matthew Williamson creation up over her head and tossed it onto the floor.

'No more empire lines! I've tried on six now and they all make me look fucking pregnant!'

'Taylor!' Megan warned in knee-jerk reaction to the swearing.

Annie was so exhausted, she was going to have to

mainline Red Bull when this ordeal was finally over. She'd already been with Taylor and her terrifying mother, Megan, for one and a half hours: they'd booked a double session.

Dressing them was like the Personal Shopper Olympics. Annie was always surprised when they came back to her, because she was sure these *Vogue, Harpers* and Net-a-porter experts, these females wealthy enough to shop for everything they could possibly need in The Store, even groceries, knew far more about up-to-the-nanosecond fashion than she ever could.

She suspected she was brought in, like the UN, to serve in a peacekeeping role when this precocious 16-year-old went frock hunting with her beautiful mama.

Taylor was, like every teenage girl, a special shopping challenge.

She was extraordinarily pretty with long flicky blond hair and the lean, perfectly proportioned body and dewy complexion born of great genes and lashings of money.

Taylor was made of fresh air, skiing holidays, summers on the beach under factor 30, sensible boarding-school food, a mild eating disorder and daily workouts on the hockey pitch.

Here to choose outfits for Taylor's father's remarriage, it didn't look as if they were ever going to agree because Megan wanted Taylor to wear something sweet and girly, whereas Taylor wanted the kind of dress a 30-year-old vamp would consider daring.

Taylor had dismissed all suits as 'bo-oh-ring', including a gorgeous pale pink Miu Miu which had inspired her to say: 'Look at me, I'm Lady Penelope,' and then do a really quite funny impersonation of the *Thunderbirds* puppet.

In pale blue velvet and lace, while Megan and Annie had sighed at how divine she was, Taylor had pulled a face and gone: 'Yeuchh! What a drip!'

All the cute empire lines had been tossed off in horror and Annie was beginning to wonder what more The Store could offer.

'I want the black wrap! Pleeeeease,' Taylor whined, sounding more and more like the spoiled and pampered princess she was.

Megan drew herself up to full height, formidable in head to toe Dior, sighed and looked at Annie for back-up before explaining once again: 'Taylor, you cannot wear black to your father's wedding. Absolutely no! Look,' she added bitchily, 'I don't think he should be marrying a twenty-two-year-old Romanian gymnast either, but we can't go in mourning and that's final.'

Annie had to turn her mind to very sad and lonely thoughts, to prevent herself from snorting with laughter at this.

The hour spent finding Megan's perfect outfit for the social and emotional ordeal of attending her ex-husband's remarriage had passed satisfyingly well.

Megan had come in with a wonderfully clear idea: 'I want a severely smart dress. Nothing soft, nothing flouncy, nothing flared. I want perfect tailoring, I want to look everything his . . .' dramatic pause to deliver these words as witheringly as possible, '*cheap, little girlfriend* is not: sophisticated, cultured, complicated, intelligent, elegant and grown-up.'

Annie, with a Parisian vision of chic in her mind, had

installed Megan in a changing room then run from floor to floor bringing her everything that could possibly comply with this description.

It hadn't taken long to find the dress: cream with an olive-coloured leaf print, narrow skirt, tight waist with a wide striped belt, close-cut bodice with a high ruffled neckline.

'It's not soft,' she'd promised Megan, 'it's supremely elegant.' It was also Missoni and comfortingly extortionate.

Wide, three-quarter-length balloon sleeves completed the dress, so Megan could display her most extravagant gold bracelet, diamond-studded watch and enormous emerald ring to full effect.

'I want suede stiletto boots to go with this and, of course, a hat,' she'd instructed.

These had taken longer to get exactly right, but finally, a vision of ex-wife perfection had been created.

'Genius.' Megan had allowed herself to smile in the mirror.

Annie had stepped back to admire her handiwork. The tiny hat with long, spiked pheasant feathers was breathtaking on top of Megan's angular silhouette. How did Megan look? She looked just what she was: an extremely beautiful, bitter brunette who was far, far from over the biggest disappointment of her life. Her marriage to Mr Fabulously Wealthy Bigwig had ended and she was still devastated by her loss of status.

Although – Annie couldn't help thinking – surely the jewels and the annual allowance, generous enough to make small African nations weep, must be of some comfort? She wondered if Megan had thought about finding a new husband yet . . . and did she dare to ask her where she was going to look?

'The best thing about this outfit,' Megan had noted with triumph, 'is that, with jewellery, it will have cost *him* five times more than what the bride will be wearing. Poor little girl, she has no idea what she's in for. Romanian gymnast!' she'd snorted. 'Let's hope that Victor and his penis will be very happy.'

'I think we need a little break,' UN Annie suggested as Taylor flung another dress on the floor. 'Why don't we go down to the vintage boutique in the basement?' she risked.

Taylor's response to this looked reasonable, but Megan's eyebrows were arched and twitching.

'Don't worry,' Annie soothed, 'it's The Store's version of vintage: exclusive one-offs and collector's items worth more now than when they were bought.'

Down in the glamorous basement floor, a section had been made over as an antique clothes shop, complete with picturesque, worn wooden shelves crammed with dainty crocodile handbags, long leather gloves, feathered and furred hats. The rails were adorned with silks, lace, taffeta, chiffon. Dresses with history. Ghosts from parties that had been held all over the city since the 1920s and on into the fifties and sixties, even the eighties.

Annie had always liked secondhand. She liked to rummage through old, and usually much better made, clothes. These were not dresses that whispered 'you shall go to the ball', these gowns had been to the ball, danced till they dropped, sipped champagne, met the man of their dreams, sneaked a cigarette or two, kissed, maybe more, and come back to tell the tale.

OK, sometimes they didn't come back too pretty – a rip here, a mud mark there, or worse, a serious sweat stain, irremovable from pastel silk satin.

But in this department, the dresses were all in mint condition. They were hung just like the new clothes, with space around them, with respect and size tags.

The walls were decked with pure silk kimonos, tiny-waisted lace wedding gowns and photographs of some of the dresses on the days so long ago when they were brand new.

Bringing Megan and Taylor down here wasn't a mistake, she was relieved to see.

Taylor was already flicking through the size 8s and 10s with a keen eye and Megan was engrossed in the jewellery display where multi-stranded pearl chokers and sparkling dangling earrings competed with intricate enamelled brooches for attention.

'Look at this.' Megan was pointing to a posy of enamelled bluebells. 'This is the prettiest brooch I've ever seen and it's thirty pounds!' she exclaimed, as if she hadn't realized anything could cost less than £100. 'Taylor, you have to have it.'

Annie knew she could get much nicer ones for under £10 at her local rummage haunts. But that was the kind of info wasted on Megan. Megan was suspicious of anything cheap. She liked to pay more, to make sure she had the very best.

As Annie stood outside the pink velvet curtain of the fitting room, Taylor tried dresses on with a more serious intent than she had before.

She fitted everything she tried. It was disconcerting.

She had the teeny little waistline needed to squeeze into 1950s suits and 1960s prom dresses.

She looked dangerously close to declaring: 'This is the one,' in a boat-necked slim taffeta dress, turquoise with big silver buttons, which made her look like an old-time Hollywood starlet.

'Oh that is pretty,' was Megan's verdict. 'With silver shoes maybe . . .'

'Hmmm . . .' Taylor was twisting in front of the mirror, sticking out her hips, critically observing the shape of her tiny little behind, not quite 100 per cent happy.

'We've still got a few more.' Annie handed over a deep sea blue satin Chinese-style dress, which she thought was very promising.

'Oh!' Taylor held it out. 'Very nice. It looks a bit big, though.'

Only Taylor could look at size 8 satin and worry about it being too big.

'It doesn't have any stretch to it,' Annie reminded her. 'Anyway, it can always be taken in.'

Taylor took it into the fitting room and after several minutes of wriggling and wrestling with hooks and eyes, she opened the curtain with something of a flourish.

'What do you think?' She looked at Annie first then her mum. Annie suspected Taylor loved it, but wanted to sound them out first.

How could she not love it? She looked incredible.

She'd pulled her hair up into a ponytail which suited the dress even more. It had a high mandarin collar; she'd buttoned it all the way to the top, and a row of tiny satin-covered buttons led all the way down to the knee where the dress stopped. It skimmed her body from her small chest over her tiny waist and narrow hips. The sleeves did not end at upper arm, like most Chinese dresses. These in an unusually modern way stopped just past the elbow.

'It's quite like the shape of your dress, Mum, without the open neck and ruffle.'

'Yes,' Megan agreed. She seemed quite mesmerized by the effect too. To her, the dress still looked girlish and charming. To Taylor it was dangerously sophisticated. So it was perfect for the wedding, and yet, of course, quite devastatingly sexy.

'Can you sit down in it?' Annie wondered. Taylor aimed slowly for the stool in the corner of the dressing room.

'Yes, it's fine,' she assured them.

'What do you think of it?' Annie wanted to know.

Taylor stood up and looked at herself in the mirror: she twisted and turned, she put her hands on her hips, she squinted at her rear again, she stood up on tiptoes to mimic the effect of heels. Finally, she declared: 'I love it. I don't care if I never get another penny of pocket money this year . . . I have to have it . . . oh and a bag and shoes to go with it, *obviously*.' She peeped up at her mama with a wheedling little smile.

Megan gave a nod: 'OK, back upstairs, we'll go and look at shoes.'

Annie made an excuse to take her safely back to her office for a few minutes where she hoovered up her entire stash of emergency chocolate. And she'd thought choosing outfits with Lana was hard work.

*   *   *

111

'She didn't want a *Matthew Williamson*?!' Lana wanted to make sure she'd heard that bit right.

'Balled it up and chucked it on the floor!' Annie elaborated, passing thirds of garlic bread over to Owen who'd already ravenously polished off everything else on his plate.

'No!' Lana sounded quite thrilled by this sacrilege. 'On the floor!'

'Miu Miu was rejected, Marc Jacobs she wouldn't even try on, Chloé was "so over" – God, she was a nightmare. Imagine being able to afford any designer dress you could imagine, plus the bag, the shoes and real jewels to go with it, and being so miserable! Such a waste.' Annie forked up the last rubbery mouthful and chewed . . . for quite a long time. She'd got home so late, there hadn't been any time to shop – even in the *extortionate* corner shop – and she'd relied on finding something, *anything* in the fridge. But the inside of the Smeg (unbelievable discount deal, but it was orange and did have a dent on the side) had been like a scene from the dating game: cold and lonely.

One fat tomato, too pale and too chilled. One slice of bacon left in its greasy packet, two potatoes, a third of an onion wrapped in clingfilm, half a mini goat's cheese, possibly past its sell-by date, but also garlic, a packet of garlic bread and, yes! Result! A boxful of eggs.

'Supper, Mum?' Owen had come into the kitchen to ask. Looking so gangly and thin, she'd felt the urge to give him a Mars bar there and then.

'Spanish omelette and garlic bread!' she'd announced, inspired. But the three of them knew that her omelettes

112

were never 'fluffy' like Dinah's, they were tough. Why was that?

'So, have you had a chance to think about what you'd like to wear to Grandma's retirement party?' Annie asked Lana, while they were on the subject of teen dress traumas.

Something about Lana's smile in response to this question made Annie slightly anxious: it was a hesitant smile, a secretive smile with a hint of triumph in there too.

Uh-oh.

Lana didn't shop with her mother any more, which was a source of both relief and sadness to Annie. If she wanted to make herself really wistful, she would think of the hours she'd once spent with little Lana trying on dresses at H&M, picking out pink blouses, stripy tights and spangled hairclips, Lana pirouetting with happiness. All day long Annie styled others while the one person she'd always loved to dress found it 'too much pressure' to go shopping with her.

Since Annie and Lana's last changing room tantrum over a five-inch-long miniskirt for school, Lana now only shopped with other members of the Syrup Six – Annie liked that nickname, it had stuck in her mind ever since Mr Leon, no, must-remember-to-call-him-Ed, had told her about it.

'Have you bought something?' Annie tried to sound pleased. 'Come on then, show me.'

She didn't really feel she'd been adequately prepared for the sheer, backless, slashed-to-the-upper-thigh frothy black lace creation hanging on the front of Lana's wardrobe, still with its Primark price tag proudly attached.

Scratchy black nylon lace . . . nice . . . if Lana went anywhere near a candle in that thing, she'd be toast.

For a moment, Annie tried to imagine what Megan's response to it would be. Megan would probably faint, or run screaming from the room, spraying pure Fracas Parfum all around to decontaminate herself.

'Oh! Well! Yes!' Annie began, trying to muster as much calm as she could from the torrent of maternal negativity pulsing through her brain.

No use, she couldn't help blurting out: 'You're fourteen, Lana! But you've gone straight from velvet with bows to see-through lace. Weren't we meant to have the taffeta years in between? You know, sweet, crackly taffeta dresses with netting underneath, worn with pale tights and ballet pumps?' Even as Annie said it, she knew it sounded unlikely.

But she'd love to see Lana shine in bright blue: an iridescent silk that exactly matched the colour of her astonishing eyes.

Annie – who had brown eyes, who had coveted Roddy from the moment he'd set his swimming-pool-blue eyes on her – could be overwhelmed by Lana's eyes. Sometimes she couldn't break her gaze from them, sometimes she couldn't do battle with the girl training this blue laser beam on her, sometimes she had to give in completely to those eyes.

Lana had sensed this weakness of course, and in an argument she did everything she could to make eye contact with her mother.

'This is the dress I want to wear,' she said fiercely.

'But why?' Annie asked.

'Because I like it.'

114

'Why?' Annie insisted.

'Because it's cool . . . and I think I look good in it.'

'Does it make you look a lot older?'

'Maybe.'

'Do you want boys to think you're older?'

'Maybe.' Her arms crossed and she huffed.

Annie was now tempted to shout all sorts of unhelpful, bossy mum warnings: *'Haven't you heard of date rape?' 'You'll look so tarty in this!' 'This is your granny's party!'* and so on, but instead, she sat down on Lana's bed and tried to restrain herself.

'I know this isn't what you want to hear, Lana,' she began, 'but there's no need to be in such a rush to grow up. Honestly. Take your time. You have years of growing up ahead of you. Try to enjoy it.'

Lana just gave an exasperated sigh. Again, Annie bit her tongue: 'Why don't you put the dress on for me?' she asked. 'Let me see how it looks.'

'No!'

'Oh please . . . go on. I'll be totally constructive. On my best behaviour, I promise.'

Once Lana was standing in front of her, hands on lace-clad hips, face in a defiant pout, Annie knew she had to proceed with caution, utmost caution, or she would never, ever be allowed to shop with Lana ever.

The dress looked . . . well . . . being totally honest . . . looking as neutrally as possible . . .

'Turn around, baby . . .' she instructed, 'I like the back. Your back looks lovely. You'll have to wear one of those backless bra contraptions . . .'

'I've already bought one,' Lana said grumpily.

'And what about shoes?'

Lana slipped on her wine-coloured suede slingbacks. They looked fine.

'Hmmm.' Annie tried to keep her professional eye on this. Not her maternal eye which was, just like Megan's earlier today, finding it hard to move past the cleavage on display, the acre of creamy teen thigh.

Lana had a good figure, Annie couldn't help but proudly notice, with Roddy's pale skin and poker-straight black hair which on Lana hung down well below her shoulders.

'Did it come in any other colours?' Annie wondered.

'Muuuum!' Lana warned, but then volunteered the information: 'Navy blue and purple.'

'And you wouldn't consider maybe . . .'

Lana just glared.

'Just a second, I have something that could . . .' Annie went out of the room, took deep breaths and counted to ten. After a few minutes, she came back in with a large, overblown fake rose, almost the exact shade of Lana's shoes.

'Can we try it pinned to the front?' Annie asked. 'It's just . . . I'm not sure you'll want Granny's boyfriends talking to your boobs all night long, will you?'

A smile almost threatened to break over Lana's face now.

Annie pinned the flower in place.

'A little sparkly, wine-coloured shrug . . . would you let me treat you to something like that?' Annie asked, although where she'd find wine in the Spring collections . . . she'd have to look secondhand.

'Maybe.' Lana didn't sound convinced.

'A little bag?' Annie added.

'Maybe.'

'And just maybe, maybe, maybe . . .' she wheedled, 'we could just pop back to the shop' – as if it would be the easiest thing in the world – 'and try . . . just *try* . . . the navy blue?'

'Maybe.' But this came with the teensiest smile that gave Annie the hope that her foot was in the door.

She would broach the subject of stitching the split to a more modest knee-high another day.

That night, in front of her computer, watching the latest Trading Station deals close, figuring out with a red pen and calculator how much money she'd made this week and whether or not it was enough, Annie let her mind wander to her own outfit for the retirement party.

There were things in the wardrobe, obviously, but she wasn't sure if she wanted to wear them. She'd tried on a four-year-old party dress in front of the full-length mirror in her bedroom, but it had brought tears to her eyes.

The dress, sky blue slippy satin with vivid red poppies printed all over it, was a Roddy dress.

She'd bought it for a first proper celebby event. Red-carpet, cameras flashing . . . not at them, of course. Back then, Roddy had been a bit part. But what a fabulous night!

At the party after the première, Roddy's eyes had popped from his head. During filming, he'd been paid £250 a week, as the production had staggered from one financial disaster to another: actors, cameramen, production staff all leaving because they couldn't afford to work on it any more.

But come the première party, there was champagne

on tap, lobsters piled in great lazy heaps, the star actress in a strapless cream knit dress made of pure cashmere.

'The publicity budget is bigger than their entire production budget,' Roddy had joked, holding both their glasses out to yet another passing waiter.

His reaction to her dress had been a frank, succinct Roddy special: 'Fucking brilliant! Take it off, immediately!'

Alone, in front of the mirror, Annie unzipped it, let it fall to the floor, then she angrily stuffed it back into its cloth cover, wondering if she would ever be able to wear it again.

Never mind, she told herself, blowing her nose firmly when the tears were over. There was the rose pink velvet dress she'd seen on eBay, she knew the label, knew the style, knew the sizing. It would definitely fit. It would be perfect, in fact: a fine, silk velvet, with a supple drape, a fitted bodice, covered buttons, bingo-wing disguising half-sleeves and a panel of lace at the front of the skirt for interest.

It was probably going to go for too much . . . but it wouldn't hurt to look, would it? Just a teensy peek? She made the mouse clicks and found it, hovering thirty-five minutes from the close of bidding at £50 below the absolute most she could afford to spend on it. If she just held steady and waited thirty-three minutes before putting in a bid just £5 higher . . . then it would be hers. Although it was well past her bedtime, she went to make herself a cup of tea.

Chapter Eight

Dress-up Dinah:

Gold Grecian goddess dress (Miss Selfridge)
White fake fur coat (Cancer Research)
Gold tap shoes (Dancewear shop)
Gold and ruby earrings (Portobello market)
Liberal amount of Fake Bake
Est. cost: £95

'I've overdone it! I'm the Fake Bake sheikh!'

'He's there! I've just spotted him, down at the front. Best seats!' Annie couldn't keep the glee from her voice as she told Dinah.

'Thank God for that,' was Dinah's response. It was obvious from the outset that Annie's outing to *After The Ball* was not purely in the interest of theatrical pleasure or even Connor support. She'd insisted Dinah dress up 'you know, properly, let's make an event of it'. Then she'd confided there was 'someone' she was hoping to 'bump into' in the audience.

'Don't you think that's just a little bit desperate?'
Dinah had asked once Annie had explained the Spencer
situation.

'Desperate? No, of course not. Wait till you meet him.
He's really quite interesting.'

Annie had turned up at the theatre looking her very
best. She'd come straight from work, but this hadn't
stopped her devoting twenty-five minutes to her outfit,
hair and make-up in the changing room. She knew
what conservative Spencer-type men liked in women.
Nothing complicated, for starters. They understood
obvious colours: black, red, white, blue . . . anything
tonal like taupe, terracotta or pistachio confused them.
They liked shapely dresses with tasteful amounts of leg
and cleavage on display. They liked small jewels, lipstick
and shiny long hair, especially if it was tied up . . .
enticingly ready to be undone.

'Oooh, very . . . Mediterranean,' Annie had greeted
her sister.

'Shut up!' an extremely tanned Dinah had told her
through gritted teeth. 'I know, I know, I've overdone it.
I'm the Fake Bake sheikh.'

The first fake tan of the season (March had just
arrived) was always an initiation. Dinah had forgotten
how much bloody scrubbing had to be done beforehand
and just how little of the stuff was needed.

'Do I look different?' Annie had asked her sister.

'You look great,' Dinah had assured her, 'I always love
you in that dress.' She surveyed the black crêpe Diane
von Furstenberg wrap approvingly.

'Yeah but look closely, babes,' Annie instructed.

Dinah peered into her face: 'Hmmm . . . something's a

bit . . . Annie! You've not had an injection or something, have you?'

Annie fluttered her eyelashes: 'Clue,' she said.

When Dinah just stared back blankly, Annie explained: 'I've had eyelash extensions. Aren't they gorgeous?' Flutter, flutter went the lashes.

'Eyelash extensions!!' Dinah had never even heard of such a thing. 'You're absolutely mad. What was wrong with your lashes before?' she'd exclaimed, but the questions had quickly followed: 'It cost how much!?' 'They use glue and sharpened tweezers?' 'How long does it last anyway?' 'You have to *trim* them when they get too long!'

'I went with Connor,' Annie had explained, scanning the foyer like a twitchy bird of prey, as they went in.

'Connor?'

'He needs them for his close-ups, apparently. It makes all the grannies swoon when McCabie bats his lovely long lashes in soft focus.'

'Ha. Will you stop looking round like that?' Dinah had hissed. 'You look like you're wanted by the Mafia or something.'

'I can't see him.' Annie had begun to worry. Maybe Spencer wasn't coming. Maybe she'd scared him off.

Although they were amongst the last to take their seats, she still hadn't spotted him; no sign of him in the interval either. It was distracting her immensely from Connor's clever, comic performance. But then she'd always thought acting was a bit of a scam: if you wanted to be a star, you just had to choose roles in which you could be a totally over-the-top version of yourself. Here was Connor on stage, being just as devastatingly handsome and witty as he'd been in her front room a few weeks ago and a rapt audience of thousands thought he was acting!

But just as the lights were starting to dim for the third act, Annie's eyes alighted on a promising-looking head of gunmetal grey hair and she watched as Spencer – minus the glasses – glanced over his shoulder.

'Bingo!' she told Dinah and began to plan for the 'accidental' meeting at the end of the show.

'Spencer, hi!' she called, frantically treading on toes in her rush to get out of her row and greet him.

'Oh, er . . . hello,' he managed once he had got her into focus. Maybe he hadn't sorted out the contacts yet.

'Did you enjoy the show? Wasn't Connor great?'

'Oh, Connor McCabe, is he the actor you . . . ?'

'Yes, yes . . .' *And who was this woman by his side, so obviously with him? Who was this attractive, raven-haired sophisticate in a sleeveless silk shell with an elegant grey pashmina draped over her arms?*

The woman was waiting expectantly, possibly wondering something similar.

'This is my sister Dinah,' Annie offered as Dinah came up behind her. 'She's been on holiday.' Well, it seemed necessary to offer some sort of explanation, although the urge to add *in her bathroom* was dangerously strong.

'Oh really, where've you been?' Spencer asked politely.

'Dubai!' Annie answered for her, inspired by the sheikh comment maybe, but also because it was the hottest and blandest destination Annie could think of that she was, fingers crossed, certain Spencer wouldn't have been to. And really, what follow-up questions could 'Dubai' provoke? 'Did you like the sand?'

'Nice,' Spencer said. And left it at that.

The elegant one cleared her throat slightly.

'Oh, Louisa, this is Annie. I met her just the other day, we were . . . um . . . introduced by a friend.'

Ah! Outwardly trendy, inwardly square Spencer was obviously embarrassed he'd been personally shopped for. Ah! It wasn't that Louisa was the object of his new affections, new love of his life or whatever . . . Annie felt a fresh burst of hope.

'This is Louisa, my date.' He turned and smiled shyly at grey pashmina girl. 'You don't mind if I call you that, do you?'

Louisa beamed.

Hopes dashed.

'Why don't you come backstage with us and meet Connor?' was Annie's fresh new idea. 'He'd love it. He's so vain, I have to keep him convinced he has an army of fans who are held back by security cordons every night.'

Spencer didn't seem so sure, but fortunately Louisa looked at him and said, 'I'd love that. It would be so glamorous. Go on, Spencer . . . I mean, if you're sure it won't be any trouble.'

Connor was slightly taken aback by the rapturous 'Darling, you were wonderful' and full-on mouth kiss that Annie treated him to when she arrived in his dressing room. 'You were brilliant, honestly! Connor, this is Spencer, and his lovely date Louisa.'

At these words, Connor understood his role completely.

123

'Pleased to meet you! Very nice of you to come back-stage to say hello.' He shook their hands and casually folded Annie in under his arm, hugging her tightly round the waist.

'You really did enjoy it, did you?'

'Oh yes,' they both gushed.

'I think Noël Coward has so much to say to twenty-first century audiences and he always says it so wittily . . .' Connor began.

And so it went on for quite a time, getting luvvier and luvvier by the minute, until Spencer took a glance at his watch and warned that they would have to make a move or else they'd be too late for the table he'd reserved at the Ivy for dinner.

Ha! The Ivy for dinner, huh? Annie couldn't help feeling a stab of jealousy. 'How lovely,' she said. Declaring that she and Connor were snuggling up for a cosy evening at home – 'Aren't we, darling?' – was probably taking things too far.

'What on earth were you two playing at?' Dinah wanted to know when Spencer and his date had left.

'Oh Dinah! You are just so sweet!' Annie teased her. 'Luckily Connor understands. It's just the same with handbags.'

'What is?'

'You only want a handbag if somebody else has it or if it's hard to get hold of, a limited edition, or collector's item preferably with a waiting list. If we have twenty-five handbags sitting in a pile with seventy per cent off emblazoned across them, we can't shift a one. I promise you.'

'Ah.'

'I'm expecting a message from Spencer on the Personal Shopping suite's answering machine tomorrow morning, guaranteed,' Annie told her.

'Hmmm.' Dinah couldn't help feeling this was a tad optimistic.

Chapter Nine

Fern's dazzling retirement outfit:

Salmon pink and white lace jacket (John Lewis)
White silk camisole (John Lewis)
Long salmon pink taffeta skirt (John Lewis)
Unspeakably awful beige, sensible-heeled
slingback sandals (John Lewis)
Pale pink nail varnish (Chanel)
Total estimated cost: £290

'I've invited someone very interesting, just for you . . .'

'Woooo hooo! We're so hot, we're smokin'! Every single one of us is going to pull tonight . . . Especially Owen,' was Connor's verdict as the party of four got out of the car and launched themselves – arm in arm, as he'd insisted – across the dark gravelled courtyard towards the country house hotel Annie's mother had chosen for her retirement party.

Annie smiled proudly at her children. Lana, negotiating heels, bag, fluffy bolero, way too much purple eye shadow and the lace dress (in navy), returned the smile a little nervously, but Owen grinned. He'd gone for a hired mini dinner suit with wing collar and red satin bow-tie. Connor had helped him gel his hair into the kind of perpendicular quiff belonging to junior Hollywood royalty and he was strutting his stuff.

Connor in black leather kilt, ruffled shirt and black leather waistcoat looked unforgettable: 100 per cent Highland hunk. He may have been from Lancashire but he was dressed for the ceilidh.

'Now remember, Owen, the fact that you are a man of few words is going to stand you in great stead tonight,' Connor was confiding in his youngest friend. 'The ladies love a bit of mystery. I could really take some tips from you. I am always saying far too much, shooting my mouth off, getting into all kinds of trouble and that's why I am sooo single.'

Owen giggled at this.

'Lana, you are a knockout,' Connor assured her. 'Obviously I'll have to be your bodyguard for the evening to keep the swarms of suitors at bay.'

'Oh ha ha,' she told him, but a smile was breaking at the corners of her mouth and threatening to run away across her face.

The sweetheart, Annie thought.

With her hair piled up glamorously, bright lipstick and highest heels, Annie felt the soft pink velvet of her breathtaking dress stroke comfortingly against her. There were going to be many people at this party that she hadn't seen for several years, that she hadn't seen since her sudden, devastating transformation from happily married to single, and she wanted to show them

127

how together she was now, how happy, how successful and how well she was coping. The dress was her suit of shining armour, although she would be selling it on . . . tonight, hopefully.

And anyway, while Annie awaited Spencer's phone call – two weeks had passed and still nothing! – and her next Discerning Dinner, what harm could there be in checking out the party talent? Not that she suspected there'd be much, despite her mother's best intentions.

'I've invited someone very interesting, just for you,' Fern had told her, when they'd met up three days ago for a pre-party nerve-calming afternoon. Fern had had to put her outfit on yet again just to make sure she was totally happy with it. Annie had been on hand to soothe and recommend make-up.

'Uh-oh!' was Annie's reaction to 'someone very interesting'. 'I've told you, Mum, our tastes in men are a little different. Me: under fifty, all own hair, teeth and seriously solvent. You: under eighty, good sense of humour, not yet incontinent. Is your fancy boy coming?' she'd asked, which had caused her mother to hoot with laughter.

'Is he?' Annie prodded. 'Mr Lubkin and his zimmer frame?'

'Walking stick, Annie!' Fern had corrected. 'He broke his leg hang-gliding and now walks with a stick. And he's a *friend*.'

'Ooooh, fancy. Mum . . .' Annie had asked her next, 'do you ever mind that you're still on your own? I mean you must have minded so much when we were younger – but do you still mind?'

'No, no,' Fern had insisted with a smile. 'We're all on our own at some point, sweetheart.'

'But I never wanted to be on my own,' Annie had confided. 'This is not the way I thought my life would be. I always thought there would be someone else to share it all with.'

'Men always let you down . . . one way or another,' Fern had replied.

'Do they?' Annie had countered.

Fern had fixed her eyes on Annie's and insisted: 'Yes, they do – even when they don't mean to. Anyway,' she'd gone on, 'I was far too busy to find someone else when you were growing up, and then I was too bossy and now I'm too old. Past it.'

'Sixty is not the same as dead, Mum,' Annie had told her.

'To most men it is,' Fern had replied.

Annie had considered telling her mother: 'I think you've missed out. You never got all the really good stuff about being a couple.' She was even tempted to blurt out: 'I'm not fine like this, I'm not fine at all and I don't want to be fine. Some days I feel like I'm missing an arm . . . like I'm hardly even alive!' Instead, she'd kept quiet, but Fern had seemed to read her feelings and had soothed:

'You've had a very hard time, sweetheart. It'll take a long time to begin to feel normal again. But you'll get there. I know you will.'

'I've brought you a present.' Annie had surprised Fern, handing over a wrapped, pink-ribboned box. 'I'm treating you . . . and I want you to know I paid full price, you old moo, because you're worth it.' Then, in a much more serious voice she'd added: 'Thank you, you know, for everything. You've been such a help to me . . .' and they'd both had to hug very tightly and squeeze back their tears.

Her mother's reaction to the pale cappuccino-coloured suede heels inside the box seemed to be very positive. She'd tried them on underneath her pink skirt, she'd looked at herself this way and that, oooohed and aaaahed, had said many, many thank-yous and had given Annie a kiss. But Annie still wasn't convinced her mother *really* liked them.

Fern had always been a grade A dresser. Since her twenties, she'd followed the fashion rules usually ascribed to Parisians: sensible, slightly stuffy, but always, always supremely elegant.

She lived in wool trousers, silk blouses and little cashmere cardigans, occasionally donning a mid-calf skirt. A fabulous coat or jacket completed the classic look. Oh, and not forgetting the mock croc bag, Gucci watch, string of pearls and weighty gold bracelet.

Now that the days of scraping together school fees were long behind her, Fern, whose mission in life had once been to economize, now had a little more money to herself. She lived in a modest bungalow but bought top quality clothes, drove a classic Jag and had never, ever been seen with her legs in need of a wax or with one single grey millimetre of root emerging from her blond bob.

Even when she was gardening, it was in well-cut jeans with a spanking white Joseph top, her blue Hunter wellies and a trug.

'If I'm not wearing lipstick, you'll know I'm dead,'

she'd once told her daughters. Such was her dedicated work ethic, she never took a day off from looking good. This was a woman whose pyjamas, dressing gown, slippers and washbag all co-ordinated.

But Fern did have one fatal dressing flaw, which Annie was constantly trying to correct. Because Fern was a podiatrist, a healer of cracked heels, balm to bunions, carer of corns, she dealt with so much footwear-inflicted misery that she would never, ever wear pretty shoes. Even her most delicate of outfits was finished off with duck feet: sensible pumps, low squared heels, or worst of all, those white comfy slingbacks, the ones which came in an extra-wide fitting, and were a great favourite with HM The Queen, a woman Fern greatly admired, by the way.

Annie, shocked by the beige, orthopaedic-looking things her mother was intending to wear with her party outfit, had decided the only way to persuade her otherwise was to buy the alternative footwear herself.

With Connor on one arm and Owen linked to Lana on the other, Annie went through the foyer of the swanky hotel and into the tasteful drawing room, already swarming with guests.

Dinah spotted them before anyone else: 'Hey, Annie and the gang are here!'

'Oh, Billie, look at you,' Annie cooed.

Billie in pink ballet slippers and a tutu obliged with a twirl while Dinah rolled her eyes and explained: 'Yes, you have a party dress, don't you, Billie? That we bought specially for Granny's party, but you changed your mind, didn't you? About ten times! As for you,

Annie Valentine, you are wearing a sensational *new* dress . . . you bad girl!' Dinah wasn't so much teasing as disapproving.

'Yeah, but I'm going to sell it tonight, so it's OK,' Annie informed her.

'You are not!'

'Watch and learn,' Annie said with a wink. 'Is that Nic, our lawyer, over there? She looks . . . not bad, considering she picked that dress herself!'

Nic was their middle sister, the lawyer, who they hardly ever saw because she lived in Cornwall and was extremely busy, being a lawyer. Oh and by the way, had she mentioned Nic was a lawyer?

'C'mon, I'll take you over.' Dinah offered Annie a bare arm with only the merest kiss of fake tan.

'She's brought her new man, Rick,' Dinah whispered. 'And guess what, he's a lawyer.'

'No! Nic and Rick?! That's amazing, because you'll never guess? Nic's a lawyer too!'

As soon as Nic caught sight of Annie, she screeched a hello, holding out her arms towards her.

They did their hugs, hellos, how are yous, how are the children . . . then Annie was properly introduced to Nic's new man and immediately asked how they'd met.

'Oh, through work,' came the reply.

'Aha . . . maybe I should retrain. Do you think I'd make a good lawyer?' Annie joked.

'No,' Nic told her, 'but you're a wonderful shopper. Tell me about this dress. I love it. Love it! Much better than this disaster.' She gestured at her long-sleeved navy and silver matronly frock – there wasn't a better word to describe it. Good grief, unless Annie was

132

actually in the shop with Nic, telling her what to buy, she got it wrong every time.

'Feel.' Annie held out her arm. 'Feel the sleeve, go on. Silk velvet. Mmmmm. And isn't this just the perfect shade of salmon pink for our skin colouring, babes?'

Nic's fingers were rubbing against the material: 'That is gorgeous. Where is it from? It looks like one of our favourite labels.'

'No, no, no, you don't, Nicky. Look at her.' Annie winked at Nic's really very impressive Rick. 'She'd have the clothes off my back. She was always like this. Stealing stuff out of my cupboard.'

'Did not!' Nic protested. 'But I do like that dress. It's a Dries, isn't it? What do you think, Rick? Would I look nice in that, or not?'

Rick looked slightly uncomfortable at having to scrutinize a woman he'd only just met and imagine her dress on his girlfriend.

'This is not for sale!' Annie insisted.

'Of course it is, Annie,' Nic countered. 'Everything you own is for sale. Always has been. And we're exactly the same size . . .'

'Speak to me later,' Annie whispered. 'You might be able to persuade me once I've had a drink or two.'

'Mum!' Annie took in the pink and white vision which was their mother making a beeline for them. 'Belle of the ball!' she added and hugged her, but then she pulled back, looked down and saw not the suede creations she'd parted with £250 of her hard-earned cash to buy, but the bloody beige orthopaedic sandals!

'Muuuum!' she scolded.

133

'Oh, I can't drive the Jag in those heels, sweetheart,' was her mother's explanation.

'Drive the Jag?!!' Annie exclaimed. 'I thought we'd agreed you were getting a taxi.'

'I hate taxis. Such a waste of money,' her mother replied, but before she could be told off further, she was swept away by a tide of new guests.

Owen and Lana were still hovering not far from Annie's side, Owen very shy in the presence of so many friends and relations.

'You're going to be fine,' Annie reassured him. 'And most people here know not to expect you to talk to them straight away, Owen . . . unless you want to . . .' she added quickly, 'then that would be fine.'

'Annie Valentine!'

They pulled to a stop in front of Aunty Hilda, the old crone, some mothballed old creation from the 1980s draped about her.

She was so hard of hearing now that she spoke in harsh silence-slicing sentences, punctuated with a top-volume *'What's that?!'* – her reply to almost anything anybody said.

She was Fern's aunt, Annie's great-aunt. She was acidic, rude and wealthy – thanks to her dead husband rather than anything she'd done – so she felt entitled to be judgemental and critical. She was also family, so was tolerated and invited.

'Aunty Hilda, how are you doing?' Annie stooped to brush her lips against a powdery cheek.

'You're looking nice, dear,' was Hilda's verdict after a lengthy up-and-down, but it came with the rider, 'For a change.'

'Oh, and Owen here' – she pulled him in with her meaty arm for a sadistically close hug: 'You're so tall and handsome, but still the deaf mute?'

'No! He's not that at all—' Annie began but Hilda chose not to hear and carried on: 'Lana? Ah, well . . .'

Annie wanted to put her arm up to defend her daughter and issue a stern: *Oh no you don't, you evil old bag, fragile teenage ego in development. Step back.*

'Hmmm . . . feathers?' Hilda remarked of Lana's bolero, in a way that conveyed her deepest disregard for plumage.

Annie hoped Lana wasn't going to say anything regrettable.

'Well now.' Hilda met Annie's gaze with cool blue eyes, misting with age: 'And where's your husband Roddy? You haven't gone and got yourself divorced as well, have you, like your mother and your sister? Don't tell me Dinah is going to be the only married woman left in this family! Ha ha.'

As if this was some kind of witty conversational gambit.

Where's Roddy? Annie turned the question over in her mind. She and Aunty Hilda weren't exactly close. Hilda was in her eighties, her memory was bound to be failing, but still . . .

The booming voice had carried Hilda's inappropriate question across the room and turned down the volume as people waited to see how she'd answer. From the corner of her eye, Annie – momentarily too stunned to reply – could see Fern powering down the room towards them, cushioned orthopaedic soles assisting her naturally vigorous stride, as she came to rescue them.

135

Suddenly Annie was grateful her mother had chosen not to wear the two-inch suedes.

'Aunty Hilda!' Fern pretended to trill with delight, 'how *lovely* to see you!' She leaned in to give the old bat a hug, while over Hilda's shoulder she winked at Annie, then pulled a gruesome face: 'No-one's even found you a glass of champagne yet, Aunty. Follow me!'

Chapter Ten

Terrifying tongue boy:

Black skinny trousers (Topshop)
Ruffled white shirt (Camden Market)
Selection of silver pirate earrings (Camden Market)
Nose piercing (his one-before-last girlfriend)
Tongue piercing (someone slightly more professional)
Total estimated cost: £75

'Whatever.'

'So, thank you all for coming tonight and making it such a fantastic evening, so far. There's going to be dancing, the bar's open till two a.m. . . . so don't even think about going home early. Not even you, Frankie!' Fern was closing the little speech she'd made and the relief on her face was obvious. 'Before I go, I just want to say thank you to my three wonderful, fabulous girls. I'm so . . .' then came the crack in the voice which gave each of her daughters a big lump in their throats: '. . . proud of you all,' she managed before sitting down abruptly.

There was warm applause and Annie might even have let a tear or two well up in the corner of her eye, except Connor touched her elbow, raised an eyebrow and directed her to look towards a window in the corner of the room.

Tucked in behind a tall green chintz curtain was a couple snogging frantically. A white-shirted teen boy was kneading his hand vigorously on a – yikes! – lacy navy breast.

'Lana?' Annie asked out loud.

Connor nodded and shot her a wicked smile.

It was several moments before Annie could tear her gaze from them. *Who is he?* she wondered. It was hard to tell from the back of his head. He still hadn't come up for air. Was he a relative? A distant cousin? Was it legal for Lana to snog him? Snog? Look at that jaw action: more like eat him alive.

She mouthed the word 'Help!' to Connor, but his response was to whisper back: 'Like you never!'

Annie turned back to Nic, hoping further conversation about the respective delights of Rick and their holiday to Rome would help take her mind off Lana. And, by the way, where was Owen? She hadn't seen him for ages.

'We're going to stay in this gorgeous little hotel not far from the Spanish Steps . . . Do you have any holidays planned, Annie?' Nic asked.

Annie thought about the school fees, the new property plan, the slow week on the Trading Station, and wanted to snort with laughter at the idea of blowing money on a holiday.

'Hmm, well, we'll see,' was her reply. She turned her attention to the pudding in front of her: chocolate profiteroles. Now these contained everything she'd renounced for the week-long detox she'd done in order to look as fabulous as possible in the pink dress: wheat, dairy, sugar and caffeine. Suddenly a bowlful of toxins had never looked so irresistible. She sunk in her spoon and necked down three big mouthfuls, barely pausing for breath.

Connor, catching sight of the choux pastry demolition, took her firmly by her spoon hand. 'Duty calls, Annie,' he said. 'They're playing our song.'

'Since when is "The Dashing White Sergeant" our song?' Annie wanted to know, bending her head to take one last lick of chocolate sauce before Connor led her onto a dance floor already lined in orderly fashion with several elderly trios.

'C'mon. The kiltie wants to dance. The kiltie wants to twirl. I'm fully in touch with my inner Highlander tonight and he wants to boogie.'

'We need a third person for this dance,' Annie warned him.

'A threesome? Excellent. Who shall we have? Spotted any handsome single men yet?'

'Not a one,' she smiled, greatly cheered at the prospect of swinging it with Connor.

She'd always loved to dance at parties with Roddy. Disco, of course, but properly, with all the moves. Or salsa. The Roddy and Annie floorshow had been semi-practised and crowd-pleasing. A little bit subtle and a little bit cool, just the right side of showy . . . just like Roddy, in fact.

Wrapped up tightly together, snaking across the dance floor, Roddy's warm hand on her bare back . . .

suddenly she was remembering one very hot dance session at a friend's wedding, when Roddy had twirled her by the hand off the dance floor, out of the party and along the stairs to their room.

With the lights off, and the noise of chatter and laughter outside in the corridor, he'd unzipped the poppy dress and let it fall silkily to the floor.

'We have to carry on just where we left off,' he'd whispered into her ear. So she'd put her hands on his buttocks, her lips to his mouth and let him salsa her all the way over to the bed.

At parties nowadays, she had to take her chances along with all the other single mothers. Sometimes, the best you could hope for was that someone not too dodgy or arthritic would ask you onto the dance floor and not make a total tit of themselves.

'Aha, just the man.' Connor had spotted Lana's tongue boy walking past with a glass of water in his hand. 'Hello there, we need you,' he said, catching the boy by his wrist and spinning him in towards them, causing an arc of water to curve from the glass: 'We need a threesome for this dance. This is Annie Valentine, Lana Valentine's mother. We noticed that you'd met Lana.'

'Oh, ermmm . . . hi there,' tongue boy mumbled. He had shoulder-length brown-blond hair and three earrings in one ear, not to mention his nose. He was way too cool for school and looked frighteningly like a 17- or even 18-year-old.

'I can't dance to this stuff,' the boy said dismissively. And that was when Annie noticed the metal stud gleaming on his tongue and shuddered.

140

'Hey, c'mon, give us a chance. It'll be fun. What's your name anyway?' Connor persisted.

'Seth.'

'Ooh, like the baddies in *Star Wars*,' Annie jumped in with an attempt to be chatty, even though she'd quite like to lock Lana away from this bad boy.

'No, that's the Sith Lords,' came the cool response.

Could he have been more huffy?

'Well, never mind, this is "The Dashing White Sergeant". You'll love it. It's easy,' she said and took hold of one of his hands.

'Whatever,' he shrugged.

Connor removed the glass of water and took hold of Seth's other hand, then they dragged him along with them.

It was a memorable dance for Annie, what with Connor on one side whooping, yeehahing, and twirling enough to give alarming flashes of dark hair – yes, under *there*, he'd gone with the traditional Scottish no pants thing – while the Seth Lord barely raised a shuffle on her other side.

Annie spotted Lana at the edge of the dance floor: arms crossed, mouth pinched, glaring at the sight of her mother dancing with her latest conquest. Lana was clearly convinced that a CIA-style interrogation was under way, with Connor on hand to administer torture.

So, Seth, what grades did you get in your last round of exams? Do you have a serious profession in mind? Have you undergone work experience within this profession? Teenage sexuality – your prevailing ethics, attitude, morality and most recent experiences: please, discuss.

Much as Annie might have liked to ask all these

questions, she managed to confine herself to a polite: 'So, how do you know my mum?' But got only a mumbled: 'She plays golf with my dad,' in reply before Seth broke away and headed off in the direction of Lana's wildly enthusiastic smile.

'Big trouble,' Annie muttered at Connor.

'Oh, c'mon, it's a snog,' he reassured her. 'No teenage relationship is going to survive the vast distance between north London and Essex.'

'Hmm.' Annie headed back to her seat to see if there was a pudding bowl around to lick.

Nic, still at the table, greeted her with the words: 'OK, how much do you want for it? But I'll have to go to the toilets with you first and try it on.'

So there was one reason to be cheerful. She wouldn't make a profit from Nic, that would be entirely unethical. But she'd break even and that was well worth it. Even though she'd miss the dress . . . maybe Nic would sell it back to her in a year or so.

As Annie stood up, she saw 'nice Mr Wilkinson' approaching.

Mr Wilkinson was 45 but, due to severe asthma and a limp, more like 75, and she'd once been set up with him by her mother. The dinner hadn't been a great success: nice Mr Wilkinson had got so nervous, he'd inhaled his entire inhaler, then had a wheezing fit and she'd ended up driving him to Casualty.

It was never a good sign when a date ended with medical intervention.

He was wheezing and limping towards her from the other side of the room. Nevertheless, she suspected he had dancing on his mind. Oh yes! Wouldn't that be lovely?! They could waltz cheek to cheek and reminisce about the very nice nurse who'd booked him in that night.

'Lovely girl,' he'd probably tell her all over again. 'All the way from the Philippines, you know.'

Ah, the kilted one was in sight. She could formulate an escape plan. He had already told her he was there to do her bidding all night long.

'I think I need to go outside, now, straight away,' she hissed at both Connor and Nic.

'Taken up smoking?' he wondered. 'Or need a wee-wee?'

'Disastrous date approaching, due north,' she explained.

Connor peeked over her head: 'Ooh, nasty, take my arm and off we go then.'

Outside, in the chilly darkness, looking through the high windows at the brightly lit fun going on, Annie felt an unwelcome moment of gloom descending on her. With her arm still through Connor's, she confided in a low voice: 'You know, there are still so many times when I really, really miss Roddy.'

Connor leaned back against the stone wall of the hotel and looked out over the dark lawn. He nodded slowly, then turned to face her. 'I still miss him too,' he said.

'The bugger!' she added, forcing a smile.

'Bastard!' Connor agreed.

'Do you think he has any idea how furious I am with him?'

'Still?' Connor wondered.

'I get angrier,' she confessed. 'As the time goes by and

the kids get older, I'm much more angry with him. Bloody, flaming furious.'

Connor paused before beginning: 'I think there's a lot more I could do for you and the children . . .'

'No, no, you're great – honestly,' she assured him. 'I don't know what we'd do without you . . . Well obviously, there's taking Owen camping,' she reminded him, hoping both to lighten this conversation and tweak at his conscience once again.

'For goodness' sake, woman, there are limits!' He flashed one of his bright white smiles. 'But I did have one idea . . .'

'Yeah?'

'What do you think about me moving in with you?'

'What!' Annie couldn't have been more surprised. But seeing the hurt look on his face, she put her hand up on his shoulder and patted him, a bit like she'd pat a dog. 'Connor, you are very, very sweet,' she told him, 'but I think you've gone a bit daft, babes.'

'But,' he insisted, 'give it some thought, Annie. You wouldn't be so lonely. You'd have me around all the time. I really love Owen and Lana. And I'd be a father figure – a man about the house.'

Momentarily, Annie pictured her and Lana discussing dresses, with Owen hanging back totally uninterested. Then she imagined the scene with Connor earnestly discussing dresses too . . . Owen still totally uninterested.

'God, I could even make an honest woman of you, darling, and we could get married,' he added.

The kilt was obviously having a very strange effect on him.

144

'Connor, aren't you overlooking something?' She couldn't stop the smile from breaking out.

'What?'

'I love you, I really do, and I'm sure you love us all too . . . and I know that you're a bit lonely . . . but we . . . you and I, we're not in love and the way you're made means we never will be,' she reminded him.

'Oh, but . . . you know . . . how important is all that other stuff in the long run?'

'Don't say that!' She smacked his shoulder. 'If we moved in together' *Why were they even talking about this? It was ridiculous* – 'it would put other people off.'

'Off what?' he asked.

'Off falling in love with us.'

'Oh God, I've given up on that.'

'Well you mustn't. Never give up. And I haven't, thank you very much.'

'Ah yes, your prince in shining armour.' He sounded a little scornful. 'Or should that be shining Armani? The one who's going to whisk you off in his Bentley to enjoy a life of leisure and taking his credit card to the max.'

'We can all dream,' she reminded him sharply.

'Anyway, putting off other lovers would be a minor inconvenience if you ask me,' he added.

'Marriage of convenience more like,' was her reply.

For a moment she allowed herself to think about the tabloid headlines.

'Think how it would be announced,' she told him: *'Love at last for McCabe of The Manor* or *Friends find love together.'*

He gave a little laugh.

'C'mon.' She yanked at Connor's arm. 'You're my best, best friend, Connor,' she told him. 'And that's enough.'

'Am I interrupting something? I do hope so,' a disembodied voice came from the doorway, then a tall man stepped out into the darkness.

'No! No!' Annie replied.

'I take it this is the smoking section.' The man held out a broad red packet of Dunhill cigarettes with one hand and a proper gold lighter – Cartier, she suspected – with the other.

Both Connor and Annie shook their heads.

'No thanks,' she told him, 'I never have. But I won't hold it against you.'

'That's very kind, I only smoke at parties, they make me nervous.'

Maybe he was another of her mother's golfing pals. Whoever he was, he was much more handsome than Spencer. Lean and smart in his soft, well-fitting dinner suit with starchy white cuffs, gold links flashing at the buttonholes.

He was very upright with a handsome tanned face and the kind of swept-back sandy grey hair that put him anywhere from 40 to 60.

'I'm Gray Holden' – he held out his hand – 'and I'm guessing that you must be Annie Valentine. I've heard so much about you.'

'That's right.' She took his hand and felt his warm, firm touch.

'Your mother told me to look out for you.'

'Oh she did, did she?' Annie smiled, but immediately felt slightly on guard; this could be another 'Nice Mr Wilkinson' in disguise.

'Connor McCabe,' Connor introduced himself.

'I know,' Gray told him, shaking his hand, 'I've seen you on TV. An honour to meet you.'

Connor looked close to purring, but then Annie gave him the kind of raised-eyebrow look which warned him to make his excuses: 'I just have to go back inside for a moment, check on my . . .' with a little wink at Annie, 'Armani.'

'His what?' Gray wondered once Connor had left them.

'Oh nothing, nothing, just his idea of a joke. So . . . you must know my mother through the Golf Club?' was Annie's starter for ten.

'No, no. Too busy for golf.' He smiled at her, flashing teeth even whiter and straighter than Connor's. 'I'm her new dentist. I've taken over the Wilson and Anderson practice.'

'Oh, right . . .' This had to be the 'interesting man' her mother had lined up for her tonight. Her flashy dentist. He wasn't bad, not bad at all, although a view of old Mr Anderson's hairy nose poked disturbingly into her mind.

'I knew Mr Anderson very well,' she told Gray. 'So he's retired then?'

Gray nodded, then to her surprise, he offered her his arm with the words, 'Can I take you back inside, Ms Valentine, and find you a fresh drink?'

She'd never expected such quaint old manners to feel so charming. But, half expecting him to bow or maybe click his heels next, she curled her hand into the crook of his elbow and allowed herself to be led back inside, momentarily feeling as if she was in a remake of *Gone*

With the Wind. Such olde worlde courtesy suited her velvet dress perfectly.

Sadly, the effect was spoiled by the sight of Nic and Dinah at one window watching them and cackling.

Then, passing a second window, Annie spotted Owen and another boy each holding a beer can, pointing at them and laughing.

Well, on the one hand, Owen had made a friend, which was a good thing. He had spoken to a stranger. But on the other hand, dear God, nine was too young to be playing with beer: she would have to go and investigate.

Chapter Eleven

Kuwaiti 'princess' daywear:

Lollipop pink suit with short skirt (Chanel)
Ruffled pink, green and white blouse (Chanel)
High pink suede heels (Jimmy Choo)
Top-to-toe jilbab (definitely not The Store)
Total estimated cost: £3,000

'Do you have it in white? Oh and yellow too!'

Annie had just finished an extended shopping session
with her two favourite Kuwaiti princesses – never before
life in The Store had she realized what sometimes went
on under a modest, Muslim jilbab: YSL, Chanel, Pucci,
short tight skirts with stockings and killer heels.

The princesses usually greeted something lovely from
Chanel with the words: 'Do you have it in white? Oh
and yellow too!' with the intention of buying all three:
great customers to have.

Now she was taking a moment of 'rest' in her
office before her next appointment. Annie's idea of a

rest meant placing eBay bids on fifteen different items and reapplying lipstick as she listened to the messages on her business phone. She regularly collected unwanted clothes, shoes and bags from many of her clients to sell on for them – taking a little slice of commission, obviously. The clients were grateful for the 'pocket money', which usually part-funded their designer habit.

Tonight, she'd have to take her Jeep on a London circuit of pick-ups and Trading Station deliveries. There was also a voicemail message from a woman wanting an at-home consultation: when was Annie available? Today, for the right price, was Annie's motto. She dialled the woman straight back.

'Annie!' Her office door opened and one of the floor assistants, Samantha, was there looking anxious. Annie suspected she knew what was coming next.

'We think we've got a lifter,' Samantha informed her. 'She's been down in handbags, there's something missing from the display and she's on our level now.'

Annie ended her call, flipped her mobile shut, stood up and smoothed down her smart tunic dress. No-one else on the floor was as awesome in the presence of shoplifters as Annie, which is why she usually got called in.

'Do Security know?' she asked.

The girl nodded. 'They've got her description, they're standing by the doors.'

'OK, let's go then.'

She followed Samantha out onto the shop floor where the suspected lifter was surreptitiously pointed out.

'Oh yes, I see her – pale blue raincoat, bags over shoulder,' Annie whispered.

Shoplifters had to be stalked carefully. They could only be 'detained' by the security guards and arrested by police if they were caught in the act of leaving the shop with unpaid items. The guards were only allowed to stop and bag-check customers who had been *seen* taking things, not just suspected of theft.

'Is she working with someone else, or on her own?' Annie wanted to know.

'Solo, we think. She did the bag counter on her own, anyway.'

'What did she take?'

'A Marc Jacobs, it's the second to go this week. Nita's going to lose her job.'

'Crap,' Annie said quietly because the woman was drawing closer.

She was smartly dressed in black trousers with high-heeled boots, the tailored blue raincoat and armful of big shopping bags possibly hiding the stolen handbag.

Now she was flipping through the rails, casually, just like any other shopper, holding out the odd item, checking the tags.

Maybe she was stealing to order, Annie thought. Occasionally several thieves at once would descend on The Store and take as much as they could of specific labels. The resale market, which she knew all about, was so good and so easy nowadays that stealing designer items was more lucrative than it had ever been.

But now the woman seemed to have tired of looking. She was starting to walk towards the escalator . . . no-one had seen her take anything yet, so maybe she'd travel down all four escalators, head out of the front door and get away with the £650 handbag scot-free, costing Nita's job in the process.

'Bugger that,' was Annie's reaction to this thought. Time to move in.

She strode confidently after the woman: 'Madam, it's your lucky day!' she told her brightly, taking a light hold of her arm.

The woman turned abruptly, freeing herself: 'I'm sorry?' She looked haughtily down at Annie, who suddenly felt her confidence waver. What if this wasn't a shoplifter? What if this was a very prestigious libel lawyer on her lunch break who would sue Annie right out of her home and onto the pavement for making this accusation?

'You're our four hundredth customer this month and that entitles you to a free style consultation in the Personal Shopping suite,' Annie offered, thinking fast.

'Thanks, but no thanks,' the woman said.

'Oh, come on,' Annie wheedled. 'It won't take long, it's a lovely treat and there's a brilliant goodie bag,' she said, wondering what she could cobble together from the back of the cupboards if this woman turned out to be no thief.

The woman considered for a moment, looked at her watch and finally relented with a grudging: 'Oh, OK then.'

Annie led her to the suite and then towards one of the changing rooms. She watched as the woman set down her shopping bags carefully. Annie couldn't make any glance or guess as to what was inside them, but then she saw a chance.

She got in behind the woman and, as she loosened her

152

coat from her shoulders, Annie took hold of it with a brisk 'Let me get that.'

It was too late for the woman to refuse the help even if she wanted to.

In Annie's hands, the raincoat felt too heavy, her confidence returned and she was now sure she had a shoplifter who could be confronted.

Quickly she turned the coat upside down and gave it a vigorous shake.

'What the hell do you think you're—' the woman began angrily.

But a pair of Dolce & Gabbana sunglasses fell to the floor, price tag still attached. Followed by a small pair of wire-cutters, two fat bottles of Aveda shampoo and a selection of chunky necklaces.

'I'd just like to get back the things you've taken which belong to us,' Annie told her firmly, 'I'm not interested in arresting you, in having to hang about a court-room for hours waiting to give evidence against you, in hearing about the distressing personal circumstances which led you to act "completely out of character" in a "moment of madness". I just want you to give back the things which are ours. Then I'd like you to leave The Store and not come back. Ever. Does that sound reasonable to you?'

The woman glared at her furiously, cheeks flushing. Undeterred, Annie bent over and reached boldly into the biggest one of the shopping bags on the floor. Her hand came back up with the Marc Jacobs bag, new season's exquisite handwork in palest lemon yellow.

'Look,' Annie began, 'down in the handbag depart-ment is a girl called Nita. She's from Poland, she works nine hours a day here, six days a week, because she always wants the overtime. She sends a big cheque home to her family every week because her little sister's ill. If she'd sold you that handbag, she'd have made an extra thirty pounds. Because you've stolen it from her, she's going to lose her job.'

'This shop can afford the odd loss,' the woman hissed. 'The prices are high enough.'

'You're not just stealing from the shop,' Annie insisted. 'You're stealing from the staff. We all work very hard here. If you want the finer things in life, then maybe you should try working hard for them too. You'll enjoy them so much more, I promise you,' she added triumphantly.

'Nita's not from Poland!' Samantha told her, when the lifter had emptied out all her bags and pockets, as instructed by Annie, and sloped out of The Store, ears ringing with the telling-off she'd been given. 'She doesn't have a baby sister either.'

'I know.' Annie winked at her. 'I may have laid it on a bit thick there, but I *hate* thieves.'

'Annie Valentine!! You're keeping me waiting, you should know better than that. I won't have time to spend as much money with you!' a familiar voice rang out from the suite.

'Got to go,' Annie told Samantha, 'Mrs B-P – one of my favourites.'

'You always say that!'

But Mrs Tilly Brosnan-Pilditch was not just one of Annie's favourite clients, she was a favourite creation.

Mrs B-P, as Annie liked to call her, had arrived in The

Store's Personal Shopping suite on Annie's third day in the job. She hadn't made an appointment, she'd just wandered in looking for help, because 'It's *terrifying* out there,' she'd confided.

Mrs B-P wasn't even Mrs B-P back then, she was Tilly Cathcart, an art lecturer in her early fifties, not shy exactly, but reserved, as if she was watching, listening, thinking it through before joining in.

When she walked in that day, she'd been dressed in self-conscious bohemian head-to-toe black: a retro astrakhan coat, big velvet beret, flat boots and long skirt.

'I have a problem,' she'd said, once Annie had settled her down on the suite sofa with a cup of tea. 'I'm about to get married.'

'Oh, congratulations,' Annie had offered. 'Lucky man.'

'Yes, a lovely man who is unfortunately . . .' she'd lowered her voice to a whisper, 'quite wealthy.'

'Oh dear!' Annie had winked.

'Everyone has a fault, don't they?' Tilly Cathcart had winked back, and they'd felt themselves warming to each other. 'I'm trying my best to overlook it.'

'Good for you!' Annie had encouraged.

'This lovely, unfortunately quite wealthy man understands many of my anxieties about becoming his new wife, about taking part in his public life of business lunches, trips to the opera, corporate things,' she'd sighed, 'and he thinks they'll be helped by a great big shopping trip . . . by dressing expensively for the part.'

'But you're not so sure?' Annie had suspected.

'No. I'm not at all sure. I've been independent for so long – and I want to stay independent within our marriage. We've talked till we're blue in the face about what he's allowed to pay for and what he isn't allowed to pay for. I don't want to suddenly be dressed from head to toe in his money, in status symbol clothes. I can't mutate into a Nancy Reagan lookalike,' she'd insisted. 'I need to remain me. And he wouldn't argue with that. That's what he would want too.'

As Annie was to learn time and time again in her new job, it was rarely simple. It was rarely a case of enter wealthy woman, exit carrying bags and bags of expensive clothes. Dressing was always fraught with all sorts of issues, meaning and hang-ups.

After Annie had heard out all the concerns of Mrs B-P-to-be she'd taken her on a tour of all three floors of women's clothing and accessories.

'At which college do you teach?' Annie had asked. On hearing the answer, she'd nodded and mentioned her own time at art school.

'The fashion school. Ever visited there?' she'd asked.

'Oh yes, I've been to the end-of-term shows, marvelling at the creations, just like everyone else.'

'You know, there are some amazing hats you should see.' Annie had steered her in their direction: 'We've taken a chance and bought them directly from a student who graduated this summer. He's done some clever little bags for us as well . . .'

And thus had begun Tilly Cathcart's transformation, not into status-laden trophy wife, but into generous patron of the arts, supporter of creative students.

Mrs B-P stood before Annie today in a funky Vivienne

Westwood green and red checked skirt-suit they'd bought together, a magnificently arty, embroidered bag, her trademark overblown beret – in olive green velvet – and wonderful red shoes which exactly matched her red lipstick.

'You're an art expert, you can be painterly about the way you dress,' Annie had encouraged her.

Definitely not Nancy Reagan. Still the intelligent, creative, thoughtful art teacher Mr B-P had fallen in love with when on a whim – his doctor having advised him to take up a stress-relieving hobby – he'd joined a night class on Medieval Painting Techniques.

'This is going to be a long session,' Mrs B-P warned Annie as they sat down together and drew up a list of her requirements. Three years into marriage, Mrs B-P wasn't quite so uncomfortable about spending her clothing allowance.

'I'm giving up suits,' was the first instruction, 'I want very soft, comfortable clothing: sensational pyjamas, loads of cashmere, but in lovely colours, wraps, shawls, your best slippers.'

'Are you going into hibernation?' Annie wondered

'Yes, that's exactly it – a spring hibernation. A rebirth, a renewal.'

'Aha! Spa visit?'

'Something like that . . . Come on, take me out there.' Mrs B-P put her arm in Annie's. 'Show me what you've got!'

Palest pink silk pyjamas met with Mrs B-P's approval. Then there were the embroidered sheepskin house-boots which she threatened never to take off again. Teal blue cashmere jogging trousers joined the pile of

157

possibilities, an aqua green cashmere long-sleeved top, a pale yellow cashmere dress. Mrs B-P couldn't get enough cashmere. She kept putting the woollens against her cheek and rubbing gently with her eyes closed.

'Oh delicious, so cosy and soothing.'

During the trying-on session, it didn't escape Annie's notice that Mrs B-P had lost weight. Her slim figure was now verging on the slight.

'You're the only person who needs to go to a spa to fatten up,' she told her. 'I hope you've picked one with sticky toffee puddings on the menu, darlin'. Get a little meat on your bones.'

Mrs B-P wasn't just shopping for herself either, she wanted birthday presents for her two stepdaughters.

'What's happening in your life anyway?' she asked Annie as they made their way down to the accessories department. 'Any news from the love life front, or is it still a no-man's-land?' she teased.

'Now funny you should ask about that,' Annie confided. 'As a matter of fact, I've met someone quite interesting.' She then proceeded to give an intrigued Mrs B-P the rundown on Gray.

'We talked and talked for the rest of the evening. He's promised to call and take me out to dinner . . . he is charming, good looking . . . I've got high hopes for this one,' Annie enthused, 'because I'm definitely ready to meet someone else . . . move on . . . have someone there for me again.'

'Of course you are.' Mrs B-P smiled at her. 'I can't think of anything better that could happen to you.'

They were standing in front of a display of the

most exquisite velvet devoré scarves. Each one hand painted, hand embroidered, with patterns painstakingly burned into the velvet and monumental price tags to match.

'These are beautiful . . .' Mrs B-P ran her fingers slowly over the pile. 'This is just what I want for Georgina and Ellie. Pinks and pale blues for my blonde Ellie' – she slithered the wide work of art scarf around her own neck – 'greens and gold for Georgie. Yes! This is just right, Annie, perfect. Then I'm going to Cartier to buy them something . . . solid.'

Annie took the two scarves and folded them carefully: 'Are you all right?' she asked finally, putting a hand on Mrs B-P's arm, intuitively worried that something was not right at all.

'I'm fine, I'm fine. I just have to spend some time in the damn hospital.' Mrs B-P turned to look her directly in the face with her sharp, blue eyes. 'Oh, it's so boring, Annie, totally dull . . . I need a mastectomy, chemotherapy and all that *dreary* stuff. I'm going to need a lot of interesting hats and scarves, I can tell you.'

She brushed away Annie's shocked look of concern with: 'It's very, very early stages. And I'm going to recover, my dear. Totally. Fully. One hundred per cent. Not a single question about that. I'm not even entertaining the possibility of not recovering. You think I'm exiting now? Just when it's got this good?!'

'I know,' she acknowledged Annie's slightly tearful eyes. 'Bummer. Now come on.' She took up Annie's arm again: 'There's a time for weeping and wailing and complaining about how unfair it all is. But now is not that time. "Chins up and straight backs," as my mother would say. Now is the time to buy a wonderful new handbag. You're to choose. I'm leaving it entirely up to you. When I'm shuffling from home to hospital and back, I want to have Archie on one arm, and something just as fabulous on the other.'

Chapter Twelve

Tor in recovery:

White blouse (M&S)
Deep red cardigan (M&S)
Jeans (no recollection)
Black boots (back of wardrobe)
Black fake fur (ditto)
Total est. cost: £360

'. . . to new men and new scarves.'

Tor, the St Vincent's mother Annie was making over for free, had met Annie at the door of the family home she was about to be kicked out of and shown her into the kitchen for tea.

'No, I think we better make it red wine, babes,' Annie had insisted, taking a bottle from her bag.

'I've made a rule never to drink by myself though,' Tor had told her, taking two water glasses out of the cupboard, already stripped of almost all its contents.

'Good thing I came round then,' was Annie's response,

before she assured Tor, 'I think a little drinking on your own might be OK right now – for a few weeks anyway – until you've got the move behind you. You better not have packed up any of your wardrobe yet, otherwise how am I going to do my job?'

Annie put her lovely jangling golden bag down on a chair, then slipped off her soft conker brown leather coat and long scarf to reveal a pink, orange and brown patterned dress elegantly set off with high brown boots.

'No, no,' Tor insisted, taking in the many details of Annie's outfit: the tights in the same shade of orange as the dress for instance, the necklace of golden leaves fanning out from her collarbone. She looked so together, so carefully considered.

'It's still three weeks away,' Tor continued. 'I've just put away kitchen stuff . . . books . . . Things that are definitely mine.'

After a bit of talk about Tor's new flat and her daughter Angela and how the divorce was affecting them (badly to say the least), Tor suddenly put her glass down on the table, ran a hand through her hair in an agitated way and blurted out: 'I don't know why you're here, Annie! I don't know why I've agreed to this. I just don't think I can. I don't want to think about clothes. I don't care! I've got no money . . . showing me some clever things to do with scarves is just not going to help! Not one bit!'

'Tor, calm down,' Annie soothed, reaching out to pat Tor's arm, 'I am so sorry about what you're going through. I am so, so sorry. I really do understand how you feel, honestly. I have been here.'

Tor looked up and met Annie's eyes.

'Yes, of course you have,' she said, 'I'm sorry. I'm trying not to think about myself and all my problems all the time . . . but it's hard.'

'I'm not a therapist,' Annie continued gently, 'I'm not a shrink – and it could be that you should see someone like that, to get you through the worst of it. God knows, I probably should have . . . But there is something I can do, I promise. I'm here to cheer you up, to make you feel just a tiny bit better about yourself, and what's so wrong with that? C'mon, drink up,' she instructed, 'then we're treating ourselves to a refill and heading to your wardrobe.'

In the bedroom, Annie took two bin bags out of her makeover kitbag and began to unroll then shake them open.

Tor looked at the black bags anxiously: 'I wasn't planning on throwing much away,' she said.

'I know.' Annie sounded brisk. 'No-one ever does, but don't worry, you will. There's a lot of dead wood in a divorce wardrobe, believe me. For starters, we're going to get rid of all the unsuitable presents *he* gave you. You know, the expensive things that didn't fit, weren't your colour, but you didn't have the heart to exchange. You know what I'm talking about. Open your underwear drawer,' Annie instructed, 'c'mon, pass it on out. I wish I could think of a good home for all the expensive underwear I have to get rid of . . . charity shops don't want it, no-one will buy it on eBay . . . maybe I should be donating it to schools for their arts and craft boxes . . .' Annie gave a little laugh. 'You know, that is a good idea.'

Tor was almost threatening to smile at this; she was also opening a drawer, stuffed full of all the usual suspects: red and pink bras and suspenders, a tiny corset, dainty peach-coloured feathery things, quarter-cup bras for breasts the size of raisins, not Tor's ample cleavage.

'What was he thinking?' Tor said, picking up the wincy bra and gazing at it in bewilderment. 'Not of me, anyway . . .' She tossed it into Annie's bin bag.

The emptied drawer seemed to have just the galvanizing effect on Tor that Annie had hoped for. Soon she was opening her cupboard doors wide and ferreting about in there for anything suspect dumped on her by her soon-to-be-ex.

A revolting primrose yellow cashmere cardigan: 'Yup, put it in the sale bag, Annie instructed. I'll put it on my web site for you and you'll get eighty-five per cent of the price paid. Sound fair?'

'Sounds bloody marvellous,' Tor told her.

Paisley scarves, dodgy brooches, a tweedy jacket and a scary loud pink cocktail dress with matching bolero followed on quickly.

Tor rooted deeper into forgotten corners of the cupboard: 'Oh God!' She picked up a cardboard box, opened it and took out a beaded, pastel-coloured wrap of sorts.

'EBay, eBay . . .' Annie instructed. 'We don't want anything hanging about that is going to make you think of Richard and weep. Obviously, I'll make an exception for very expensive jewellery and handbags.'

'Hah!' Tor snorted and took another gulp of wine. 'My engagement ring was the one and only decent bit of jewellery I got from him.'

'Ah well,' Annie said, 'I never even got an engagement ring. We were young and couldn't afford it.'

'Do you think I should still wear it?' Tor wondered, holding out her hand and the triple-stone ring for inspection. 'On my other hand, maybe?'

'If you love it, why not? It's your badge of honour. Reminder of the better times before . . . or then again you could have the stones reset . . . or sell it off and buy something just for you.'

'Hmmm.' Tor turned back to her wardrobe and knelt in front of the shelves. 'Everything in here is utter crap,' she announced, the wine now loosening up any inhibitions about this task. 'I don't know if I can even bear to show you these things. I sort of rummage around in here every day and bring something out and just plonk it on.'

Now this was just so heart-breakingly sad, it made Annie want to cry.

Today, Tor was wearing washed-out jeans, a T-shirt with a sagging neck and a bobbly grey fleece cardigan.

'Babes, if I gave that cardigan to Gisele Bundchen, she'd struggle to make it look good,' Annie told Tor gently. 'You've got to stop with the lucky dip going on in here every morning and find some things that are a little easier to work with.'

'I'm not going shopping,' Tor said firmly. 'I can't face it and I can't afford it.'

'I know, I know. But c'mon, let's get it all out and see what's hiding in there . . . and by the way, what is this nice little collection hanging up here on the rail?' She made a quick rifle through the smart black skirts and jackets, sparkly tops and silky summer dresses.

'Oh, you know, work clothes. Then dress-up things, I never wear any of those, I never go out any more.'

165

Annie tutted and shook her head. She brought down a lovely knee-length dress and held it up against Tor.

'Bet you've lost weight . . . all the stress?' she asked.

Tor nodded.

'So, think how fabulous you'd look in this now. You know, once a week, babes, you've got to dress up: hair, make-up, shoes, the full monty, and get out there.'

When Tor scoffed at this, Annie insisted: 'Not on the pull. Not yet anyway. Just nicely turned out for a special occasion. And then you make the occasion happen. You take your daughter out for coffee at a nice hotel . . . you go to the cinema in town . . . you ask your friends out for a drink. Once a week, girl, you have to dress up, treat yourself and remember how great you can look when you want to. You have to remind yourself that life is still out there, fun is still to be had. Otherwise, all these beautiful things, they're just hanging here with nowhere to go. Look.' She took down a turquoise silk blouse: 'Wear it with jeans to do the supermarket run. Wear it to work, just don't leave it up there all alone!'

Tor's shoulders seemed to droop at the thought of having to make this effort.

'OK, work with me,' Annie encouraged her, 'let's get rid of the unwearables and see what's left, shall we?'

They spent the next ten minutes or so sifting through Tor's daily lucky dip outfits. Everything worn, saggy, ratty and baggy hit the bin bag, including the tragic knickers and mismatched ankle socks.

'You do not need me to tell you that you need new underwear, Tor. You can afford new pants, OK? Every-

166

one can afford new pants,' Annie told her. 'Buy them on the internet or at the supermarket if you don't want to go into a lingerie shop.'

Annie looked carefully through the clothes that remained and could see that there was going to be enough . . . just.

'You need a uniform, don't you? You don't want to think about outfits every morning yet, you've got enough going on in your head. You're not quite ready to come shopping with me to try on swing jackets and tunics and figure out how the new season is going to work for you.'

Tor just shook her head.

'But you will be soon!' Annie told her.

'So, in the meantime what we need is an easy uniform . . .' Annie began to lay the remaining clothes out on the bed. 'I'm looking at your nice white shirts, and this little red cardigan here and the two woollen V-necks and these jeans, which are almost passable, and your nifty black trousers . . . but please, Tor, a skirt at least twice a week, not just for work. Anyway, I'm thinking, here is the beginning of a chic French mama uniform. White shirts, *ironed*,' she warned, 'are very morale boosting, so c'mon, into the first outfit.'

Tor seemed taken aback at the request, but Annie insisted: 'Get on with it! I won't look, not that there isn't anything I haven't seen before, believe me.' So Tor undressed quickly then put on the white shirt, jeans and red cardigan.

'Right.' Annie turned her in the direction of the mirror. 'Feeling a little bit more together?'

When Tor nodded, Annie moved in and undid the

shirt one button lower: 'You're not teaching at Sunday school. Now, show me your jewellery box.'

Tor pointed to the corner of the bedroom and Annie asked: 'May I?' before rummaging about inside then returning to Tor with several long-forgotten treasures.

She clipped a red and silver necklace round Tor's neck, instructed her to put on earrings, then Annie took Tor's hairbrush from the bedside table and brushed out her scrappy bob before securing it with an elaborate silver clip she'd found in the jewellery box. Then she went into her handbag and brought out blusher and rosy lip gloss.

Once this was applied, they both looked at the effect in the mirror.

'Better?' Annie asked.

Tor examined herself and nodded slowly. But she didn't seem convinced.

'I really do understand why you don't want to care about how you look, babes,' Annie began. 'Sometimes when everything's turned to crap, we want it to show on the outside too. It seems just too frivolous to care about hair and nails and colour co-ordinating. But the problem is . . . the big problem is, it's not good for morale. If you hide inside a baggy grey fleece every day, believe me, it's much harder for things to get better again. Great things do not happen to people hidden inside grey fleeces . . . they don't land exciting new jobs, or meet brilliant new friends or have amazing ideas or get invited out spontaneously. They just don't. They get greyer and fleecier, you've got to believe me here. Maybe the best piece of advice I can give you is to dress for how you want to feel again. Because then it will happen more quickly.'

Annie squeezed Tor's shoulders because she could see her eyes welling up.

'You're going to be fine, Tor,' she assured her. 'In a year's time, this is going to feel like the best thing that ever happened to you. And the more you keep it together, the easier it will be for Angela. Don't let her think of her dad as the man who kicked the stuffing out of her mum.'

Annie let Tor blow her nose while she turned her eyes in the direction of the wardrobe again: 'And what is this lovely coat doing hiding in here?' she asked, taking out a cosy, black fake fur which looked almost brand new. 'And these boots!' Her hand reached for the black suede mid-heels, again almost unworn.

'Well, they're special occasion . . .' Tor began.

Annie shook her head vigorously. 'No, no, no! Not any more, they're not. You need all your special things around you right now. For support,' she insisted, handing over the coat and boots.

Tor put them both on. And now Annie could see she was more convinced. The boots gave her an extra inch or so and forced her to straighten up, her hands were sunk into the coat pockets and she was turning just a little, this way and that in front of the mirror, actually admiring herself, if only slightly.

'Oh yes!' Annie raved. 'Now you're good to go!'

Tor's smile suddenly appeared and she gave a relieved giggle, which made her seem so much younger than the weighed-down 46 or so that she was.

'More wine for the lady!' Annie teased.

'No, no, I need to concentrate or I'm going to forget everything you've told me,' Tor replied.

Annie made her fetch a notebook and a pen ('No, in the boots! Don't take off the boots now!') and together they wrote down all the outfits Annie had put together for her and lots of Annie's top tips including: 'New pants, for God's sake!' . . . 'Lip gloss, tinted moisturizer and blusher, it's not rocket science' . . . 'Smile more – laugh, even' . . . 'Cheap but glamorous sunglasses for bad eye days' . . . 'White shirts, IRONED, to boost morale' . . . 'Always, *always*, jewellery to make you sparkle.'

'Semi-permanent hair dye, Tor, ever heard of it?' Annie asked. 'You can buy it at the chemist's for a fiver, no need for a hairdresser, no need for an inch of grey root.'

'OK, OK!' was Tor's reaction.

'Clever ways with scarves,' Annie scribbled down in the notebook. 'Let your sexy new boyfriends teach you these.'

'Oh, ha ha,' Tor responded.

'It's true though,' Annie insisted. 'There will be new men – and think how exciting that's going to be. But you do need new scarves, honestly, babes: soft velvety ones, bright cashmere ones, you need the colour and the comfort, something to snuggle up in, a buffer between you and your jackets, you and your coats, you and the world . . . a sprinkle of colour when you're feeling totally monochrome.'

'Well then,' Tor met her eye and smiled broadly, as if she was finally enjoying herself, 'here's to new men and new scarves.' She held up her tumbler of wine.

'I'll drink to that.' Annie clinked glasses with her.

When Tor's session was over, Annie buttoned herself back into her leather coat. She ran a hairbrush through her locks, applied lipstick, a little spritz of perfume and set her shoulders back. This meant that when she was out of the front door, she was ready to face her mobile phone.

She switched it on and looked for the voicemail symbol. Nothing there. She checked her inbox just in case.

No. Nine days had passed and Gray had not called her. What a total, utter bummer. She couldn't understand it. He'd seemed so keen. He'd promised! He'd even put her number directly into his mobile.

She wasn't sure what she was going to do now. Going back to Tor's house to rescue the grey fleece from the bin bag for herself was a tempting idea.

Chapter Thirteen

Annie's 'accidental' date outfit:

Pink cardigan (Whistles sale)
Flowered pink and camel skirt (same)
Camel trenchcoat (the trusty eBay Valentino)
Pink pashmina (so out of fashion, but still so good)
Flower necklace (Topshop)
New high-heeled camel T-bars (Chanel, oops . . . but
with a staff discount . . . and consider the Trading
Station resale value)
Cloud of Chanel's Cristalle
Est. cost: £490

'Gray! What are you doing here?!'

'So when is your date with Gray?' Dinah had barely been able to contain her excitement. Dinah hadn't just seen Gray at the party, she'd been introduced to him, she'd chatted to him, she'd watched carefully how he'd reacted to Annie. Then she'd pulled Annie off to the loos to tell her that Gray was 'very promising' and that Annie was to use all her available charms to 'go, go, go for it, girl!'

'Well, he's coming into town this week . . .' Annie had fudged, 'and he said he would call to arrange something.'

'So? What's arranged?'

The pause that followed told Dinah all she needed to know: 'He hasn't called?' she asked, outraged. 'Oh Annie! Have you got his number? Aren't you going to call him? It's not like you to—'

'I thought about it,' Annie cut in, 'and I decided it wasn't cool. I mean it's never cool to be the one phoning to say' – she put on a whiny voice – '"Why haven't you called me?"'

'So you're not going to see him?' Dinah sounded very disappointed for her.

'No. I didn't say that. I have a plan,' Annie confided.

'Uh-oh.' Dinah didn't sound convinced. But then this was a crucial difference between Dinah and her older sister. Dinah liked to leave things to fate, to chance, to instinct or luck, whereas Annie liked to plan and scheme. Annie always had a plan . . . she always thought it was better if she was in charge.

'The conference he's going to, I've found out it's at Claridge's,' Annie told her.

'Claridge's?' The name of one of the most luxurious old hotels in London seemed to take Dinah by surprise. 'Why would dentists book a conference at Claridge's?'

'Are you joking?' Annie countered. 'Have you been to the dentist's lately? The prices they charge? The boundaries between cosmetic dentistry and plastic surgery are blurring.'

'Bet Gray told you that,' Dinah teased.

'Anyway . . .' Yes, Gray *had* told her that. 'I'm going to think up a very good, very glamorous reason for me to be at Claridge's at the same time. So we'll meet by accident . . . me looking fabulous. He'll be really, really sorry he didn't call me and the rest will be easy!'

'Hmmm . . . it sounds a bit obvious.'

'It won't be obvious. You forget what a brilliant actress I am. Haven't I learned from the masters, Roddy and Connor?'

'Annie!' Dinah warned and then began to list all the reasons why Annie should not get beautifully dressed up and hang out at the Claridge's bar in the hope of 'accidentally' bumping into Gray: it was too desperate, it would look like too much of a coincidence, what if he wasn't pleased to see her? And so on.

'I hear what you're saying,' Annie said once the list was over.

'And you're going to ignore it.'

'Yeah, but I'll keep you posted.'

'You're going to embarrass yourself.'

'No, no, no,' Annie insisted. 'He'll be delighted to see me. I'm sure of it! We got on so well at the party. He's just one of those men who doesn't rush in, he needs a push. Honestly! He needs to be shown the way. Trust me on this. He needs some surprises in his life and some fun. He needs *me*!'

'Oh boy,' Dinah sighed.

Annie had never set foot in Claridge's before. Although she'd left work early in a fresh, painstakingly chosen camel and pink outfit with new (Chanel!) shoes, as soon as she passed the top-hat-and-tails footman and entered the marbled, chandeliered lobby, she felt a little unequal to the occasion.

This was true early twentieth-century splendour. This was a hotel where women should still be wearing veiled cocktail hats and lizard-skin heels, toting alligator handbags and silver cigarette cases.

Only sleek black bobs, real diamonds and thick scarlet lipstick were appropriate here.

After asking directions, as casually and as bravely as she could, Annie made her way to one of the most elegant bars she'd ever encountered. It was dark and snug, but the mahogany table tops, brass lamps, glittering mirrors and glasses meant it sparkled with very expensive glamour. The seats were low slung, comfortable leather, the tables decked with heavy glass ashtrays and flowers. There was the gentle buzz of just a select handful of guests talking quietly.

This was the perfect rendezvous for would-be lovers. With a little pang, she wished Gray had called and that they were meeting here on purpose. How romantic that could have been.

Never mind . . . she brushed the thought aside. He was a man who needed to be told what was good for him, just as she'd explained to Dinah.

She approached the handsome dark-haired barman and smiled winningly.

'Hello, how are you? Quiet afternoon?'

Once he'd made his reply, she asked for a gin and tonic.

'A double, madam?' he wanted to know, because this was, of course, the kind of place where everything came with a possible upgrade.

'No, thanks. And can I have a mineral water too, please?'

Once further clarification had been made as to which of the five available sparkling or still mineral waters she wished to drink, Annie had another question for the barman: 'I just wondered if I could ask a little favour?'

'No problem, madam,' he assured her, when she'd explained what she wanted. 'Please, take a seat, make yourself comfortable and I'll bring your drinks.'

He also brought the bill, which proved this was one of the most expensive bars in Europe as well as one of the loveliest.

But the drinks were beautiful: they sparked and fizzled from real crystal tumblers with fresh lime slices and so many chunky ice cubes that they went all the way down to the bottom of the glasses, like the acrylic ice used in movie drinks.

But Annie wasn't so lost in her admiration of the place that she didn't notice the small stream of people heading from the direction she'd carefully positioned her chair to observe.

OK – she took a steadying sip of her G&T – time to be cool.

She watched as Gray came into the lobby. He looked good: dark navy suit, crisp white shirt, navy tie with subtle polka dots. He was several inches taller than the people he was talking to and had that proud, upright posture of a confident man. A good profile, she noted once again, nice nose, strong chin.

Yes, he would do. He would most definitely do.

Annie turned her head slightly to the side and willed him to look over. She had a back-up plan in case he didn't, but it would be so much easier if he just did.

Several long seconds went by. She took another sip of her drink.

'Annie?' came his voice finally. 'Annie? Is that you?'

She turned to see him striding purposefully towards her, while the small group of men he'd been talking to hung back.

'Gray! What are you doing here?!'

'Annie, what are *you* doing here?' he countered, adding quickly, 'I mean, my God, that's fantastic' – he looked almost flustered – 'I've been trying to call you for days but I must have got your number wrong and I haven't been able to get hold of your mother to—'

'You could easily have got me through The Store,' she reminded him, not willing to fall for the old 'I tried to call' chestnut.

'The Store!' He smacked his forehead lightly. 'I've been phoning Selfridges'!'

Ah! Now he was forgiven.

Annie smiled broadly at him: 'That's very sweet of you. Is this where your conference is being held?' she asked, succeeding in sounding just the right kind of surprised.

He nodded.

'Bit posh, innit?' she teased.

'Why are you here?' he asked, still standing, but leaning towards her, with both hands on the back of the chair opposite hers, which was surely very positive body language.

'Well, obviously, I'm stalking you,' she said, an eyebrow arched.

When he just smiled in response to this, she quickly corrected him: 'No! Don't flatter yourself! I've got a job on here.' Her voice dropping low, she elaborated: 'An American actress, far too famous to actually come into The Store, is upstairs in the honeymoon suite trying on a load of our clothes and any moment now I'm going to be summoned up to help her and her stylist with the final decisions. That's why I need a quick drink, believe me.' She winked at him.

'Who?' he was desperate to know.

'I can't tell you!' she teased. 'Goodness me, we've only just met. I can't let you into any state secrets.'

'But we're going to meet again, aren't we?' he asked, then took a quick glance back at the huddle of dentists still in the lobby waiting for him. 'I'm a bit tied up right now . . . but could we get together for dinner later? There's something on but I can get out of it and I'd love to take you out. You are looking fabulous, by the way.'

See? She was right, he was delighted to see her. Dinner?! But no. It was time to be cool. He had not phoned, so she was not available. Basic dating rules.

'Oh! I'm going out tonight . . . What a shame.' She didn't explain further. Let him think she was on a scorching hot date, it would do him good.

At that moment, bang on cue, as previously arranged, the barman approached the table: 'Madam, I'm so sorry to interrupt . . .'

'No, no problem,' she assured him.

'There's a call for you from suite number one. You're to make your way up.'

'Thanks,' she told him with a smile. A great tip really did buy you fabulous service here.

'I have to go,' she told Gray. 'Wish me luck!'

'At least let me make sure I've got the right number for you, so we can set something up soon.' He was almost pleading. This was excellent progress.

'Hmmm . . . my evenings are a bit tied up for the next week or two,' she told him, just to dangle the carrot a little longer. 'But . . . how about Sunday? Would you like to meet for lunch?'

'I'd love to,' he told her.

'Well, let's meet on Tower Bridge at one p.m., Sunday then, I know a nice place round there. And here' – she reached into her handbag – 'this is my card. You can phone me if you're going to be late.'

'I won't be late!' he assured her. Then, as she stood up to leave for her phantom appointment at suite number one, he leaned over and kissed her on both sides of the face, giving her a hit of sexy citrus aftershave and coffee breath.

'Is there something . . . ? Umm, on your cheek? What is that?' He brushed at her face, while her toes curled up as much as they could in tight Chanel.

On the tip of his little finger was a frazzled clump of eyelash extension, which he was examining with great curiosity. She thought she'd felt something odd happening out there at the corner of her eye. The acrylic debris looked like a squashed spider.

'Ah! It's my new mascara,' she managed. 'I think I'm allergic to it or something. It's doing very strange things to my lashes. Anyway,' she brushed the offensive item from his fingertip, 'thanks for telling me. Well . . . I'd better head off.'

On reflection, her sashay through the lobby, past the

group of dentists and towards the grand staircase would have been so much more elegant and effective if her brand new, staggeringly high heels hadn't caused her a vicious ankle twist and her mobile hadn't been trilling with the latest Crazy Frog anthem. Thank you, Owen.

'Dinah!' she hissed into the phone, once she was safely at the top of the stairs, into a corridor and out of sight. 'I said *I'd* phone *you*!'

Chapter Fourteen

Silver fox Gray's date wear:

Black lightweight wool suit (Armani)
White T-shirt (Paul Smith)
Thick white shirt (Gant)
Black socks (Paul Smith)
Boxers (Paul Smith)
Black lace-up ankle boots (Oliver Sweeney)
Aviator shades (Ray-Ban)
Est. cost: £890

'And how would you make me over?'

Annie leaned on the metal railing of Tower Bridge and marvelled at the great swollen 'gherkin' building which rose up and swaggered high above all the other office blocks surrounding it. The gherkin? Really? Why not just name it 'the willy' and be done with it? The Tower of London, once so monumental and impressive, was now squeezed underneath a skyline dominated by vast modern towers.

But this was where to come and cloud-watch in London. Today grey cumulus stacks were sweeping in quickly from the west, chasing shafts of sunlight over the dark water surface.

She turned to take in the view on the other side, just in time to see Gray walking briskly along on the opposite pavement. He was early too but he obviously hadn't spotted her yet. His face and gold-rimmed aviator shades were set against the frisky wind, his jacket was flapping and he had a hand on his head as if to keep an invisible hat in place.

'Hey, Gray!' she called out. For late forties, he looked fit. Worked out, she thought, watching the wind push his T-shirt against his flat stomach – definitely.

'Gray!' she called again, louder this time, as he hadn't heard her and was still marching purposefully on in his head-to-toe black.

Giving her own outfit an automatic, anxious little smooth-over, Annie prepared to cross the road to catch up with him. For the occasion, she'd chosen a full-skirted black and white dress, black high-heeled ankle boots and one of her key spring items – a wide-sleeved, cropped orange jacket. A lipstick that matched the orangey red of the jacket exactly had been the one special date purchase she'd allowed herself. Well . . . er . . . the boots were new too . . . but . . . they'd been too hard to resist. And footwear was so important on dates, she'd reminded herself as she'd handed over the credit card. Men always noticed footwear, even if they didn't think they did. Boots and shoes seemed to play on their imagination like nothing else, so if the new boots meant she landed Gray . . . wasn't that practically an investment?

'Gray!'

Finally, he turned and his slightly surprised expression changed to a smile.

'Annie! Hello there!' He pushed his shades up into his hair and walked over, moving straight in to give her a kiss not on each cheek, but on the lips as he put a bunch of flowers into her hands.

The brush of lip, hit of mint breath and spicy aftershave was a very pleasant experience Annie thought she'd definitely like to repeat soon.

'Flowers! Thank you. You really shouldn't have!' she gushed with a big smile although the waxy white lilies, fat white roses and green garlanding were so stark and funereal that she would have quite liked to throw the bouquet off the bridge. She liked colourful, cheerful flowers. Nothing poncy. But never mind, she could drop those hints another day.

'So,' she began, 'we meet on the bridge. Me and the master of bridgework.'

'Oh ho! Very good. Look at that building.' He pointed to the gherkin as if it had just popped up into view. 'Fantastic.'

'Well, I suppose,' she offered grudgingly. 'If you like that sort of thing. How was your journey?' she asked.

'Fantastic!' he told her with a smile. 'Roof down all the way, first nice day of the season for it. How about you?'

She didn't think her forty minutes spent on the underground merited such a rapturous reply.

'And your children?' was his next question. 'What are they up to today?'

'Oh, they're busy,' she told him. 'Hectic schedule . . .'

Annie had arranged for Dinah to take them for lunch,

183

then Lana had agreed to walk Owen up to his karate lesson and wait for him there. This meant her home was empty . . . so if lunch went well, she was going to invite Gray back for coffee and a little light canoodling.

With small talk, lots of smiling, sizing up and eye contact, Annie held the arm he'd offered her as they crossed Tower Bridge and made their way down to Butler's Wharf where she'd booked a table for two at the Chop House.

Gray kept up a pleasantly steady flow of chat and with the anxious butterflies in her stomach settling, she began to enjoy herself.

When he asked if she'd been on many dates 'since your husband . . . erm . . .' she quickly cut in with: 'Oh, loads. I like to get out in the evenings. Keep busy. It's easy to get a date, you know, Gray.'

'For you, I'm sure it is,' he offered gallantly.

'But it's not so easy to get a *good* one,' she told him, eyebrow arching.

Their table came with the riverside view she'd requested.

'I love it down here on the river,' she said once the menus had been studied, the food and drinks ordered. 'It doesn't feel like London, it feels European but this is one of the oldest parts of the city, you know. This is where the first kings and queens lived, where they kept the prisoners, hanged the pirates. This is where ships set sail hoping to return laden down with goodies from all over the world. I like to think that this' – she gestured to the stretch of river – 'is where shopping began.'

It made him laugh.

When the wine was poured, they clinked glasses and

he asked her to tell him more about her work: 'It sounds very intriguing. Basically, you help people to shop?' He sounded a little incredulous, as if he couldn't quite believe this counted as a job. Annie had weathered this reaction plenty of times before.

'It's an American concept,' she told him. 'America is the home of good service, after all . . . Think of me as a super-enhanced sales assistant. Customers book an appointment with me, we discuss what clothes they're looking for, what lifestyle, what budget they have, then I take them through the relevant sections and departments, making suggestions until we find all the outfits they want. In short, I'm there to give my clients a happy shopping experience. I help people make great wardrobe investments, not expensive mistakes.'

'And you're on commission?'

'On top of my wages, yes.'

'And you do this on a freelance basis as well?'

'The thing you'll get to know about me, Gray,' Annie teased, 'is that I have fingers in many pies. I do home consultations, because they pay well and because they're such great fun. Who wouldn't love to have a good old rummage through other people's wardrobes?! I also buy and sell used designer clothes and accessories on the internet and I'm a trained stylist, believe it or not.'

'Oh yes! You told me when we met that you'd worked on films.'

'Aha . . . the film days . . .' She smiled, carefully picking a large cooked prawn out of its shell. 'My globetrotting twenties. Roddy, me and our surprise baby Lana. We were always happy to go wherever the work was: France, Romania, Poland, Morocco . . . wherever.'

'Sounds incredibly glamorous,' Gray said.

'It was,' she agreed. 'I think I probably took it for granted, thought life would always be as simple and as much fun as it was then. But babies grow up, they get baby brothers, everyone has to go to nursery and then to school, suddenly you need a bigger home and a regular income. Roddy landed a string of good theatre jobs based in London, so we stopped travelling so much. Finally he got his soap role, I had my nice job at The Store and we got grounded, just like everyone else I suppose . . .' But this came with a cheerful smile. 'I don't regret it,' she told him truthfully, 'I've done my wandering and it's nice to be home again. And I'll tell you one thing, it's much more fun making the not-so-beautiful look wonderful than dealing with leading ladies all the time. Everything you've ever heard about actresses is true,' she exaggerated, but only slightly. 'They are only so talented and so supernaturally beautiful because they've sold their souls to the devil!'

'So how would you make *me* over?' he challenged her, propping his chin up with his hand and giving her a look that made her suspect the intensely green eyes leaping from his tanned face were created by tinted contact lenses.

'I don't think *you* need a stylist,' she told him, hearing the flirty little purr in her voice.

'Oh, well . . . that's very nice, but we could all improve, couldn't we? Take tips from the masters.'

'You've got very good taste, Gray.'

'Hmmm,' he nodded in agreement. 'And not just in clothes.' He kept his gaze trained directly at Annie, until she couldn't help giggling.

'So,' he unfolded his hands, 'you should venture out, start your own big business. How about a shop? A makeover boutique? A chain of personal dressing stores where customers can go to get much more than the usual shop assistant input? Or what about your own clothing collection? The perfect black trousers, smart jacket or white shirt? Annie's Essentials?'

'A shop?' she teased. 'So very last century. You should look up my virtual store some time, Annie V's Trading Station. Who wants to pay staff and rates and overheads when you can create your own cyber shop-front?'

'You're very good,' he told her with a smile. 'Maybe I should get you to look over my business, see if you can think of any improvements.'

'I'd be delighted. So are you into cosmetic dentistry as well as fillings, extractions and root canals?'

'Oh yes,' he assured her, as their plates were cleared away by an attentive waiter. 'Teeth straightening, veneers, dental implants, all the high-end stuff. I'm hoping to add Botox® to our range of treatments very soon.'

'Really? But my ladies tell me Botox® is over and everyone's doing Restylane® now,' she informed him.

'Yes, well, possibly. I'm looking into that. I'm going over to LA in a couple of weeks to find out what's on offer in the home of cosmetic surgery. But you've not had anything done, have you?' He was scrutinizing her just a little too closely for comfort.

'No! I'm not ruling it out though. If I wake up one morning and make-up alone can't save me from looking like a haggard old witch, then I might just come to you to see what you can do about it.'

187

'Well . . .'

She'd meant this as a cheeky, flirty comment, but now his scrutiny of her face was too professional for her liking.

'Not everyone looks as fantastic in their thirties as you do.' It was his turn to purr now, she noticed with a delicious little shiver: 'But a tiny hit, just in there between your brows,' he pointed, 'would work wonders. But what I'd really love to make over is your mouth.'

No, no, no! This wasn't sexy. Now she wanted to put her hands over her face and never part her lips again. What was wrong with her teeth, exactly? They weren't perfect but they weren't too bad either.

'The overcrowding on the bottom row could be cured with wisdom tooth extraction and a gentle brace. On the top, I'd put in two or three veneers to smooth out those slightly crooked angles, then whiten everything up two or three shades. You'd be stunning. I'd give you a great rate,' he offered.

'Erm, well . . . that's very kind of you . . . let me think that one over,' she hesitated. Despite the tempting offer of a discount, lying back in a dental chair with her tonsils and all her fillings on display didn't strike her as the best of wooing techniques.

Annie wondered what he'd had done. Well, obviously his teeth were pearly white and perfect, but she guessed that he kept the other little touch-ups a trade secret, so she didn't ask.

As their coffees arrived – both of them had waved away the suggestion of dessert – he turned the conversation from teeth to ask: 'So you like it down here on the river?'

She nodded.

'I'm thinking of buying a flat down here to rent out.'

Aha, a budding property mogul. Her ears perked with interest.

'I've got a viewing at about three p.m. Would you like to come along? You know I'd value your opinion.'

The flat was smart if a little boxy: maple flooring, recessed lighting, two small bedrooms, two high-tech bathrooms of dark greenish slate, one a wet room with a rain-bath shower. The living area had a glitzy open plan kitchen and big floor-to-ceiling windows offering views of . . . well, another development.

It was obvious quite quickly that Gray was not impressed.

'That's a very small bedroom,' he told the estate agent, then, 'It's hardly a view, is it? The kitchen's part of the living room, I wasn't expecting that.'

'This is a very prestigious address,' the estate agent argued. 'Excellent area for shopping, eating out, you're so close to the City – only a ten-minute walk over the bridge to the tube . . .'

Clearly wherever Gray lived, he was getting a much better deal than this. But he lived out of town. He was a 'burbs man, probably the proud owner of a driveway, a front lawn and French windows out onto his own back garden. This was city living – more luxury, less square feet – and clearly it was a shock to the system.

'What did you think?' he canvassed Annie's opinion once they were out of the flat and had bid the agent farewell.

'Complete rip-off,' she informed him confidently. 'Don't touch it with a bargepole.'

'And what makes you so knowledgeable?' he asked, casually draping an arm over her shoulders, where it sat comfortably, if a little self-consciously.

'Well, Gray, if you offer to drive me home, I might tell you all about my successful scramble up the London property ladder,' she said, imagining the two of them cosied up together on her big white sofa.

'It's a deal,' he agreed. 'But only if you invite me in.'
Result!

As he opened the passenger's door, so she could climb aboard his sleek, low-slung, silver Merc convertible, she surveyed the black leather seats, high-tech dashboard, GPS navigation device, not to mention the suave gentleman in the driver's seat and she thought: I could get used to this.

Chapter Fifteen

Lana at home:

Black vest top (Miss Selfridge)
Black jeans (Evisu via eBay)
Black nail varnish (Topshop)
Black eyeliner (Chanel)
Black mood (model's own)
Est. cost: £75

'D'uhhh.'

As Annie pushed open her flat door, she wasn't exactly thrilled to hear the sound of the television in Lana's room and the noise of the kettle coming to the boil in the kitchen.

'Lana?' she called into the hallway. 'I thought you were at karate with Owen?'

Lana in head-to-toe clinging black appeared in the kitchen doorway: 'He didn't want to go,' she said grumpily, 'I couldn't make him.'

'No? No . . . well . . . right.' She tried to keep her

annoyance under control. She loved her children dearly and was, on the whole, fiercely proud of them, but the meeting of children with prospective boyfriends was something that had to be carefully managed, not just sprung on her, because of the potentially explosive emotions.

'Well, now you'll get a chance to say hello to my friend Gray.' With these words, Annie ushered Gray in through the door, as Lana's mouth opened and forgot to shut.

'Hello there, Lana,' Gray offered a hand for her to shake, 'I remember seeing you at your grandmother's party – but you were a little busy . . .'

Lana blushed, shook Gray's hand and managed a mumbled hello.

'Come into the sitting room,' Annie offered. 'I'll just go and dig Owen out of his room, but he's a little shy,' she reminded Gray in a quiet voice.

He nodded with understanding.

Owen waved at Gray from the doorway then fled back to his room. Annie left it at that. She was trying to enjoy Gray's many compliments about her home rather than worry too much about how her children were going to react to him and vice versa.

'Shall we go into the kitchen and have some coffee?' she asked.

'Yes, definitely . . .' Gray got up from the sofa arm he'd perched on. Annie was still thinking she'd like to push him back onto the cushions and rumple him quite a lot, but the presence of children made that impossible.

At the kitchen table, Lana was chewing at the skin round her nails and texting frantically.

'Everything OK?' Annie wondered.

'Yeah, fine, everything's fine,' she answered, not breaking eye contact with the screen.

'Does the Seth Lord still rule?' Annie couldn't help herself.

But she shouldn't have, she just got a black look and deepest scowl in reply: 'At least he doesn't use hair dye and fake tan,' Lana snapped.

'Hopefully it won't *kill* you to be nice,' Annie whispered at her, just before Gray was in earshot.

'D'uhhh,' came the great grudging sigh. Annie decided to stay calm. Lana was a confused 14 and the prospect of a real, live man in her mother's life, rather than a faceless date, was bound to be unsettling.

Once the kettle was on for the coffee, Annie felt an unusual desire to play domestic goddess. She brought out a tablecloth then shooed Lana and her things out of the way so she could put it on the table. She set out cups, saucers, cake plates and shook almond biscuits out of the packet.

The milk went into a little blue jug, brown sugar into a matching bowl. She warmed the rarely used cafetière before adding the ground coffee she'd unearthed at the back of a cupboard.

Then, using the typical parental combination of threats and bribes, she made Owen and Lana sit up at the table properly to meet Gray.

'I hear you're both at St Vincent's?' was Gray's ice-breaker, once he was settled into his chair. But the question didn't go down so well.

Lana scowled, rolled her eyes and came out with: 'Godawful place, I absolutely hate it.'

'No you don't,' Annie said with her nicest smile. 'Tell Gray about the fund-raising website. They're hoping to make ten thousand pounds for charity by the end of the summer.'

Lana pulled a face, but then her phone bleeped with a reply text and she pounced on it, snatching it up, eyes lighting.

Gray and Annie watched as Owen picked up four biscuits and crammed them all into his mouth, forcing his lips to part as he crunched down on them.

'Of course we won't be at St Vincent's for long,' Lana fired out, taking Annie completely by surprise. 'Mum's totally broke and we'll either have to sell the flat or leave school.'

'Or both,' Owen added for emphasis, spraying crumbs across the tablecloth. Despite her embarrassment, for a moment Annie managed to feel proud that Owen had actually spoken two words despite the presence of a stranger. Just a few months ago, this would never have happened.

'Er . . . well,' she smiled at Gray and twisted the coffee cup round in her hands. Maybe last night hadn't been such great timing for the earnest little conversation she'd had with the children about the hole in the family finances. 'It's hardly as bad as that.'

'But you said—' Lana began.

'I may have to free up a little equity,' she breezed, seeing what she read as concern in Gray's face, 'but St Vincent's is a great school. They're both going to be there for many years to come.'

She shot a look at Lana, who slumped melo-dramatically over her phone. The phone Annie would right at this moment like to rip from her daughter's hands and toss out of the window.

Then the landline began to ring and to Annie's surprise, Owen stood up and ran out of the room to answer it.

He picked up, said, 'Hello,' in a very calm-sounding voice and then carried on something resembling a normal conversation.

This was very unusual.

'Oh yeah . . . hi . . . aha . . . that's really cool,' she overheard.

Then came: 'Hmmm . . . Wednesday? This Wednesday? Muuum!' came the shout.

'Yes?' she answered.

'Are we doing anything on Wednesday evening?'

Annie flicked mentally through the following week's family schedule: Sunday karate, Tuesday Billie babysit, Thursday swimming lessons. Wednesday? Was anything planned for Wednesday? Annie glanced at Gray, in case he wanted to jump in with a suggestion: helicopter trip to Paris for rooftop dinner, perhaps? No. He wasn't saying anything.

'No,' she said finally, 'I don't think we're doing anything – but why? Who?'

Owen didn't answer her, he was back on the phone: 'Wednesday's fine. Great . . . So about seven p.m.?'

This was positively chatty, startling for Annie.

'OK cool. Yup. See ya tomorrow, sir. OK.'

'Who was that?' Annie asked as soon as Owen came back into the kitchen, although the 'sir' at the end of the call had been a good clue.

'Ed,' Owen replied.

195

'Mr Leon?'

'Yeah.' There was a pause and Annie thought the presence of Gray was going to silence Owen once again, but instead she watched as he took a breath or two to calm himself, as he'd been taught to do but rarely remembered, then he continued, stumbling over the odd word: 'There's this singer, Rufus Wainwright, and he's doing an . . . an . . . acoustic thing at the National Theatre. Ed said he'd look into getting tickets for us. It's going to be cool!'

'All of us?' Annie wondered.

'You, me, Lana.'

'Oh no,' came the groan from Lana.

Rufus Wainwright wasn't registering on Annie's radar. She looked at Lana, to see if she could spot any signs of recognition there.

'He's gay, took crystal meth . . . folk-type god,' was Lana's helpful biog, delivered in tones of deepest uninterest.

'Don't you want to go?' Annie asked.

'Oh yeah . . . well, Ed the Shed is so not cool, but Rufus is crack!'

Annie worried for about the tenth time that day if her children were watching too much American TV.

Gray's contribution to this new turn in the conversation was to ask what crystal meth was, which earned him the kind of scowls and shrugs Lana usually reserved for *total losers* such as children's TV presenters, people in cagoules, members of the Conservative Party or the Royal Family.

This caused Gray to look at his watch (stainless steel Tag Heuer) and announce his imminent departure.

196

Annie suspected he still wasn't over the 'Mum's totally broke' comment and she would have to do something to remedy the situation or she wasn't going to see him again for dust.

As he got up, she ushered him through into the sitting room, saying she wanted to show him something.

'Take a look at that building over there.' She pointed it out from her window. 'Now that is really worth investing in.' Her tone was cosy and confidential now: 'Lovely part of town, great views, good school catchment, right on the tube. It will rent like a dream. I happen to know that the developer is right on the verge of going down the tubes. He desperately needs money coming in to finish the project off. I'm absolutely certain that he'd take a very low bid on a two-bedroom flat, so long as you were willing to pay a big deposit up front, before the place was even finished. I would be investing in that right now . . . except, as my children have so helpfully explained,' she tried to make light of it, 'I'm not exactly so flexibly . . . liquid at the moment.'

'Great tip.' To her relief, Gray was purring again. 'I'll look into it,' he added. 'And by the way, what are you doing next weekend?'

Yes!

'Well, let me see . . . There's the shopping trip to buy gags for Lana and Owen . . . but otherwise . . .'

Chapter Sixteen

Ed dressing for the occasion:

Yellow polo shirt (drawer)
Red polo shirt (drawer)
Green tweed jacket (can't remember)
Baggy khakis (Army and Navy stores)
Heavy boots (same)
Est. cost: £45

'Music always gives me an appetite!'

'There you are!' were Ed's opening words as Annie, Lana and Owen arrived wet and slightly bedraggled at the doors to the concert hall.

They were twenty minutes late and now there was barely time to say hello because the performance was just about to begin.

'Sorry, Ed,' Annie began. 'It's taken us ages . . . We got totally lost out there.'

This wasn't untrue, there had been some confusion about directions, but she decided she'd bypass an

198

explanation about the enormous Lana row which had really held them up.

Just your standard mother–teenage daughter 'you're not going out like that' argument, which had of course escalated to great, hurtful, all-encompassing insults being tossed around at random.

Lana: 'You're such a cow! I hate you!'

Annie: 'You're just a spoiled brat, I'm not buying you anything, ever again! This time I mean it!' And so on.

Owen had quietly put on his shoes and anorak, then he'd gone to stand by the door, headphones in, iPod cranked up, foot tapping to the rhythm, as he'd waited for the storm to finally blow over.

The sight of him had taken the wind out of Annie's sails.

'Right, Lana, that's it, I'm done,' she'd announced in the coolest voice she could summon: 'Just put on the sparkly boob tube, skinny jeans and platform boots if you want. I'm not saying another word about it. Just make sure . . .' See? She was already saying another word about it, but she couldn't resist: 'Make sure you've got something waterproof on top because it's definitely going to rain.'

There. Words her own father could have been saying to her twenty years ago. He'd barely been around enough for her to remember many of his words of supposed wisdom, but she could definitely recall the nagging: 'Put something warm over that or you'll freeze.'

But then wasn't this the most totally irritating thing about parenthood? Just as you came to appreciate how caring and sensible some of your parents' advice had been, that's when your very own little teenage spawn was throwing it all back in your face, exactly as you'd done too.

Annie sometimes understood Lana too perfectly, felt her pain, felt her burning desire for the boots and jeans and cleavage display. Felt her outraged injustice. And sometimes Annie couldn't decide which side she was on: parent or child?

So this was how it was: she usually ranted but then relented. Her children could ultimately do as they wanted, but at least they would know how she felt about it.

She'd been tempted to grab the camera and take a quick photo of Lana's outfit to torment her with in about three months' time, when this look was so *over*!

'We're going out with your *teacher*!' she'd reminded her daughter. 'I don't think we're likely to bump into the living god that is Seth, are we?'

In the concert hall, they had to squeeze past twenty people or so to get into their seats: Ed leading the way, then Lana, Owen and finally Annie.

During the performance Annie kept catching sight of Ed's face appearing over the top of teen boobs hoicked up in a padded bra underneath a boob tube. They were listening to a song about a teenager being in love with an art teacher. Another time Annie might have loved this song, all haunting and melodic, moody drumming piano in the background, but instead, she felt her world view shift a little uncomfortably.

Was Lana attracted to Ed? Despite her cool disdain, maybe she had a little crush? That wouldn't be so surprising, any teacher slightly more attractive than Frankenstein could usually be guaranteed a decent pupil fan base.

But . . . she looked over at the two of them again closely. Did Ed have any sort of thing for Lana?! Just the thought of this made little prickles of anxiety stand up on the back of her neck. Lana was at that tricky teen age: she looked older than she was and tonight she looked lovely, sexy even, but hopefully she didn't have much of a clue about the admiring glances she was attracting. But not from Ed, surely?

Annie turned her head and watched the two of them to see if there was any sort of . . . well . . . what? A look? Nudge? Communication between them?

Ed was leaning forward, totally wrapped up in the performance. Lana was scratching at her bare arm in a slightly distracted way.

There was nothing obvious. She'd give it a few minutes then try again.

The next time she looked, Ed turned his head and looked not at Lana and her overexposed teen boobies, but at Annie.

She felt caught out and gave an automatic little smile which he returned with something much broader and kinder. He tilted his head in the direction of the music and raised his eyebrows as if to ask her: Is this OK? Are you enjoying it? And she nodded enthusiastically back.

'You've got to come to the café with me,' he insisted when the performance was over. 'It's fantastic! Honestly. And I bet you've not had time to eat.'

This was true.

Then he gave one of his spectacular sneezes and took

a big cotton handkerchief from a pocket to blow his nose.

'Still not over your cold?' Annie asked.

'Doh, dot really,' came from the depths of the hankie. 'Think I'm allergic to London,' he added when the hankie was out of the way.

It was a self-service café, so they got their plastic trays and stood in line. Despite Ed's rave review, Annie didn't feel tempted by any of the main courses on offer, so decided to go for lentil soup with a roll. She watched Lana make the same choice, while Owen plumped for an open sandwich with prawns, lettuce and pink mayonnaise sprinkled with cayenne pepper. Annie decided not to intervene, just offered up a silent prayer that there was nothing nasty lurking in the dish.

While Ed got caught up in the ordering process for a hot meal, Annie paid for her family's food and drinks and went to find a table for four.

As they sat down, she wondered if, like her, the children were registering the empty fourth seat. The fourth chair was usually something she would quickly move away to another table, so that it wasn't staring at them, glaring with emptiness as they ate. But tonight there would be a fourth person. The fourth chair would be filled.

When Ed joined them, his tray was laden. He had a steaming plate of steak and kidney pie with mashed potatoes, a separate dish of vegetables, an orange juice, a glass of red wine, a side dish of bread and butter.

'God! I love the food here,' he announced settling himself into the seat, 'I'm absolutely starving. Music always gives me an appetite! Don't you agree, Owen?'

Owen, midway through a prawny mouthful, nodded in smiley agreement.

If Ed had noticed that no-one else had such a big meal in front of them, he didn't draw attention to it and he certainly didn't feel shy about it. He was tucking in with an enthusiasm bordering on the alarming.

Annie, on his left, felt a touch on her hand and realized it was a splash of Ed's gravy: 'Steady on!' she warned him.

'Mmm . . . mm . . . mmmm . . .' Heaped fork poised, he made the sound of a contented man.

When his plate was a little emptier and he could turn his attention to the business of conversation he focused on the children, very interested to know what they thought of the music. Owen gave it a rave review and Ed even managed to coax some words of enthusiasm from Lana. Annie could see he was a natural at his job.

'Yes, that was very clever,' he was telling Lana, 'and you know, I don't think it was based on any more than three different piano chords. You could probably teach yourself that in ten minutes.'

'Really?!' Lana was close to sounding impressed.

'But obviously I'm not sure if it's going to be appropriate for me to teach you a song about falling in love with your teacher!' he pointed out.

When Lana made a groaning sound, both Ed and Owen laughed and Annie felt herself relax. If he was just going to come out and joke about it like this, then there couldn't be anything to worry about, could there? She could put her mind to rest.

He was chewing vigorously again, loading up the next forkful, trying to balance two green beans on top of it.

'Do you go to many concerts?' Annie asked him, then wished she'd left it a few moments. Ed's mouth was full and he was doing the 'mmm . . . mmm' sound of someone about to answer, just as soon as they'd swallowed down enough to be able to talk coherently.

Annie wondered where he put it all. He had a squarish build with broad shoulders, long body and stocky legs, but he didn't give the impression of being at all chubby, although under the monumentally baggy khaki trousers and hairy tweed jacket chosen for tonight, it was hard to tell. And why had green tweed been paired with a double layer of red and yellow polo shirts? Annie wondered. Was he in some sort of competition for worst-dressed man in London? There was no consistency to his look: it was skinny cords one week, over-baggy trews the next. He probably shopped at Oxfam but not in the caring and considered style of Dinah.

'I try and do two a week,' came Ed's answer finally. There was a fleck of gravy on his chin and Annie wiped her own chin in the hope that maybe he'd be inspired to do the same.

'No preference, all types of things.' He waved his knife and fork expansively and she saw Lana dodge slightly to avoid being sprayed. 'The cheap seats at the big operas, folk and classical here and at the Barbican, jazz nights, dodgy gigs in pubs. I just like to see the action, hear what's going on. What about you people? What kind of things do you like to go to?'

Before Annie could even consider her answer, Owen shook his head and said sadly, 'We never go to anything like this. It's the first time I've been out in ages.'

'That's not true, Owen!' Annie was quick to deny, but she couldn't help smiling because she'd never seen Owen so at home with someone from outside the immediate family and friends circle. Her son had been seven when his dad had left and the debilitating shyness had set in almost immediately. Despite all sorts of expert advice and opinion, there had been little real improvement until Ed had become his teacher. Now, Owen seemed to be coming on in leaps and bounds, flourishing. She would have to take Ed aside and thank him for his help.

'Yes it is!' Owen retorted.

'We go out!' Annie insisted, but the more she tried to think of an example to prove Owen wrong, the more she couldn't. Plenty of memorable family outings with Roddy were filling her mind, but her and the children . . . at a concert . . . at a play or something . . .

'Help me out, Lana!' she said.

'We go to the cinema a lot,' Lana reminded Owen. 'We go to Dinah's, Connor's, we visit friends and relatives . . . so we go out. But we don't do the concert, theatre, art gallery thing hardly at all.'

'Well, you have to,' Ed told them. 'You have to get out there.' He looked at them all in turn, so Annie didn't feel as if she was being singled out for criticism: 'Rub shoulders with the world, find out what's goin' down.'

This was met with smiles from both Lana and Owen, even though they always shuddered and rolled their eyes if Annie dared to use this phrase.

'So you're more a cinema person?' He directed this at Annie, as he used a thickly buttered roll to mop up the last of the gravy from his plate.

'I suppose so,' Annie replied.

'And what kind of films do you like?'

'Oh . . . stylish films,' she told him, 'with lovely clothes, beautiful people and beautiful settings, a touch of romance and there always, always has to be something to make me laugh. I like a great story with a happy ending, but, you know, I don't mind a bit of art house, high-minded stuff as well.'

Ed was nodding vigorously.

'Just no horror,' Annie told him, 'I don't do horror. And I tend to give heavy, tragic subjects a bit of a miss as well.'

'I love comedies,' he confided. 'Love them! And I love good music in films . . . but films of musicals, well, unless they were made before 1960, forget it. Although there was a Tina Turner biopic. That wasn't bad at all.'

'Oh I remember that. That was very good! Totally over the top,' Annie added.

'What was the song?' Ed's brows scrunched up in concentration and the hand with the roll paused midway to his mouth.

'"Nutbush"?' she asked, certain this was what he was thinking of: actress Angela Bassett shaking her booty in a very tight, very short, fringed dress and great shaggy wig.

'"Nutbush"! Thank you!'

They both laughed.

'Something very . . .' He paused, brows scrunching again.

'Sexy?' she offered.

'Sexy,' he agreed, 'very sexy about that song. Pudding!' He smiled at Owen and Lana in turn, while

Annie struggled with the connection between 'Nutbush' and pudding.

'The pudding is sensational here,' Ed enthused, 'and it's my treat. No, really' – he raised a hand against Annie's objections, both to eating pudding and having Ed pay for it – 'I won't take no for an answer.'

He returned to the table, tray loaded with four bowls. Some sort of crumble dripping with cream: a calorific disaster.

'Ah!' was Ed's benediction over the plateful before he sank his spoon in. 'Like it?' he asked Owen, who was already wolfing down his third or fourth spoonful.

'Oh yeah!' came Owen's answer through a full mouth. 'This is the best crumble I've ever had. What's in it?'

The small spoonful Annie had taken was just hitting her taste buds, so she was too late to save Owen.

'Rhubarb,' came Ed's reply.

Annie could only watch, hoping he'd be fine. Hadn't he just declared this the best crumble he'd ever eaten? Which, yes, had dented her pride slightly, although she'd be the first to admit she wasn't exactly gifted in the kitchen department.

Owen stopped chewing and began to change colour. Pink first, then red, then a deep purple-tinged scarlet.

'He's not allergic?' Ed asked anxiously, dropping his spoon.

Annie shook her head and explained: 'Only in his mind. Owen, you're going to be fine,' she soothed, reaching to pat Owen's hand. 'It's delicious, you just said it was delicious.'

But Lana couldn't resist: 'I don't think so,' she teased. 'Rhubarb, Owen, rhoooooo-barb.'

'Lana!' Annie hissed.

Scarlet, Owen made choky, gagging noises before a soggy lump of the offending crumble landed unceremoniously back in his plate.

Now it was Annie's turn to blush, but Ed, entirely unruffled, sprang into action.

'Oh dear, oh dear.' He got a little closer to the plate so he could scrutinize the remains. 'No need to panic. I'm so sorry, Owen, I didn't know anything about your dislike of this fruit . . . or is it in fact a vegetable? Anyway . . .' He quickly filled Owen's glass with water from Annie's bottle: 'Have a little sip of water and let me take that away.' He stood up and whisked the offending plateful out of sight as quickly as possible.

When he got back to the table, Ed was determined to put the abashed Owen back at ease: 'Did you know there is a great long list of foods that have exactly the same effect on the Queen?' he asked Owen. 'Oh yes,' he added, without waiting for an answer, 'if she's eating away from home, or one of her many homes, the list gets sent out in advance. Then all the dishes are personally inspected by her footman before they get to her, just to make sure she doesn't barf at a state banquet, while she's sitting between the President of Russia and the King of Swaziland or something.'

A teacher talking about the Queen barfing was enough to make Owen grin despite the unfortunate rhubarb incident.

'So if you could draw up a list of your hate foods, Owen, and pass it on to me, I'd be most grateful and then maybe I could act as your personal taster, you know, check out your food before it gets to you . . .

mmm . . .' Ed picked up his spoon, once again ready to tackle his bowl of the crumble everyone else had lost their appetite for. 'I would enjoy being a personal taster. Two dinners . . . three . . . four . . .'

When Owen had exited to the loo, Ed told Annie: 'I've been a teacher for nine years now. If there's any regurgitating, vomiting, fainting, losing control of bladder or any other bodily functions to be done in public, I'm your man.'

'Well, that's very reassuring,' Annie told him. 'You know, I have to thank you for all your help with Owen. He's coming on so well . . . and you handled that . . . well. Better than I would have.'

'No problem, honestly . . .' Ed was threatening to blush. 'Now' – he went quickly for a change of subject – 'shall I get the tube back to Highgate with you charming people? See you safely to your door?'

Then, just as Annie had thought she was beginning to warm to Ed, he plucked a vibrant yellow cagoule from his backpack, pulled it over his head and – although they were still indoors – put the hood up and pulled the toggles tight so that his face was framed with scrunched yellow nylon.

This gave Annie something close to a rhubarb moment of her own.

She quickly looked away. Owen's admiration for Ed had given her an idea. She'd ask the teacher in and sound him out over coffee.

Chapter Seventeen

Science kit Owen:

> *Grey T-shirt (Asda)*
> *Enormous jeans (Gap sale)*
> *Belt (St Vincent's uniform shop)*
> *Socks (Asda)*
> *Very well-equipped science kit (Connor)*
> *Total est. cost: £60*

'Er . . . I think there's a slight problem.'

Ed lived in Highgate too ('I must show you my grimy little abode . . . maybe next time, when I've arranged for the industrial cleaners to come round') so he insisted on walking them home and Annie, in turn, insisted he come in for a coffee.

Even if she hadn't had something she wanted to ask him, she wouldn't have liked the thought of sending him straight back to a grimy little abode without something in the way of thanks, so she guided him into the kitchen, while her children splintered off to their rooms.

'I need to make a call,' Lana explained.

'Yes, I know, darlin', you've not spoken to Seth for at least two hours now, obviously you'll want to snuggle down for a long chat and fill him in on everything that's happened,' was what Annie wanted to say, but didn't.

'There's something I want to show you, just give me a minute,' Owen told Ed.

Annie put the kettle on and made a quick check on her emails and her eBays at the kitchen table while she chatted to Ed.

As she poured hot water over the instant coffee plonked into the bottom of two large mugs, her mobile rang.

To Ed's bemusement, she seemed to be taking an emergency call of the wardrobe variety: 'Ruby, darlin', of course I can come tomorrow evening. Not tonight. No, it's a bit late. Yeah . . . we'll look through the cupboards and we will find something . . . No . . . Of course not . . . What about the black and red one that we bought together last month? No? Well . . . Yes . . . I'll see you tomorrow and don't panic!'

As she talked, Annie brandished a small bottle of brandy and made tipping gestures to ask if Ed wanted some in his coffee.

He gave her the thumbs up so she slugged a little into both mugs.

'OK, nighty night then, Rubes. Bye,' she said and put down the phone.

'I didn't realize you were on call,' he teased as she placed the mugs on the table and pulled up a chair.

'Oh yeah, twenty-four seven,' she told him. 'A wardrobe emergency can strike at any time,' she said and took her first sip of coffee, curling her hands round the mug. 'Aah! The brandy takes the edge off the caffeine – you'll sleep better,' she explained.

'Right.'

'So, how long have you lived round here then?' Annie asked, able to meet his eyes again now that the cagoule was off.

'Oh, ages,' Ed replied. 'But on and off. My mum bought her place here years and years ago and I used it as a base whenever I needed to. I've only been here full-time for a year and a half. Mum got ill. I took the job at St Vincent's so I could move in and look after her.'

'Oh . . . and how's she getting on?' was Annie's next question.

With a sad little smile, Ed told her: 'I'm afraid she died. Six months ago now.'

'Oh! I'm ever so sorry, Ed. I'm sorry,' she repeated, trying for one moment to imagine life without Fern, and having to push the horrible thought away, 'I didn't know.'

'No, don't worry, honestly . . .' Ed tailed off and took a mouthful of coffee.

'And how are you coping?' Annie asked, full of concern for him now.

'Well, I'm . . . you know . . . just getting on with things.'

He leaned back in his chair and ruffled his hair before continuing. 'Hannah, that's my sister, and I . . . we were looking after Mum full-time at the end, which was fine, it was what we all wanted, but it was pretty hard going . . . My Italian girlfriend left me and went back to

212

Italy . . . my rubbish car got nicked . . . the usual triple whammy stuff.'

'Oh dear, oh dear,' Annie sympathized.

'Obviously we miss her . . . miss her a lot.'

Annie heard the involuntary swallow that this caused him.

'But,' he went on, 'I'm trying to focus on how great it is to be back out here again. Back teaching, getting out again . . . meeting new people.' He nodded, as if in her direction. 'It's very nice to be taking part in life again.'

'How old was she?' Annie wondered.

Owen's head popped round the corner of the kitchen door and he asked, 'Can Ed come to my room for a minute? There's something I want to show him.'

'Hang on a minute, Owen,' Annie told him. The head disappeared.

She turned her attention back to Ed and he replied, 'Mum was fifty-nine, four weeks from her sixtieth birthday. It was such a bugger. It was all a bugger.' He let out a sigh and turned his attention to his coffee cup.

'I'm really, really sorry,' Annie said once again.

'Anyway' – he looked up at her and gave a smile, hoping to draw a line under this conversation and start afresh in a new direction – 'I have a favour I want to ask you. It is a bit bizarre, though.'

It was her turn to smile: 'Now that's funny,' she told him, 'because I have a favour I want to ask you . . . and it's really bizarre.'

'You first then,' he said.

'No, no, definitely you.'

'Well, I was just wondering, if you'd consider . . . I

213

mean, if it's not too much . . .' The request was turning him slightly pink. 'I just thought since it was the kind of thing—'

Owen's head popped up at the door again: 'Ed? Could you come and see—'

'Just a minute!' Annie cut him off and he skulked back out again.

'Ed,' she reassured the teacher, 'it's OK, we're all friends here, just spit it out.'

She wondered what on earth was coming next.

'Boston, USA. Job interview. Well, not job, exactly . . . a term's paid research into the roots of rhythm and blues.'

Her eyebrows knitted: what was he talking about?

'I'm desperate to go. I was supposed to go last year, but because of poor old Mum . . . well . . . but so, there . . . you see?'

No, she did not see at all. Boston? His mother? What?!

'I need a suit,' he clarified. 'A proper, decent suit that will stand up to interview with American academics.'

Ah! The fog was clearing.

'I need not just the suit, I need the whole outfit, you know, quite the thing. I think Americans take all that pretty seriously, don't they? And anyway, I have no clue. But you, you're always so wonderfully' – he waved his hand in her direction, taking in the happy pairing of red lipstick, red Topshop jacket, black ankle boots and Dries Van Noten skirt – 'wonderful. And you work in that scary place. So I thought, you'll know all about this. You'll be just the right person to help me. There.' He looked really very embarrassed about it. 'Bizarre request. What's yours?'

Wonderfully wonderful? He was a case this man, no doubt about it.

'I'd be happy to help you find a suit, Ed,' she assured him. 'It would be no problem at all, it would be a pleasure. You tell me when and I'll book you in an appointment. Now . . .' she hesitated, feeling slight embarrassment of her own creeping up, 'I know you like to camp . . . have you heard of the Man and Boy Orienteering weekend by any chance?'

'Heard of it? My friend Clyde runs it! It's brilliant,' came Ed's answer. 'I'm desperate to take my nephew Sid, but he's only six. Does Owen want to go?' Ed guessed straight away. 'Are you looking for someone to go with him? Because I am definitely your man. You know, so long as you're OK with that . . .' He backed down quickly. 'And obviously so long as Owen . . .'

She waved away his reservations and told him that she would of course check Owen was happy with the idea, but he was certain to be delighted.

Such was Ed's enthusiasm for the project, she began to think he wasn't just a case; he was, in fact, bonkers.

'What tog rating is his sleeping bag?' Ed asked, along with other incomprehensible questions. 'It's just, if he has a thick one, we could bivouac. We could do without the tent altogether. Spend the night under the stars. Really bivvy down with nature. Provided it's dry of course, although the modern bag can cope with a stiff shower or two.'

Annie had been thinking camp-site, with hot showers, a restaurant, possibly even Tourist Board stars. She was now feeling nervous.

'Owen's got all the details. Maps, plans and projects. He'll love talking to someone else about it who can make out one end of a compass from another. What is Owen up to anyway? Owen!' Annie called sharply in the direction of the hall.

'How's your dentist?' Ed asked all of a sudden, taking her by surprise. In response to her raised eyebrows, he explained: 'Owen told me about him.'

'Oh! Well, he's not "my" dentist. It's early days. Very early. I'd forgotten how stressful the whole dating, getting-to-know-someone thing is . . . trying to say and do the right thing all the time. God, it's exhausting! Tonight has been great fun. So relaxing.'

Ed held up his coffee mug to her in a toast-salute: 'To relaxing fun,' he said.

Lana slouched into the kitchen and crumpled melodramatically into a chair, head slumping to the table.

'You can only get voicemail?' Annie guessed.

'Why won't he answer his phone?' Lana wailed, obviously so stricken that she wasn't embarrassed to mention this in front of a teacher.

'I'm sure there's a perfectly good reason,' Annie soothed. 'The battery's probably flat. Please, stop worrying about it.'

Although secretly, she suspected Seth was not phoning as often as he had before. She wasn't sure whether to be relieved about this, or worried.

Gray, on the other hand, was phoning very regularly and had already lined up several intriguing meetings.

'Er . . . I think there's a slight problem in here!' came the sound of Owen's voice.

With a lurch, Annie thought she detected a note of

fear in those words. As she got up from her chair, there was a bang. Not a loud, startling bang, but a whoosh that climaxed in a surprising pop.

She rushed for Owen's room, Ed on her heels.

Pulling his door ajar, she registered the smell: smoky, of bitter burnt toast. 'Owen!' she called out. 'Are you OK!?'

'Well, erm, I had a little problem,' he said shakily, coming to the doorway to meet her, 'I mean it's fine now . . . fine . . . but . . . a bit messy.'

Annie stepped inside, where the sight took her by surprise. Owen had a desk propped against the back wall of his room. It was usually stacked with half-read books, scribbled and scrunched papers, blunt pencils, empty CD cases, the bits and pieces of Owen's busy, messy life. But tonight, it looked as if he had built a bonfire there and the desk-top was strewn with the charcoaled remnants of whatever had been in the bonfire.

Even more alarming was the big sooty black scorch mark that covered the white wall from desk to ceiling, three feet wide at the bottom, tapering to a tip at the top.

'Oh. My. God,' was Annie's first reaction. 'What on earth?!'

But then she saw the science kit box upturned, contents scattered about on the floor of the room.

'Owen! You're not supposed to get that out when Connor's not around,' she snapped.

'I know. But I was a bit bored . . . and I wanted to show . . .' He tailed off, but it was obvious he'd wanted to show Ed some experiment from the kit.

'What happened?' she demanded. 'I can't imagine this

was supposed to be the end result. What were you trying to do? Build the indoor atomic bomb?'

'I went a little bit off plan,' Owen shrugged, looking annoyingly unapologetic.

'Off plan? Off the planet more like,' was Annie's snappy answer. 'You're lucky you didn't take out an eye, Owen, or burn down the house.'

'It was quite scary when it went off.' He let out a nervous giggle.

There was a big glass of water, full to the brim, standing in the middle of the floor. Annie pointed at it questioningly.

'Yeah, I thought I should have that on stand-by. But then I worried I'd make it worse.'

Knowing the chemical mixture would be wasted on his mother, he lobbed an explanation over to Ed, who had come to the door too and was looking on wordlessly, wondering if he should offer a comment.

It was indeed lost on Annie, but Ed gave a whistle: 'You took a risk there, Owen,' he said. 'That could have been very nasty. And the water! Water would have . . . well, never mind,' he decided seeing the look on Annie's face.

'We'll have to speak about this later,' she told Owen. 'Anyway, you should be in bed.' She flicked a glance at her watch. 'It's almost eleven o'clock! You should definitely be in bed.'

She turned on her heel and headed back to the kitchen.

Ed decided he would risk a few words of his own to Owen, of the teacherish sternly soothing variety, then he followed Annie.

She had her back turned to him and Ed was surprised to see she was shaking slightly. He hadn't realized how much the incident had upset her.

'Don't worry about it,' he began, coming up behind her. 'I'm sure he won't do that again.'

'Oh,' she turned and wiped her eyes, 'I bloody hope not!' she said just as Ed realized she was shaking with silent laughter.

His arm, which had been raised slightly to offer her a comforting touch on the shoulder, fell back to his side and he gave something of a laugh himself: 'At least he didn't add the water . . .' Ed said. 'I think you could have been looking at . . . well . . .' he didn't want to frighten her, '. . . a fairly extensive bit of redecoration.'

Chapter Eighteen

The funky paramedic:

Green boiler suit, but worn top off, arms tied
round the waist (NHS)
Skimpy white vest top (Primark)
Deep tan (surfing in Fuerteventura)
Leather and shell choker (stall in Fuerteventura)
Hiking boots (Tiso)
Blond hair in plaits
Est. cost: £28

'A romantic moment gone wrong here, then.'

After the Tower Bridge date, Gray had taken Annie out for lunch again and then came a big, swanky dinner. A dazzling, high-end, intimate restaurant with attentive waiters and truly superb food and wine.

That night, she had found Gray quite irresistibly attractive. Ordering the wine, making menu suggestions for her, sweeping up the bill with his platinum card – debit not credit, she'd noticed – he'd been the suave, witty grown-up she was absolutely certain she wanted.

Strolling along the streets of Knightsbridge afterwards with his arm tucked around her, Annie had felt a wave of happiness wash over her. This felt like togetherness, real closeness. At last, she was beginning to allow herself to think that she had found a person she could share her life with once again.

They'd looked in furniture shop windows and he'd wanted to know her opinion about everything: 'Now, I like that white chair, the big leather one over there . . . But what do you think? Too showy for a home?'

Each time they agreed on something, she'd felt a little internal 'yes!' and in her mind the domestic fantasy of being Gray's stay-at-home wife had cranked up again.

La-la-la, she would wear dresses all the time, because he'd complimented her on her legs. (And of course they'd always be freshly waxed, because she would have so much time to pamper herself.) She would learn to cook, beautifully, from scratch every day and be able to lavish her undivided attention on Gray and her children.

When her family was out, she would housekeep to perfection: ironing sheets with lavender water, folding fluffy towels, baking bread and keeping the kind of kitchen where matching tea towels, tablecloths and oven gloves are all fresh and fragrant and changed every day. La-la-la. There would be no more house renovating, no more moving, no more dealing with Donna the total bitch. Life would just be so peachy and perfect . . . wouldn't it?

Having just agreed with her that the sofa in the window of the Conran Shop was far superior to anything else they'd seen the length of the street, Gray had wrapped both arms around her and said, 'Annie, I think I'm going to have to kiss you. I hope that's OK?'

The formality of the request had caused her to tease, 'Well . . . depends what your kissing's like. Shall we see?'

He'd moved in with a dry, lip-on-lip kiss before, on her cue, mouths had opened and begun a hesitant exploration. Very minty breath, moist, but the moves needed a little practice, was Annie's first thought.

The kiss didn't go on for long and she was aware of the carefulness of it. For instance, a full six inches apart at the hip had been maintained at all times.

Maybe Gray, being fourteen years older than her, was going to be very formal and measured about wooing her. There would be no getting swept away with your passions here. He was too grown-up. They were both testing the waters and cautious about the decisions ahead.

She liked his old-fashioned charm anyway. Gray was like a suitor from a 1940s movie: he was courteous, always in a suit and cufflinks, always close shaven, smelling just the right side of citrusy. He was the serious man she was sure she wanted and she was beginning to think she could fall in love with him.

'So what are you doing tomorrow?' he'd asked after a second, slightly more intimate kiss.

'Nothing I can't get out of – if it's for a very good reason,' she'd decided to answer.

'Why don't you come and have lunch at my house?'

'I'd love to,' she told him, wondering how to bribe Lana to look after Owen . . . and Dinah to supervise Lana.

They kissed again, and this time Annie wrapped her arms around Gray's waist and pulled him in close. They would finally be alone and undisturbed in a private place tomorrow. She hoped he had a lot more than lunch on his mind, because she certainly did.

When they broke off from the kiss, she looked at his face closely. He still had great bone structure but must have been gorgeous when he was younger. Maybe it was hard for him to grow middle-aged and lose that power over people that extremely good-looking people have.

That might explain the green contact lenses, perfect teeth and just slightly odd-looking hair; it was a little too coppery and too smooth. But she had run her hands through it several times and was certain that Owen and Lana were wrong. He didn't deserve the nickname 'rug boy'.

Just before noon the next day, Sunday, Annie climbed into her Jeep, fully briefed with directions from Gray, and set off to find his home in a bijou Essex village.

She was depilated, exfoliated, moisturized and fragrant from top to toe. All twenty nails were manicured and painted, her underwear was luxuriously fancy, she was wearing stockings and her teeth were flossed. She even had condoms stashed in a zip-up compartment of her handbag and she was as ready for seduction as she was ever going to be.

She cranked up the car radio and drove, singing along, with the windows down a little to recreate the breezy convertible effect she was getting used to.

After forty minutes of driving, the scrappy retail

parks, mega-bowl complexes and car sales showrooms gave way to something more definitely resembling countryside. The sky was cloudless, the landscape spring's fresh, bright green and Annie felt her mood lift and soar.

The traffic on the M25 was good and her car zipped along in the fast lane. As she drew nearer to Gray's village, she called him up on the in-car mobile.

'Hello, Sexy Suburban Man,' she greeted him, 'I'm on the outskirts of your village, so you'll have to talk me though the final turns.'

'This is not a suburb!' he insisted. 'Upper Ploxley is the most expensive village in Essex.'

'Gray, I'm driving through a housing estate!' she countered. 'Anyway, I hope you've got the wine on ice.'

'Champagne, my dear. Champagne.'

'Ooooh . . . even better.'

'Have you brought your swimsuit?' he asked. He hadn't explained why she needed a swimsuit, had only said, 'Wait and see!' She suspected a small kidney-, maybe heart-shaped, outdoor pool. But it better be bloody well heated, it was only April. Not exactly skinny-dipping weather.

'That must be you now, coming down the road in your small armoured tank,' he joked. 'I'm the white house, third on your left.'

She indicated, made the left turn and slid the Jeep into a short driveway before an impressive 1970s boxy glass and concrete construction, painted bright white.

It was so neat, was her first impression. Every piece of gravel was raked into place on a driveway that bordered a smooth, green crew cut of lawn. Crisp, white blinds came halfway down the windows of the house and even the plants inside the windowboxes, two doorway tubs and little strip of border were standing to attention against a background of flawless brown earth.

Gray was already at the front door.

'What a lovely house,' she said immediately, as she climbed out of the Jeep. 'Your garden is so immaculate, you must be at it all the time.'

'I use a weekly gardening service,' he batted the compliment away. 'They're really good.'

Of course he did.

'Come here.' He waved her over. 'I'm so glad you could come.'

He waited until she'd stepped inside to give her one of his careful kisses. 'Come on in,' he said, breaking off, 'I want to show you round.'

Much as she wanted to untuck his white shirt from his blue chinos and mess him up a bit, she was desperate to look round too. Desperate to glean all the clues she could, not just about Gray but also, very importantly, about his estranged wife. Annie felt sure that the taste stamped all over this expensive 1970s home would not in fact be Gray's but, much more intriguingly, Marilyn's.

Gray did not like to talk about Marilyn. All Annie had been able to find out had come from her own, fairly blunt questioning.

The ongoing divorce was not exactly a happy one.

'She'd made my life extremely miserable by the end,' Gray had told Annie over their second date lunch. 'Now we're fighting over every little detail. Sometimes, I would just like to let her have what she wants and be done with it. Start again, start over, an all-new,

Marilyn-free life. But then I remind myself that she never *did* anything. She never had a job, we didn't have children, all she did was spend my money and now she wants to be left with half of all the things she spent my money on and half of the home she didn't contribute one penny towards.'

Staying at home to bake for Gray with the crisp and shiny oven gloves had suddenly not looked quite so rosy to Annie.

'My lawyer has prepared a more than generous clean break settlement for her and still she's refusing to take it,' Gray had added angrily. 'She's upping the stakes all the time, wanting a little slice of this, part of that . . . a share in my business! She's not prepared to go with any dignity.'

They'd been married for five years. Marilyn – originally called Tracey, she'd changed it by deed poll, he'd told her just a little cattily – had been with him from the age of 34 until she was 40. Apparently the neurotic dread with which she'd approached her fortieth birthday had been the final straw to tipped their marriage into irretrievable breakdown.

'You know, forty is just a number. Get over it, I'd tell her. But she acted as if she was going to die on the day, not reach her fifth decade. You seem so much more relaxed,' Gray had told her, 'about life in general. Marilyn was in a frenzy about everything! From which colour to paint her fingernails to how to arrange the plant pots at the front door. It was totally exhausting!'

'I'm not forty yet,' Annie had warned him. 'It could all change!'

But to Annie's slight disappointment, there didn't

seem to be any clue to Marilyn left in Gray's home now. Well, unless her taste had been very masculine, but it looked as if he'd completely redecorated since she'd gone.

There was a huge dark brown leather sofa in the calm, bright sitting room and one of those swooping chrome lamps embedded in a marble plinth. On the floor was a rug made of plaited leather and a great fluffy sheepskin-covered beanbag. Floor-to-ceiling windows overlooked the neat front garden, and a wide opening in the back wall led through to a dazzling slate and stainless steel kitchen, divided from the back garden by another huge window.

'Wow,' she kept telling him. 'This is amazing.'

He was such a gadget man: he showed her how the blinds slid down by remote control, how the kitchen back wall moved up like an electrically powered garage door, so that on warm days the room could be transformed to an outdoor space.

'Now, let me show you the roof terrace,' was the way Gray framed his invitation to upstairs. Annie got a peek of his beige-and-chocolate, neat-as-a-hotel-suite master bedroom on the way past the door, but he carried on to the roof terrace, the highlight of the house tour.

Out on the terrace, surrounded by dark decking, tall shrubs in pots and ornamental marble balls, was a generous, two-metre-wide jacuzzi.

'It's a bit of fun, isn't it?' Gray said, unlocking the glass windows so they could go out. 'It's heated, obviously . . . I worried it was a bit too James Bond, but now I'm a total convert. Sitting out here, glass of champagne in one hand, watching the sunset over there, believe me, it's breathtaking. Maybe we'll do that later,' he added gently.

'Oh bollocks to later!' she announced, only partly because staying here too late was going to cause her a babysitting headache. 'Let's get into the water and build up an appetite for lunch!'

She reached for him and as they kissed, she began to unbutton his shirt, but, to her disappointment, he broke off, took a step backwards and told her: 'There's a big dressing gown and towels for you in here.' Then he opened the door to his spare room and ushered her in: 'I'll see you out there in a few minutes.'

Well, it wasn't the giggly stripping off and jumping in stark naked she'd envisaged, but then this was Gray's old-fashioned charm, wasn't it? The reserve she'd seen in him and found so likeable?

Annie took her clothes off in the neutral hotel-like room. There was even a cushion on the immaculate bed which matched the fabric of the curtains. She hated, *hated* that. No-one should ever do that. Bet that was a Tracey-turned-Marilyn touch.

She pulled on her red with white polka dots swimsuit and hoicked herself into it. It was a glamorous 1950s style with a hefty 40 per cent Lycra. No swimsuit should come with less. With its eye-distracting dots and elastic cling, this baby did almost as much for her as a corset and was worth every penny she'd spent on it.

Now if she'd just thought to buy the matching Joan Collins sarong and wide-brimmed straw hat . . . but then, it was April out there. The thick dressing gown was probably completely necessary.

Just for good measure, from her handbag she slid two

flesh-coloured silicone breast enhancers and stuffed them underneath her boobs in the swimsuit cups. Oh yes! That was better. Check out that cleavage. How could Gray resist? Maybe one day she'd treat herself to a boob job . . . stick two fingers up to the forces of gravity.

She looked herself over in the mirror, readjusted her ponytail and reapplied the red lipstick chosen to match the swimsuit exactly. What a dish – even if she had to say it herself.

Stepping out into the hall, Annie saw that the roof terrace door was open, the jacuzzi was bubbling fiercely, but Gray was not there and his bedroom door was shut.

Never mind, she would get in first. She walked out onto the decking, feeling the smooth wood beneath her feet. A toe-test assured her that the water was bathtub warm, so she let her dressing gown fall to the deck and slipped into the pool.

Oh! Delicious! There was a curved comfortable bench beneath the surface so she could sit and look up at the sky as her body was pummelled with surprisingly vigorous jets of water.

She threw her head back, tits out, and waited for Gray to catch her looking utterly irresistible. But long minutes passed and there was still no sign of him. Her neck was stiffening, so she relaxed the pose and her eyes fell on the stacked pyramid of large black marble balls between the potted palms.

Surely this was another Tracey-Marilyn thing? No man went into a shop and came out with marble balls.

Now she remembered being in a design shop with Roddy and asking his opinion on the vogue for polished marble balls.

'If you're buying marble balls, it means you have far too much money,' had been his pithy verdict. 'Then again,' he'd added, 'maybe it means you have balls of marble.'

What was keeping Gray? She must have been in the water on her own for at least ten minutes now. Maybe he was showering? Applying a fresh coat of aftershave?

And what would he look like naked? she couldn't help wondering. He would be lean, quite muscular and tanned, she suspected, but as he was almost at the 50 mark, there would probably be those tell-tale age signs: slightly shrunken buttocks, little baggy wrinkles at the armpit, elbow and knees, skin not clinging quite so firmly to the muscles . . . *OK, no need to panic!*

On a whim, she reached over to pick up one of the marble balls: it was much heavier than she'd expected. The great chunk of slippery stone wobbled between her damp palms, she felt it slip just slightly and panicked that she was about to drop it to the bottom of the pool where it would cause a crack and thousands of pounds' worth of damage. She tightened her grip on it and quickly turned to put it back into the pile.

But the marble ornaments had been stacked with far more skill than she'd appreciated and the ball she returned was still for only a moment before it rolled off, taking down another five balls with it in a loud, cracking tumble.

For solid marble, they rolled away at a surprising rate in three different directions – which didn't say much for the skills of the joiner who'd done the decking.

Annie leapt out of the pool to herd them.

She had three balls under control and was bending

over trying to reassemble the pile when she heard Gray asking: 'How's the water?'

Peering over her shoulder, she saw him swathed in a dressing gown at the terrace door, balancing a small tray with a bottle of champagne and two delicate glasses.

Instead of finding her in the pool looking fabulous with a come-hither smile upon her face, he was subjected to a full-on rear-end view as she wrestled with the slippery ornaments.

'Oh dear, what's happened?' he asked.

'Nothing, nothing . . . no damage done,' she rushed to assure him and turned quickly to get her bum out of the spotlight, 'I just . . . well, the marbles . . . they've rolled about a bit.' She spotted the fourth and kneeled gracefully this time to pick it up.

'Here, let me help you,' Gray insisted, setting the tray down on the floor.

He put his hands out to take the ball from her, but misjudged and made contact with her enhanced swimming costume cleavage. He jerked his hands back again, which was a mistake, as Annie had now let go of the ball, thinking Gray had it.

It crashed down, landing squarely on Gray's foot.

'Aaaargh!' he cried out, understandably, and instinctively brought his knee up so that, hopping slightly, he could clutch at the mashed toes. Another error, as he slipped on the now wet decking and lost his balance.

He wobbled mid-air for a moment, arms flailing, Annie reading the shock in his look, and then with a resounding CRASH!!! he went down, falling backwards into the champagne tray and knocking himself out cold.

'Gray! Crap! Bloody *crap*! *Gray*!!' was Annie's cool, collected response.

Her rearranging of the ornaments had killed him: it was Ms Scarlett on the decking with the marble ball.

'Gray!!' She crouched down beside him. His head had crunched into one of the glasses, the overturned bottle had rolled away and was now glugging its contents into the jacuzzi. She'd always wanted to try a champagne jacuzzi . . . but this was obviously not the moment.

His lips were white, which didn't strike her as a good sign, but there was definitely breath coming from his nose, so she let her panic subside slightly.

What was she supposed to do? Nothing she'd ever learned about first aid (from watching *Casualty*) came to mind.

Maybe she should splash him with a little water? She leaned over to the pool, scooped up a handful of water and dripped it over his temple. It ran off his forehead and into his hair.

She couldn't help taking just a nanosecond to scrutinize his hair, now that she had the opportunity. Leaning in, she took a closer look and satisfied herself once and for all that Gray didn't wear a toupee. It was all natural – but he did use hair dye: there was just the tiniest millimetre or so of grey root visible on inspection. Fair enough, he liked to look good.

But anyway . . . she had to get on and do something to help him. She decided to roll him gently onto his side – the recovery position, wasn't it? – then she'd phone for an ambulance.

As she began to pull him over, she saw that his head was bleeding at the back from the little shards of glass embedded in it. It didn't look too serious, but they definitely needed medical assistance.

Once he was in position, a fold of his dressing gown fell open to reveal a fresh surprise.

Was that a . . . ? Could that really be . . . ?

One part fascinated, one part horrified, Annie moved her head down to examine this new development.

There was no mistaking it: poking up from the thick white cloth of the dressing gown was a rigid, pink erection.

That wasn't right, was it? You couldn't be unconscious and have a boner like that. Could you?

She wanted to touch it, to make sure it was real. But it looked real enough, pointing at the potted palms, sure and solid as a tent pole.

This could not be a natural phenomenon, could it? No. Gray must have taken something. One of those products everyone with an email address opened up to every morning: Viagra, Cialis, soft tabs . . .

Gray gave just the slightest of groans and Annie quickly got to her feet. It wouldn't do to get caught examining a man's penis while he was unconscious. No, that wouldn't look good at all.

His eyes were still closed, so she ran to find her mobile, snatching it from her handbag as it started ringing.

'Yes?'

'Mum?'

'Lana, I can't—'

'Muuuum, Owen's being really, really annoying—'

'Lana, I have to go, Gray has—'

'God!' Lana screamed. 'Gray this, Gray that. Who

cares about your stupid boyfriend? I'm not babysitting for you any longer! I'm going out! Owen can just wait in for Dinah.'

'Lana! Give Dinah a call, please. I have to use the phone now. Please, Lana, please! Don't leave Owen at home on his own, he might play with the science kit and blow the entire place up,' she pleaded.

A huge, martyred teenage sigh came back down the line at her. Then Lana hung up.

Annie could not worry about Lana and Owen. Right now she had to dial 999.

She was back on the roof terrace trying to put her folded gown underneath Gray's head, when he came round. He jerked his head up too quickly and almost passed out again. Annie was trying to explain what had happened, but it was taking some time to sink in.

'What do you mean, hit my head?' he asked in a voice that sounded a little slurred.

'You've had a fall . . . please, just stay still, there's an ambulance on its way.'

'An ambulance!!'

There was no ignoring the Bone. It was still there, long and pink, poking well clear of his dressing gown. She shifted position a little to get away from it.

'Gray, you've been unconscious, you've got pieces of glass in your head, you need to go to hospital.'

He lay still, absorbing this information.

'Oh God,' he groaned. 'This wasn't supposed to happen.'

'I know, I know,' she soothed. 'Don't worry about it.'

Annie had just spotted her towel and was about to throw it over his middle to stop him from realizing about the very embarrassing little situation going on down there, but then came a much deeper groan and the pulling up of his knees and rearranging of his dressing gown as he noticed.

'Oh Jesus!' he exclaimed and curled himself foetally around the unforgiving, undisguisable Bone.

'Hey, don't worry about that . . . I'm flattered,' Annie joked, trying to put him at ease. 'Would you like a drink of water?'

He just closed his eyes and groaned again.

'Look, Gray, if it makes you feel any better, I've got chicken fillets in my swimsuit.'

He open his eyes and looked at her in bewilderment.

She reached down the front of her costume and matter-of-factly pulled out one of her silicone breast enhancers, wibbling it in front of his face. 'Viagra for girls,' she assured him. 'At our age,' she added, chummily, 'we need all the help we can get.'

He just groaned again.

The ambulance crew of three arrived and included Brenda, a visual feast from Tasmania. Deeply tanned, tomboyish and gorgeous, she at least perked Gray up slightly.

'A romantic moment gone wrong here, then,' she summed up, surveying the bubbling jacuzzi, Annie still in glamourpuss swimsuit and pole-axed, tent-pole Gray.

One crew member spoke into his radio: 'Middle-aged male: champagne glass injuries to the scalp, injury by a spherical marble ornament to the left foot, suspected concussion and a possible Viagra reaction. Yes, I am in Upper Ploxley . . . How did you guess?' He did at least try to keep the chuckle from his voice.

'Could you pack a bag for your boyfriend?' they asked Annie.

'Erm . . . Gray? What do you want me to get for you – and where will I find it?' she had to ask, causing more stifled sniggering from the ambulance crew.

Gray was finally carried out on a stretcher with the weight of three towels over his middle in an attempt to keep the Bone at bay.

Once they'd all left, Annie switched off the jacuzzi, swept the broken glass from the decking, drank down the mouthful or so of champagne left in the bottle, locked the terrace doors, changed out of her swimsuit and exited the house, pulling the front door shut behind her.

Back in her Jeep, she sat in the driver's seat for a few moments to consider the events of the afternoon. Well, that hadn't exactly gone to plan, had it? She wondered if she should have accompanied Gray to hospital, but he'd told her not to. She wondered if she would ever hear from him again . . . She'd get in touch first, make sure that somehow they pick up again from here.

It was an accident . . . these things happen . . . *but why today?!* was her next thought. Finally Annie had to give in and allowed herself to do the one thing she hadn't been able to do ever since the marble boulder had slipped from Gray's grip: she began to rock with laughter.

'That's the best story I've heard all week,' was Connor's verdict, when she rang to share it with him later: 'The man with marble balls and a rod of iron.'

Chapter Nineteen

New, improved Martha:

Orange, red and white dress (Issa)
Slouchy brown boots (Miu Miu)
Caramel tote (Chloé)
Est. cost: £1,400

'Don't you think I'm transvestite tall?'

Paula, now back on the shop floor, was the assistant who led Martha Cooper into the Personal Shopping suite for her second visit with the words: 'Wow! I can't believe it's really you!'

Annie, who was trying to fit in several quick computer bids and her stone-cold Starbucks latte, not to mention arrange a delivery of flowers to Gray at his hospital bed, took her feet off her desk and began to clap.

'Oh, very good!' she told Martha, who was smiling from ear to ear.

The mum who'd turned up in old jeans and a parka now stood before them in the sharp trousers and swing jacket she'd bought on her first visit, nicely grunged down with a pair of green gymmies. But the biggest change was the healthy, make-up-assisted glow on her face and the hair. The lank overgrown mop was now a tousled, tonged, caramel-coloured mane.

'Grrrrrrr,' Annie purred. 'Look at you. Good enough to eat. And are you back at work now?'

Martha nodded.

'So you've returned to spend lots of your new lolly?'

'Oh yes. I want a raincoat . . . and a dress . . . and maybe some boots . . . and *possibly* a bag.'

'Oh, you are so in the right place, babes. And it's me looking after you this afternoon, hope that's OK? Right . . . follow me, we'll do a little tour of the shop floor and bring back a bundle of things for you to try.'

After a speed search of the collections Annie thought would work for Martha, they were back in the suite. A vibrant orange and red Issa dress with high-heeled boots and a fab bag were the choices Annie was nudging Martha towards.

The dress was beautiful on. Although it was patterned, it wasn't floral because, as Martha had warned Annie: 'A tall girl in big flowers . . .'

'Is a sofa,' Annie had agreed straight away.

Unfortunately the high-heeled brown slouchy boots which went so brilliantly with the dress seemed to be the problem for Martha.

'I know everything looks better with heels,' she began, 'but don't you think I'm now transvestite tall?'

'No,' Annie assured her, but, well . . . she was about six foot four in those boots, which was a little scary. It also pitched the dress to well above her knees.

238

'There's no use telling me how tall Cindy, Lindy, Elle etc. are, I just don't want to be the tallest thing in a room bar the column holding up the ceiling. And . . .' she gave the slightly confused hand gestures which Annie had seen in so many clients before, 'I just don't think this—'

'Is really you?' Annie jumped in. 'Too smart, too dressy . . . too much, too soon! Sorry, I'm rushing you in there. OK. We like the dress? Agreed? So maybe we need to style it down. And we need to bring you down too, don't we?'

She disappeared off into the store and came back with several accessories.

The dress was tried on again, but this time with a white vest underneath, brown footless tights and flat gold pumps.

'Oh yes! Yes. So much better!' was Martha's verdict.

Then Annie handed over the killer accessory. The power bag which would ensure that even if Martha turned up at her office in the unspeakable parka, she would still have a shred of cred: a Chloé tote bag – big, astronomically expensive in a go-with-everything tan leather.

'No, no!' Martha didn't even want to hold it.

'It comes in six different colours,' Annie wheedled. 'Just try it, girl, get it onto your arm . . . it won't bite.'

Annie handed it over and was too fascinated to see what Martha would think of herself with a bit of almost four-figured kit in the crook of her elbow to notice Donna stalking into the suite.

Martha was holding the bag, this way and that, staring back at her reflection. 'I have a handbag morality,' she explained. 'I draw the line at two hundred pounds. You should be able to get a fantastic bag for no more than two hundred pounds. When I see price tags above that, I just think: this is madness! I can't walk about with a month's salary slung from my shoulder, inviting muggers from far and wide to have a go. I certainly can't carry my packed lunch in it, or baby wipes, or beakers.'

'OK . . . well, then you know where you have to shop?'

'Where?' Martha wondered.

'EBay! You could probably get this bag for two hundred pounds on eBay, but you have to accept that it's a fake. Hopefully the kind of really, really clever fake that even Ms Chloé herself might be pushed to spot. Worth thinking about. Or then again, downstairs we have wipedown PVC Orla Kiely bags, very, very popular with the Yummy Mummy. But I love you in that bag!' she added.

Annie also did not see Donna stalking out of the suite with an expression on her face that was hard to read: part sour, part satisfied.

'The bag is absolutely stunning, baby.' Annie took it back from Martha and held it up to her: 'A real investment . . . But no pressure. I've got three lovely raincoats here for you to try on while you think about the bag. Orange? Great with that dress. Or classic light beige? Or maybe both?'

'Annie, *stop*! You are so good, you are very, very bad. I'm going for a strong, sobering coffee before I decide about the bag. Maybe I'll buy a fake like you said.'

'It's just not the same though, babes, *you'll* always know . . .'

'Yeah, but if I buy the real one, my husband will always know – and kill me.'

'But you're back at work,' Annie wheedled. 'There have to be some compensations . . .'

'Coffee,' Martha insisted. 'I'll buy the dress, the tights, the flats, probably a raincoat too . . . but I need coffee for the bag decision!'

'OK, OK.' Annie smiled at her. 'You know where we are!' She heard the swish of the metal bead curtains at the entrance to the suite parting, then Ed Leon was standing there, looking sheepish. 'Sorry, am I a bit . . . erm . . . early?' He looked as if he was about to walk out again.

'No, no. Take a seat,' Annie instructed. 'I just have to sell this nice lady here a raincoat, then I'm all yours,' she told him.

When Martha had paid for the purchases she was certain about and gone for her bag-decider coffee, Annie was able to turn her attention to the dweeby teacher, perched, a little nervously, in skinny cords on the suite sofa.

'So,' she said, settling onto the sofa beside him, 'tell me all about your tailoring requirements.'

'Top-to-toe overhaul,' was Ed's verdict. He'd chosen a worn navy blue jacket today, instead of his typical tweed, as if in the spirit of dressing up and making an effort. But it looked cheap and didn't fit.

'Where do you usually shop?' she wondered.

'Oh' – he shrugged his shoulders – 'here and there,' was all he could manage.

'Where?' Annie pressed the point.

'Well, er, Burtons . . . and what's that place? Mister

241

Byrite. There's the Highgate Cancer Research once in a while, it's pretty good . . .' Watching her melodramatic eye roll, he didn't like to continue. 'You're not impressed, are you?'

'It's OK, you are here now,' she told him, teasing slightly. 'I'm here to cure you of the madness. This is where I begin to convince you of the merits of investment dressing. I have an investment dressing lecture, if you'd like to hear it.'

Ed leaned back in the sofa, crossed his ankle over his knee – tricky in those cords, surely – and said, 'I'd like to hear any lecture of yours very much.'

In the cool and quiet menswear department, Annie assembled suits, shirts and ties for Ed, while he was held hostage, stripped to his underwear in the changing room.

He kept appearing at the fitting room door in a slightly alarming pair of crinkled purple boxer shorts and short red socks to ask how it was going.

Annie couldn't help catching a glimpse of his unexpectedly muscular stomach and the flash of white skin over his hip bones where the boxers had slipped below his tan line.

'Do you work out?' She tried to keep the incredulity from her voice.

'No!' He was equally incredulous.

'You look . . . fit,' she justified her remark.

'Rugby coaching . . . keeps the gut at bay,' was his reply.

In every one of the suit, shirt and tie ensembles, Ed would step out and Annie would give a businesslike appraisal: shoulders too broad or too tight, jacket too long . . . trousers too tight. He was proving a difficult figure to fit.

Finally, a deep navy blue suit, matched with pale pink shirt and blue tie, ticked every box in Annie's checklist.

'Goodness!' was Ed's verdict as he walked around the shop floor a little, then surveyed himself in the full-length mirror. 'Look at that! Old Ketteringham-Smith won't recognize me. I hardly recognize myself! Just wait till I get my hair cut, then all traces of the old Ed Leon will be erased. I might have to post up a photo on Friends Reunited.'

Annie was looking at him closely, professionally. There was no denying that the jacket shoulders were a perfect fit; that the straight trousers brought his legs into better proportion, that pink and blue were a great colour combination for him. He had bright blue eyes, summer-sky blue, and she'd not noticed that until she'd held shirts up to his face to check for colour matching.

He also had rosy cheeks and very pink lips. These details hadn't come into such sharp focus before. No. Before the blue suit and pink shirt effect, she'd seen only Ed's woolly hair, bushy eyebrows and tweed.

'Haircut?' she asked, not sounding convinced.

'Yup, short back and sides. I'm taking this very seriously. Do you have any idea how much I'd like to go to Boston?'

She tried to imagine how his hair would look short. He'd be certain to go to a £5-a-pop barber who'd massacre it, so she told him firmly: 'No. Definitely no haircut – and you know what?' This wasn't exactly good business, but she felt she had to say it: 'I don't think you should buy this suit either, Ed, because it's just not you. In fact it's so not you that I'm really not sure what I was thinking.'

Just as Martha had looked great in the high-heeled boots, so Ed looked good in the suit. Really, she'd been quite taken aback with how good he looked. But it was as if she'd extinguished everything that was Ed. Everything that was sparky and quirky about Ed was buried now that she'd put him into this regulation dark blue suit, teamed with the required pink shirt and plain tie.

How was anyone going to know the slightest thing about him in this outfit? How were they going to know that he could play ten different stringed instruments? Or that he had a folk and blues LP collection to rival any New Orleans DJ's?

Worst of all, he looked uncomfortable. He kept tugging his cuffs and smoothing his lapels. The stiff black shoes he had on his feet weren't helping either. They seemed to weigh him down; he'd had a funny, lolloping spring to his step before, a bounciness which went with his mad hair.

She checked her watch: ten past five. She could slip out early, there were other places . . .

'I think we need to try somewhere else. C'mon.' Her instructions were brisk: 'Put your things back on and we'll head out.'

He raised his eyebrows questioningly. He'd never been in and out of so many outfits in his life, he'd never before experienced such a zealous quest for perfection and besides, he quite liked this blue suit. He thought he looked like, well . . . someone with an office job, someone with means . . . someone who could be seen with a woman as gloriously elegant as Annie.

But she was frowning and the frown, which made a captivating little 'v' between her eyebrows, was not directed at him. No, her eyes were firmly on the suit and she wasn't happy with it at all, so he pulled the plush velvet curtain of the changing room closed and began to undress and re-dress all over again.

From one of The Store's side exits, which just happened to be overlooked by Donna's office, they set off in the direction of Jermyn Street to an enormous corner building entirely devoted to the fitting out of 'gentlemen'.

'We'll just wander for a little,' Annie instructed him. 'Tell me if anything catches your eye.'

She loved this shop. It was living, breathing proof of the very different way men and women approached clothes. Whereas women wanted to know what was new and what was now and didn't care what it was made of, how it was sewn, how tight or ill-fitting it was; men wanted the traditional, the familiar, the hard-wearing, the long-lasting, the comfortable and the practical.

The difference always struck Annie most at black tie events when men wore beautiful suits they could put on year after year, which made them look fantastic but kept them warm and allowed them to enjoy the food to the full. Whereas women flitted like butterflies in wonderful chilly creations they couldn't sit in, let alone eat in, only intended like Cinderella's dress to last till the stroke of midnight.

In this shop there were socks in cotton, wool or

cashmere blends, available in three leg lengths, eight different sizes and twenty different colours. There were racks filled with the kind of suits and overcoats which would last for the next fifteen years and beyond.

The ties didn't just come in a multi-hued rainbow of colours, they came in different widths, different silks, different weaves.

There were scarves, gloves and hats, waistcoats, button-down shirts, winged-collar shirts, cutaway collars, half-cutaways, Windsor cutaways. Only the sober, quietly spoken male assistants could possibly know the full range of collars available here.

'If sir requires any assistance, he should not hesitate to ask,' came the gentle instruction from one of the impeccably dressed staff.

'Yes, erm . . . right,' was Ed's slightly tense reply.

Sensing he was out of his depth now, Annie stepped in and directed him towards the long rails packed with tweed jackets.

'Have a look through . . .' She was running her hand along their rough cloth. 'See if anything jumps out at you.'

There was a small check in beige and brown with an accent of maroon, which she homed in on, pulling the jacket out with its hanger.

'Like this, maybe?' she wondered.

'Nice,' he agreed. 'Very nice,' then put his hands on something way too yellowy with a bold black check.

'I dunno,' she warned him. 'Rupert Bear?'

'You might be right.'

Together they picked out jackets and toning checked shirts and moleskin trousers. She let him rifle through every tie, engaging the salesman in earnest tie discussion and tie comparison.

Long minutes passed as they discussed knot count and the superiority of the traditional English 'worsted'.

In and out of the changing room Ed went, as Annie checked everything over for fit, for colour, for proportion.

The blinds were being drawn on the shop windows, the tills were being closed down and counted out for the night, but their salesman insisted: 'No trouble, sir, take your time. One must have the right apparel. Seize the day.'

Finally Ed and his stylist were finished. Their work was done, their creation was complete.

Even the salesman, George, as they'd come to know him, admired the effect: 'A little eccentric, but very pleasing, sir.'

Ed stood before them smartly and appropriately dressed but also still totally Ed.

'Brilliant!' Annie allowed herself to grin at the outfit; no more frowning and letting the furrows form between her eyebrows.

Ed was in the beige, brown and maroon tweed jacket, the very first one Annie had picked out, a white with a pale brown check country shirt underneath. A very thin finest spun silk golden tie with ducks flying upside down was tied into his trademark tight knot at his neck. Most striking of all were the close-cut bright maroon moleskin trousers. Very rock and roll star retires to country estate, Annie had thought.

The long trouser legs rested and rumpled against softest caramel suede punched brogue boots. And on top of all this was a swinging short beige mac with a bright green padded lining and a scarf: sober beige wool on one side, crazy paisley maroon, gold and orange patterns on the other with long silky orange fringing.

The ensemble broke all of Annie's rules – few things matched, well, OK, the maroons and the beiges matched just enough to hold it all together – but it looked fantastic.

Ed was going to buy two more checked shirts, a maroon tie and a pair of beige moleskins, on Annie's instruction, to make sure he had plenty of different ways to wear the jacket.

He was also going to be getting another pair of glasses – small gold rims – and a 'really funky bag', she had informed him.

Turning to look at himself in the mirror, he told her: 'You're really good at this, you know. Have you ever thought about doing it for a living?! I look just like myself . . . but much better.'

He'd wow them, he'd definitely get the post, she knew.

'Ed,' she made eye contact with his reflection, 'you're hot, baby.'

Ed began to blush, then didn't seem to be able to stop. He turned a deep burgundy red.

'Steady on!' she instructed him. 'George! I think you might have to loosen his tie!'

Annie's phone began to ring.

When she answered, she heard Gray's voice on the other end of the line: 'Annie, what beautiful flowers,' he began in a low purr. 'You shouldn't have. You really shouldn't have . . . Now how am I going to make up to you for that *fiasco* the other day?'

'Oh Gray, hello. I'm sure I can think of a few ways.'

Ed was obviously tired of the shopping session. As she made arrangements to meet Gray, he went back into the changing room and pulled the curtain shut behind him.

Chapter Twenty

Connor's friend Henrik:

Bright pink polo shirt (Ralph Lauren)
Jeans (Paul Smith)
Top-stitched loafers (Office)
Est. cost: £220

'Hey, Connor, my man, you've made my day!'

'Now, we know all about your first attempt and the trip to Casualty with the tent pole . . .' Connor was leaning over the table, talking quietly as Annie and Dinah moved their heads closer to catch what he was saying. 'But the million-dollar question, what Dinah and I are gagging to know is, have you and the dirty dentist done the deed yet? We know you went to his place again last weekend, Annie, so come on . . . time to confess. How was he? Does he have an impressive instrument?'

Annie just smiled as Dinah ticked him off with the words: 'Hey! This is an old-fashioned romance. It's progressing nicely, slowly, in a ladylike and gentlemanly way. Keep your overactive sex drive out of it.'

Connor just snorted.

Their first courses arrived, delivered by a waiter with splendid buttocks and a quite Parisian level of rudeness.

'The soup?' he snapped and dumped the dish in front of Connor, so that the liquid slopped over the edges of the bowl.

Annie was not sure about this restaurant. It was in its first week and had been opened by friends of Connor's who'd had the novel idea of combining a hairdressing salon with a restaurant. As you walked in there were chairs and smart white-linen-covered tables ready for diners, but on a raised platform beyond were chairs, mirrors, washbasins and all the accoutrements of a hair salon. It didn't make for a happy combination.

Annie could not imagine wanting to be spotted in a headful of highlight foils by people eating their lunch.

Nor would she want to eat in a place filled with the smell of hair dye, with hair clippings on the loose.

'Do you dare me to tell the waiter there's a hair in my soup?' Connor whispered at them.

But this plan was thwarted by the appearance at their table of one of the owners. 'Hey, Connor, my man, you've made my day!' came the greeting from the tall, very blond, tight-pink-T-shirted man now hovering over their table.

'Henrik!' Connor greeted him like a long lost friend, standing up to give him a big hug. 'This place is great!' he gushed.

Henrik wanted to know what Connor and his guests thought of the food, the décor, the venue, everything.

All three told him as many complimentary and flattering things as possible until finally he went away, promising the chef would be out to meet them later.

Connor tried to look as thrilled as he could at the prospect of this.

'So, c'mon,' Connor urged Annie, 'cough! It's Sunday afternoon, you arrive at Gray's house for lunch and . . . ? Take us from there.'

'OK, OK . . . Gray was looking good,' she relented. 'He'd obviously made a full recovery from . . . the jacuzzi moment.'

'Wearing?' Dinah asked, suppressing a smirk.

'Black,' Annie replied. 'Black jeans, black shirt, black leather flip-flops and really nice feet.'

'Mmmm.' Connor was impressed with the detail. 'And how's his hair? Real? Or rug?'

'It's just hair dye,' Annie replied, a little coolly, 'I've already told you that.'

'Never mind, anyway, Annie gets the hots . . . for Mr Grecian 2000. Excellent!' Connor noted. 'So did you get down to it straight away or was there alcohol involved first?'

'You don't have to tell him!' Dinah insisted.

'Yes you do!' Connor insisted. 'We're family. Think of all we've done for you. We deserve to know about Annie's first shag since . . . he who shall not be named.'

'We had lunch,' Annie continued, ignoring as many of Connor's remarks as she could. 'Gray made seafood risotto with champagne. He *cooked* with the Taittinger!'

Connor looked impressed.

'Then we ate, and talked and drank the rest of the bottle.'

'Aha . . .' Connor prompted, scraping up the last mouthful of soup from the bottom of his bowl. 'And then? Were you ready for some dental work? An intricate mouth examination?'

Dinah dug her elbow into his ribs sharply.

'We went to the sofa . . . Steady!' Annie put her hand over her wine glass, so Connor couldn't top it up any further. 'And it got . . . nicely steamy,' she decided on.

She'd liked Gray's kisses. His mouth was very clean and probing. The black leather sofa had been too slippery though. She'd kept having to put an arm down on the floor to keep them both from sliding right off and this had been distracting.

His careful questioning – 'Can I undo this? Would that be OK with you?' – had been a mixture of charming and annoying.

But the prospect of undoing his perfectly ironed black Hugo Boss shirt and running her tongue along the fragrant, freshly showered, tanned skin beneath had begun to make her feel pleasantly hot and bothered.

Opening one button at a time, she'd discovered that his nipples were small and his chest smooth and hair-less.

'And did ya?' Connor asked.

'Kinda,' Annie replied.

'Oh, no, the Viagra didn't let him down again, did it?' Connor cut to the chase.

'No!' Annie insisted. Lowering her voice, she added, 'They've worked out a new dose for him at the hospital, one which won't make him dizzy . . . and believe me, it's quite impressive.'

'Oh yeah!' Connor encouraged.

253

'Like a ramrod,' Annie added.

'You lucky girl! Maybe you should introduce us,' Connor couldn't help himself.

There was a pause and even Dinah had to admit to herself she was quite interested in hearing the rest now.

'Well . . . were you ramrodded?' Connor asked with a wicked grin. 'Brace yourself, Annie, I'm a dentist. Brace yourself . . . geddit?'

'Oh ha ha,' came from Dinah.

'Er . . . no. It was all a bit too much, too soon. I ducked out,' Annie confessed.

Did she want Connor to know the nitty-gritty? That making use of the shiny sofa surface, she'd slid herself out of Gray's heated kissing and easily towards his navel.

'You went oral on the dentist, didn't you?' came Connor's merciless question.

'I'm not answering,' she told him.

'Did he ask you to open wide? And try not to swallow?' he teased, paying no attention to the waiter who was dumping their main courses in front of them now. 'No. Let me guess, he made you rinse and spit?' Connor couldn't help laughing at his own joke.

'I'm *not* answering!' she told him.

'Stop it, Connor,' Dinah warned. She wasn't sure how much Annie was or wasn't enjoying this.

'It's been a little confusing,' Annie confided. 'There I was, convinced I was desperate to have sex with the guy . . . desperate to have sex full stop . . . And when it came down to it . . . well . . . it was too big a step to take all at once.'

'How did he react?' Dinah asked.

254

'He was fine. Charming . . . very grateful,' Annie told them.

'I bet he was,' said Connor, and Annie's cheeky smile returned. 'And afterwards?' he prompted.

'It was very comfortable. We snuggled on the sofa, cuddled up and we were able to talk about things. He's really nice, you know. I wish you two would give him a break. He said he really missed having a wife.'

'His wife?' Dinah checked.

'No. A wife.'

Annie had asked Gray the same question. 'No, definitely not missing my wife,' he'd told her. 'She was . . . difficult to live with. But someone to come home to, someone to share even the very small things with – I miss that.'

His fingers had found hers and he'd squeezed her hand tightly.

'I miss that too,' she'd told him. 'Obviously I have the children, and they're fantastic . . . don't know what I'd do without them, but being part of a couple, sharing your life . . . it's very special,' she'd said, feeling slightly nervous that she'd overexposed herself, overstepped a line.

But Gray had just nodded and squeezed her hand again.

'We got into his rooftop jacuzzi,' she told Connor and Dinah.

'Nice. Very nice,' said Dinah. 'Left the ornaments in peace this time.'

'Naked or costumes?' Connor asked.

'Costumes. I told you, he's very gentlemanly and very proper.'

'Then he drove me home, but we made a bit of a detour via the shops.'

'Mmmm, this sounds good,' was Connor's comment.

'Aha – it *was* good,' Annie agreed. 'He bought me a very nice pair of shoes.'

'Show,' said Dinah.

This was easy, Annie just lifted a foot up into the air. All her waking hours since Sunday had been spent with her feet in these adorable pointy pumps, palest biscuity gold leather with just a hint of glitter to them.

'Nice. Marc Jacobs?' Dinah guessed.

'Miu Miu.' She gazed at them fondly. They were just so pretty: girlish, ready to party, light-hearted and Gray had been very good at shoe-shopping. Seemed to understand why shoes were such a tonic: because you were never too fat for shoes . . . you'd never crept up a size without noticing. They were the perfect present to yourself, they came in a box, wrapped in tissue paper, all pristine and unbroken.

'Look and be jealous, Dinah,' said Connor, stroking the shoe. 'Bryan could really learn from this man.'

'How?' Dinah asked a little sharply.

'He'd get so much more sex if he took you out shopping afterwards, wouldn't he? For Miu Miu, you'd probably do some very filthy things.'

'Bryan doesn't need to buy me anything,' Dinah huffed, but quickly followed it with, 'But if Gray wants to treat Annie, that's lovely. Now we're asking you about your sex life,' she told him, because for three whole weeks now (surely a record?) Connor had had a lover he was crazily excited about. 'And you will not be spared,' she added.

Connor looked at them in a seriously unusual, blissed-out kind of way, then tugged up his white T-shirt. Right across his rippling stomach from hip bone to armpit was a fine red line – intermittent, as if caused by a slim chain rather than a cord. There were also deep red pinch marks on either side of his rosy nipples and a brand new raw-looking metal stud in his navel.

'It's love, definitely love,' Connor said. 'Where would you like me to start?'

Dinah let out a little scream before saying, 'It's OK, we're fine. Really.'

Connor got hold of his wine glass and held it up, Dinah did likewise, then Annie too.

'To falling in love,' Connor offered.

Annie was sitting, feet up, on the big sofa holding a vast bowl of popcorn, with Owen curled up on one side of her and Lana on the other. The two takeaway pizza boxes were on the floor in front of them and all three were in their pyjamas, because it was Tuesday night, DVD night. Whenever possible on Tuesdays, the three of them snuggled up together for a pizza and an evening of giggling through something as hilarious as Blockbuster had to offer.

When the phone began to ring, Annie leaned forward, but Lana instructed her: 'Leave it to the answering machine. This is a really good bit, I don't want to pause it.'

'No, you don't have to,' Annie insisted. 'But I think I better—'

'Muuuum,' Lana complained. 'Don't! I'll have to move my feet, I'll get all uncomfortable.'

'Lana!' Annie stood up, pushing Lana's legs away from her lap. 'I won't be long.'

Lana didn't make any reply, Owen stayed glued to the screen, so Annie hurried out of the room to take the call in her bedroom before it was too late.

'Hello there, lovely to hear your voice . . .'

When Annie heard those words, she was delighted to have guessed correctly: it was Gray calling.

She lay back on her bed to enjoy the chat, listening with interest to what had been going on in the Holden dental world today.

After she'd imparted her news, they began to plan their next meeting.

'I'd like to see a lot more of you,' Gray purred. 'A lot, lot more.'

Annie's attention was distracted by Lana coming into the room.

'Are you on your own?' Gray was asking.

'No, not any more.'

'Now that is a shame,' came his reply. 'I was wanting to have a private chat with you . . . very private.'

No mistaking the sauciness in his voice. That kind of phone call . . .

'Sounds very interesting,' she told him, 'I think I'm definitely going to phone you back later.'

'I'll look forward to it.'

'Bye for now.'

'Bye.'

'How's your auction website going these days?' Annie asked Lana, who was still hovering by the door, neutral questions were best when Lana was sulky.

'Great, you should check it out some time, there's stuff

258

even you'd consider buying,' came the offhand reply. 'That was the dentist, wasn't it?' Lana said next, throwing herself over the available space on her mother's silky lilac bed.

'It was *Gray*, yes, Lana,' Annie said pointedly and smoothed her hand over the head that was now lying level with her elbow.

Lana gave a deep sigh and told her: 'I don't like your boyfriend. But I'm trying to give him the benefit of the doubt.'

'Well, that's very kind of you. I'm trying to do the same for your boyfriend.' Annie tried to leave it there, but then several moments later felt the irritated need to ask: 'What don't you like about Gray?'

'Well, his name for a start,' Lana told her. 'You do know he's called Gary really, don't you?'

'Oh.' No! Much as she'd suspected Gray was too exotic, too suave to be a real first name, she hadn't suspected quite so mundane a reality. Gary??!

'How do you know?' Annie wondered, a little suspicious that Lana had made this up just as a strike against Gray.

'Gran told me.'

'When?'

'When I asked her.'

Hmmm. Annie would check with Fern. Find out her source. Maybe it was a guess.

'Gary is just a bit full of himself, don't you think?' Lana added, scratching one bare foot with the black painted toenails of the other.

'He's a successful man. He's proud of himself and he has a certain confidence,' Annie told her. 'Don't say "full of himself" because that sounds nasty and really, I think he's pretty nice.'

Lana's sulky response was the inevitable: 'He's not the same as Dad though, is he?'

'No,' Annie told her gently. 'But your dad isn't exactly here right now, is he? So you've got to give someone else, someone like Gray, a bit of a chance. Please?'

This almost made Lana smile.

'I think we could all be happy with someone who is nice and caring, and who could look after us all. Someone who'd make me feel a lot less worried . . .'

'Someone rich,' Lana interpreted.

Annie turned to her daughter so she could speak to her eye to eye: 'You know, that's another nasty thing to say, Lana. Do you honestly think the only thing that interests me about Gray is his money?'

'I can't see what else there is.' Lana was definitely sulking now, her arms were crossed so tightly over her black vest top that her many silver wrist chains and bangles must have been digging into her skin.

'He's handsome, he's caring, he's interesting. I like to talk to him. He's got really good taste. We have lots of things in common.' None of this was convincing Lana, who was staring straight ahead over her crossed arms now.

'I don't know . . . He makes me feel interesting too . . . appreciated . . .' Annie said with some exasperation. 'Unlike some people I could mention,' came the little dig.

'He's so *old!*' came Lana's scornful response. 'And it doesn't exactly sound like mad passionate love.'

'No. It's not!' Annie was trying not to raise her voice.

'I'm not expecting that. I'd be happy with something a bit more comfortable and companionable.'

'You still have to sleep with him though,' came Lana's retort. 'Wonder if he'll take his wig off. Have you had sex with him yet?'

Annie felt a surprisingly powerful flash of anger at this and snapped back: 'He doesn't have a wig! And how would you feel if I asked about your sex life like that?'

She regretted it immediately. This wasn't the way she'd rehearsed the close and confiding mother and daughter chat she'd been mentally preparing for, ever since Seth had come onto the scene.

Lana offered a scornful scowl in response to this.

'Look,' Annie began, trying to find the reasonable, friendly voice she knew she should be using: 'I haven't slept with Gray. But if I do, it will be for all the right reasons.'

'Ditto,' Lana said.

'Fourteen is too young for sex, Lana.' Annie tried to keep her tone friendly and encouraging. She couldn't believe that she was already discussing the very real possibility of her little girl . . . well, they'd had all sorts of sex talks before in the past, but they'd been so much more abstract. Much easier to deal with. Annie was trying to reason with her instinctive desire to shout out: *No!* Don't do this. It's too soon, for you and for me.

'Did I ask you for advice?'

The pale little face beside her was pointy, facing away and closed off from her for the moment.

'I'd be so happy if you came to me for advice, Lana. And I will try to be as open-minded about it as I can be,'

Annie told her as calmly as she could. She felt as if she'd just aged about five years.

After a burning silence, Lana decided to air a different sore point: 'Why do we have to sell this flat, Mum? I don't want to move again. I don't want to be living in some grotty dump all over again with rotten carpets and a hideous toilet and a horrible bedroom. I don't want to do it. And this isn't just any old flat! This was our home with Dad!' she burst out. 'Doesn't that mean anything to you?! Don't you think me and Owen might like to stay in our family home? All you can think about is yourself and how to earn more money for yourself.'

'I don't think that's very fair, Lana,' Annie warned, 'I have to look after you both on my own and that's very expensive.'

'Yeah well, but you're very expensive too.' With that Lana got up, flung open the white door of Annie's fitted wardrobe and pushed all the clothes on the rail over to one side.

'Lana!' Annie's warning not to go any further was clear now, but Lana began flicking through the hangers one by one.

'Gucci!' she read from the label of the first top. 'Valentino, Nicole Farhi, Paul Smith, Westwood, Diane Von Furstenberg, McQueen, Farhi, Smith, Smith, Westwood, Whistles, Karen Millen – you were slumming it that week – and back to Gucci. My God, this one's Chanel! Do I have to go on or do you get my point?'

'Lana!' Annie could barely contain her fury at this little lecture: 'You know how hard I work and you know where I work. You know perfectly well I get a great deal on all the clothes I buy and that I have to dress really smartly for The Store. Yes, we might have to sell the flat, just to be practical, just to make sure there's plenty of money in the bank to pay for the great school I send you to, which you are so determined to piss off and run down and undermine all the time. You know what? Maybe one of these days you should try working hard too. No-one's going to give you great exam results because you're cool, Lana! No-one's going to give you a great job because you were one of the school rebels! You get out what you put in, Lana, and maybe it's about time you understood that!'

A furious 'Huh!' came back from Lana. 'And I suppose you're planning to solve all your problems by marrying Mr Rich Dentist, are you?'

'Shut up, Lana!' Annie shot back. 'I've been on some dates with Gray and I like him. Who said anything about him being rich? Because I haven't asked to see his bank accounts . . . And who has said one word about marriage? Don't you think that maybe you're being really rude?'

'I'm not moving out of here!' Lana shouted at her. 'You can't make me. I am not leaving this flat and that is final. I'd rather leave school!'

'Oh, you would, would you? Well, that's fine, tomorrow morning I'll take you along to . . .' Annie shoved in the name of the worst comprehensive in the area she could think of and watched for her daughter's reaction.

'Yes, that will be fine. Suzie's boyfriend goes there and he says it's cool.'

'Enough about *cool*,' Annie practically shrieked. 'No-one cares what's cool. No-one gives a . . . a . . .' she managed to tone down the word which sprang to mind to: 'toss.'

But with that Lana stormed to the bedroom door, slammed it shut behind her and shouted: 'I'm getting out of here!'

Annie stayed on her bed, heart pounding.

Twenty minutes or so later, when a bit of vigorous nail filing had calmed her down slightly, she decided to go out of the bedroom to see what was happening.

In the sitting room, Owen had turned off the TV, tidied away the pizza and popcorn debris and was reading on the sofa.

'Hey, Owen,' she ran her fingers over his hair, 'you're a star for clearing up. I'm really sorry about all that. I'm sorry. We spoiled the film, we spoiled the evening . . . and we shouldn't have done all that shouting.'

'I know,' Owen said. He didn't look up from his book. 'Mum?'

'Yes?'

'Did you know that jellyfish have been on the planet for five hundred and thirty million years?'

'Well, babes, that could be because you can't eat them, you can't burn them, you can't wear them and you definitely can't make them into shoes. Is Lana in her room?'

'No. She went out,' came the reply.

'What?! Out of the flat?'

'Yeah.'

'When?!'

'Not long after the fight.'

'Did she say where she was going?'

'She didn't say anything.'

'Why didn't you tell me?'

'You sounded scary,' was Owen's answer to this and now Annie felt like the worst parent in the world.

She hurried to the telephone, dialled Lana's number and got straight through to voicemail: 'Lana, don't be so stupid, phone me up and let me know where you are.' Clunk. She put the phone down and began the ring-round of all the home numbers of Lana's friends.

An hour later, Annie was almost in tears. Despite the soothing words of the six parents she'd spoken to, she was panicking about her daughter.

'She'll be fine,' Lana's friend Greta's mother had assured her. 'Greta did this a few weeks ago, stormed off to someone's house and didn't come back for hours, just to scare me. There isn't any big problem, is there?'

'No,' Annie had assured her, 'I don't think so. It was just one of those usual stupid arguments.'

'Could she have gone to her boyfriend's?' Greta's mother asked.

'He lives in Essex. She'd have had to go to the station, catch a train . . . I don't know,' Annie admitted, 'I don't have his number, his mobile . . . I don't even know his surname!'

'I'll see if I can find out, and if Greta hears anything at all, I'll phone you, OK. Try not to worry too much.'

But when Annie put the phone down after leaving another message on Lana's mobile, she realized she was scared and flooded with guilt.

It was 11.40 p.m. when the phone rang.

Annie snatched it up with a hopeful 'Hello?'

'You're alone now, aren't you?' came the husky voice.

'I'm alone too and I can't stop thinking about you and all the things I'd like to do with you . . .'

'Gray, now's not a good time,' she told him briskly. 'Sorry. Lana's gone out . . . without permission and I'm waiting for her to phone and tell me she's OK.'

'Oh.'

There was a pause.

'Sorry,' she repeated. 'Can I speak to you tomorrow?'

'Yeah, no problem.' He hung up abruptly.

If Gray never called her again, it would be Lana's fault . . . and wouldn't Lana be pleased? Annie felt a surge of anger. Had she been this unsupportive about Seth? But that was so different! Seth was 17! Far too old for a 14-year-old. Lana had to be with Seth now, didn't she?

It was almost 12.30 a.m. when the phone rang again and Annie, sitting wide awake in bed, anxiously picking at her nail polish, shot out her hand to pick up the receiver.

'Lana! For God's sake—' she began.

'Ermm,' came a male voice.

'Gray! Not now!' she snapped.

'My name's Matthew Laurence,' the voice informed her, 'I'm sorry to phone you so late at night. It's about Lana.'

'Oh!' Annie felt nothing but blind fear – mind racing with all the terrible things that could have happened to Lana.

'I'm Seth's dad and she's here with us,' Matthew continued calmly.

'Oh, thank God for that!' The tight squeeze on Annie's heart began to loosen just slightly.

'Umm, I'm sorry this is so late. I didn't know she was here because I've been out. She was upstairs with Seth and they've fallen asleep . . . in front of the TV,' he added, although this wasn't allaying Annie's fears about underage teen sex one little bit.

'I've woken her up and told her to give you a call but . . . erm . . . she doesn't want to.' There was no denying the embarrassment in his voice as he said this. 'I gather you've had a row.'

'Oh.' Annie was suddenly trying very hard not to cry.

'Anyway, I told her I would phone to let you know she's safe. She can spend the night here, if that's OK with you . . . she can sleep in my daughter Libby's room,' he added quickly.

'I'm so sorry about this,' Annie began.

'No, honestly, Mrs Valentine. Seth's our third and we've seen it all before.'

There was no mistaking the loud sniffle Annie now made down the phone.

'It'll all blow over,' Seth's father assured her. 'I can give her a lift into London early tomorrow morning, she should make it to school in time.'

'Are you sure? I don't want to put you out . . .'

'No, it's fine,' he replied.

'She's only fourteen,' Annie heard herself blurting out, 'I don't even know if Seth knows that.'

'Well, I'll make sure he does and don't worry, we'll look after her.'

There was nothing more Annie could do other than trust this kind parental voice on the other end of the line and wish Seth's father good night.

When the call was over, she turned her face into her pillow and let out the long, hard sobs which had been building all night.

How did anyone manage to parent on their own? How did anyone do it?

Chapter Twenty-one

Annie goes yachting:

White cropped jeans (Tesco)
Red boatneck top (Joseph)
Red and white plimsolls (La Redoute)
Red, white and black scarf tied into ponytail (Tie Rack)
Thin black raincoat (Miss Selfridge)
Est. cost: £110

'Does anyone have a plastic bag? Quickly!!'

Gray came to pick the three of them up in his car. His beautiful, new £45,000-plus red Mercedes with steel fold-down roof, bright red upholstery and a jet black dashboard studded with dials. Annie wasn't sure what was wrong with the silver one he'd traded in, but apparently every year for the last decade, he'd upgraded his car. Must be an irrepressible male urge . . . just like the one for a new handbag, only so much, much more expensive.

Since Lana's runaway stunt, Gray and Annie had

decided he should make a concerted effort to get to know her children better and as the attempts to go out for cosy lunches and little excursions round town hadn't gone so well – Owen silent and Lana sullen – Gray had made a bold new plan for a day trip.

'A friend of mine has a yacht,' he'd announced. 'He's offered to take us all out for a day, as soon as the weather's good. Ever been yachting, Annie?' he'd wanted to know, adding, 'It's fantastic. Blasts the cobwebs away . . . Might even get a little boat of my own one of these days.'

Despite her father's seafaring background, Annie could not recall setting foot on a boat, bar a rowing trip round the Serpentine in Hyde Park or grim ferry rides from London to Calais and back. But 'yachting' sounded fantastic. It sounded like sun sparkling on the water, gin and tonics fizzing on deck and everyone clad in Persilwhite Ralph Lauren.

Now that April was well under way, the better weather had arrived and along with it, Gray's yachting day trip.

His car swept into their Highgate street early one morning and he came up to the flat laden with flowers for Annie and Lana and an oversized slab of chocolate for Owen.

'You mustn't always think you have to bring us presents,' Annie ticked him off.

'Shhh!' he told her. 'There are many things you can tell me off for, but this isn't one of them.'

'Owen!' she warned. 'Don't even think about eating any of that before we get into the car. Go put it in your room.'

It took some time to load up the Mercedes. Annie had three big cool bags full of picnic stuff and the holdall of spare clothes and shoes that Gray had instructed her to take: 'It can get very wet on board a yacht.'

'Oh, really?' she'd responded as cheekily as she could, because since the leather sofa moment there had been very little frolicking with Gray and she'd decided she would have to take the matter in hand and do some seducing of her own: 'Why don't you let me make you dinner at my house after the yachting trip . . . stay over with me?'

'Well . . .' His eyebrow had twitched.

So, once the car was packed, she was buckled into the passenger's seat and Lana and Owen were installed comfortably in the back.

Gray, in a stunning gesture of child-friendliness, had decided to take the option of the built-in back seat DVD player and screens, so they just needed to agree on a film to watch (Annie's UN-level negotiator skills were required), put their headphones on and enjoy. Although Gray had insisted the children take their shoes off, so as not to dirty the carpet or the backs of the front seat, which Annie had found a little over the top. It had obviously pained him to take the polythene covers off the passenger seats and let mere mortals sit on them.

'Erm . . . Lana?' he was now asking awkwardly. 'I don't want any eating in the car, if that's OK.'

'It's just gum,' Lana snapped.

'Well, I'm sorry, I hope you don't mind, but could you take it out? Just in case it somehow by accident lands on the carpet?' He did ask very nicely, but the sigh it provoked showed how annoyed Lana was.

For a moment, Annie couldn't decide who she should ask to back down . . . but the thought that he'd installed back seat DVD players *just for her children* clinched it.

'Lana!' she growled.

Once the offending gum had been deposited, they set off.

'Shame about the drizzle,' Gray told her as they made their way through the streets heading for the motorway out of town. 'Otherwise we could have had the roof down and fresh air.'

'Don't know how much fresh air there is in north London, matey,' she reminded him.

'You should think about moving to the country,' was his reply. 'Fresh air, greenery, much more space . . .'

A light-hearted debate broke out between them as they batted about the pros and cons. Annie felt an undercurrent of excitement because she wondered if he was sounding her out – if he had in mind asking her to move out to the Essex countryside with him . . . one of these days.

What would she do if he asked her? As she argued playfully with him against long-distance commuting 'even in a stunning car like this' she tried to give some thought to her answer.

The M25 was clogged with traffic, even this early on a Saturday morning, so their progress was slow and jerky, but finally they got onto the M11 and Gray was able to move up through the gears and nose his red beauty into the fast lane, where she belonged.

'Mum, I'm feeling a bit dizzy,' was the first warning to come from Owen.

'Oh dear.' Annie looked over at him. He looked fine.

Maybe the back seat DVD wasn't such a great idea. He'd had the odd bout of travel sickness in the past, but it had all settled down now. 'Maybe you should switch your screen off and just lean back in the seat for a while,' she suggested.

'Is he OK?' Gray asked.

'He looks fine,' she assured him.

Ten minutes later, when Owen told her he *really* wasn't feeling great, Annie was spurred into action by the sight of him. His face was white with an unmistakable green tinge to the edges and there was a faint moustache of sweat on his upper lip. He was going to puke, no doubt about it.

Sitting bolt upright now, she instructed Gray to pull over: 'Just as soon as you can!' but they were on a three-lane motorway, in the fast lane: she could see it would take time.

'Does anyone have a plastic bag? Quickly!! Lana? Anything at all?!'

She was in such a panic about Gray's new car seats that it crossed her mind to dump out the contents of her handbag and let Owen use that. But it was vintage Mulberry, with a tartan lining. Surely that had to be much more difficult to clean than car upholstery?

Annie, and of course Roddy, had learned how to drive in a travel sickness crisis: as smoothly as possible, without any sudden movements or any unnecessary braking. But Gray swooped the car into the middle lane, which made Owen puke down his T-shirt. Gray then made a panicky lunge for the slow lane, causing Owen to vomit harder: all the way down to his knees. The abrupt ABS-induced halt in the hard shoulder . . . well, Owen bravely tried to cup his hands to contain it, but it overflowed, splatting all over the crisp red seat beside him.

Defeated, Owen let his hands drop and two puddles of vomit dripped to the seat then down his trouser legs and onto the dense black carpet.

'Oh sh-sugar!' Annie managed to restrain herself.

A strained expression was pulled tight across Gray's face. She couldn't decide if it was a smile or a grimace. Maybe it was a grimace trying to pretend it was a smile.

'Don't worry,' she said, aiming it at both Owen and Gray, 'I'll deal with this, it'll be fine. We'll get as much off here as we can, but we might have to stop at the service station ahead.'

Gray just nodded: 'Yes . . . OK,' he said, sounding in pain.

Annie shot her blackest look at Lana, who'd begun to have a giggling fit.

Cars and lorries whizzing past her so fast they shook the car as they passed, Annie opened Owen's door and surveyed the damage.

He'd obviously made serious inroads into the chocolate slab. The vomit wasn't just chocolate coloured, it smelled sweet and sticky too.

'Owen!' Seeing his pale damp face, it was hard to be angry with him. But with just a small packet of pocket tissues in her handbag it was difficult to know what she could do in the face of this violent eruption.

She got Owen out of the car and away from the road, she helped him change into his spare clothes, even though this did involve him standing by a motorway in just his pants . . . briefly. She dabbed hopelessly at the enormous brown stains on the back seat with her tissues.

Vomit staining was bad . . . chocolate-flavoured vomit staining? Oh boy, there was a pair of cream trousers from Whistles she'd once had . . . they'd been rushed to intensive care at London's top dry cleaners but even then . . .

The next forty minutes of the drive were a tad tense. Instead of smelling like new, the car stank of spew. Owen still felt bad, he was curled in his seat groaning into one of the six plastic bags secured for him at the service station. Lana's attempts to giggle-stifle would fail every so often in a snotty explosion.

'I'm sorry to be just a little ticked off,' Gray tried to justify his barely contained fury. 'I was just looking forward to showing the car to John.' Ah, the man with the 30-foot, interior-designed yacht . . . Ah. Annie understood now. A bit of man-to-man size-comparing had been in the offing.

The drizzle cleared, the sea sparkled, the yacht bobbed up and down on the water, desperate to play, John appeared in top-to-toe white with a sailor's cap and a sunburnt face, but still Owen felt horrible.

'I think Owen and I will have to sit this one out,' Annie, almost sick herself – but with regret – told a dumbfounded Gray and Lana.

Gray and Lana looked at each other in undisguised confusion. Neither felt they could say: 'I'm not going with you – without her!

Annie managed to persuade Gray that she should take the keys to the car and find a valeting service in the little town, once Owen had recovered.

With hindsight, the day went extremely well: Annie and Owen spent hours walking along the beach, talking, throwing stones, finding shells, enjoying each other's company, then eating ice-creams on a wall together. ('*At least there won't be lumps, if you throw up on the way home!*')

Lana and Gray came back from the yacht trip glowing with excitement and finally comfortable together. Jim of the Washaway Valet had not flinched from the stains on the Mercedes back seat; no, he'd claimed it was an honour to work on a car so showroom new. He'd managed to turn the deep brown marks into something much more biscuity and he'd used a fine internal 'cleansing' mist to reduce the nostril-clogging stink.

That evening, Owen went to bed very early, worn out by holding it together on the journey home. Lana left before dinner in a great full-of-the-joys-of-yachting mood, for her friend's Suzie's house for a pre-arranged sleepover.

So Annie and Gray ate alone together: a gourmet curry meal for two, bought specially from M&S.

There was a scented candle burning in her room and the string of extremely flattering pale pink flower lights looped above the bed was already switched on. Annie had a sleepover of her own in mind.

Kissing in the kitchen led to kissing in the bedroom.

Gray's cheeks were warm and dry, still salty from the sea. As she licked his neck and began to unbutton his shirt, he excused himself and in the moments he was gone, Annie whipped off her clothes and brought out the brand new lilac satin knickers and bra she'd selected for this little scene, then tied a silky, matching kimono on top. Her legs and bikini line were newly done, her room smelled delicious, there was moody jazz on the stereo. She applied lip gloss and arranged herself attractively across her bed waiting for the good time she was determined would follow.

And waited . . .

And waited . . .

Once a full fifteen minutes had passed, she got up and went out into the hallway. Although she'd thought Gray might be trying to slip in one of his many showers, no sound was coming from the bathroom.

'Gray?' she asked, tapping lightly on the door. 'Is everything all right?'

'Yes, well . . .' came a hesitant, slightly strained reply, 'not really.'

'Are you OK? Can you come out?' she wondered, really hoping this wasn't some troubling bowel situation. It was too early in their relationship for all that. It really was.

It had been all very well for Roddy to lure her into the bedroom with the words: 'Darlin', I really want to shag you, but I've got to do a big dump first,' but you had to have at least ten years of marriage under your belt before you could get away with that.

There was deep sigh, then she heard Gray's footsteps coming towards her. He undid the lock and put his head round the door, but for several moments just looked at her, as if he wasn't sure what to say.

'It's OK,' she assured him. 'If you don't want to talk about it . . .' *the painful piles . . . constipation . . . whatever*, 'don't worry.'

'Oh . . . well . . . I forgot my medication, you know, the love drug.' He hurried the words out, trying to make a little joke of it, but still looked tense.

Oh God, he meant his Viagra. He'd obviously been in here searching his overnight bag ten times over and maybe trying to kick things off naturally on his own.

They'd had a little chat about the Viagra recently, and he'd assured her it was more of a psychological prop than a physical necessity.

'You're fine,' she told him, reaching out to take hold of his hand. 'Just come into the bedroom with me and we'll . . . play.'

There was a strange moment when Annie found herself lying on her back, with her head hanging from the bed and an extremely willing, able and raring to go Gray on top of her. But other thoughts kept crowding into her mind to distract her from fully taking part: she remembered lying right here, but with Roddy, an ice cube squeezed between her breasts . . . and then . . . next thought, reading in a magazine that women should hang their heads from the bed during orgasm because it made the experience more extreme.

She was trying to decide if this was because the blood rush was speeded up or slowed down. But anyway . . . back to the man at hand. He was looking very pleased with himself and definitely wanted to put the non-medically enhanced Bone to good use.

But . . . but . . . looking up at her very own familiar ceiling, headboard and pink lights, she knew she definitely didn't want to do this here, on her marital bed.

No, no, definitely not.

But Gray was keen. Well, how could he know what she was thinking? She was wearing a smile and murmuring 'Oooooh yes, yes' to him.

But really, she was wondering how to get off the bed before they were too involved.

She began to pull slightly against him, down towards the floor. Her bed had a satin bedspread, so once she'd begun the slide, it was easy to keep it going. Already her head was touching the carpet, now her neck and shoulders were following.

'Whoaaaa . . . where are you going?' Gray asked, still holding on and sliding with her.

Her elbows took her weight and as she giggled at him, her hips and legs followed a little too quickly as she brought both herself and her would-be lover down onto the floor with a thud.

The angle of Gray's bodysurf to the floor was much steeper than hers and as his hands were behind her back, he couldn't put them out to save himself. He hit the carpet, chin first, and gave a cry of pain.

'Whooops, sorry!' She was still giggling.

But Gray was lying face down on the floor, groaning slightly.

'Are you OK?' she asked him, slight flicker of worry now. Were all her romantic encounters with Gray going to end with a 999 call?

He raised a hand and put it gingerly onto the small of his back: 'My sacroiliac!' he gasped, 'it's popped out before . . . I'm going to have to get you to roll me over.'

She did, but to the slightly concerning soundtrack of Gray going 'Aaaaaaaaaaargh!' over the moody jazz.

Once he was on his back, he raised his right knee slowly and painfully, finally managing to pull it towards his chest, where he held it tight and began to rock from side to side. Whatever ardour Annie may have had for Gray, it was a little quenched at the sight of this.

He made the 'Aaaah!' sound again. Then finally, there was a look of relief on his face. He stood up and walked gingerly, not to mention butt-naked, in a semicircle. He was limping slightly, but declared, 'Don't worry, it'll settle down.'

Annie put on her kimono and went in search of wine, deciding it was time for a civilized glass of Tesco's finest under the covers. She didn't want to risk killing him with a further lovemaking attempt.

Snuggled up under the covers together, relaxed by the wine, Annie began to touch him again. She started with gentle strokes on his chest, which was muscular, because he kept fit and looked after himself. She played with his nipples then began to work her way down, watching the changing expression on his face. She was enjoying this: teasing him, coaxing his reluctant cock back into life.

Suddenly, she found she was more than interested herself, wanted him to play all the same games with her, make her just as excited and breathlessly ready as he was now.

Then they were making love, properly . . . and it was OK, she was telling herself. It really was OK. Not amazing, but not disastrous. It reminded her of 'sex: the early attempts' . . . because she was suddenly optimistic that from here on in, it would get a lot better.

Later, when they were both almost ready to fall asleep, Gray startled her with the words: 'I don't really like doing this.'

'What? Sex?' she asked, wondering what big self-revelation was to follow.

'No, no . . . Are you joking? That was great!'

Always nice to be appreciated.

'No,' he went on, 'I mean coming here, sleeping over . . . you visiting my home every now and then. It's all quite stressful and inconvenient. Your children must be wondering what's going on.'

'Oh, I think they know,' Annie responded. And she began to have a nasty suspicion: *was he telling her it was over? Surely not?*

'Annie, I'm taking a risk, I know we've only been seeing each other for six weeks or so, but we're grown-ups . . . I think we both know what we want.' He paused, then came right out and asked, 'Why don't you rent out your flat for a bit and move in with me? Give me a trial period. Properly. Nothing ventured, nothing gained.'

She was glad he was cuddled in behind her, talking into her neck, so that he couldn't see the look of astonishment cross her face at this suggestion.

'I've got a big house,' he added, 'I'm rattling around in it. Why don't you move in? The three of you. Please at least tell me you'll consider it?'

There was a long, long pause, as all sorts of arguments, thoughts and emotions raced through her mind.

Finally, after several swallows, listening to the nervously shallow breathing Gray was making as he awaited her reply, she told him: 'That is a very kind, very generous offer, Gray. Really. You're just going to have to give me some time to think about this.'

Chapter Twenty-two

Footballer's wife in spring:

Black tight top (D&G)
Boyfriend cut jeans (Sass and Bide)
Black strappy wedges (Gucci)
Black raincoat (Burberry Prorsum)
Gold bag (Balenciaga)
Huge black shades (Chanel)
Est. cost: £2,700

'Black's so slimming, innit?'

'Look, babes, it's spring. And I know spring is hard to get right in London, but it is our duty to try,' were Annie's words of encouragement to Dannii, as she arrived at the changing room door with another armful of clothes.

Dannii (yes, with a double 'i') was 20, the luscious (obviously), blonde (predictably) girlfriend of a Chelsea FC midfielder with – according to WAG bible, *heat* – £4,000 of 'pocket money' a week to spend on herself.

Although, at the rate Dannii was burning her cash,

£4,000 a week wouldn't be enough and she'd soon be asking her 21-year-old lover-boy for a raise: 'So long as I keep him very happy, he pays up and keeps me very happy,' she'd cheerfully confided.

Dannii had not yet realized that owning ten Louis Vuitton handbags is not ten times as thrilling as owning one.

This was the third week in a row she'd been in for a personal shopping session and although she spent lashings of money, Annie's enthusiasm for her was waning. A big part of the problem was that the magazines Dannii had been so keen to appear in had now started to poke fun at her. Snide captions were appearing, along with hideously unflattering photographs: *Dannii shows off another new £3,000 outfit, but don't be jealous, girls, on her it still looks cheap!*

Despite Dannii's pleas to Annie that she wanted to look 'a bit classy, right', she'd so far turned all of Annie's suggestions down and was drawn like a moth to the gold, the glittering, the fussy, the sequinned and the spangly and on her surgically enhanced E-cups . . . well . . . even in Diane Von Furstenburg, she looked like the wrong kind of working girl.

Dannii had recently taken to squeezing her voluptuous self into tight black in an effort to counteract the 'cheap' accusations and, in her words, 'Black's so slimming, innit?' But Annie's pet hate was clients who dressed in monochrome. It was so draining on the complexion (Dannii had already gone several shades blonder and browner to compensate) and as Annie was trying to explain . . . it was spring!

'Yeah, but it's not like it's actually warm out there,'

Dannii insisted, plump pink lips pouting. 'I mean if we move to Milan this year, because Jakey is talking to someone about a transfer, that'll be different. But in London . . .'

Annie wondered for a moment if there was a tabloid newspaper she should ring with the Jakey transfer information . . . but then it was her job to be discreet, even if her customers weren't.

'I know spring is unpredictable here,' Annie replied. 'One minute it's blazing hot and everyone's dying a death in their woollen trousers, boots and coats, the next minute, just as you've changed into your frock and flip-flops, it's chucking it down and there's a wind from Siberia howling round your ankles. But your spring/ summer wardrobe plan cannot be black. It just can't!' she insisted. 'You've got to blossom, Dannii. You've got to be in tune with the seasons. I've brought a beautiful pale green raincoat down for you, and some gorgeous new handbags in lemon and in pink. Look, I've got white jeans, pale blue jeans, pink jeans, violet jeans. I've got really sweet, demure little blouses – Missoni, Paul & Joe – which are sexy, but not quite so . . . in your face. I've got three-quarter-sleeved Prada cocktail dresses, because believe me, less flesh is sometimes so much more . . . and I think platform-heeled loafer-style shoes for you, my darlin', for daywear at least. The thing about always having your pedicure on display is that it's just not elegant. I know you have a driver to take you everywhere, Dannii love, but you're always getting photographed with your tits and your toes hanging out.'

'Come on then, pass me the coat,' Dannii relented.

With her inch-long pink nails, she attempted to tie the belt round her waist.

'Ooh, that is very pale,' was her verdict. 'God! Look at my tan now! I look like a blooming *Efiopian*, wish I was as skinny as one an' all.'

Annie cringed slightly. Clearly an invitation to fundraise for Oxfam wasn't going to be heading Dannii's way too soon.

'With all my clients, babes, it's easy to get people to pile on the layers and dress dark for autumn and winter,' Annie told her. 'But nobody wants to lighten and brighten up for spring because we think it's never going to happen. Then the first hot days are a fashion disaster: sparkly sandals and raincoats, wool trousers with vests, summer skirts with black boots . . . it's horrible.'

As Annie finished her lecture, she began to wonder if she was just talking about clothes. The words suddenly had another meaning for her. It was beginning to occur to her that she could be caught in the 20 plus degrees of Gray's sunshine in her emotional equivalent of thick jeans and a black jumper. Was she ready to go to the next stage with Gray? Should she be ready? Was she holding herself back? She'd been on her own for nearly three years . . . no-one could accuse her of not leaving enough time. She hadn't been with Gray for long, but as he'd said, they were grown-ups – they knew what they wanted, they didn't need to play games, maybe they should just move on to the next stage.

It took another hour of concerted effort, but Dannii finally headed tillwards with two tasteful dresses, two blouses, three pairs of coloured jeans, new shoes, a new bag and the raincoat. A fortnight's worth of pocket money, at least. Annie hoped she'd stay away that long and wondered whether she should risk giving this lucrative new client the advice to change hair salons and slash her daily dose of St Tropez bronzing gel.

'I am so sorry, can you just give me five?' she asked her next customer, who was already waiting on the sofa. 'Have a little wander out on the shop floor and I'll join you there . . . or I can send someone along with tea? Coffee? Mineral water?'

The woman decided to head for the shop floor and Annie made straight for her office, closing the door tightly behind her.

In front of her computer, she made her quick email and website checks. Three great offers were in on Trading Station items. Buoyed by this, she clicked over to Lana's school charity website to see what her daughter's fund-raising gang had managed to get hold of this week.

Just as Ed had suspected, Lana and her friends loved running the auction website and had begged, wheedled and hustled all sorts of goodies to flog on it.

Meanwhile, Annie opened her mobile and speed-dialled Gray.

'Hello there, girlfriend!' he answered. 'Having a moment off? Thinking about me?'

'Yes I was . . . I was thinking about you. Where are you? Have you got a minute or are you about to excavate a root canal?'

'I always, always have a minute for you,' he assured her, 'I'm in the car. You're on hands-free.'

'I'm a bloody hands-full, babes, you should be warned . . .' She took a deep breath and then began: 'I've been thinking about what you said . . . you know . . . the *big* question . . .' She paused and so did Gray.

'Have you talked to Owen and Lana about it?' he wondered, which was the right thing to ask. Annie felt a surge of affection that he'd thought to ask about her children's opinion before he heard her own.

'I've not had a big discussion with them, to be honest,' she told him, 'I've been trying to sort out my own thoughts about it all. But I've mentioned it, as a possibility. They're . . . well . . . I think "curious" is the best word. They've not said yes, they've not said no. I think we might need to persuade them that we think it's a good idea – if we do think it's a good idea,' she added quickly. 'They'll have a long commute to school . . . but they might want to give it a go.'

'My offer stands, Annie,' was Gray's response to this. 'You and your children are all very, very welcome to come and live with me, even on a trial basis. I think we'd all get along really well.'

With the mobile clamped so tightly to her head that her ear was beginning to throb, Annie took another steadying breath before telling him: 'OK, Gray, I'll have to talk to Lana and Owen, but I'm thinking we should give it a whirl.'

When the call was over, Annie put her phone back down on her desk, then her professional eye took over, directing her attention to the item on the screen in front of her: yes, it really was this season's BNWT Marc Jacobs handbag with serial number for sale on Lana's charity website. The top bid was £120 and the deal was closing at the end of the day.

She speed-dialled Lana and left a message on her phone: 'Babes, I've just put in two hundred pounds for your handbag, but tell me if I need more to get it, I'll sell it for you on my site and give your charity the extra money. You should get four hundred and fifty for that bag at the very, very least, if it's genuine. Call me.'

Then her phone rang and she saw it was Owen, who did have his own mobile but it was for emergency use only.

'Everything OK, Owen?' she asked before he'd even said hello.

'*Yes!* I just wanted to tell you . . .' He was breathless.

'My God! What's the matter? Are you OK?'

'*Yes!* It's just I've been picked . . . I auditioned . . . it was so scary . . . but I've been picked for the school show . . .'

'To do what?' Annie was only slightly conscious that she'd kept her client waiting a full ten minutes by now and she never, ever did that, but the client would have to wait just a little longer.

'A guitar solo . . . and a song!'

He didn't need to say another thing, the happiness that beamed from those words was so radiant, she could feel the warmth of it down the line.

'That's just fantastic,' she told him. 'A solo! I can't believe it!' This was how far he'd come, her little boy, the boy who'd once only spoken six words at school in an entire term. 'I am so, so proud of you, that's amazing! I was proud of you anyway, Owen,' she added, 'I think you're just fab.'

*   *   *

Arriving home just after 7.30 p.m., Annie saw a notice warning that the lift was out of order, so with the last burst of physical energy she had left for the day, she took the stairs up to the third floor.

She walked quickly, taking the treads at a steady pace. Just as she approached the top of the last flight of stairs, the stairwell door burst open and Ed Leon was at the top of the steps.

'Ed, hello. I was hoping to catch you!' she greeted him.

'Oh, Mrs . . . erm . . . Annie. I take it the lift's still out of action?'

'Yeah, but I try and do the stairs once a day anyway.' There was a slight breathlessness to her voice by now because she'd taken them at a brisk trot. 'Keeps my bum at the top of my legs, where I'd like it to stay.'

'Right, well . . .' He seemed at a loss to know what to add to that, and clasped his hands tightly together in front of him.

'Owen!' they exclaimed together.

'Fantastic news about Owen,' Ed said next. 'I waited to speak to you about that but I thought' – he looked at his watch – 'thought you must have been held up.'

'I know, I'm later than usual. Anyway, he phoned to tell me. Singing with the guitar, solo?' She wanted to check she'd understood it right.

'Yes. Not a whole song, he does the first verse, then the group join in, but still . . .' Ed smiled at her, before adding, 'I worried it might be too much too soon, but his reaction is so positive that I think he'll be fine. And he did the audition brilliantly, put himself in for it. Nothing to do with me.'

'Thank you, Ed.' Annie had made it up to his level now. 'Thank you so much. But don't be so modest: it is all down to you, no question about it. You've been the best thing that's happened to Owen for a long time and I'm thrilled for him!'

She gave Ed a broad smile and wondered how she could show her gratitude. This nerdy but very kind man had taken her shy and wobbly son under his wing for no reason other than he seemed to really like Owen and wanted to help him progress.

Quite spontaneously, Annie opened up her arms and threw Ed a generous hug and a kiss on the cheek.

The effect of this on Ed was unexpected.

He kissed her back, first on the cheek and then, turning his head slightly, he sought her mouth.

His eyes turned down to level with hers and she caught a glimpse of how darkly blue they were in the dim light of the stairwell. She thought she saw something questioning there, but before she could read it properly, their lips had brushed together and they *seemed* to be kissing.

Her lips were pressed against his, his arms were tightly around her back, her mouth was feeling for more and yes, they did definitely seem to be kissing.

She felt the prickle of stubble at the corner of his mouth . . . her hands moved to his warm neck, then underneath his jacket, under his arms and down to the small of his back. Her tongue quite of its own accord ventured past his teeth. There she had found a reassuringly warm tinged with coffee taste.

His tongue responded and she found it textured, on the drier side of damp, interestingly mobile and very,

very satisfyingly kissable. Yes, this was definitely kissing.

Owen's class teacher's hand was on her arse. There may have been a raincoat, a skirt, tights and a pair of knickers to go, but Ed had definitely moved his hand onto her derrière.

Annie would have quite liked to have stopped for a moment to assess the situation. The kissing of Ed. To debate it a little. Think it through. She wasn't sure if she would like to be in this situation, if she had time to consider it carefully. She would probably tell herself that this was not a good situation, this was a situation fraught with problems. Totally off-track. It could even have something to do with telling Gray this afternoon that she was going to move in with him. Surely this was a reaction? A strange and unexpected reaction . . . but nevertheless a definite reaction.

But there was no chance of stopping to think for even a moment because she was enjoying this so much. Her toes were curling in her boots, there was a hungry tingle starting up in the very pit of her stomach and it was threatening to get warmer, hungrier, tinglier and to spread.

Her hands had pulled up his shirt and were now against the very soft, warm skin at his sides. How had this happened? She was in the process of undressing the poor man in the stairwell.

Ed was squeezing at her bottom in a particularly tickly and quite fascinating way. She did not want him to stop. But he really should stop . . .

Finally, she broke off from the intense exploration of his mouth and briefly leaned her head against his shoulder.

But she found she wanted his mouth again, the warmth of it, the way his tongue moving against hers made her body tingle spread. So then they were kissing again. With urgency.

Her fingers wound themselves into his tangly hair. His hands behind her back pulled her closer towards him.

When she realized her hand was on the smooth leather of his belt, sliding along towards the buckle with intent, with a purpose all of its own, she opened her eyes.

She pulled back from the kiss and took a small step backwards. His eyes were very dark blue now, his lips not just full and pink but also damp. His cheeks were flushed, but there was no frantic blushing, a smile was just about to break and he was much, much better looking than she'd noticed before. Now she got a glimpse of what all the fuss was with the St Vincent's mothers and Ed. He was genuinely cute . . . when he didn't have a yellow cagoule tied around his head, obviously.

'Ed,' she said, trying to keep her voice as level as she could and making a small adjustment to the angle of the beret she was wearing (yup, blame the red beret), 'I think we may have overstepped the parent–teacher relationship here.'

'Completely,' was his reply. His eyes were still on hers and he gave a little smile.

'I'm sorry, I have to go,' she said abruptly, suddenly not wanting to be in this situation at all. For goodness' sake, she'd just agreed to move in with Gray . . . what was she playing at? Did she want to sabotage the new

292

happiness she was so sure was just around the corner for her?

As quickly as she could, not looking back, not giving him any reason to think she might want him to follow, or call after her, or in fact do anything at all, she hurried past him, out of the stairwell door, pulling it firmly shut behind her. Because really, anything else would have been far too complicated.

With great care and attention, Gray reversed his red, still slightly smelly, Merc into the slightly too small parking space in front of Annie's block. It took him three attempts to make the manoeuvre and he could feel sweat pricking from his armpits by the end of it. He would not miss visiting this cramped corner of London for one moment. Thank God she'd agreed to move.

On the passenger's seat beside him was the enormous bunch of flowers he'd ordered as soon as she'd phoned him with her decision. He'd considered having it delivered to her home, but then he'd decided it would be far, far more romantic to take the flowers in person.

He locked the car with the remote, then, flowers in one hand, bottle of champagne in the other, he strode along the pavement to her door. There was a guy ahead of him who was approaching the block as well. A scruffy-looking bloke: washed-out jeans, baggy shirt and a godawful green cord jacket, he needed a haircut as well. This man too was carrying a bunch of flowers but it was the sorriest, scrappiest bunch Gray had ever seen. Limp weeds from the back of the garden compared with the fat lilies, prime pink roses and scented stocks packed into his bouquet.

'You after the Valentines?' Gray asked, noticing the man's finger head towards Annie's buzzer.

'Yes I am. You too?' The man turned to face him for the first time and moved his hand from the buzzer without pressing it.

'Oh! Are you the music teacher? Ed the Shed? That's what they call you, isn't it?' Gray was trying to remember what Annie had told him about this character: one of those slightly nutty professor types by the look of him.

'I'm Owen's teacher . . . yes,' Ed replied, 'Ed Leon. I've not heard the other name before,' he added with some irritation.

'Have you got a lesson on?' Gray asked.

'No. No. That was earlier in the evening. I was just . . . ermm . . .' He lifted his bunch of flowers slightly.

'Those aren't for Lana are they, mate?' A note of concern had entered Gray's voice now. 'Annie's very protective of Lana and you wouldn't want to give either of them the wrong idea.'

There was a very cool tone to Ed's pointed 'These aren't for Lana.' *Who was this arrogant shit who'd just got out of the flashy Merc?*

As Ed hadn't offered any further explanation, Gray felt compelled to ask a baffled 'Are they for Owen?'

'No!' Ed really didn't want to add more, but felt forced into admitting, 'They're for Annie.'

Gray managed to check the laugh he wanted to make in response to this and lifting his own extravagant bouquet and champagne bottle up slightly said, 'These are for Annie too, she's agreed to move in with me. Her and the children. So I've brought these to celebrate.'

There was a pause as Ed seemed to struggle slightly with his response to this. He put his hand to his head and scratched at an imaginary itch.

'Tell you what,' Gray leaned in chummily. 'Would you like me to take yours up too? Save you the journey?'

Ed looked up at him: the guy was tall, his aftershave expensive but just a touch too noticeable. 'No, no,' he waved the offer away; his grip on the flowers had loosened and they were now pointing towards the ground. 'It's just a bunch from the garden, I'll pick some another day. No big deal. I was just passing. If you two are celebrating . . . I'll leave you to it. Honestly.'

'Sure?' came Gray's question, friendly now.

'No, no . . . congratulations. She's a . . .' Once again he found himself struggling for the words. 'They're a . . . lovely family.'

'Thank you.'

If Gray had followed Ed round the corner, he'd have seen him throw the flowers, fiercely, with a bowler's overarm, over a hedge and into a neighbouring garden.

Chapter Twenty-three

Donna on the warpath:

Red and white tunic (Anna Sui)
Linen trousers (Whistles)
White heels (Gucci)
Gold tassel necklace (Erickson Beamon)
Est. cost: £730

'Flouncing round here like you own the place.'

Fern had a wedding to go to. Annie's mother always had weddings to go to. As soon as the summer loomed, she was in need of one new wedding outfit or, at least, new accessories to 'refresh' older wedding outfits.

Annie never went to weddings any more: her friends had either been married for years or had no intention of ever marrying. Annie went to divorce mop-ups rather than wedding celebrations.

Whereas Fern had a busy schedule of remarriages and the weddings of her children's friends, at least three, sometimes even five or six a year.

Fern was that woman of a certain age in a wonderful hat who propped up a wedding, who could be counted on to give an expensive gift from the gift list – not something radical and alternative – who would look good in the church and good in the photos without in any way upstaging the bride, bridesmaids or, more likely, the bride's and groom's mothers.

She was a moral support guest, who understood her role as part of the glamorous backdrop. She was your classic third guest on the left, who enjoyed every wedding she attended.

'I'm not shopping in your shop,' she'd instructed Annie on the phone. 'Even with your discount, the prices are absolutely ridiculous. Jaeger, Annie. That's where we'll go. I want something beige . . .' Before Annie could groan in response, Fern added, 'I've got this sensational hat, cocoa straw with a wonderful cream gardenia, you want to smell it, it's so lifelike. A beige jacket will be just the thing.'

Jaeger was a disaster, though. 'Just office clothes,' Fern had sniffed at the selection. 'Black and white, white and black, black stripes, black spots, geometrics, where's the fun in that? And so brutal on the complexion.'

Annie's mother was a faded brunette. She'd once had creamy skin, auburn brown hair and sumptuous brown eyes, so she'd never liked black. She'd always set herself off in plum, fuchsia, red, beige, white and dusty greens.

As she'd gone grey, she'd also begun to highlight with caramel blond. The colour change had demanded new lipsticks and new clothes colours.

Plum had been replaced by burgundy and rust,

fuchsia with rose pink, red with pale orange and egg yolk yellow.

Fern had an enviable understanding of which colours suited her. Most of the people Annie dressed had never got to grips with colour and wondered why they always looked so washed out or so flushed . . .

As Annie shopped with her mother, she enjoyed another admirable trait: her mother never once uttered the words: 'I look so' – insert derogatory word – 'bad', 'fat', 'hippy', 'short', 'stumpy', 'frumpy' (you name it, Annie had heard it) 'in this.'

No. With Fern it was always reversed: the garment was to blame.

'Annie! Look how badly they've cut the back,' or 'Oh these seams don't sit well at all', 'The shoulders are a disaster', 'This colour does nothing for me.'

It was another message Annie tried to impart to her more timid, understated shoppers.

'Blame the clothes! Not yourself! Let's find the right thing. The cut and the colour that does you justice. And if it's still not right, you know what? We'll get it altered.'

Her mother pulled back the curtain and came out onto the shop floor in a beautiful creamy-beige suit. A very simple cut: nipped-in jacket, no lapels, a just-below-the-knee panelled skirt.

She would wear her hat, the inevitable hideous sandals, a pink rose corsage and a ruffle-necked blouse underneath.

'Maybe in pink as well?' she wondered out loud. 'Or cocoa . . . so as not to be too matchy? What do you think?'

'Cocoa . . . or creamy, something to highlight the

gardenia? Or beige, toning, so's not to introduce too many colours?'

'Hmmm.' Fern contemplated herself carefully in the mirror, taking in all the angles.

'Handbag?' Annie wondered.

'The little brown alligator, you know, the secondhand shop one you gave me. It's a treasure. It goes with everything.'

Annie felt the nice glow of giving the right gift.

'Oh, I met the dentist's wife, you know. Marilyn,' Fern said all of a sudden.

'Oh right, yes . . .' Annie tried to sound as casual as possible, but could not have been more interested. She'd still not even seen a photograph of Marilyn but imagined her as this impossibly slim, glamorous, fragile Jackie O type creature so weak with hunger and fraught with mental torture that she rarely had the energy to get off the sofa for anything other than a taxi ride to the shops.

'Because you've been out with Gray a few times, haven't you?' Fern was still turning herself carefully before the mirror.

'Aha . . . yeah.' Annie had not exactly kept her mother up to speed with the rapid developments on the Gray front. Why? Maybe just because she didn't want another opinion on it. Her own vacillations and Dinah's strident views (*You're going to do what?! You're moving to Essex for him?! Are you out of your MIND?!!!!'*) were quite enough to be getting on with.

'Well, Marilyn did not have one good thing to say about him,' Fern forged ahead. 'And you have to admit, Annie, he may be charming, but he is a pernickety fusspot. I mean, those are good qualities in a dentist, but not necessarily in a man. I know I invited him to that party for you . . . but with hindsight. Anyway, Marilyn was terribly upset. She'd always assumed Gray was going to sell their house and split the proceeds with her. In fact she has Ronald on the case – so you can be sure she'll be getting as much as she possibly can.'

Ronald being another family friend. In fact, Fern went to their youngest daughter's wedding just last year.

'So Gray's decided not to sell?' Annie prompted her.

'According to Marilyn, Gray has told Ronald he has a new partner, it's serious, they're getting married just as soon as the divorce is through and he's moving this person into the house as soon as possible. So he's claiming he needs the house, this new person has children . . . it's his asset, he's paid for it, he's keeping it.'

'Well, he has a point,' Annie decided to wade in on behalf of Gray. 'Marilyn has no children and has never worked.'

'Hmmm.' Her mother sniffed just a little, as if this was absolutely no excuse for anyone to be turfed out by their husband.

'He's not exactly planning to leave her destitute . . . I'm sure,' she added quickly, not to make it seem as if she had too much insider information on the case.

'No. I'm sure there's a valuable settlement to be made. Gray is a very wealthy man. You've no idea how much money there is to be made in dentistry. It's not just fillings, you know: veneers, implants, bleaching. People are going quite crazily American about their teeth.'

There was a moment's pause and Annie was just about to take that deep breath and tell her mother that she was Gray's new woman, that she was seriously considering the move to Gray's rooftop-jacuzzied corner of Essex, when her mother added: 'Of course Ronald, whom I met out at dinner the other week, at Eloise's, you know, the Clarks, wonderful cook . . . really, superb food. Although pumpkin risotto as a starter is not my absolute favourite, bit autumnal, heavy stodge—

'Ronald?' Annie reminded her, sensing the danger close at hand of having to hear Eloise's entire menu for the night.

'Yes, Ronald is convinced it's a total scam by Gray. Move some poor woman in, keep the house, then ditch her again.'

'I thought you said he was a charming man!' Annie could barely contain her outrage.

'Well, people do get funny about money though, don't they? Always brings out the worst in everyone, arguing about money.'

'So what do you think?' Annie wondered. 'You know him fairly well, don't you?'

'Oh, God knows. I've not seen him for months. I'm overdue a check-up in fact. Maybe I'll book in and try and hear it from the horse's mouth.'

Move some poor woman in . . . keep the house . . . then ditch her . . . Just the thought of this happening . . . just the thought of people thinking it might happen. It was totally riling her.

'Mum. It's me,' Annie blurted out. 'It's us. We're moving in with Gray.'

'What!' Fern exclaimed, looking astonished at this news. 'My God, why haven't you told me anything about this? Last I heard, you were dinner dating and then . . . you know . . . you went all quiet about him and I didn't like to ask. Good grief, Annie, isn't this a bit soon? I mean you have to think about the children.' She sat down abruptly on the changing room stool.

'Of course I've thought about the children. A big part of the reason I'm doing this is for them. But you know, it's a trial period. I'm going to rent our flat out for six months and see how it goes.'

Her mother did not look impressed.

'Is he serious though, love? You don't think he's doing this for the money?' she asked.

'No! Of course I don't. Maybe he's a bit desperate for the company. Maybe he's speeding things along for that reason, but you know . . . we get on very well,' came Annie's reply.

What Annie didn't add was how much she wanted the company too. The best thing about moving in with Gray was that she would no longer be the only adult in the household. She would have someone to kiss good night, someone right there next to her when she woke up every morning.

There would be someone to sit and open a bottle of wine with, someone to really talk to. She would no longer, every day, have to cope and battle and try to pretend that everything was just great and she was getting along just fine. If she moved in with Gray, she would have someone else there, to help her through. She would have back-up. A security net. Her children would no longer have to rely on just her. Right now, these reasons were more important to her than anything else.

Back at The Store after shopping with her mother, Annie was hardly pleased to be told on arrival at the Personal Shopping suite that Donna wanted to see her. She climbed the escalator and tried not to worry too much about what Donna might have to say to her today. Like it or not, she was still Donna's very best sales assistant and that had to count for something.

She knocked on Donna's office door and was asked to come in.

One look at Donna's sucking-on-a-sour-plum face and she felt her heart sink. This wasn't going to go well, she just knew it.

'You've been taking The Store's customers to other shops,' Donna began.

Before Annie could even get a question in, Donna continued: 'Don't even bother trying to deny it. Apparently you were doing a consultation in Jaeger this morning, during time you're employed by The Store.'

'I had a couple of hours off this morning to meet my mum,' Annie defended herself. 'She's shopped in Jaeger since I was knee-high, I'm not going to stop her now.'

Undeterred, Donna carried on: 'I've seen you leave our shop with customers so you can take them some-where else. I've seen you, Annie. I saw you leave with a male customer who bought nothing in the menswear department, and head off for Jermyn Street.'

For a moment Annie was confused. Then it dawned on her that Donna had seen her with Ed that day.

'But that was . . .' she began, not sure what she was

303

going to say next. *A special case? An eccentric individual who could find nothing right here?* It was a slightly lunatic defence, even she could see that.

But Donna wasn't even stopping to listen. 'Although you're in possession of a written warning from me, you're constantly advising people to shop elsewhere. I heard you telling one woman to get her dresses at Topshop and buy her Chloé bag on eBay!'

Like this was the worst crime in the world. Like Donna had never, ever snapped up a little bargain here or there; as if she'd only ever bought every single item including her toilet paper at The Store.

'You can't *sack* me for any of these things,' Annie told her, still standing, hackles up, more than ready to fight.

'No,' Donna said, leaning forward in her chair now, eyes locking on to Annie's. 'But I can sack you for theft.'

'Theft?' Annie almost laughed. 'I'd like to see you try. I've never stolen anything in my entire life. Not even an unpaid grape from the greengrocer's.'

'Oh, really?'

There was something so ominously catty about this that Annie could only suspect Donna had something on her. But what? She did honestly believe that she'd never, ever stolen anything . . . not knowingly.

Donna picked a sheet of paper up from her desk. Annie had a bad feeling as it was handed over to her.

'Recognize this?' Donna asked.

It was a printout of a computer page. The image was faint but Annie could still make out a digital photograph of a handbag, a Marc Jacobs handbag, BNWT and serial number. It was the one she'd bought from Lana's website and had sold on the Trading Station for £490 last week.

Annie felt a lurching sensation in her stomach.

'Thanks to the serial number you've displayed so nicely here . . .' the note of triumph in Donna's voice was unbearable, 'I can tell you that this bag was stolen from our accessories department on the eighteenth of February. Maybe you'd like to explain how you ended up selling it?'

'I did not steal it, Donna.'

That much Annie could say, but her mind raced as she tried to work out what explanation she could offer. The bag had come from Lana and Lana's friends, the Syrup Six, who were in quite enough trouble at school. Running the charity website had been their last chance to make good. If it came out they'd been fencing stolen goods – or actually stealing them . . . Had one of the Syrup Six dared to come into The Store and walk off with a top designer handbag? That would mean police involvement and instant expulsion. Although Annie was certain Lana would not have stolen the bag, maybe she'd be expelled too for playing a part in the sales team.

The thing that was just so utterly infuriating was that usually Annie checked everything she sold as scrupulously as she could. She could count on one hand the number of fakes she'd flogged on by mistake. But this bag . . . of course she'd seen straight away it was genuine, and she'd assumed (Argh! Assume and be damned) that some incredibly rich pupil or their in-credibly rich parent had made a little retail mistake and decided to be generous and offload it on the website.

It hadn't crossed her mind for a moment (and she was

usually so careful!) that the bag could be stolen . . . and from her own shop. Jesus. There was nothing she could tell Donna without landing Lana and her friends in huge trouble. And even then, couldn't Donna imply that she'd somehow put the girls up to it? Then she considered the rumours that would stir up at St Vincent's. Lana's mother had stolen an expensive bag from her shop to put on the charity website . . . It was all horrible.

'I had no idea the bag was stolen. I never, ever knowingly sell stolen items,' Annie told Donna. 'I can't explain to you how I got that bag because someone, who couldn't have known about it, would get into trouble,' she continued. 'I did not steal it, Donna. At least show me you believe that!'

Donna just kept her gaze trained on Annie's face.

There was a Roman expression, wasn't there? To fall on your sword. Annie saw that her moment of sword-falling had arrived: completely out of the blue. She was going to have to leave. Right now. Without a fuss. Cave in to Donna completely. Even though Donna's sales figures for the next few months would be on the floor, she wouldn't care because she'd be rid of the one person who consistently dared to stand up to her.

Annie would have to leave her white-walled, pink-sofa-ed suite, her daily dose of rubbing shoulders with Yves St Laurent workmanship, Paul Smith tailoring and multi Missoni colours. Even worse, she would have to leave The Store's staff: Avril, Delia, Paula, Janie in Accounts. There would be no more weekly happy hour sessions, no more staff discount, no more sale rail bargains, no more Tupperware boxes from the staff canteen.

'I'll get my things.' Annie's voice was so husky, she barely recognized it.

Donna just nodded.

It was only sinking in for Annie that if she were to leave in disgrace, there'd be no pay-off, no severance pay. She might not even be paid for the rest of the month.

'You have to give me references!' Annie exclaimed, feeling a wave of panic. 'You can't put me down as leaving for theft. I'll never get another job and you know, Donna, you know that I would never, ever have done something like this. Everything I get from The Store I pay for, fair and square. Does HR know about this?' she asked anxiously.

There was almost a smile playing about Donna's lips. Annie would love to have smacked her, right there and then.

'I suppose I could tell HR you left for personal reasons . . . a personality clash, maybe?'

'Well, that wouldn't be a lie, would it?' Annie retorted. Then as something of the enormity of losing her job of six years, when she was the sole provider for her children, began to dawn on her, she suddenly found herself appealing: 'You can't do this, Donna. Are you really going to sack me? I'm your best sales assistant. Couldn't you at least give me time to find something somewhere else? I've got my children's—'

'School fees to pay . . . oh yes, yes, Annie, my heart bleeds,' Donna snapped. 'No. I've had enough of you. Flouncing round here like you own the place, like The Store owes you a living, like everyone should be constantly doing you a favour, giving you a discount, letting you claim all the damaged goods and sell them right under our noses because we should all feel so, so sorry for you . . . just because your husband . . .' She broke off abruptly and the rest of her words hung in the air.

'Donna,' Annie said, pulling herself up straight, feeling her fight and her fire return, 'I might be many things and wrong in many ways, but at least I'm not a heartless, ruthless bitch like you.'

She should of course have thought to phone Gray first, but instead she phoned the man who'd been her first port of call for several years now.

'You've been *what*?!' was Connor's astonished response. 'OK, sweetheart, you know what to do. If you've been fucked over, you've got to be Dog and Ducked over. And quickly. Name the drinking establishment of your choice and I can be there within the hour.'

Chapter Twenty-four

Gray at home:

Pink V-neck golfing sweater (Pringle)
Beige chinos (Gant)
White T-shirt (Gap)
Crested velvet slippers (Jermyn Street)
Est. cost: £270

'But they're comfortable!'

Gray's immaculate house was not looking quite so good these days. His hotel-tidy master bedroom was lined with the racks and stacks of clothes, accessories and items currently for sale on the new and improved Annie V Trading Station. His once super-orderly walk-in wardrobe was crammed as Annie's many, many belongings fought with his for shelf and rail space.

The guest bedrooms had become home to Owen and all his paraphernalia – most of it still in cardboard boxes – and Lana and her endless clothes, make-up, CDs, DVDs and currently atrocious teen tantrums.

Several things had gone wrong at once for Lana: Seth had finally snipped off their budding romance, plus her allowance had been severely docked for her part in fencing the stolen bag which had cost Annie her job at The Store: *'Suzie's boyfriend!? The bag came from Suzie's dodgy boyfriend?!'* Annie had shrieked at her. *'Why didn't you tell me? Why didn't it cross your mind that there might be something not right about it? Boyfriends don't just show up with six-hundred-pound bags! I thought it was from some loaded St Vincent's mum.'*

It was obvious from Lana's long face and even longer sulks that she missed Highgate, especially the regular after-school visits with friends. Having a friend over was now a weekend-only event involving an overnight stay.

'Give it a chance here,' Annie kept urging her. 'You'll meet some people. Maybe you should join the tennis club? You love tennis.'

But suggestions like this were met with slammed doors and shouts of 'It's OK for you, but what about us?'

At least Owen seemed fine, but then he'd always liked the company of his family and himself best. He was playing the guitar a lot, listening to music and could sometimes be found at the very top of the apple tree in Gray's garden.

Gray was finding family life something of a change. He had never experienced noise or mess on a scale like this. Because it was a school holiday, the children were always around, underfoot, when he came back from work. He stumbled about his home, tripping over new piles of stuff in unexpected places. He found his sofa already occupied, his plasma TV screen blaring out end-less reruns of *Friends*, his jacuzzi filled with three embarrassingly nubile teen girls, his kitchen utterly void of anything edible, although it was now stacked with Annie's cash and carry treasures: industrial sized boxes of clingfilm and tinfoil, 80 rolls of kitchen towel, 1,000 bin bags. His new live-in lover was surprisingly unavailable: either on her mobile, at her computer or out again, making another round of house calls, con-sultations, drop-offs or pick-ups.

Ever since she'd left The Store, Annie had woken up every morning ready to hustle. Within four days, her flat had been stripped of everything personal, redecorated with the vigorous application of Dulux Once, and she and the children had moved to Gray's while tenants paying top dollar had moved in.

With her mortgage payments covered, Annie had turned her attention to earning enough money to keep the children at St Vincent's and her with the monthly income she was accustomed to. This meant a rapid expansion of the Trading Station and her own Dress to Express makeover and personal shopping service.

Things weren't looking too bad; she was learning that Gray's corner of Essex was ripe with well-heeled women who hadn't the slightest clue how to accessorize and weren't shy about recommending her services to all their friends. The only downside to drumming up all this business was that Gray didn't seem to like it very much.

'You know, Annie, I don't really want you to work so hard,' he was telling her again, one evening over a glass of red wine as they sought sanctuary out on the garden terrace from the noisy goings-on in the sitting room.

Several days ago, he'd suggested she become his PA; now he was bringing the subject up again.

'You could help me with my admin, keep track of all my meetings, appointments . . .' he said. 'It won't keep you as busy as you are now, so you'll be around a lot more, for me and your children. Obviously, I'll keep on my secretary at work . . . and I'll pay you.'

Of course the idea of not working so hard was appealing, but did she want to work for Gray? Would that be a good plan? There were quite enough teething problems: arguments about food on the sofa (last night's) and using a spoon for the jam (this morning's) without Annie risking a move into Gray's work life and being told off for not doing things quite the way he wanted there as well.

'I'll have to think about it,' she said. 'What would you pay me anyway? . . . What!?' was her undisguised surprise at the figure. 'How do you expect me and mine to survive on that?'

'Well' Gray was flustered, taken aback by her reaction. 'Now that you live with me there are lots of things you don't have to pay for. I don't expect you to pay anything towards the house, I'm happy to pay the bills, groceries, this is money just for you.'

'My pin money?' she'd asked with more than a touch of sarcasm.

'Well, that's a bit old-fashioned,' he replied. 'What I mean is . . . Marilyn was my PA, she spent her wages on herself and I paid for everything else—'

'Gray . . .' Annie cut him off, 'don't misunderstand me,

312

it's lovely that you're well-off and that you want to help us out, but Marilyn did not have two children of her own to keep in school. I have always, *always* supported myself and the children and often Roddy too when his parts were few and far between and his shitty employers took months to pay. Relying on you to pay for us and to give me a tax-deductible little allowance is out of the question.' She drained her glass, set it down on the table between them and gave him the stern look which he was learning meant: no further discussion.

In slight need of a change of subject, he decided to ask: 'Are you doing much tomorrow?'

'I've got a home consultation in the morning, but I'm not too busy after that. I'll just be at my day job, buying and selling.' With a smile she added: 'I'm a stockbroker of used commodities. Like my job description? Anyway, why? Have you got something planned for tomorrow?'

'I've invited my parents round. I mean, I said I'd check with you first, obviously . . .'

'For drinks?'

'Well, no. I think I might have said dinner . . .'

Annie had not yet met Gray's parents, although she'd heard plenty about them. They were in their early eighties, but apparently this had not dimmed their sharp opinions, pointed criticism of and interminable stream of advice to their precious one and only son.

'They were very fond of Marilyn,' he had warned her earlier. 'I'm afraid moving you three in has put them in a huff. It's going to take weeks to talk them round.'

Now, obviously, they had been talked round and were to meet over a civilized dinner – which Annie was to provide, presumably, as Gray had a full day's work ahead of him.

'Why don't we all go out for dinner?' she suggested.

'Well, I just thought for Lana and Owen's sake . . . they can go off and do their own thing . . . won't have to sit and listen to us talk all evening.'

He had a point.

'I mean, if it's a problem . . .'

Hadn't Gray noticed that she couldn't cook? Hadn't he realized that most of her meals came in a plastic tray with a wrapper ready to be heated in the microwave?

'No, no, it's not a problem,' she insisted, wondering in which removals box one of her three barely touched cookbooks might be found – and what kind of simple, but nevertheless impressive, dish could be served up for six.

'I'll go and phone them then?' Gray asked. 'They're looking forward to meeting you.'

'Oh yes. I bet they are. Are you feeling cold?' she wondered. 'Why don't we go inside?'

Such was Gray's horror of the mess and mayhem going on in his sitting room that he replied: 'No, no, I'm fine, but I can bring you out a jacket if you like.'

Annie didn't make it back to Gray's house until after 2 p.m. the next day, later than she'd intended, considering his parents were due at seven. The home consultation had been long and involved: a woman in her fifties who had found it very hard to see beyond navy blue and even harder to see beyond her – admittedly substantial, but hardly disastrous – thighs and hips.

'I don't have any tricks to disguise hips,' Annie had informed her. 'That's not my thing, darlin'. What we want to do is bring your lovely blue eyes to the fore, your shapely calves and wrists, not to mention your beautiful pale neck and upper chest and when we've done all that, you'll find the hips quieten right down.'

After the consultation, Annie had rushed over to one of her latest suppliers to secure her trump card for tonight.

Laid out across the back seat of the Jeep, carefully wrapped in many layers of damp newspaper, was a whopping great fish.

In her regular trips to the cash and carries of Essex, her endless quest for trade suppliers, discount outlets and bargains, she'd made quite a few new friends. One of them, who was a fishmonger, had supplied tonight's centrepiece at a superb price.

An enormous line-caught wild Scottish salmon. The beast was so long and so heavy, she'd barely been able to wrestle it into the back seat. The plan was to make new potatoes, a lovely salad, hollandaise sauce – if Dinah was available to talk her through it step by step on the telephone – then strawberries, cream and meringues to follow.

She would start on the meringues just as soon as she got back. She would keep calm. She had a full four hours ahead of her. It was simple enough, nothing too complicated. There was plenty of time for everything to turn out fine. What could go wrong?

'Jesus! Owen! Could you have made any more mess? Where's Lana?' was Annie's reaction on surveying the state of the front room, strewn with crisp packets, DVD boxes, socks, sheet music and whatever else. *How much longer was half-term going to go on for?* she couldn't help asking herself.

'In her room, crying,' came Owen's reply.

'What now?'

'Nothing, just the same as usual. *Seth, Seth . . . I'll never love anyone as much as you . . . waaaah,*' he mocked.

'Stop it. That's mean. Can you please start clearing up in here? Gray's parents are coming for dinner, remember? I better go and talk to her.'

It took thirty vital minutes to talk Lana from blotchy-faced misery into some sort of useful state:

'There, there, babes . . . You will start to feel better really soon, I promise. I know everyone says it, but there really are plenty more fish in the sea . . . Young hearts do mend quickly, I promise you . . . In a couple of weeks you're going to be over him.'

And in exasperation when that didn't work: *'He was far too old for you . . . boys that age are just totally unreliable . . . and anyway, he was covered in acne . . . even on his back.'*

And finally losing all patience: *'I'm sorry, I don't care any more! You'll just have to blow your nose, bring your tissues and come and help me downstairs.'*

At last, Annie had Lana employed in the house along with Owen, hoovering, plumping cushions, cunningly disguising packing boxes with tablecloths and throws.

With a great deal of concentration, Annie managed to separate one dozen eggs: whites into one bowl for the meringues, yolks into another for the hollandaise.

Then her mobile rang and she was very surprised to hear Svetlana on the line.

In a few breathless sentences the former Miss Ukraine spelled out the crisis going on in her life. Potato-faced Igor, who had doubtless cheated on her in the past, had now inevitably met someone much younger, much more beautiful and willing, so he had filed for *divorce*!

But the billionaire gas baron, with an eye towards safeguarding every penny of his fortune, had filed in Russia, leaving Svetlana convinced she was going to get nothing.

'I am phoning all my Russian friends, they are putting me into a panic,' Svetlana was blurting into Annie's ear. 'I think: I must phone an English friend and I think of you.'

Annie couldn't help but be flattered by this elevation in status from stylist to friend. Although it didn't say much about the multiculturalism of Svetlana's inner circle.

'Darlin', you've got to calm down, right now,' Annie said as soothingly as she could. 'You live in London. Your children were both born here, right?'

'Yes, at the Portland, yes.'

'Darlin', the boys are English. I'm certain, absolutely certain he can't mess you about. He can't divorce you in Russia, I'm sure you can make sure it goes through the English courts.'

'But his fortune, his estate is Russian, all in Russia,' Svetlana went on, her voice rising. 'He can hide things, hide everything from the English courts. He's told me this before. Annie, if I don't agree, I'm going to lose everything. He will threaten to take the boys away . . .'

'Svetlana, calm down, calm down, darlin'.' The Russian had Annie's full attention now: the bowls of separated eggs had been completely forgotten. 'You've been talking to your Russian pals, haven't you? But this is not a Dostoevsky novel . . .' Somewhere up there, her late Francis Holland English teacher was smiling. 'Babes, you live in a sixteen-bedroomed mansion in Mayfair, Igor would have a job hiding that, and that alone would probably see you comfortably all the way through retirement.'

There was a pause while Annie thought hard about what Svetlana needed to do next. Suddenly, it was obvious.

'You know what?' she began. 'I know someone who has been through a very nasty divorce with big money at stake. I'm sure I can ask her which lawyer you need, so keep your phone close and I'll come back to you just as soon as I can.'

It hadn't occurred to Annie before just how powerful the women who formed her client base at The Store could be . . . and she had all of their mobiles on speed-dial, in order to inform them at the press of a button when something new and perfect for them had come in.

Aha . . . and here was the number of the very glamorous forty-something whose monumental divorce settlement had made headlines. Now, she would just explain Svetlana's situation, get the name of the QC who had done the business and call the soon to be ex-billionaire's wife straight back.

'Hi! Megan? How are you? Yes, it's Annie Valentine. Not of The Store any more . . .'

When Annie got back on the line to Svetlana, she was in for a surprise.

'Got a pen and paper, babes?' she asked. 'His name is Harry Roscoff, of Roscoff, Barry and Mosse . . . How will you pay for him?!' It had never occurred to Annie that Svetlana would have no money – that Potato-face would already have cut off her allowance precisely so she couldn't cruise the streets of London in her chauffeured Bentley, chequebook in hand, in search of expert legal advice.

'You've no money?!' Annie asked incredulously.

'Not one penny.'

Once this had taken its moment or two to sink in, Annie issued the following instructions: 'OK, darlin', here's what you have to do. You fill up a big suitcase with some of the things in your wardrobe you don't want any more, the more bags, boots, shoes and labels the better. Then you tell me where I come to collect it from you and I will turn it into cash. I'll sell everything for the best possible rates. And absolutely not one penny of commission, babes. I'm doing this one for you.'

Now she didn't envy Svetlana her army of staff, her gilded lifestyle and her utter dependency on a total arsehole quite so much.

When she'd hung up, a glance at the clock caused Annie to swear and ram the slightly runny meringue mix into the oven, set the timer and begin to hunt round the still unfamiliar kitchen for a pot to cook the fish in.

'Dinah!!!!!! Why haven't I been able to get you on the phone for twenty minutes? Heeeeelp!'

'What's the matter?' Dinah exclaimed, totally panicked by an emergency call from her sister.

'I need you here. I can't cope. I can't do this on my own. I've only got two hours left.'

'Annie, what are you talking about?'

'I have to make dinner for Gray's parents and it's a total cock-up, everything's going wrong.'

'OK.' Dinah breathed something of a sigh of relief. 'Talk me through it.'

The bloody, blinking hollandaise had curdled . . . Annie was going to have to go out again in the car in search of more eggs . . . oh and the cream she'd forgotten. There was no pot in the entire house big enough for the fish . . . but Dinah was assuring her that salmon could be cooked in the dishwasher.

'The dishwasher!?' Annie did not sound convinced.

'Yes – provided you've got enough tinfoil. But you always do.'

'Oh yeah, I have no more eggs and no more cream, but I have enough bloody tinfoil to build the Tin bloody Man and his entire tin family.'

'That's my girl. You just put it on the hottest wash for thirty-five minutes and you must, *must* make sure there's no powder in the dispenser, obviously.'

It sounded simple enough.

'Will you talk me through the sauce on the phone when I get back with the eggs? Where are you? I can hear music.'

'I'm in the Rialto, hiding from the builders, I've got half an hour before I get Billie from ballet.'

Because the strangest things had happened to Dinah and Bryan just as soon as Annie had left London: Dinah had been offered the part-time job (doing admin at an art college) she'd always said she never wanted and Bryan had gone out and landed himself a major contract. Now, believe it or not, Dinah was having a new kitchen installed.

'Oh . . . how's the Rialto?' Suddenly Annie felt a swoop of longing for the bustling Italian café she and Dinah liked best for coffee.

'Oh, you know, same old, same old, the bacon got left in the grill so it's pretty smoky today. What do you do in Upper Ploxley for coffee?'

'DIY,' was Annie's gloomy reply. 'Café culture has not made it this far east, sadly. Bugger. Damn . . .'

'Charming,' Dinah commented.

'I've just realized that bleeping's the oven. Balls! The meringues! Call you later.'

'Eton mess, remember, Annie!' were Dinah's parting words. 'If your meringues are crap, scrunch them up with strawbs and cream and call it Eton mess.'

It wasn't the colour of the meringues which was so bad – well, more roasted than lightly toasted – it was the shape. They'd merged, they'd moulded . . . they'd become as one. She had a baking tray entirely covered in one great big sandy brown, slightly crispy meringue.

'Never mind . . . Eton mess,' she told herself as she scratched and scraped large chunks into a bowl. Mix with cream, loads of strawberries and . . . Bob's your uncle.

She loaded up the dishwasher, put in the powder and turned it on, so she could empty it out later, all ready for the wrapped fish, then she rushed out to get eggs and cream.

Back into the Jeep, back down the road, through the eight junctions and three sets of traffic lights, into the mega-supermarket, right down the aisles, locate eggs and cream, also buy more wine, party nibbles and other things to make the basket leaden heavy. As she bowled the Jeep back through the roads, eight junctions and three sets of traffic lights, she considered the convenience of life in Highgate: there, she'd have sent Owen out for eggs and cream and he'd have been back in under five minutes.

It was already approaching 5.30 as she stepped back into Gray's house to the sound of Connor calling out a hello from the kitchen.

'What the bloody hell are you doing here?' were her first words as she emerged from the bear hug he treated her to.

'Just passing – well, filming – not a million miles away,' he managed through a full mouth. He swallowed then turned to pick up the glass of wine on the table behind him and swilled it down: 'Mmm . . . gorgeous,' he said.

'You've made yourself at home,' Annie said. 'That's not anything too fancy, is it?' She turned the wine bottle and saw a new-looking Spanish label. No, fortunately Connor hadn't broken into Gray's vintage French burgundies . . . or whatever they were, all neatly stacked from floor to ceiling in the pantry.

'Yup, Owen's an excellent host.' Connor gave her son, who was seated at the table with an empty bowl in front of him, a hearty pat on the back. 'So, what's for dinner? You're quite the little suburban Nigella these days, then?' he teased and she was tempted to punch him.

'You can't stay for dinner,' Annie told him. 'Gray's parents are coming. I'm meeting them for the first time and I'm totally stressed.'

Connor's reaction was to sit down, put his long legs up on the kitchen table, fold his arms behind his head and utter the challenge: 'Just try and make me leave, babes, just try and make me.'

Owen giggled as Annie told Connor, 'You can stay for a bit but by seven p.m., you are out of here.'

'C'mon . . . I'll help break the ice.'

'Shut up, will you! I have to get on . . . Owen, you do the salad, Connor, scrub the potatoes and I'll think about it . . . I have to phone Dinah about the sauce again.'

The next hour did not go happily. As Annie tried to make hollandaise again, Connor snuck up behind her and asked her heavy questions quietly.

'How's it working out?'

'It's fine. We're settling in . . . I think it's going to work out really well.'

'Aha . . . *fine* . . . *well* . . .' Then standing close behind her he whispered into her ear: 'And how's it going in the bedroom?' and made several pelvic thrusts against her hip for emphasis.

Unfortunately he chose the moment she was carefully pouring a spoonful of vinegar into the sauce.

'Jesus! Connor!' She tried to spoon the vinegar overflow out of the bowl as quickly as she could. 'It's fine, thank you,' she snapped. 'I'm not talking about it right now. I'm busy!'

'Oooooh tetchy . . . another "fine" from Annie.' Then in a suddenly serious voice, he added: 'He's got to be right, Annie, he's got to be the *Next* One . . . absolutely no-one says you have to settle.'

'Go away, Connor,' she growled, 'I can't have this conversation now. Open the dishwasher and check my fish.'

'What?!'

Connor opened the machine and let a cloud of scalding steam into the kitchen as Annie pulled back the fridge door to bring out her meringue mess and beaten cream.

'Smells lovely and lemony,' Connor commented.

'Lemony?! What??' Just as it was dawning on Annie that maybe she should have double-checked the powder drawer hadn't jammed shut on the last wash only to open and tip soap over her salmon, she also spotted the meringue bowl, totally empty, standing by the kitchen sink: 'Where the bloody hell are my . . . CONNOR! Did you and Owen eat the meringues?' she shouted.

'The scrapings . . . the leftovers, I told Owen those had to be . . .' Connor broke off. He could tell by Annie's face that it hadn't been a bowlful of scrapings they'd wolfed down.

'They were very good,' he said sheepishly.

'Aaaaaaargh!' She ran at him, but at the last minute veered to the dishwasher, which stank of lemony-bleachy dishwasher powder.

'Aaaaaaaargh!' she cried again.

Only for Gray to walk in, still in his raincoat, and ask what was the matter? And hello, Connor, and . . . could he smell fish? Didn't she remember his father was allergic to fish?

Annie ran out of the kitchen and into her bedroom where, in a melodramatically Lana-like style, she threw herself across the bed, right on top of the chic red and white Marc by Marc Jacobs dress she'd laid out for tonight, and began to sob noisily.

It wasn't just that she was exhausted, or a crappy

cook, or that she'd washed the salmon instead of cooking it, or that she'd completely forgotten about the fish
allergy. There was something else. She was frightened.
For the past few days she had been trying to suppress
the worry, but now it was bubbling up uncontrollably.
She was frightened that she'd made a mistake.

She was beginning to suspect that she didn't like
Upper Ploxley, didn't like suburban Essex life and all the
endless trips on the M11 ferrying grumpy children to
school.

And then there was Gray. It was only when she'd
moved in that she'd got a sense of how set in his ways
he was. How – dare she use the word? – old and
old-fashioned he seemed to her and the children.

He wore shabby purple velvet slippers round the
house ('But they're comfortable!') and wouldn't listen
to her protestations about them. Although he looked
dapper in a suit and tie, in his preferred golf V-neck
and chinos he didn't. He liked to read the paper,
undisturbed, from cover to cover, taking a full two
hours over it. The children bugged him. They made too
much noise for him, too much mess. They required
too much of her time and attention. He was used to a
pampering wife, who kept a neat house, had meals on
the table, and who ironed, and fussed over him. Maybe
he was sorry too. Maybe he was wondering what the
hell he'd got into. Maybe Fern's worst fears were true:
maybe Annie *was* being used as a tactic in the divorce
battle.

Annie found herself regularly replaying Roddy the
Early Days in her mind to try and remember if she'd felt
all the same worries then too. Had she experienced the

same feelings of claustrophobia and uncertainty when she and Roddy had first moved in together?

Now, when she thought back to that time, she remembered only delirious happiness: painting their tiny bedroom sexy pink . . . Roddy nursing her through appalling morning sickness because she got pregnant so soon . . . buying babygros and baby shoes, spending entire evenings entwined on the sofa, listening to each other's music collections with mock disgust and debating baby names.

But maybe she had been just as unsure, she kept telling herself, there must have been some moments of doubt. But she'd been so young. Nothing mattered so much when you were young. The stakes were not so high. You could give someone a whirl, you could back out and walk away. Well, OK . . . baby Lana would have made that more tricky, but still . . .

Now there was no denying that she'd made a great big, important decision, which affected both her and her children's lives, far too quickly.

But she couldn't just walk away . . . she had to be a grown-up and give it a real, considered chance.

In the kitchen, Gray made the mistake of telling Lana, Owen and Connor that he'd better go upstairs to see 'if I can calm down this tantrum'.

This caused Lana to jump up and shout: '*No*! No, you will not go up to my mum. How dare you call it a tantrum! Maybe if you hadn't asked your parents round on a day when my mum's working! Just expecting her to cook for you all like some sort of housekeeper! She can't cook! Haven't you noticed that yet? Haven't you worked out the slightest thing about her?'

'Lana,' Connor intervened, 'I think you're being a bit—'

'But look at him,' Lana raged. 'He doesn't do anything for himself, he's the most unreconstructed chauvinist pig I've ever met. He just wants to turn Mum into his housewife!'

'Lana, that is not true,' Gray insisted, riled by the accusation. 'I think you should stop, right now.'

'I'm going up to her,' Lana stormed. 'You can just keep away!'

With that she rushed out of the room.

Connor and Owen looked at each other in the ensuing silence. Owen shrugged his shoulders. It was hardly the first time Lana had shot her mouth off.

'Why don't you have a glass of wine?' Connor said amiably. 'Then probably best if you cancel your parents for tonight. Don't worry about all this. I'm sure it'll blow over . . . Teenagers! Total nightmare,' he tried to sympathize.

Gray let out a deep sigh, pulled up a chair and turned the bottle of wine towards him. His face grew several shades paler: 'For God's sake!' he exclaimed. 'That's my Dominio de Pingus 1996!'

When Connor's face failed to register any recognition, Gray spluttered: 'Very rare, Spanish . . . three hundred pounds a bottle . . . with excellent investment potential.'

'Ah . . . sorry . . .' Connor hung his head apologetically, then, reaching for a fresh glass, he added, 'I think you'd better have some.'

Chapter Twenty-five

Annie back in town:

Orangey red linen wrap dress (Joseph sale)
Beige mac (the trusty Valentino)
Large orange leather tote (Coccinelle on eBay)
Caramel heels (the Chanels, for morale)
Orangey red lipstick (Mac)
Est. cost: £390

'You're not dead yet, woman.'

Annie walked down the charming flagstoned pavement of one of her favourite Highgate streets. Smartly painted fences enclosed gardens brimming with blossoming lilac bushes, buddleia and honeysuckle.

Almost all of the three-storey Georgian houses had been beautifully and expensively renovated: lime mortar pointing restored, old wooden windows and doors repaired, fresh coats of historically appropriate Farrow and Ball paint applied, bright hanging baskets and windowboxes attached.

To buy a whole house on this street . . . at least £1.5 million, she reckoned, which is why most were carved up into bijou flats. It was still her property dream to own a house in Highgate – but maybe it would have to be something a little smaller than one of these. Just two storeys and a garden would be fine. She wasn't greedy.

She passed a plump thirty-something woman striding briskly along in navy blue shorts, a pale floral blouse and black pumps. A black shoulder bag with a narrow strap was strung diagonally across her chest, bisecting her cleavage to horrible effect.

Annie considered stopping her there and then to hand over a business card and urge her with the words: 'C'mon . . . you're not dead yet, woman, why have you given up?' What was it with some women and their attachment to black shoes and a matching black bag, anyway? Was it a hangover from school uniform? Or were they still clinging to the mistaken belief that black went with everything? Although black had a chance of going with lots of things in the winter, in summer it was hopeless.

Number 39 was not a house that had been renovated yet. The paint was flaking, the stonework was grubby, parts of the fence had rotted away. Absent landlord, she guessed, or maybe landlord down on his luck.

She'd been told to follow the garden path round to the back of the house where the entrance to the basement flat could be found: 39B.

Through the overgrown garden she went, damp flower stalks and shrub branches whipping at her legs as she negotiated the mossy, slippery path.

The black door was flaking paint and all the windows needed not just repainting but cleaning too. She pressed hard on the buzzer and after a few moments Ed appeared at the door, looking – despite her efforts – as much in need of care and attention as his home.

'Hello there, erm, Annie . . . why don't you come on in?' Ed gave her a smile and waved her into the cramped hallway.

A rack stuffed with coats, anoraks, walking boots, shoes and wellingtons had to be shuffled past before she could follow him into a tiny, low-ceilinged kitchen also crammed to bursting.

She took in the overflow of pots, pans, jars rammed with utensils, piles of newspaper, small table overwhelmed with a burden of books, pens and papers, as Ed made welcoming but slightly apologetic chat.

'Sorry . . . always such a mess . . . hopeless . . . can I get you a tea? Hope you don't have to rush off . . . Owen's getting on great . . .' and so on. His words were punctuated with several sneezes, smaller than the ones he used to startle them with.

She was here to collect Owen from his music lesson. Now that Ed could no longer swing round to their address, the new arrangement was that Owen would go home with Ed after school on Thursdays and Annie would pick him up at 7 p.m. But she'd been held up twice and had had to send Dinah, so this was her first visit to Ed's.

'Tea would be great, thanks,' Annie told him and knocked over a dish of cat food on the floor as she tried to get out of his way. Once he'd mopped up the spill with a dishcloth that went back into the sink, she noticed unhappily, he filled up a battered aluminium kettle and put it down on the ring of an ancient electric cooker.

'Come on, I'll take you through,' he offered and she followed gingerly, wondering what housekeeping horrors lay ahead.

The sitting room was reached by way of a tiny corridor lined with bookshelves so packed that books were stacked double thickness, and also piled up on the floor. The ceiling lamp hung so low that Annie bumped her head not just once but again when the lamp swung back at her.

The room had been painted dark pink and the curtains and sofa were of a faded and threadbare floral pattern. Some tartan rugs had been thrown about, to cosy things up a little, and the fireplace looked as if it had been used recently.

'Hi, Owen!' she called to her son, who was sitting cross-legged on the sofa, a guitar cradled between his knees.

'Listen to this,' was his response and he strummed her a complicated-sounding chord sequence.

'Brilliant,' she told him, still taking in the room around her. The upright piano, three guitars and a framed collection of concert posters were the kind of belongings Annie might have expect Ed to have. The breathtaking, voluptuous oil painting of a nude woman was a little more unexpected.

The frilly ornaments and porcelain figurines clogging up the mantelpiece and windowsills were also out of keeping and Annie was guessing that Ed was still curating every single item that had once belonged to his mother. He had not yet learned to let go of anything of hers.

The low ceiling above their heads dipped slightly in the middle. For how many decades had it been like that? she wondered. There was no denying the character of the place, even if it was a little dark and gloomy and in serious need of brilliant white paint. The doors all hung at a wonky angle, the floor squeaked and if she were to drop a marble, she suspected it would roll right towards the black fireplace at the side of the room.

As Owen played on, Ed came in bearing a little tray with two mugs and a teapot.

'Please, take a seat,' he insisted and as she settled herself into a saggy armchair, her amateur property developer's eye fell on the buckled skirting board and the peeling sheet of wallpaper working itself away from it. Turning her head, she surveyed the rest of the stretch of skirting board, also buckled with blistering paint and peeling paper above.

'Looks like you've got damp,' she told him.

'Oh . . .' Ed landed on the sofa, close to Owen's feet: 'These old places' – he waved a biscuit in the air – 'always have a touch of something.'

'No, Ed.' Annie lifted the flap of wallpaper and saw across the back, as she'd suspected, a plume of black mould. 'You've got damp and a serious mould situation and – '

With perfect timing, Ed gave one of his spectacular sneezes, so she could tell him, very convincingly, 'You're allergic to it. Most people would be.'

'You're joking!' he said and he came over to look at

332

the paper she was holding up. He sneezed again as soon as he was up close.

Owen came too and declared the situation 'gross' but nevertheless went on to tell Ed in detail all about the dry rot 'fruiting body' which had been discovered in the basement of their previous home.

'It was orangey-brown and huge and mushroomy, alive! It looked like it had just come down from outer space and was about to evolve into another life form,' he told them in an excited voice, a smile on his face, eyes twinkly with mischief.

'That's just lovely, Owen. Maybe you'd like to come into my coal-hole and we'll see if we can find something like that down there?'

'Yeah!'

'Right, well . . . something to look forward to for next week, I think.'

Owen's face fell, so Ed cheered him up with the request: 'Would you like to see if you can find Hoover and Dyson in the garden for me? My cats,' he said in response to Annie's raised eyebrows. 'They're the closest thing I have to a cleaner.'

'Erm . . . there's something I need to talk to you about,' Ed began a little awkwardly, once Owen was out of the back door and into the garden.

Annie felt just a flicker of nervousness. She looked at this increasingly familiar, yet still quite unknown, man on the sofa just a foot or so away and couldn't help but remember kissing – well, make that snogging – him in the stairwell.

Neither of them had ever referred to that . . . incident and she'd not given it a thought since it had happened.

333

Well . . . not really. But now her toes were tightly curled at the thought of him bringing it up.

He sat forward, elbows resting on his knees, and looked directly at her, terribly seriously.

'How's it going in Upper Ploxley?' he asked.

'It's fine,' she replied. 'Good,' she added quickly but then followed it up with, 'The commuting's a bit of a pain, but we'll get used to it.'

When he made no reply, but kept on looking at her questioningly, she felt compelled to add: 'I suppose we're all having some teething problems . . . settling in . . . finding our feet. But I really think it's going to work out for the best.'

'Do you?' he asked, still very serious. He leaned forward and looked directly at her. Oh brother, he was definitely about to mention the kissing, she knew it.

'Look, Ed,' she jumped in, 'if this is about what I – what we . . . you know, in the stairwell . . .' she stumbled. 'Look, I didn't mean anything by it. I don't want you to get the wrong idea. I was just very excited about Owen . . . and his solo . . . and I got carried away. I'm very happy with Gray,' she said with emphasis.

Ed's face seemed to cloud over. She'd tried to clear the air, but her words seemed to have had the opposite effect. He looked almost angry.

'No, I wasn't going to talk about that,' he said, making her want to kick herself hard. 'I thought I should tell you, in case you hadn't noticed, that Owen is not happy. He's stopped speaking in class and judging by how well his guitar playing is coming along, he must be in his room practising for hours every day. I'm delighted when pupils practise, but I don't think that amount of time on his own can be very good for him.'

For a moment Annie didn't know what to say, she was so taken aback. Had she overlooked Owen? He'd seemed to settle into Gray's home quite well, compared with Lana, but if he wasn't talking in class again, that was a big setback.

'Don't you think it was a bit soon to move them?' Ed asked her. 'Don't you think you've maybe rushed into things for your own reasons?'

That was too much. He had totally overstepped the line and she felt a surge of annoyance.

'I don't think that's any of your business, Ed,' she told him angrily, then added in a raised voice: 'Don't think that I don't worry about the children, because I do! All the time! Of course I only want what's best for them. I made the move to give us all some more security. Saying I did it for my own reasons is just completely wrong!'

'I'm sorry,' Ed replied, which took the wind out of her sails a little.

'I'm helping Owen as much as I can,' she added, voice not so angry now. 'I hadn't realized what was going on at school. You were right to tell me about that.'

His head was bowed and he was rubbing his hands together, agitated by this conversation.

'Well, maybe this isn't my business either,' he began, not looking up at her, 'but I think you should know that there's about two thousand pounds missing from the school's charity fund-raising account. I haven't spoken to Lana and her friends about it yet, but obviously I'm going to have to.'

'Two thousand pounds!' Annie repeated in astonishment. 'How much is in the account?'

'There's over eight thousand left, but there have been three withdrawals which have added up to two grand. Only Lana and one other girl are signatories entitled to make withdrawals,' he told her gravely.

'Oh no!' was Annie's stunned reaction. Immediately she wondered what Lana was planning to do with the money. Run away? This was her first panicky thought.

'Ed? Can you give me the chance to speak to Lana about this first?' Annie asked. 'She's being so difficult at the moment. She doesn't like it at Gray's, her boyfriend's dumped her, she's missing her friends . . . It looks like she's done something totally out of order, but can you just give me a couple of days to pick the right moment and find out what she knows about it?'

And if she's got £2,000 on her, she could just take off were the words Annie didn't add.

'Right, well . . .' Ed stood up. 'I'll see Owen at the weekend then?' He was referring to the long-planned camping expedition.

Annie got up too and felt awkward, now that Ed had landed all these difficulties on her: 'I will understand if you don't want to do the trip any more,' she told him.

He looked at her with surprise. 'Why wouldn't I want to do it? Owen would be gutted.'

She gave Ed a smile, grateful that he at least understood this.

Chapter Twenty-six

Owen's camping pyjamas:

Socks (Asda)
Pants (Asda)
Jogging bottoms (Asda)
Long-sleeved top (Gap sale)
Est. cost: £12

'Yeah . . . Too many beans.'

Owen was uncomfortable in his sleeping bag. He felt too hot, too tight and too bundled up. Also, his right thumb, carefully wrapped in a clean plaster, was starting to throb.

Opening a family-sized tin of beans with his penknife turned out to have been a bad idea. The tin had opened easily enough, but the knife had left a cruelly jagged edge, which had ripped his thumb open as he was tipping the beans out into the pot.

For a few moments, Owen hadn't registered the pain and his blood had dripped noiselessly down onto the beans. But as soon as he'd uttered his first 'Owww!' Ed, on cooking duty at the camp along with two dads and four other boys, had sprung into action.

The cut had quickly been assessed, cleaned with disinfectant wipes and held up high to stem the blood flow. Once the plaster had been expertly applied and soothing words administered, they'd both gone back to the gas stove to check over the beans.

There was a small, but unmistakable puddle of blood sitting on top of them.

'Do you think we should throw them out?' Owen had asked.

'No, no, no,' Ed had heartily assured him. 'Of course not – as long as they get a good boil. Extra iron for everyone.'

He made several jokes about it to jolly Owen along: 'Bloody great beans . . . I'm bloody hungry . . . these are going to be bloody delicious,' and so on.

But the cut finger had been Owen's third injury of the day and he was beginning to feel like the clutz of the camp. During the stick-whittling session, he'd accidentally whittled his left index finger, so now he had a plaster on both hands.

Drystone dyke building hadn't gone much better; he'd struggled with a stone which was too heavy, and it had slipped from his hands and landed on his toe.

'Never mind,' Ed had assured him when he was assessing the damage to a tearful Owen. 'You're going to have a really cool black toenail. Very Ozzy Osbourne.'

Ed had sat next to him at supper, chatting with him and some of the other boys, telling jokes, playing some of the clever word games he was so good at.

When Owen's yawns had come thick and fast Ed had suggested he head for his sleeping bag in one of the boys' tents.

This is where Owen, overdressed in socks, pants, jogging bottoms and a long-sleeved T-shirt, now wriggled uncomfortably.

On one side of his stomach there was a slightly sore patch – too many beans, he suspected.

Then he found he couldn't help thinking about his dad, a cheerful and extrovert farter who'd had about fifty different words for the process, Owen's favourites being 'humming' and 'letting off steam'.

And he was thinking about the other thing and worrying quite a lot more. He'd thought he'd be able to keep it to himself, make it his own little project, but now he wasn't so sure.

Then he saw Ed, in cord trousers and a frazzled old stripy pyjama top, coming into the tent with an old-fashioned storm lantern in one hand and one of Owen's books in the other.

'Thought you might want this,' he said, crouching down beside Owen's sleeping bag and handing over the book. 'How are you doing? Comfy?' He looked around: there were three other boys in the other corner of this big Boy-Scout-sized tent.

'Do you think you'll get any sleep? Or will it be ghost stories all night long?'

'Don't know,' Owen said.

'But you're not sleepy yet?'

'No, not yet,' Owen told him, then promptly gave a huge yawn.

'You're warm enough though?' Ed asked.

'Yeah . . . hmmm . . . fine.'

Something about Owen's slightly pained face made Ed ask: 'Sore tummy?' When this got a nod, he suggested: 'Too many beans maybe?'

'Yeah . . . too many beans.'

'I'm sure everyone in here will understand if you need to release a little . . .' he raised an eyebrow, 'pressure. Just keep your bag pulled tight.'

This made Owen grin and he suddenly found himself telling Ed: 'The maps that I made for this trip – the special walk that I'd planned along Even Ridge – I've forgotten to bring them. I left them on my bed.'

'It's OK,' Ed assured him, surprised to see such an anxious look on Owen's face. 'We'll buy an Ordnance Survey first thing in the morning and plot it out with that.'

'Yeah, well, but the thing is . . .' Owen continued, 'I'm worried my mum or my sister will find them.'

'Now why would you worry about that?' Ed asked with a puzzled look.

'Well, you see . . . the thing is . . .' Owen made a long pause, but Ed gave him such an encouraging look and nod of the head that in a tense little burst of words, he began to explain: 'It's about my dad.'

It wasn't nearly as hard to tell someone as he'd expected.

Ed listened carefully, asked just a question or two, then told Owen he should try and get off to sleep now and have another think about it all in the morning.

Chapter Twenty-seven

Lana goes outdoors:

Fuchsia rebel girl T-shirt (Camden market)
Pale grey skater trousers (Quicksilver sale)
Silver parka (Topshop)
Fuchsia trainers (Rocket Dog)
Est. cost: £110

'There's no way I can tell you about it . . .'

'Mum!'

There was an unusual note of urgency to Lana's voice as she walked into Gray's kitchen, clad in skimpy pink pyjamas and holding out several sheets of paper.

'What is it?' Annie, still in her dressing gown, uncurled her newly painted fingernails from the mug of coffee she was enjoying in front of the large sunny window. 'It's eight fifteen! What are you doing up so early?' she asked as Lana handed her the pages covered with Owen's cramped handwriting and intricately detailed pencil drawings.

'Trying to find my iPod, but Owen must have taken it,' Lana snapped.

Lana liked to wire up for sound first thing on a Saturday morning, then dive back under the duvet for at least another hour or two.

Annie leafed through the pages, but couldn't see what was exciting her daughter so much. 'These are Owen's little maps and drawings of the camp-site he's at with Ed,' she said.

The plans were so detailed and so careful – each with a little compass drawn in at the top – she could picture Owen sitting at the kitchen table, hunched over them, tongue poking slightly from the corner of his mouth.

She felt the wave of worry about him break over her again. The same feeling she'd had as he'd climbed into the dodgy little hatchback Ed had turned up in. Borrowed from a friend, apparently.

It hadn't occurred to Annie that Ed didn't own a car until the trip was in the final stages of preparation.

She'd watched as Owen had settled into the front passenger's seat and snapped his belt into place. Her eyes had moved all over the body of the well-worn Ford Fiesta as she'd tried not to dwell on the fact that it probably didn't have a passenger air bag, or side impact bars or even ABS brakes.

They'd taken so much stuff that the boot was packed to capacity. Would Ed even be able to see out of the back window?

Ed, already dressed to hike in muddy blue waterproof trousers and walking boots, seemed to catch wind of her anxiety, and as he'd opened the driver's door and prepared to get inside, he'd assured her, 'I'm a very careful driver. I don't want you to worry about that. OK? Not for a mood. I'll take very good care of him. Won't I, Owen?' Then he'd given her a wink, to lighten the moment. And maybe to show he was sorry for the harsh criticisms he'd laid on her the last time they'd met.

Watching Owen cheerfully buckle himself into the car, Annie was glad she hadn't phoned Ed up and told him not to bother, as she'd considered doing. She was also glad Ed hadn't made the same call.

They'd both obviously decided to put their disagreement on hold for Owen's sake.

'OK. Well, goodbye . . . goodbye, Owen.' She'd gone round to her son's side of the car and tried not to wave and smile too frantically.

'Did you have any idea where they were going?' Lana now asked her accusingly as Annie continued to look at the drawings.

'Of course I know where they are! They've gone to the Black Mountains.'

'And do you know where that is?'

'It's in Wales.'

'Yeah . . . the bit otherwise known as the Brecon Beacons.'

Annie could feel her heart rate speed up at these words.

'This map . . .' Lana began, but Annie's eyes had now picked out the words *Even Ridge* in tiny writing running along one of the contours Owen had copied onto his plan.

'Oh my God!' she exclaimed. Even Ridge was known for only one reason in their family. It was Roddy's place.

343

'Don't you get it?' Lana was almost shouting at her: 'Owen wants to visit Dad's—'

'Why does he want to do that?!' Annie cut her off, her voice now urgent too. But she already knew of this deep-seated wish of Owen's. He had asked her to take him many times before and she had always assured him they would go, the three of them would travel there together as a family, 'when they were all ready'.

What she'd really meant was when *she* was ready. And she was not.

She didn't even like to think about when she could face this trip and had put Owen's request so far to the back of her mind that she had succeeded in forgetting about it altogether.

But clearly, Owen was determined to go and had hatched this clever little plan all on his own. She was certain Ed could have had nothing to do with it.

Annie snatched up the kitchen phone and punched in the number of the mobile Owen had with him. Ed, of course, infuriatingly, did not have a mobile.

'I'm not a brain surgeon,' he'd informed her. 'Nobody will ever need to contact me that urgently!'

But now she did.

She heard her own voice coming down the line at her: 'Hi, it's Annie, I can't take your call right now . . .'

'Owen, it's Mum,' she began her message. 'Please phone me, straight away.'

As soon as she'd hung up, she told Lana: 'Get dressed. We have to go there. If Owen's going to do this today, he needs us to be there with him.'

Lana didn't argue, even though Annie knew she'd planned to spend the day in London with her school friends . . . and there was another conversation Annie had to have with her daughter.

Gray came downstairs for breakfast just as Annie, fully dressed and all set to head off with Lana, was about to wake him and explain what was happening.

'There's a problem with Owen,' Annie told him. 'Lana and I have to head up there and be with him.'

'Is he OK?' Gray asked, double-checking the wrap and cord tension of his dressing gown at the sight of Lana in the hallway.

'He's not hurt, it's nothing medical . . . look, we really have to go . . . do you mind if I explain it to you later?'

'Right, well,' Gray looked grumpy about this, 'I'll have a quiet little day to myself, will I? Maybe I'll do some tidying up in this pigsty of a home.'

'Sorry, I was going to do . . .' Annie shrugged her shoulders apologetically. There was a lot of stuff lying about everywhere. Something about Gray's open plan house didn't really lend itself well to family life. There just wasn't any room to put anything. Maybe they needed storage boxes; maybe a trip to Ikea would solve everything.

'Perhaps if I search hard enough, *Lana*,' he said pointedly, 'I'll come across the two boxes of medicine currently missing from my supplies.'

'What?!' Annie and her daughter chorused together.

'Yes, that's right.' Gray was still several steps above them on the stairs, his face clearly furious, but trying to do an impression of calm: 'One box of fifty Valium tablets, one box of fifty Temazepams. Both missing from

345

my locked office cabinet. A nice little earner for some-body.'

'Do you know anything about this?' Annie snapped at Lana.

She shook her head emphatically, not taking her eyes from Gray.

'Gray, if there's a problem with my children, you come and talk to me about it first,' Annie told him, now furious too. 'Don't just go about making completely unfounded accusations.'

'But we know Lana's dishonest!' he exclaimed. 'Didn't she cost you your job? And the way she's been behaving the past few weeks, it wouldn't surprise me one bit to find out she's on drugs!'

This was too much for Annie. She took Lana by the arm and hustled her out of the front door, giving it a great dramatic slam for good measure.

Once they were in the Jeep, she revved the engine and roared out of the driveway, creating two deep ruts in Gray's neatly raked gravel.

No words passed between mother and daughter until they were miles out of Upper Ploxley and on the motor-way heading west, then finally Annie asked first about the dental drugs, to which she got an emphatic: 'I don't know anything about that, I promise.'

Then she began her enquiry into the missing £2,000.

At first she was met with silence. Lana turned her head, folded her arms and stared out of the passenger's window at the passing scenery.

After a long pause, she asked her mother a question in return: 'How do you know about that?'

'Ed told me.'

346

'Ed! How does he know?'

'He checked the bank account. The money's been taken out. It's not rocket science, Lana.'

'I didn't think he ever looked!'

Annie let this completely incriminating remark pass without comment. She kept her eyes on the road, drove steadily and waited.

'There's no way I can tell you about it . . .' Lana said slowly. 'No way.'

'Of course there is,' Annie said gently, feeling her heartbeat accelerate with fear, 'I'm your mum. I care about you more than anyone else in the world does.'

Then Lana began to sob.

And Annie began to feel very afraid. Lana had obviously done something terrible, or something terrible had happened. Wild thoughts raced through her mind. An abortion? Gambling? Drugs? Guilt that she hadn't paid close enough attention to her stroppy, difficult, but nevertheless fragile, about-to-turn-15-year-old was coursing through Annie's veins.

'Lana, whatever it is, you're here with me. You're safe and I'm going to look after you. Whatever it is.'

'It was for Suzie . . .' the words began, in between tears and sniffs and fresh sobs. 'She's in such a mess . . . her parents have split up and her boyfriend's a . . . total . . . he's just a cokehead, Mum. No other word for it . . .'

Annie was nodding encouragingly, but her grip on the steering wheel was knuckle-white.

'She was just doing it at the weekends,' Lana went on, 'but . . . it got to her. She started bringing it into school. She was a mess! We kept telling her to split up with him and get some help.'

Annie moved the Jeep over into the slow lane so she could give Lana's story better attention.

'She persuaded us to lend her money from the fund. She said she needed it to get treatment and she'd get it back from her dad, as soon as he was back in the country. But I think . . . we all think . . . she's taken the money and spent it with her boyfriend. She's never going to ask her dad now and I've no idea how we're going to get it back and' – her voice raised to a desperate crescendo – 'we're all going to get expelled once this comes out.'

The sobbing broke out anew.

Although this was a problem, Annie couldn't help breathing something of a sigh of relief that, for Lana at least, it wasn't nearly as awful as Annie had imagined.

'Lana,' Annie began, 'don't worry. OK? Try not to worry. I wish you'd told me sooner.'

'You've been so busy with Gray,' came the accusation.

'I am never, ever too busy for you, OK?' Annie looked over at her daughter. 'But we will sort this out. Blimey,' she added several moments later. 'There's never a dull moment with you around, is there?'

'Mum?' Lana asked, wiping her face and looking over at the person she now wished she'd confided in weeks ago. 'Are we going to carry on living with Gray?'

Annie, looking straight ahead, nudging the Jeep back over into the fast lane and putting it up into sixth gear, let out a deep sigh before confiding, 'No, babes, and I'm so, so sorry. I thought he was going to be really good for all of us. I wouldn't have put you through another move if I hadn't thought it was the best thing to do. I am so sorry.'

348

'We'll have to move again,' Lana pointed out.

'I know.'

'Where to?' Lana wondered, knowing full well that they couldn't go back to their flat for months.

'I'm working on that,' Annie told her and began to chew her lip. 'We'll go back to town though . . . definitely. I can't stand Upper Ploxley,' she added with feeling. 'Where am I supposed to go for a coffee? Let alone a nice pair of shoes.'

Lana giggled at her, which made Annie feel slightly better about the decisions ahead.

Chapter Twenty-eight

Annie outdoors:

Maroon cagoule (village shop)
Maroon waterproof trousers (village shop)
Navy hiking boots (village shop)
Est. cost: £50

'I can't . . . I just can't!'

Lana tried and failed to reach Owen on the mobile as the Jeep ate up the miles between them. Close to two hours had passed when Annie exited the motorway and, using the map they'd bought at a service station, began to navigate the smaller, twisty roads that led to the campsite.

The towns and red-roofed housing estates had fallen away now and they'd entered gentle green countryside: first farms with patchwork fields and then the roll of hills began.

It was damp weather. The highest peaks had wispy cloud clinging to their summits and the smell of fresh, moss-scented air was coming in through the Jeep's heating system.

Annie wanted to know if Lana was all right about a visit to Even Ridge.

'If Owen's going to do it – or if he's already done it – then I will too,' came the quiet reply. But after a little while, Lana asked: 'Mum? It's OK to be nervous, isn't it?'

'Yes, of course it's OK to be nervous,' Annie assured her, 'I'm absolutely terrified.'

Soon, the Jeep was moving slowing through the high street of the small town closest to the camp-site as Lana tried to decipher Owen's map. They'd decided to look for Ed and Owen at the camp-site first, then if there was no sign of them, head on to Even Ridge by themselves.

But suddenly Lana shouted: 'Look, over there! I think that's Owen!'

Sure enough, walking with his back turned to them was her brother and several feet behind him, recognizable by his nest of hair, was Ed.

Annie sped up a little to get ahead of them and after a quick pause and indication, pulled up on the left. Moments later, she and Lana were on the pavement, standing in front of the surprised campers.

'Mum?' Owen spoke first. 'What are you doing here?'

'We came into town to look for a phone box,' Ed began, in no doubt as to why Annie was here. 'But we've not been able to get through to you.'

'Owen has a phone,' was Annie's irritated response. 'Why couldn't he have used that?'

'No reception,' Ed answered, a picture of calm.

'Owen!' She turned all her attention on her son. 'Don't

351

you think it would have been a good idea to tell me about your plan?'

'What plan?' Owen asked, trying for just one moment longer to avoid the inevitable showdown he'd been dreading ever since Ed had told him, kindly but firmly, that no, he couldn't possibly take him up to Even Ridge without his mother's full permission and blessing.

Annie took Owen's drawings out of the back pocket of her trousers and held them out to him.

'I knew you'd say no,' Owen burst out. 'I wasn't going to tell Ed either . . . and I have . . . and now it's all ruined.'

His face was suddenly pale with a bright spot of red in each cheek. Annie knew this meant he was very upset, or very angry, maybe both.

'I should be allowed to see Dad's place!' he added in a surprisingly loud voice.

'I haven't driven all this way to tell you no,' she said, hugely relieved to realize that they hadn't gone up to the ridge yet. 'Lana and I came here because if it's so important to you to go, then we'll go with you.'

Annie saw Owen's shoulders loosen a little and for a moment she thought he was going to cry.

'I was about to take Owen for a scone,' Ed chipped in, patting Owen on the shoulder. 'It's still too misty to do any serious hill walking. But it looks like it's going to clear up nicely, so in the meantime I think we should hide out at "Edna's tea corner" over there. Great cakes in the window,' he added cheerfully.

All three Valentines felt deeply grateful for Ed's tension-breaking enthusiasm for home baking.

*   *   *

Annie looked at herself in the mirror with undisguised horror: 'An anorak? An anorak??!!' she repeated. 'I don't do anoraks.'

Especially, she thought to herself, when they are maroon cagoules paired with – *horror of horrors* – maroon waterproof trousers, tucked into – *this can't be happening* – hiking boots.

The whole outfit was available for £50. Double discount day special in the town's little outward-bound clothing shop.

Her children were giggling. Ed had one arm folded across his woolly-jumpered chest, the other was propped up as, chin in hand, blue eyes twinkly, he scrutinized her a little too carefully.

'Oh, now that is sooo you,' he said, displaying a hitherto undiscovered talent for camping it up. 'Brings out the colour in your cheeks, wouldn't you say, Lana?'

Lana's giggles grew louder.

'And the trousers, they co-ordinate so well,' he added. 'Who'd have thought of putting those two together? Very clever.'

Annie couldn't decide whether to laugh at him or hit him.

'Do I have to wear this? All of it?' she pleaded once again.

He nodded his head: 'Oh yes. Strictly necessary. I'm going to insist you put the hood up and tie it tightly round your face as well.'

'But we're just walking up a hill . . .' she tried one last time.

He shook his head and told her: 'You need proper kit.'

'Mum, you look fine,' Lana encouraged her, although

353

Annie couldn't help feeling this was a bare-faced lie. Maroon? Why did the only things left on the bargain rail in her size have to be *maroon*? The colour she'd over-dosed on in those vulnerable years aged 13 to 15. She remembered 'pleather' pixie boots in almost this exact shade.

Ed had broken the news to her gently after the teas had been drunk and an impressive amount of Edna's home baking consumed: 'If we're going to go up Even Ridge, Annie, then you'll have to get some waterproofs and a pair of walking boots.'

Although Lana had left the house in an unusually sensible outfit, Annie had dressed for a day's window-shopping in a short belted mac and leather trainers. But obviously that wasn't going to do. To her horror, Ed had explained that in this drizzly wet, she'd need water-proofs to stay dry and a cheap pair of hiking boots for grip.

'Cagoules can get a bit sweaty,' he was warning her now, 'I like a nice breathable anorak, myself, Gore-Tex lined.' He held up his bright yellow and navy serious mountaineer's bit of kit for her examination, but added, 'That really adds to the price though and if you're not planning on doing much . . .'

'No.' Annie shook her head. 'Definitely not planning on doing much hill walking, especially if it involves getting dressed up like this. Couldn't they just have made a nod or two to passing trends?' she wondered aloud. 'Skinny trouser bottoms? Colours from this century's palette?'

'It's practical,' Ed told her.

'It's criminal,' she insisted.

She pulled the maroon hood on and tied the draw-string tight round her face so that she peered out like an owl.

'I can't . . . I just can't,' she made one final protest.

'Twit-to-woo,' Owen teased.

'All set then?' Ed asked, ignoring her pleas.

Chapter Twenty-nine

Ed up a hill:

Navy blue waterproof trousers (Tiso)
Ancient hiking boots (Army and Navy Stores)
Two long-sleeved T-shirts (vintage)
Yellow Gore-Tex anorak (Tiso)
Small waterproof backpack (Tiso)
Est. cost: £160

'Let's try and enjoy the ride.'

The walk towards Even Ridge began straight after the purchase of the maroon waterproofs, once Ed had satisfied himself that every single person definitely wanted to go, and that they were all absolutely sure they wanted him to come with them.

There was some chatter at the start, but it was of the nervous, rather than the cheerful kind.

Twenty minutes or so into the climb, the talk dried up and the four were walking along in silence, in single file, concentrating on the narrow, steadily rising path.

Annie found herself thinking hard in the quiet.

Ed had showed them on the map the way the ridged path curved right along the face of the hill, moving slowly up to the summit and then bringing walkers back down by a different route.

'It's about two and a half hours' walk, all in,' he'd told them. 'Do you know roughly where we're aiming for?' he'd asked.

Annie had shaken her head in reply to this, but told him: 'I don't think it's far from the top.'

'OK, fine.' Ed had smiled at them encouragingly as he'd pulled up the zip on his neon yellow jacket: 'We'll just put one foot in front of the other. Keep going . . . Let's try and enjoy the ride.'

A gentle grey drizzle was still blanking out both sky and sun and wrapping itself all around them. Within fifteen minutes of starting the walk, Annie felt damp everywhere. Her face was running with drizzly wet, her body underneath the waterproof outfit was clammy. Suddenly Gore-Tex wasn't looking like such a bad investment.

She watched her feet moving for a while, clumpy in the brand new navy hiking boots. Put one foot in front of the other, as Ed had instructed. She tried to concentrate hard on this rather than think too much about where they were heading. It wasn't a difficult walk. The path was about three feet wide and stony: it was damp but only very slightly slippery.

As they got higher, every so often she lifted her head to take in the view, which was much more pleasant than she'd expected. As the drizzle began to lift, she could make out calm, green hills and valleys stretching out ahead of them. Where sunlight had broken through the clouds in the distance, roads, cars and windows gleamed gold.

She was also on the lookout for some clue that they were in the right place, although she had no idea what this clue was going to be.

She had expected to feel very anxious up here, panicky even . . . so close to Roddy. About to see the place where . . .

But she was surprised to find that a sense of calm had come over her. The act of walking was helping. As she walked on and gradually up, she felt a growing sense of purpose.

She looked back at Owen and Lana and wondered what they were thinking. Owen broke into a jog; he quickly pulled up level with her, then flashed her a smile before passing.

'Are you going to be first to the top?' she asked him, cheered by the irrepressible fun he was managing to squeeze from this.

'Definitely,' he called back over his shoulder. His red anorak was unzipped and flapped in the wind behind him as he jogged on ahead.

She automatically wanted to call out to him: Be careful, but she didn't.

They had been walking for about fifty minutes and seemed to be making good time towards the summit when Owen, eighty feet or so ahead of her, called out: 'Muuum! Mum, come and look at this!'

Annie, Lana and Ed hurried up the pathway to reach him and followed his pointing finger to a colourful bundle propped next to a large grey boulder. The side of the hill was much steeper here, so if they wanted to take a closer look they would have to scramble carefully down the grass, to get down to the rock which was about thirty feet below the path.

'Owen!' Annie called out to steady her son, who'd already left the path and was crawling his way down backwards: hands, knees and toecaps in the grass for grip.

'I think he'll be OK,' Ed reassured her, climbing down from the path himself and holding out a hand to Lana, who clearly wanted to join them. 'It's grassy, but I don't think it'll be too slippery.'

So all four of them moved, sliding and crawling, down the steep bank towards the stone. Annie, face pressed hard into the wet grass as she tried to slow her descent, wondered how on earth she'd got herself into this . . . and how would they ever get back up?

By the time she made it down to the boulder, the colourful bundle had come into focus as a weather-beaten bunch of flowers. Owen had picked it up and as Lana scrutinized the wrapping paper, Ed stood at a distance, not wanting to intrude.

'Can I have a look?' Annie asked and Owen put the wet bundle into her hands. About ten days ago, or so, this had been a sensational bunch of flowers. The significance of the date did not pass her by.

She had done her very, very best to try and forget the anniversary of Roddy's death this year, but still the date had come round and slapped her hard in the face.

The bunch was sodden wet and browning. These had once been fat pink and orange roses, prettily arranged with evergreen branches. The smart cellophane was

359

shredded in places, but Annie could make out a London, WC1 postcode.

She was certain this had something to do with Roddy. At the inquest, it had been stated that no other serious accident had happened on Even Ridge in living memory; unless there had been something since, of course.

Lana pointed down into the flower stems: 'Look, there's a card.'

Annie peeled back the wrapper and brought out a small silver envelope. For a moment she didn't know if she dared. What if this was something she didn't know about? Shouldn't know about? What if it was private to Roddy? Or even to do with someone else entirely?

But Owen and Lana were crowding close and urging her on, so she put a fingernail under the miniature flap and pulled out a tiny white card no more than two inches square. Scribbled over the front and back in a handwriting she recognized were the words:

> *The third anniversary, my friend . . . Three*
> *whole years without you. I just hope wherever*
> *you are that you have some idea how*
> *much we all miss you.*

Annie stared at the card. The words were blurring and she knew she would have to take rapid tear intervention action immediately.

'Who's it from?' Owen wanted to know.

'It's from Connor, isn't it?' came from Lana.

Annie just nodded, could feel the tears overflow from the bottom lid of her eye.

'Yes,' she managed.

'Did Daddy fall off the path and hit his head here?' Owen asked.

'Yes.' Her voice was down to a husky whisper. 'He was so unlucky, babes, so very, very unlucky.'

Unlucky . . . this was the way she chose to describe it now. There was nothing to be gained from thinking about whether it was 'fair' or 'unfair'. She had only come to realize this after long and pointless hours raging about how unfair it had been.

Why had Connor never told her he was making this journey? Had he made it the years before as well? She tucked the card into the flowers, then carefully placed the bunch back at the foot of the stone, moved to tears by Connor's gesture.

Now she suspected they were going to have to do the thing she'd been dreading, halfway up a hillside with the odd passer-by to see them. They were going to have to huddle together and cry.

With her nose pressed into the top of Lana's head, with Owen tucked in against her cagoule, they cried together.

She thought at first she would just have a short cry: a let it out, blow nose, then move back to the path sort of thing.

She thought she had to be strong for the children, she had to hold it together. *They're the ones who are really, really upset, they need me to keep it together here.* But she began to feel horrible, big, wrenching sobs bursting out of her lungs. She couldn't do anything to stop them.

Roddy was not away on location as she so often tried

361

to fool herself. He was gone. Taken away for ever. He wasn't ever, ever going to come back to them. Her mobile was never again going to flash with his number, he was never going to be in the doorway back from a trip laden down with presents for them all and she was never, ever going to wake up in the morning and find the nightmare over and him safely back home beside her.

Standing here on the hillside at the very place for the first time, it was as if she at last understood the finality. It broke over her and it hurt so much, so intensely she didn't know if she could stand the pain, she was struggling for breath, struggling to stand.

Lana and Owen's father, her lovely husband, Roddy, had been fatally injured on this walk. Right here on Even Ridge.

A 'freak fall', apparently, so everyone involved in the accident had told her at the time.

'Accidental death' was the coroner's final verdict.

As if the words 'freak fall . . . could have happened to anyone' had made it any easier to bear. In fact, she often thought it made it much harder.

If Roddy had set off that weekend to scale an Alpine glacier, she might have been more prepared for a terrible accident. But he'd left with three of his mates for a beer-drinking and hill-walking weekend: 'It'll be much more about beers than hills, I can tell you that,' he'd joked as he'd flung his overnight bag into the boot of Connor's car.

After a big night out, a little bit hungover, Roddy and his friends had set off for a pick-me-up jaunt up to the top of Even Ridge.

Close to the summit, Roddy had stumbled, lost his footing and fallen. He'd rolled down this steep bit of hill and should have come to a laughing standstill just a few metres further down. His misfortune had been to hit his head hard enough against this boulder right here to cause a massive brain haemorrhage.

A helicopter had been scrambled and he'd been airlifted to the nearest intensive care unit, but he'd never regained consciousness and after a week on life support, he'd died.

Annie could wish and wish all she liked that he'd died immediately. But the reality of Roddy's death had been a battery of extensive tests and then the devastating news that he was brain dead. His family and his closest friends had all come to visit. They had talked to him and held him and told him things they wished they'd told him so much more often when he could still have heard. They'd cried over him, touched him, kissed him, curled up in bed beside him.

Until finally Annie, fully conscious, vaguely wondering why she was not entitled to pain relief – an anaesthetic, or at the very least gas and air – had signed the forms.

With Lana and Owen in the fiercest embrace of Fern next door, with her own arms too tight around the waist of Roddy's mother, Penny, Annie had watched the nurses quietly and sensitively switch off the machines, take out the tubes, unhook the drips and remove the needles.

With his wife holding one hand, his mother clinging to the other, it had taken Roddy several excruciatingly long minutes to die. The moment she knew it had happened, Annie had felt a dreadful, physical snap. Something inside her had broken irreparably.

She had sat with him, gripping his hand, for almost two hours afterwards, so lost and so shocked, she hadn't even noticed Penny leave the room.

Until someone, specially trained, had come in to talk her through what happened next.

What happened next, it turned out, was on a par with a big family wedding except she had just a week to get it organized.

There were hundreds of phone calls to make, flowers, church, selection books, catalogues, relatives – both liked and disliked – to deal with. There were daily arrivals of more flowers, more cards, and still more phone calls to make and the endlessly ringing phone to answer, like a permanent ringing in her ears.

After all that, after all the noise and the bustle and the deadlines and the plans and preparations and the great rush and swell of emotion on the day . . . after that came the most deafening silence.

Annie's days and evenings became totally silent. She undressed in silence, she went to bed in silence, she woke up to silence. Whole weekends passed in silence. She could talk to her children, she could hear her children, she could put on the television, the radio, play music loudly, she could phone her mother, visit her sister. It didn't make any difference. All she could hear, for months on end, was the silence in her life where before there had been Roddy.

Now that she was here on the hillside, now that she could see the slope she and their children had just scrambled down had killed Roddy, she realized how furious she was.

How outraged, how totally, totally livid she was about this.

How dare this stupid, innocuous bit of ground, this hard grey useless stone, how dare they take Roddy away from them?

How dare they?

She kicked furiously against the stone.

'HOW DARE THEY? HOW DARE THEY?!!'

Annie realized she was saying it aloud, over and over again. She was squeezing Lana and Owen too tightly, could feel them both pushing slightly against her.

She let go of them and sat down heavily on the ground, hearing the weird scrunch of the waterproofs underneath her. She cried and cried. Didn't care now that Lana and Owen had stopped crying, didn't care whether anyone on the path up there was looking down at them or what Ed, the outsider, was making of it all.

She howled. She keened.

She wiped at her streaming nose uselessly with the sleeve of the cagoule. Now there was a shiny patch of snot on her waterproof sleeve, but she didn't care.

She didn't care about anything: not the school fees, not the flat, not Gray, not what was in fashion, or out, or who looked good in what. She cared about nothing but these two dear, dear people standing looking distraught in front of her and the fact that this stupid, bloody useless, heartless, mindless lump of grey stone had taken away their dad. The man who had loved them most in the whole world.

'I don't care . . . I don't care . . . I just don't care . . .' She realized she was repeating a new phrase over and over in between gulps and choking, snot-laden sobs.

Then there was an arm round her shoulders. Not Lana's soft comforting one, or Owen's light arm which just made it from one of her shoulders to the other and no more. No, this was a heavy arm, holding her tight.

With her eyes shut, she briefly leaned her head on the shoulder the arm was attached to and felt supported enough to cry more. Cry hard, really hard, cry with some intention of crying herself out.

Because she was going to have to cry about something else now too: how much she missed her job.

All day long, she caught herself thinking about little things happening at The Store. About unpeeling the cellophane from the new season's arrivals, about the excitement of the first day of the bright pink 50 per cent off tickets. Walking past racks of new shoes, inhaling the smell of unbroken leather.

The flow of women in through her suite every day, the transformations in front of the mirror . . . even tidying up at the end of the day, seeing the place in the dimness of the night half-lights. She missed it all so much.

She liked the fact that this solid arm and shoulder didn't come with words. It didn't say: 'There, there', or, 'It's going to be OK', or 'Don't cry', or 'Shhhhh now.' It was just there. Holding her shoulders tightly. Giving her heavy head a place to rest.

Long enough to catch her breath again, to grope for the sides in this pool of grief and begin to pull herself up, out of the water for a little bit.

Eyes closed, head still leaning, she waited for the heavy breaths and gulps, the rasping feeling in her lungs to die down.

After a long time, she felt able to open her swollen eyes again. Slowly, she released herself from the grip of the arm and she stood up.

When she could manage the words, she said, 'I'm really sorry,' to Ed, the owner of the arm.

'No need to be, I understand,' he said gently.

'Where are the children?' she asked, surprised to see they were no longer around.

'They've gone on to the top of the hill. Do you feel ready to walk up after them?'

When she nodded in reply to this, but looked anxiously at the steep slope they'd have to scramble up to get back onto the path, Ed held out his hand and told her: 'Don't worry, I'll help you up.'

She took hold of the hand offered and let him pull her up the steep slope. On the summit of the hill, she could see Lana and Owen standing close together, pointing out the things they could see in the distance.

When Annie finally got up beside them, she looked out over the wide open view with them, ruffled Owen's overgrown hair, and asked him, 'What do you think of this?'

Eyes fixed on the distance, he slipped his hand into hers, and told her, 'Thanks, Mum. I always wanted to finish Daddy's walk for him.'

When Lana heard this, she told her brother in a voice close to a whisper, 'That's really nice, Owen. I never thought of it like that . . . I'm glad you brought us here.'

Chapter Thirty

Spare clothes Annie:

Wide, short, worn-out jeans (Ed)
Belt (hers)
Tennis socks (Ed)
White boxers (Ed)
Navy blue sweatshirt (Ed)
Est. cost: £0

'I'm bloody soaked!'

'Are you OK?' Ed had asked Annie with concern as she'd scrambled to her feet after a backwards-on-her-bottom skid down a substantial chunk of hill in the torrential rain which had accompanied them all the way down.

The smooth waterproof trousers had tobogganed her furiously over several fierce dips, bumps and tufts until, pained and winded, she'd skidded to a standstill. The force of the slide had split the trousers in two and caused her anorak to ride up, wetting all her clothes underneath.

'I'm fine,' she'd told the little crowd of three around her, 'but I'm bloody soaked!'

'Oh don't worry,' Ed had assured her. 'I've got some spare things in my tent.'

She'd worried about that all the way down the rest of the hill.

Back at the camp-site, Ed's tent had collapsed under the weight of the downpour. A handful of boys and their dads were taking down one of the big tents before it did the same.

'I think we might call it a day,' one of the dads called out to Ed as they walked past. 'Forecast is for heavy rain.'

Nevertheless, Ed managed to fish out his holdall from the jumble of tent fabric, sleeping bags and assorted belongings and told Annie to take whatever she needed.

In the dank toilet and shower block, she undid the zip on the ancient sports bag and looked inside.

Chaos.

She felt in gingerly, but at least it seemed to be a clean sort of chaos. The dirty pants and socks she'd feared must have been tucked away somewhere else. She pulled out a pair of faded jeans, which were going to be too wide and too short, but there was nothing else in the trouser department. A white T-shirt, wafting washing powder, although it was saggy and almost threadbare, and a worn-out, frayed-at-the-edges sweatshirt were the items she decided would have to do for her top half. She'd need those socks and boxers, too. Should she risk wearing his boxers? They looked clean.

She scrambled out of her wet clothes and into the dry ones as quickly as she could, trying not to look at the cold room around her, walls damp to the touch with a persistent dripping sound. She used her belt to hitch up the trousers, making the denim bunch and gape.

Then her phone, tucked into the wet trousers she'd just peeled off, began to ring.

'Mum! Hi! How are you?'

'Where are you, Annie?'

'I'm with Owen and Lana and their music teacher . . .' she began. 'Owen was at this camp-site and it's right beside the hill where Roddy fell.' She talked Fern through the journey they'd just made.

'Oh my God!' was Fern's reaction. 'Are you OK?'

'Yes,' Annie assured her, 'we're fine. It was . . .' she paused, 'I think it was a good thing to do. The children got a lot out of it.'

'Oh Annie, I'm sorry,' Fern sympathized.

'How are you? What are you phoning me for at three p.m. on a Saturday anyway?' Annie wondered.

'I've just seen Gray,' Fern told her, 'but now maybe isn't the time to tell you about this . . .' She paused.

'What do you mean?'

'Do you know where he is?' Fern asked her.

'Not really. He said he was having a quiet day at home – but he might go out. Why? Where have you seen him?'

'Well, maybe you should phone him up, sweetheart. See if he tells you that he's in a cosy little booth at Le Pont d'Or having a three-course meal and two bottles of wine with his . . .' Annie could hear the irritation in Fern's voice now, '. . . *wife*, Marilyn,' she added.

'Really??!' Annie could hardly believe it. 'You've just seen them *there*?'

'Yes. Went in to meet Netty for a lunchtime special – that's all I can afford in Le Pont d'Or – and only when I was leaving did I see them. I'd love to be mistaken . . . and maybe there's a completely innocent reason for it . . . but there we are.'

As soon as Annie had hung up on Fern, she dialled Gray's number. She felt slightly caught out when he answered straight away.

'Hi!'

'Hi!'

'How's it going?' he wanted to know. 'Where did you rush off to? Is everything OK with Owen?'

He sounded so concerned that for a moment she thought her mother must have been wrong. Gray was surely at home, waiting for her to call him. She felt a pang of guilt that she hadn't phoned him earlier, he must have been worrying about them.

'Everything's fine. Really. Are you still at home?' she asked.

'No. I couldn't face the tidying up so I headed into town.'

'Southend?' she asked.

'Yeah . . . I gave John a call and we met up for lunch.'

'John?'

'You know, yachtie John. We had a bit of a blowout at the Pont d'Or. Very nice it was too. I'm just heading out of the Gents to settle the bill.'

'Great . . . Sorry, babes, I've got to go . . .' was all Annie could manage in response to this. 'Speak to you later.'

'When do you think you'll be back?' he asked.

'Sorry, no idea yet. OK.' She hung up abruptly.

Bloody hell!

It was one thing for her to decide that moving in with Gray had been a mistake. It was something else for him to be sneaking off to see his soon-to-be-ex-wife behind her back.

She opened the make-up section of her handbag and took out her hairbrush and a new lipstick.

After brushing carefully through her wet hair, she tied it up tightly and took several minutes to apply the lipstick perfectly. Like a soldier in a combat zone, she never let rough times get in the way of a bit of grooming or shoe polishing. That would be bad for morale.

Unfortunately, she had to pull her soggy walking boots back on and the wet cagoule because the stair-rod rain had not eased.

Out on the camp-site field she located Ed's tent, which had been pulled back to rights, and guessed that her children were inside with him.

Opening the tent flap, she saw the three of them sitting on rolled sleeping bags, backs hunched against the nylon sides, listening to the pelt of rain. She crawled in, trying to avoid putting her hand into the wet mud on the crackling plastic floor of the tent.

'Pull up a sleeping bag.' Ed moved from his seat and sat on the floor, so Annie inched in a crouching position over to the bag and perched her bum on it, grateful for the slight warmth it radiated.

Casting a glance round at the quiet, thoughtful faces surrounding her, she raised her voice to be heard above the drumming raindrops to say: 'Well, here we are. Everyone OK?'

When they all nodded, she couldn't help adding, 'This is fun, isn't it? I hadn't realized how much fun camping could be.'

Although Lana and Owen giggled, Ed was the first to speak. 'Owen, do you want to do another night under canvas?' he asked. 'Or should we think about packing up and doing this another time when it's not so wet? Totally up to you,' he added.

Once the four of them had tossed about the pros and cons of staying or going and decided to go, there came an unexpected offer.

'Can I make you all supper tonight? At my place. Yes.' He waved away Annie's protests, although she was wondering whether she could face going back to Gray tonight . . . having to have the row about his Lana accusations and his expensive lunch, on top of the day she'd already had.

'It's the least I can do, honestly. No trouble at all,' Ed was insisting. 'Well, I'll have to do something with all the beans I bought for this trip.'

Annie hoped this was a joke.

Cross-legged on the floor, Annie was contemplating her row of letters with as much concentration as she could manage with a fourth glass of wine in her hand. KLJWKIU. Impossible. The sadistic Scrabble sack had landed her with a hand that couldn't be played.

Ed had somehow managed to cram them all into his tiny kitchen and feed them, even though Annie had stood in the cat's bowl this time, cat food had stuck to her socks and the fresh pair Ed had brought her turned out to have an enormous hole at the toe, but she'd decided not to cause him further agitation, because the catering hadn't been going well.

The potatoes baked in the microwave had taken a surprisingly long time.

'I'm just used to making one,' Ed had flustered. 'I forgot it would take four times as long.'

When they were finally served up, they were tough, dry and chewy and they came with baked beans, grated bright orange cheddar cheese and, inexplicably, tinned sardines.

But Annie and her children were so starvingly hungry after the walk, the rain and the long drive back that they ate everything and scraped their plates, causing Ed to scratch his head, look around his cupboards for something else then declare he was going to make scones. Annie had been sceptical, expecting little cremated lumps of flour and fat to emerge from his decrepit oven. But instead they came out beautifully and Ed was totally redeemed.

After dinner, he'd opened wine and settled them all into his sitting room, stoking up the fire which the damp and chilly May evening seemed to require.

Annie glanced at her row of letters again despondently, then looked up to see Owen laying the word 'zenith' down right across the triple letter and triple word score boxes, earning himself about 1,000 points.

'Owen!' she groaned. 'You don't even know what zenith means.'

'A summit or peak. Just like the one we reached today,' came Owen's reply, a little thickly, as he tried to talk through a mouthful of chocolate biscuits he'd just scooped from the dish on the low table they were playing at.

'Are you trying to argue with my budding Junior Scrabble champion here?' Ed asked, as he coolly placed three tiles down, extending two words and creating a third, collecting about 10,000 points in the process.

'We never play Scrabble,' she said, as if that wasn't obvious from her pathetic three-letter offerings so far. 'How did you learn to play, Owen?'

'Ed's Scrabble club at school,' came the short, chocolatey response.

'Wednesday lunchtimes,' Ed explained. 'He's never mentioned it?!'

Annie gave a little shrug, which was meant to convey: Boys? What can you do?

'I am constantly asking Owen about school,' she explained, 'but I probably only know about fifteen per cent of what goes on there.'

'It's best that way, believe me,' came Lana's comment from the sofa. At Annie's insistence, Lana had had a private, slightly shamefaced conversation in the kitchen with Ed, in which she'd explained enough about the missing funds and what she would do to get them back for Ed to feel relieved that he didn't have to take the matter up officially.

Lana had opted out of the Scrabble – 'No, not exactly my thing' – and was now rummaging through a pile of heavy books stacked up against the sofa.

'Those are my sister's,' Ed explained. 'She used to be into all sorts of arty stuff. But I seem to have landed up with most of it.'

This wasn't really a surprise. Ed's flat was the kind of place where stuff landed, never to escape again.

'Where does your sister live?' Annie asked, curious to learn a little more.

'In London,' came the response, but perhaps because Ed was focused on the Scrabble, no further information was offered.

'But you didn't grow up in London, did you?' she prompted, noticing S and T on the board and putting her new tiles in front to make the word 'resist'. But this only netted her about eight points.

'Mum, that is feeble,' Owen didn't spare her.

'No, no, we grew up all over the place. Dad was in the army,' came Ed's reply to her question. 'Home sweet home for me was boarding school . . . seriously!' he added when she laughed.

Scooping up a big handful of biscuits, he told them how he was sent to boarding school the week after his seventh birthday: 'Seems so barbaric now, but that was the norm, all the army kids went. We left on the plane together, went off to our various schools, then met up again on the plane home at the end of term.'

When they all looked at him with various shades of surprise, he added: 'I don't really remember being homesick . . . Maybe I was too young. But my mum was totally traumatized. Especially later. When Hannah's son, Sid, started school Mum kept telling me, "I sent you away, when you were hardly any older than him. There should have been a law against it!" She thinks I'm institutionalized.'

'What do you mean?' Annie was smiling, sure he was joking about this.

'I've never really left school. I've been teaching at boarding schools most of my adult life. St Vincent's is a real departure, believe me. I have my own home . . . well, Mum's old home. I have to cook for myself and clean . . . well, in my own way . . . Believe me, these are big steps! I mean,' he went on, 'I have tried to break free before. For a year or two I was in this travelling band . . .'

Owen looked up at him with something approaching awe.

'But I don't know, I think I must have missed the custard and steamed pudding too much. Come September, I feel a real longing for the smell of fresh radiator paint and newly kicked-up rugby pitches. Sad.' He shook his head at himself. 'Very sad, but true.'

'But you're getting over it?' she reminded him.

'Trying to. There's something so appealing about boarding schools though. Especially the remote ones. I've worked in schools in the middle of nowhere, so you're in this hermetically sealed little community. You don't have to worry about all the things other people have to worry about. The bell rings, the next part of the day arrives, meals are served on the dot . . .'

'Clearly a big attraction,' Annie teased.

'You never have to shop for anything, ever. There are cupboards all over the school with everything you need: food, stationery.'

'Clothes?' she wondered.

'You can always raid the lost property box – find an old rugby shirt.'

'This is really explaining a lot about you.' Annie was smiling at him over her wine glass. 'What about your dad?' She decided to come out and just ask, because the desire to know was burning.

She heard Owen give a little sigh before Ed began his answer: 'My poor old dad got himself killed. Occupational hazard of being in the army, obviously.'

'I'm so sorry,' Annie offered.

'I was just about to sit my O levels. My sister and I flew out to my mum, then after a few days we flew back to school again and life carried on as normal. See, that's the thing about boarding schools – these enormous shocks can happen, but you're totally buffered. My daily life was just the same as if nothing had happened.'

'Not very healthy,' Lana informed him.

'No.' He shook his head. 'Maybe that's why Mum dying was such a . . . blow . . . I had some catching up to do.'

With these words, Annie, who'd previously found the mess, clutter and chaos of Ed's home so irritating and proof that he was hopelessly stuck in a groove, suddenly felt some real understanding and sympathy for what he was going through.

When she took herself off to his bathroom, which had one of those highly unsatisfactory electric shower over the bath arrangements, she saw a bar of soap on the sink, worn down to a sliver hardly bigger than a thumbnail. Presumably this was the kind of thing Ed would have found in one of those cupboards at boarding school.

Now she felt a pang of protectiveness towards him.

Back in the sitting room, when she settled down to her tiles again, she found that Ed had switched seats. He'd come down off the sofa and had pulled up an old corduroy beanbag next to her cushion.

'You're wasting your time trying to cheat off me,' she teased.

'Who says I need to cheat?' he asked, tipping his tiles out into his hand and using them to change her 'resist' into 'irresistible'.

He caught her eye and gave such a tiny quirk with his eyebrow that she wasn't sure if she'd seen it or not.

Two more rounds of the game were played, with Owen and Ed in an increasingly vicious and competitive battle, while Annie trailed hundreds of points behind. Secretly she was bursting with pride at her son. When did he get so clever? she wondered. Clearly, his many hours spent watching *Countdown* had paid off.

Ed seemed to be trying to lose, as his final offerings – 'dreamy' and 'date' – didn't seem up to his usual standard at all.

Suddenly a shrill alarm clock sounded in the room and Ed leapt up to his feet.

'Is that your bedtime bell, Ed?' Lana asked, which made them all laugh.

'No, no . . . got to let the cats out,' Ed explained, clearly embarrassed he'd been so startled.

When they laughed even more at his explanation, he felt he had to elaborate: 'If I'm playing the guitar or something, hours can go by and they've not been out and—'

'Don't cats let themselves out? Haven't you got a cat flap?' Owen wanted to know.

'Oh no, not my cats, they're too lazy. I have to chase them out,' he confided. 'So . . . you're all heading back to Essex now?' he asked when Annie saw to her surprise that it was close to midnight and announced that they really would have to go, although she was tired and too cosy and comfortable here.

'No. Not after this much wine,' she reminded him. 'We're going to stay with Connor. I spoke to him earlier.' And now she was going to have to turn her attention to the difficult phone call ahead of her. Already there were voicemail messages and five missed calls from Gray's numbers.

'Annie and family!' was Connor's greeting as he held open his front door for them. Looking straight at Annie, with undisguised sympathy for the long and gruelling day he knew she'd had, he added: 'Yes, well . . . come on in, I've been expecting you.'

'We've been up Daddy's hill,' Lana told him.

'Yeah,' Connor smoothed her hair with his hand, 'I heard.'

Chapter Thirty-one

Hector in love (with Connor):

Organic cords (Howies)
Eco-slogan T-shirt (Howies)
Two-strap vegan sandals (Birkenstock)
Sheer black net boxers (La Redoute)
Est. cost: £180

'Darlings, isn't it a wonderful evening!'

Annie left her children in Connor's care and drove alone to Essex through quiet Sunday morning traffic to face Gray.

All the way there, she convinced herself it wouldn't be a big problem . . . it wouldn't be so hard. But on arrival at Gray's house, at the sight of his tragically apologetic face at the opened front door, she realized nothing about this would be easy.

Gray kissed her gently on the cheek, touching her shoulder as he did, and showed her in. He'd been tidying, that was obvious. The sitting room had been almost restored to the immaculate minimalism of her first visit, apart from a few packing cases tucked away into the corners.

Immediately he offered coffee and she followed him through into the kitchen, where the taps gleamed and surfaces sparkled in a way they'd never done while she was in residence.

While the coffee was brewing he began with a string of apologies.

He was sorry he'd been so grumpy and difficult to live with . . . he was finding it hard to adjust to having so many people living in his home, but he promised he was getting used to the idea and he was enjoying so much about it: *'honestly'*, he assured her.

His dazzling chrome Gaggia machine chuffed and glugged in the background as he went on. Although personally, Annie liked coffee made in a 20-quid cafetière (was Gaggia coffee really £500 or so more tasty?) or even instant if she was in a hurry. What was wrong with instant, anyway? Especially the first cup from a new jar.

'I found the Valium and the Temazepam,' Gray told her, shamefaced, 'under a pile of stuff in the sitting room. I must have put them down . . . then something went on top . . . then something else. Anyway, I owe Lana an apology.'

'You do,' Annie agreed. 'A big one. You can't go around making accusations like that. You have to tread carefully with children, build up their confidence and their trust, not take great swipes at them like that.'

'I'm so sorry,' he sighed. The sound of coffee trickling into his dainty white cups began.

'I'm going to do much better at all of this, I promise you,' he said and squeezed her hands.

Now Annie's big bold decision to tell him goodbye, pack up some of their things and leave him wasn't so certain. It didn't feel so clear-cut. He wasn't a bad person. He saw what had gone wrong, didn't he? And he wanted to try for them. This was a man who had a lot to offer.

She looked out through the windows into the big garden, where green branches were swaying in the gentle breeze, and she imagined Lana on a sun-lounger reading, Owen digging up earth to conduct a biological experiment. In London, they didn't even have a garden. They had windowboxes and trips to the park.

Gray set her coffee before her and poured in just the right amount of milk without asking, which struck her as a caring action.

Then he turned and opened a cupboard, but instead of bringing out a packet of biscuits, he came back with a small leather-covered box, which he held out to her. No prizes for guessing what was in there, she told herself, taking a deep and steadying breath.

Wordlessly, she took the box from him and carefully opened the lid.

From the dark velvet bed inside, a bright white diamond – oval, maquise cut, she recognized – shone back at her. At least one carat, she estimated, maybe even 1.2. Very, very white and clear. She couldn't help but turn the box slightly to catch the light and make the surface sparkle.

It was absolutely breathtaking. She'd waited patiently all her adult life for a ring like this. Roddy's promise to her when she turned 30 (didn't happen then) . . . well, maybe when the big job came (didn't happen then) . . . well, maybe with the profits of the next house move (didn't happen then) . . . the day had never come. It turned out to be too hard to lash out hard-earned money on a diamond once they had children and a mortgage.

She'd even briefly considered buying herself the ring out of Roddy's small life insurance – but that had seemed far too frivolous.

'Oh . . . my . . . God,' she managed finally in a low and breathy voice.

Gray's eyes were trained on her face, waiting for the smile to break and the overwhelming 'yes' of renewed commitment to come.

Instead, Annie asked, 'What about Marilyn?'

Before he could make any excuse or fresh fib or cover up, she added simply, 'I know you saw her yesterday.' And with those words she wondered when he had bought the ring. Before seeing his wife? Afterwards? Today? At some early morning fabulous diamond store? Or in the days before the big row? It seemed important to know.

A splutter emerged from Gray in response to her question.

'Marilyn . . . well . . .' he stammered, 'she wanted to have a chat about the divorce . . . how things were going with me. And I didn't tell you because I didn't want you to think—'

'There's never any need to lie to me about anything . . . I hope,' Annie told him coolly. 'If you lie and I find out then I'm going to think all sorts of things. Right now,

I'm thinking: your ex-wife wanted to talk, so you take her for a cosy lunch at Le Pont d'Or? Hmmm. Then you offer me a big, stunning diamond. Hmmm. This is strange behaviour, Gray. This is a man who's not sure what he wants.'

Something about his flickering look – it went from her to his coffee cup, to the ring box in her hand and back to her – made her decision clear to her once again. Carefully she closed the box on the breathtaking, once-in-a-lifetime diamond and placed it gently down on the table, then she slid it slowly back towards him.

Feeling tears of regret pricking at the back of her eyes, she told him: 'I'm sorry, Gray. I'm really sorry, but we're not going to work out.' Catching the gasp these words seemed to have provoked at the back of her throat, she added, 'We need someone for the three of us . . . someone to take us all on. You're a very special person' – the tears were slipping freely down her cheeks now – 'you'll be really good for someone else. But you're not the one for us. I'm sorry.'

He hung his head at these words and may even have been squeezing back some tears of his own. Annie wiped at her cheeks, then took several tissues from the box Gray was holding out for her and blew her nose hard.

After several moments, she felt together enough to ask, 'You will get a refund on that ring, won't you? You didn't buy it off a dodgy internet site?'

'Don't worry, I'll get a refund,' he told her before putting his hand on her arm and asking if she was absolutely sure . . . wouldn't she like some time to think this over?

'No. This is the right thing,' she assured him. 'Hard to do, but still the right thing. Bloody hell!' she added after a moment's pause. 'Packing again!'

'Where are you going to go?' he asked. 'Your flat's—'

'Rented out for another five months, I know. Well . . .' She'd worked through a plan on the way up the motorway. 'We'll stay at Connor's till I've hustled up a deposit, then I mortgage myself to the hilt and buy the place in need of a makeover I was planning to get anyway – so it'll be fine,' she assured him.

'You don't have a job right now, Annie,' he reminded her.

'That's never stopped me before,' she told him firmly.

'You can stay here as long as you need to,' Gray offered, maybe in some last hope that he'd be able to persuade her to stay . . . or maybe just because he felt guilty.

'No, no. It's best we go. I might have to leave some boxes here for bit, just till we get sorted. But I'll load up now with whatever I can.'

She stood up, leaving both the coffee and the diamond untouched on the table.

Shame, she couldn't help thinking. But you weren't allowed to take the ring and then leave, were you?

'Strong drink required,' was Connor's verdict when Annie arrived back at his place looking pale and tired, laden down with most of her and her children's possessions.

'Is that your answer to everything?' she wondered.

'In what situations does strong drink not work?' he wondered back.

She, Connor and his boyfriend, Hector, got a little tipsy on fizzy wine he'd blagged from some photo shoot and all shared giant man-sized pizzas with Lana and Owen.

Annie hadn't realized, until she, her children and most of their belongings had arrived, that Hector was now a live-in fixture at Connor's. Usually she would be very happy for Connor, but right now it was another irritation to cope with.

But tonight, tipsy on the fizz and conscious that Annie might not want to have to talk about Gray, or moving, or not being able to go home, or the general chaos, Connor and Hector drummed up enthusiasm for a ruthless card game with truth or dare as the consequence of failure.

It involved Connor having to reveal who he'd first kissed (a girl, of course, way back in the days before he'd admitted he was gay), and Hector having to lean out of the window and shout 'Darlings, isn't it a wonderful evening!' Lana, who under no circumstances was choosing 'truth', had to promise she would go to school in the morning with her shirt tucked in, her cardigan done up all the way and pigtails.

Owen had no problem with imitating five different farmyard animals on the balcony and then finally it was Annie's turn.

'Truth! Truth!' Lana chanted. 'We want to know everything.'

'No way!' was Annie's response. 'Oh . . . it'll all come out in the wash anyway . . . eventually. Cover your ears, Owen.' In a whisper she added, 'Yes, he was rubbish in bed . . . you already know that though, don't you?'

Connor and Lana nodded, while Owen added: 'I heard that!'

'Anyway, dare. I chose dare, go on . . . bet you can't think of anything I'm scared to do. I ain't scared of anything now, Connor McCabe.'

A slow, cunning smile began to spread across Connor's face. 'Oh-oh! Nothing I like more than a challenge. Right, Annie Valentine . . . here's your dare.'

He paused for a moment, for entirely dramatic effect.

'You have to kiss again the last person you kissed passionately.'

'Ha!' she laughed. 'Well that's impossible. I've broken off with Gray, Roddy's . . . unavailable. I haven't kept the numbers of any previous dates . . .'

'Mum!' came from Lana.

'No, no, no, my girl,' Connor interrupted, 'I don't mean any of them.'

Annie looked at him blankly.

'Can't think?' he asked.

'No idea what you're talking about,' she insisted. 'Oh, not the One Night Wonder! Just a little snog,' she added quickly, seeing the surprise on Lana's face.

'I heard that!' came from Owen.

'No, no, no, not him. I'm going to tell you a little story, Annie,' Connor began. 'One afternoon, I took the tube up to Highgate to see my friends Annie, Lana and Owen. When I arrived at their lovely little mansion block, the lift was out of action, so I swung open the heavy door at the foot of the stairs and began my climb up . . .' In full dramatic flight now with voice modulation and eye rolling in the style of a murder-mystery narrator, Connor went on: 'I was wearing rubber-soled shoes and as I climbed up, noticing how noiseless they were against the beautiful stone steps, I thought I heard your voice high up in the stairwell above me. Yes, it was definitely you and you were talking to someone . . . Is it starting to come back now?'

Annie made no reply, so he went on: 'Yes, you were talking, then all of a sudden there was total silence. I sped up, taking the steps two at a time, wondering what was happening, and that's when I got a glimpse of you, two flights above me, totally entangled with someone. The kiss went on and on and on, my girl. Remember now?'

Annie was starting to look a little strange: slightly too pale but with a pink flush across her cheeks.

'I tiptoed as quietly as I could back down the staircase so that I didn't interrupt anything, then I waited for a few minutes. Imagine my surprise when tripping down the stairs, with a great spring in his step, came—'

'That's enough utter nonsense, Connor!' Annie stopped him. 'What a complete fantasist you are.'

She looked over at her children, who were glued to Connor with expectation.

'Who?!' asked Lana.

'All I'm saying,' Connor looked squarely at Annie, 'is that if you want to stay here any longer, you better go and kiss *that* man again. That's my dare.'

'Huh!' Annie huffed, looking thunderous. 'I need to go to bed,' and with that, she picked herself up from the sofa and headed towards the door.

But then she turned and added angrily: 'Here's my dare to you, Connor McCabe. Grow up, and you know what else? Come out properly, for God's sake. Don't fudge it in the interviews any more. In the twenty-first century it's a bad career move to be an actor who isn't gay.'

She slammed the door hard behind her.

'Some people,' said Connor, 'are just stubborn. They have no idea what's good for them and they have to be taken firmly in hand.'

Chapter Thirty-two

Annie in action:

Pale grey and silver striped trousers (Toast sale)
Crisp white wrap blouse, big collars and
cuffs (last year's MaxMara)
Shiny silver and turquoise neck cuff (Camden market)
Pale caramel shoes (Chanel)
Light red nail varnish (Chanel)
Light red lipstick (Chanel)
Tight ponytail
Est. cost: Don't even think about it

'It's a waste of money to economize on yourself.'

It was close to 1.30 a.m., but Annie was still hunched over her laptop putting the finishing touches to the introductory paragraphs on her Annie V Trading Station web-pages.

This was the largest amount of goods she'd ever tried to sell, but she was hoping to raise money just as quickly as she could. Life with the actor boys could not be tolerated for more than a few more weeks at the most and she wasn't quite ready to accept a family loan, although it was nice to know it had been offered: 'Annie, I'm your sister!' Nic had insisted, when she'd called. 'I'm also a lawyer, in case you hadn't noticed. I can lend you the money for a flat deposit, or to rent somewhere else for a while.'

'Annie, if you need any help, financially . . .' Fern had begun.

'We have more money now, you could borrow some . . .' was Dinah's offer.

But no, Annie had to try to get there on her own first.

Now, she just needed to finalize her sales pitch because she had a pile of cracking stuff to shift – she had scoured secondhand shops and sale rails across London, plus approached every client she could think of and offered to sell on their cast-offs for commission.

Hello girls, her website note began, as usual.

Do I have some fabulous, fabulous things in store for you today. It's the on-line equivalent of Opening Day at the Harrods sale. There's going to be tussling and handbags at dawn. Put your very best bids in, girls, nothing will be left on the shelf.

Today, I'm bringing you the property of:

One Russian fashion maven (Svetlana's divorce fighting fund)

Several wealthy young ladies (the Syrup Six's prized personal possessions, rustled up to plug the hole in the charity account)

A footballer's moll (Dannii was ridding her life of bling after another bitching in *heat*)

An unbowed divorcee (Megan had been talked into selling off some of the clothes from her married years)

A Lady of the Arts (These were very special things. The one client she'd asked for a short-term loan: Mrs B-P – recovering nicely and determined to live life to the full – had handed over designer labels, expensive classics, several collectable handbags and wouldn't hear of taking a penny for them. Not now and not in the future: 'Annie, I can help, I want to help, so be a good girl and let me help.')

As well as the treasures unearthed for you this week by me, your very own on-line Personal Shopper.

As I said before, girls . . . do not hang about. Grab yourself a bargain! Remember always that it's a waste of money to economize on yourself. I think Coco Chanel said that.

Keep it coming . . .

Annie V xxxx

Annie pressed the return button and posted the words up. Her room at Connor's house was crammed to bursting with boxes of things she still had to photograph and post up before she went to bed.

And she had an early start. Her ring-round of all her former Store clients to tell them she was now freelance and could shop with them anywhere in London, and by the way did they have any old things they wanted to sell through her, had resulted in twelve appointments for the week ahead. Somehow she would also have to squeeze in attendance at Lana and Owen's speech day.

*   *   *

Speech Day was a big event at St Vincent's. It was held two days before the end of term and even the most stressed and frantically busy London parent pulled out all the stops in order to attend.

This was St Vincent's on parade. Every pupil was scrubbed and combed, the lawns were freshly mown, every one of the building's Victorian windows washed; even the gold lettering beaming down from the walls of the impressive assembly hall looked freshly polished.

Annie had persuaded Dinah to come with her despite their little debate:

'I'm not sending Billie there, you know.'

'But you've got enough money now.'

'But it's the principle.'

'Fine, fine . . . and where is the principle in moving out of your flat and into the catchment of the best church school in the city? Just don't tell me you've started going to church too . . .'

'The church is nice.'

'But you're an atheist!'

'It's still nice.'

Both Dinah and Annie were in knee-length dresses with bold prints and fashionable cuts (Annie: TK Maxx, Dinah: Marc Jacobs full price! *'I could have got that for you for less.' 'I don't care!'*). They had pastel macs folded over their arms (Annie: Primark, Dinah: Jigsaw), carried good bags and wore status shoes. It was that kind of event.

'Think chic summer wedding. But no corsage or hat,' Annie had instructed.

Settled into the middle of a row, not too far from the

front, Annie and her sister watched the prizes being handed out: Athletics, Cricket, Tennis, Badminton, French, German, English, History, Maths, Science, Latin, Greek, Music, House Cup for this, House Cup for that, Chess, Debating, Dominoes, Tiddlywinks. It went on for ever.

Dinah sighed and rolled her eyes in disapproval. But finally it was time for Lana and the other members of the Syrup Six to cross the stage and hand over a cheque for £11,000 to Mr Ketteringham-Smith.

Two days ago, Annie had written the girls a cheque for £500: the money raised by the sale of their stuff on her website.

The other £1,500 had come from Suzie's father, who had now been brought fully up to speed with his daughter's personal problems.

'Lana looks adorable,' Dinah whispered in Annie's ear and it was true. On Speech Day, senior girls were allowed to wear dresses and Lana had chosen (from Miss Selfridge) a short-sleeved white cotton wrap with cornflowers strewn about it. When in doubt, pick out your eye colouring with your clothes – a classic Annie rule.

Lana's hair was tied back loosely with strands flying as she walked shyly across the stage to deafening applause. Despite the hiccups with the fund-raising, Annie still felt a rush of pride in her daughter.

Now it was time for the musical performance. Annie could feel her stomach knot with tension. The school orchestra struck up with a collection of jaunty and un-usual numbers, all Ed's choice, no doubt.

He was conducting the young musicians – she was

pleased to see – wearing one of the outfits they'd chosen on the interview shopping trip.

With a great clumping of heavy black shoes on wood, the school choir filed on stage, then a much smaller group of musicians in front of them: two violin players, a drummer and finally Owen, clutching his guitar, looking small and skinny way up there on stage.

Annie could see he was pale with anxiety. Her stomach knots pulled tighter, she could feel her throat drying and clenching, so she gave a concerted swallow. Her hand felt for Dinah's and she gave it a nervous squeeze. Dinah squeezed back.

Ed glanced behind him and gave the audience a smile. It was a confidently reassuring kind of smile, which made Annie feel much better. He was going to be right there, standing in front of the performers. Owen would look at Ed and remember to breathe and his solo bit would happen and be over and Annie would be clapping before she knew it. It was OK.

The music began: verse one, then the chorus, then the strummed solo guitar intro to verse two and then Owen's solo . . .

If Annie had thought it would go quickly, she was wrong. Time slowed to a standstill and every one of Owen's notes hung and wavered in the air for her, every one of his breaths between notes seemed to take an entire minute: it was as if he could only sing if she willed it to happen.

She never breathed once during the entire verse, as his clear voice sailed over the crowd, then his lone guitar chords followed, and finally the choir and other musicians joined in.

Owen was still singing but now there was a delighted flush of pink and a smile trying to run away all over his face.

Annie let out a great sigh of relief and an irrepressible smile of her own broke out.

'Wasn't he amazing!' She sought Ed out in the crush of parents and staff jockeying for cream teas afterwards.

'I don't know if I can ever thank you enough,' Annie told him, squeezing his arm.

Ed, balancing teacup, saucer and a tiny plate overloaded with three scones and a mountain of cream, gave one of his blushes, then sneezed, spilling tea all over the floor.

'Whooops, I didn't hit you, did I?'

'Not with tea,' she assured him. 'Just snot . . . I'm joking, Ed,' she added quickly, when his blush threatened to go nuclear.

'This is my sister Dinah,' Annie introduced her. 'Lana and Owen's music teacher, Ed Leon.'

Ed nodded awkwardly, indicating that hands full made shaking impossible.

'So when are you heading to Boston?' Annie asked, adding for Dinah's benefit, 'Ed's very clever, he's got a term's placement at Harvard to study American folk music and he's spending the summer travelling round the States.'

'Wow!' Dinah told him. 'That's great.'

'Day after tomorrow,' he told them, but looked more anxious at the prospect than excited. 'First day of the school holidays, I'm away.'

He was looking at Annie in a slightly troubled way, as if there was something he wanted to say to her.

'Well, we should be saying our goodbyes then,' Annie said with a smile. 'I hope you have a great time. Really great.' She met his eyes and held them for a moment: 'You deserve this, Ed, enjoy it. We'll look forward to hearing all about it when you get back.'

She was just about to lean over his full hands and give him a little kiss on the cheek when he said, 'Yeah, well . . . have a good summer . . . all of you,' then teacup, saucer, scones and all, he turned away from them and headed into the crowd.

'Huh? That was a little cool, considering how much we've seen of him – how friendly he's been with the children,' Annie couldn't help telling her sister.

'Maybe he's just stressed out by this whole school show-off event thing going on here. But great talent-spotting venue, Annie?' Dinah rallied. 'We should circle the room, picking off all the single dads for you.'

'Hmmm . . .' Annie, although she'd dressed and made up with extreme care and attention for the afternoon, wasn't at all keen.

'Annie!'

Her thoughts were disrupted by the sight of Tor in front of her. Tor in a summer dress and heels, Tor with pink nail varnish and lip gloss. Tor looking slightly unrecognizable.

'Good grief!' was Annie's first reaction, quickly followed by, 'Good girl!'

She asked about the new flat, about Angela, and then she couldn't help asking: 'New job?'

Tor shook her head.

'Greatly improved love life?'

Tor shook her head again and confided: 'Just new scarves, Annie! Like this one?' She held up the wisp of pale pink chiffon for Annie's approval. 'I'm working on the other things . . . I'll get there.'

'Good girl!' Annie repeated with a grin.

Chapter Thirty-three

Martha on Oxford Street:

White and green flowery summer dress (Topshop)
Green leggings (Topshop)
Orange sandals (Miu Miu)
Orange tote bag (Accessorize)
Orange flower hairclip (Accessorize)
Green and silver necklace (Topshop)
Est. cost: £190

'You were right, I was spending far too much
money on the kids' clothes.'

'Annie? Hello, it's Ed.'

'Oh . . . Ed? Hi.' Annie was slightly taken aback to hear from him, especially after his abrupt goodbye yesterday. 'You must be busy packing.'

'Yes . . . yeah . . . look . . . There's something I wanted to ask you.'

Annie put a hand over her left ear, blocking out the noise of traffic on Oxford Street.

'Yup, fire away,' she said, wondering if this was going to be a 'which tie goes with which shirt?' query. She made a quick check on her watch, 9.50 a.m., just ten minutes before she was due to hook up with Indira Clifford (long-term client, wealthy lawyer) in Selfridge's. She quickened her pace along the pavement.

'Well, it's just . . .' Ed began, 'I was thinking . . . you and the children could do with a temporary home. Well, so I understand . . . Lana's explained you've moved back to London. Anyway . . . I really need to get my place redecorated because I'm planning to sell it, so while I'm away in the States I just wondered . . . I mean obviously, totally up to you . . . it would be a hassle for you, but you'd obviously not pay any rent and I'd pay for all the decorating . . . well, I need help with it and I just thought maybe it would tide you over . . .'

She understood exactly what he was suggesting and immediately thought it was a perfect short-term solution: 'Brilliant idea, Ed! Brilliant!' she exclaimed. 'We probably won't even be there long, just enough time to sort it all out for you and find a place of our own. Fantastic!'

Recently, Annie had begun to think that even a few more nights of the heavy drinking, fun and games of living on top of Connor and Hector was going to kill her. But she was still some time away from being able to stump up the deposit on a new place. Here was this fantastic, unexpected solution coming at her out of the blue, proof that one should always wear lipstick, perfume, nice heels and stay positive.

'I'd need to see you before I go,' Ed was saying. 'Give you keys, show you round, ask what you think should be done, see what kind of budget is needed.'

Yes, of course Ed should have thought of this earlier, so they could have looked through brochures together, picked out kitchen cupboards, talked colour schemes, all that kind of thing. But never mind, she liked a plan that fell together at the last moment. Her mind was already racing ahead to redesigning the layout . . . to where Lana and Owen would sleep in the flat when the damp course was being put in . . .

She told Ed she would come round to his just after 1 p.m., so she would have an hour or two to talk to him before the children broke off from school for the summer holidays.

'How come you're not at school today, anyway?' she wondered.

'They gave me the day off to get organized. Maybe they had some idea how long it would take me.'

'Aha.'

Then Annie almost dropped her phone at the sight of the woman walking – no, make that sashaying – towards her. Was that . . . ? Could that be . . . ?

'I have to go,' she told Ed. 'See you later.'

'Hey! Nit girl!' Annie shouted once she'd hung up. She gave a vigorous wave. 'Get you!'

Martha Cooper's head turned and when she spotted Annie, she began to laugh. She'd lost weight, her hair was even lighter than the last time Annie had seen her. She looked great.

'Look at you!' Annie said coming up to her. 'You look fabulous. And it's only . . .' she gave Martha a quick up and down, 'only the shoes I can take credit for! Wow, good work! I hope you're going to recommend me to all your friends.'

'They are clamouring for your number!' Martha told her.

After a quick chat about Martha's children, Martha's work, Martha's new exercise regime, Martha thanked Annie sincerely for her advice.

'You were right,' she told her, 'I was spending far too much money on the kids' clothes. God! I was spending far too much time obsessing over the kids, full stop. Me and all the other haggard mothers hanging out at Baby Gymnastics. Those days are over . . . well, not entirely, obviously . . .' she added quickly, 'but at least I no longer look like their scruffy au pair.'

Ed answered his battered door and showed Annie into the kitchen. He was wearing trousers and a shirt from the clothes they'd chosen together, his hair had been trimmed rather than hacked off and she couldn't help thinking how well he looked. He was obviously preparing for his big US adventure and she was proud of her handiwork.

Fleetingly she wondered if he might land himself an American girlfriend and maybe not come back to St Vincent's again. That would be so nice for him, she told herself. She wasn't sure what Owen would do but . . .

'What time's your flight tomorrow?' she asked him, stepping well away from the cats' dishes which she'd landed in twice before.

'Four p.m.,' he replied.

There was something of a restlessness to him she hadn't seen before, because usually he was so calm. His hair-rummaging had increased, he spilled water on the kettle's journey from the sink to the hob and couldn't seem to locate a cloth to wipe the puddle away.

'I'm fine for tea,' she assured him. 'Shall we make a start on looking round?'

After a pause he said, 'Yes, yes, no problem,' but his voice sounded uncertain, almost as if he'd forgotten what she was here for.

They went into the sitting room where Annie wasted no time getting down on her knees to lift the peeling wallpaper and inspect the damp again. 'This will have to be treated first,' she told him. 'We can't do any decorating in here till that's been sorted.'

Then she began her knowledgeable damp talk. Did he want to put in a chemical damp-proof course, or did he want to go the conservation route and look into lime plasters and porous paint?

'Oh, right . . . well, whatever you think,' was his distracted answer, then he began talking about what time his plane would arrive in Boston and how he'd travel on from there.

'OK, focus, Ed!' she reminded him. 'If you don't want to finalize the damp issue today, we could at least talk about kitchen units and sub-floor insulation and colour schemes. I need to know your budget . . . whether you want to repaper, replaster or just paint over the old stuff . . . all that kind of thing.'

'No, no,' he shook his head, 'I'm going to leave it up to you. I'm selling anyway, so I'll write a cheque and then you just make it look as nice as you can. As nice as you will,' he added. 'I know your flat, it's lovely.'

'Aha, very trusting.' Annie was wondering why someone who hadn't been able to clear out even a bookshelf

405

for years was suddenly planning an entire home renovation and move. The imminent American sabbatical was obviously having a motivating effect on him. She wondered also where he planned to go next.

'OK, I've seen your kitchen, your sitting room, your bathroom . . . if it's not too personal, can I see your bedroom?' she asked him.

Ed rummaged with his hair, gave a strange sort of half-yawn, then a sneeze. 'It's obviously fairly untidy . . . what with all the packing and everything,' he warned her.

'You're really nervous about the trip, aren't you?' Annie ventured. She hadn't seen him look agitated before; usually he was so laid back.

'Kind of,' was all the response he made to this.

'Hey.' She stood up from the sofa arm she'd perched on briefly and walked over towards him. 'You're going to be fine,' she reassured him with a smile. 'You're going to have the time of your life and I promise I'll take care of everything here, including the storage of all your mother's things. I'll look after it all for you.'

'Right.' He gave her a tight little smile, then turned. 'My bedroom,' he said and she followed him into the corridor.

She wondered why she was feeling a flicker of nervousness herself now. Watching how he bent down to avoid the low ceiling light, she did likewise, then he had to angle his broad shoulders from the narrow corridor into the bedroom door.

'Here we go.'

Then they were both in the dark green room, standing side by side, arms almost touching. She looked round briefly, taking in the wooden double bed, the jumble of clothes and cases on top of it, the framed posters, piles of books, overflowing cupboard and drawers. It was messy, just like Ed, but it was also welcoming and comforting . . . just like Ed.

A narrow French window led out to a dainty garden in as luscious and unkempt a state as Ed's hair. A rose bush, bent over with heavy yellow-pink heads, was bobbing up and down in the breeze, scattering petals onto the path below.

'Very nice,' Annie said, 'but a much lighter green . . . maybe?'

'Maybe,' came back, the word sounding as if it had been forced through a dry throat.

'It's OK,' she assured him again. 'You're going to have a great time!' and then, in what she felt was a kind and maternal sort of gesture, she put her arm round Ed's waist and squeezed a little.

The result of this was that he turned, moved his arms around her and, not for the first time, they *seemed* to be kissing.

Mouth against mouth, they touched each other. That definitely counted as kissing, didn't it?

She realized he tasted the same as before and that she had a clear memory of the taste of him. His warm body, pushed against her, was now not just new or hesitant and awkward, it was welcomingly familiar. She'd held him before. But this time was better. This time they pulled each other close.

'How are you doing?' she said against his soft, slightly downy ear when they stopped for a moment, to pause for breath.

'I'm extremely, extremely nervous,' he whispered back to her.

'Where's your sense of adventure?' she asked in between landing little licks and kisses against his warm neck. 'It's the trip of a lifetime.'

With his hands on her shoulders, he pulled her just slightly away from him so he could look at her face properly: 'It's not the trip,' he said with a smile. 'It's you . . . I'm in a total state about you.'

'Oh!' This was unexpected . . . to say the least.

Annie didn't know what to say next, so she leaned forward to press her lips against his; her hands moved to the small of his back and held him tightly as his lips parted. She moved her tongue against his and enjoyed the slow slide. The roll and gentle chase. Their teeth touched just slightly. His mouth pushed at hers and she felt the hungry tingle start to buzz through her body.

'Does kissing help?' she broke off to ask.

'Uh-huh,' he told her.

She pulled his shirt from his waistband and put her cool fingertips against his skin, felt his soft side goose-pimpling at her touch.

He was holding her chin in his hands and kissing down her neck. Strands of his hair were tickling her neck and shivers were travelling over her shoulders and down her arms. Gently, he pushed her shirt and bra strap away so he could kiss the top of her shoulders.

She loosened her arm from the strap and the sleeve so that the top of her breast was visible now.

Putting his nose against the fold of her arm, he kissed her there. His hand drew the fabric over her nipple, brushing past the hardening tip on the way.

Everywhere he touched or stroked or brushed against was hair on end, desperate to be felt by him again.

Unbuttoning his shirt as quickly as she could, she pulled his warm body against hers.

They were both topless and kissing frantically at mouths, nipples, necks and shoulders, feeling each other over and over at once quickly and yet tenderly.

When her hands moved to undo his belt buckle, his hands moved on top of hers, holding them still.

'Annie?' he said into her neck. 'I don't want you to rush into—'

'Well I do,' she cut him off and gave a vigorous tug at the belt, which was surprisingly unyielding.

'Annie!' His hand held on to hers again.

'Ed! Please!' She began to rub against the obvious swelling underneath the fabric of his trousers, causing him to groan against her ear.

'Ed,' she began, 'do you have any idea . . . ?' She'd found the fly buttons buried in the fabric below the belt buckle and her fingertips were busy trying to loosen them.

'Do you have any idea how much I want you?' she continued. True. She hadn't realized until the moment they'd started kissing – well, maybe that last kiss on the stairwell had been an inkling – but now that they were half naked together there was going to be no backing out. She wasn't going to let him. She had to have him. Please!

The first button was undone, then the second, her fingers were already inside his trousers, his teeth were biting gently at her shoulder, but his back was arched away from her.

'Ed,' she said into his hair, 'my husband died when I was thirty-two, I've got to make up for so much lost time . . . you've no idea . . .'

The third button sprang open and she could fit her hand in now, move past the thin material of his boxers and feel for him. Firmly, insistently touch him, causing the bite against her shoulder to intensify.

'I'm not letting you get away. No way. I can't let you . . .'

The back moved in now, pushing his stomach and his erection in towards her. His warm, bare arms closed in round her and she was squashed up against him.

He'd finally agreed to go with the flow. Then they were busy: stripping off their clothes as quickly as they could.

He pushed her skirt up and in the following moments he transformed in Annie's mind from the person she'd thought he was into someone much more interesting.

Before, she'd found him boyish, chaotic, incapable and needy . . . but no, no, no, it turned out he was someone much more grown up than that. Much more insistent and yet tender, much more practised and yet still so very, very kind.

In his every move against her and with her was the fine balance of intention and question. As if he were asking her over and over again, but without words: I'm going to do this, I'm going to go here, and move in here . . . but only if it's OK. Is this OK? Is this what you want? Yes? And this too?

They took off every shred of clothing, although she'd thought she didn't want to be so exposed to him. She moved her hands away and let him kiss her all the way down her stomach until he was kneeling in front of her and his tongue was where she'd thought she wouldn't want him yet.

She had to let him keep on moving and touching and moving there until she felt the tiny rush build and knew she was going to come when she hadn't meant to. Not at all, she'd wanted to keep that to herself, in reserve. Hold back from him. But he hadn't let her. He wanted all of her, every centimetre, and deep into her mind too.

Shuddering over him, hands sinking into his springy hair, she now wanted to know all about him, everything, every little past moment, kink and detail, and definitely all about his past lovers.

'You're very interesting to me . . . do you know that?' she told him with the edge of her voice.

His response was to sweep all the jumble of stuff off his bed so they could fall down on top of it together.

Tangling into him, she sniffed at his armpits and realized the acute anxiety she must have caused him because he smelled of fresh, nervous sweat. She'd forgotten how delicious the smell of male sweat was . . . Well, Gray had never let the slightest whiff of it hang about him.

It hit the back of her throat and made her feel warm, dizzy and turned on. She buried her nose right against him, making him release a throaty laugh.

She sat on top of him and briefly took him inside as they looked at each other with their eyes wide open, still full of surprise.

Afterwards, she lay she stretched out on the bed

beside him, utterly naked, with unselfconscious stubble on her upflung armpit, and remembered how glorious sex could be, because she'd been in serious danger of forgetting.

A long, deep silence followed.

He tucked her in under his arm and then they lay side by side looking at the ceiling, not wanting to break the silence.

But Annie couldn't resist lifting her head and leaning over to kiss him again and the kiss broke the spell.

He smiled broadly, crinkling the skin round his eyes, and told her: 'Parent–teacher relationship . . . we've really overstepped it this time.'

'Did you know you liked me?' she asked him, feeling with her hand for his and running her fingers across it. It was a broad hand with big thumb joints and finger-tips hardened with guitar playing, not that this had roughened his touch in the slightest.

'Did I know I liked you? Let me see . . .' Ed began, eyes fixed on the ceiling, a fresh smile on his face, 'I've considered taking up smoking for the first time in five years, I'm playing Elvis ballads till two in the morning, not to mention "My funny Valentine", I can't think about anything else except your face and the way you flick your ponytail and walk very, very fast and call everyone around you "babes" . . . yes, I think we can safely say I knew I liked you . . . but you' – he put his finger on the tip of her nose – 'you didn't know you liked me, did you?'

'I liked you, Ed,' she told him, running her hand across his stomach. 'I just hadn't realized until today that I fancied the pants off you.'

'What about that kiss?' he wanted to know. 'Before, on your stairwell. The one I've been thinking about maybe ten, twenty times an hour ever since.'

She let out a shriek of laughter at this then told him cheekily: 'I put that one down to hunger. I was on a detox that week, it can have strange effects.'

They turned, rolled into one another and began to kiss again.

'It's after two p.m.,' she told him, raising her arm to catch a glimpse of her watch behind his head.

'You're going to be very late,' he warned her. 'Better phone Lana, tell her to walk over here with Owen very, very slowly.' He was licking at her again.

She put her hands against his cheeks and pulled his face up to look into it properly: 'Do I really know you?' she asked him. 'You seem so different in bed.'

'Do I?' he asked as his hand moved to her tummy button then downwards with deft little strokes.

'Aha,' she nodded. 'But I like you. I do, definitely, like you.'

After the second time came not a spellbound silence, but tears.

Annie curled away from Ed in the bed and couldn't stop herself from crying.

'What's the matter?' He leaned over her, stroking her arm, desperately concerned.

'Please don't go away now,' she heard herself say, although she hated how small and sad her voice sounded. 'Don't leave me now . . . You're going to be away for ages and what if something happens?'

What was she saying? Suddenly, she was going to

413

pieces! She wanted to stop herself but instead, found she was wailing, 'What if I lose you too?' Then general blubbing noises followed. It was horrible. Horrible.

But Ed's arm was around her, holding her together through this, just as it had done before. What was it about this man? Without ever asking, he seemed to bring her defences down every time.

He got to her. Got through to her. Connected. Got past the shell she'd built tightly around herself and saw how she really was. Drew the inner Annie out and made love to her. In a way no-one had since Roddy. That's why it felt so breathtaking. So private and close. So real.

'I'm away for four and a half months,' he was telling her gently, kissing her hair. 'I've always wanted to do this trip and I think I should. I think it's good . . . for . . . us.' He said the word as lightly as possible, hardly daring to use it. 'You shouldn't be rushed into anything, Annie,' he said and tightened his grip on her. 'You should take things very slowly. 'I'll come back and visit you at half-term,' he added. 'That's just ten weeks away. No time, no time at all. You can come out and see me . . . if you want to.'

'But I'll miss you . . . we'll miss you so much.' She was still crying. Still feeling great confusion about why she suddenly cared so very much about this man. This morning she'd have waved him off happily at the airport: now she felt prepared to lie down in front of the plane.

He brushed her tears carefully away and held her close for several long, quiet minutes. Then he got down from the bed and went round the room retrieving her clothes.

'Time to get dressed,' he told her. 'Come on – I want

to show you where Owen and Lana can sleep, before they get back here.'

'I've already planned it,' Annie told him as she pulled on her clothes and tried to sound brighter than she felt. 'Owen and I will share your room, Lana can have a sofa bed in the sitting room.'

'No, no,' Ed told her. 'There's some space upstairs.'

'Oh.'

This was obviously one of those wonky conversions where neighbours had done deals in the past and a cupboard full of stairs would lead to a stairwell converted into a poky little room.

Once they were both in their clothes, Ed un-shyly led her by the hand to a door in the sitting room: the cupboard full of stairs, as she'd guessed.

He opened the door and a stone staircase, lit by a window from above, was in front of them.

'This connected the basement kitchen to the dining room, back in ye olde days,' he explained.

She followed him up and they came out into a big, pale yellow room, flooded with light from the tall Georgian windows at both ends

Plaster from the small holes in the ceiling had splattered the bare floorboards, but she didn't dwell on that. It was a fabulous room, and so empty compared with the rest of Ed's flat.

'There's a roof problem,' he began, 'I've had to take loads of stuff downstairs from the other rooms.'

'Other rooms?' Annie repeated.

'Yeah, there's this dining room, well, it was Mum's sitting room, then there's her kitchen next door and then her bedroom upstairs and two little attic bedrooms.'

Annie gaped at him, eyes wide, mouth hanging – not entirely flatteringly – wide open.

Finally, when her power of speech had returned she asked him in utter amazement: *'You own the whole house?!'*

'Well, I owe my sister a third . . . Mum helped her buy her flat . . . so the arrangement was Hannah would get a third when it was time to sell up.'

But Annie didn't seem to take this in.

'You own the whole house?' she repeated. 'A whole house, on my favourite street . . .' Annie was heading towards the dining room door, eager to see the rest of the rooms. 'Ed, baby,' she said over her shoulder, 'do you realize? All this time you've been hiding your most attractive feature from me!'

Chapter Thirty-four

The Preppie returns:

White cotton button-down shirt (Brooks Brothers)
Slim-fit khaki chinos (Banana Republic)
Midnight blue cashmere V-neck (Brooks Brothers)
Hiking boots (some things are harder to change)
Est. cost: $390

'Are you sure, Annie? I mean, are you really, really sure?'

'You look brilliant. Absolutely fantastic! Completely shaggable – and take that as a big compliment because I'm a gay man. Very gay,' Connor added, waving a copy of the *Daily Mail* at them.

Right across the top of page five was a photo of him and Hector attending a film première in matching kilts with the caption: *The Manor's Connor McCabe shows off the new man in his life.*

'Shut up will you!' Annie shot at him. 'You were supposed to stay in the kitchen with Dinah and keep out of our way.'

But Svetlana was laughing: 'Is fine,' she said in her melodious alto. 'I miss a man's opinion of how I look.'

'OK, come and see in the mirror,' Annie instructed, stepping back to admire her handiwork.

She directed Svetlana towards the huge three-sided mirror in the corner of her bright white office. The room, which had once been Ed's tatty sitting room, was now transformed. There was a desk with computer and telephone in one corner with a filing cabinet next to it topped with a monumental stack of fashion magazines. The room's centrepiece was a comfortable pink sofa, with close at hand the mirror and several all-important clothes rails on wheels. The rails were for clients to hang up their many, many clothes: the ones they'd bought with Annie, the ones they'd dragged from the back of the wardrobe, the ones they needed help to part with or help to dare to wear.

'Oh this is very good,' Svetlana declared as she took a careful look at herself from all possible angles.

She was in a tight white Chanel suit with black trim on the jacket lapels. Black and white T-bar shoes and a small black patent bag completed the look.

The gas baron's soon-to-be-ex-wife had her hair pulled back, soberly but softly, and her make-up had been under-applied by Annie in a way intended to make her look beautiful but vulnerable.

This was a dress rehearsal for her day in the divorce court. Annie liked to clothe her very wealthy divorcees in white Chanel: 'White is a rite of passage colour. Chanel is as smart and appropriate as you can get, plus a couture suit costs reassuringly more than your wedding dress did. And it always seems to have a winning effect on the judge: male or female.'

'Perfect,' Annie agreed with Svetlana, smoothing the back of the jacket down. 'You go kick Igor in the balls tomorrow. Just make sure,' she added with a twinkle, 'that you do it . . .' her voice dropped low, *'sexy but ladylike.'*

This made both Connor and Svetlana laugh. Then the Russian's eye fell on the big black and white framed portrait photograph which dominated one of the white walls.

She walked towards it: 'A client?' she asked. 'He is very handsome, no?'

'Oh yes, babes, isn't he?' Annie agreed and felt . . . well . . . She walked over to stand beside Svetlana, so they were both looking at the photo of the roguish man in a black leather jacket leaning his chin on a balled-up fist, suppressing a grin and unmistakably hamming it for the camera.

'That's Roddy,' Annie said and she felt OK. She was even able to smile proudly and add: 'That's a gorgeous photo of my late husband, Lana and Owen's daddy.' She looked at Svetlana and gave a wink. 'We were very lucky to have had him. Weren't we, Connor?'

That's how Annie thought of it now. She had made peace with the reality that Roddy was no longer with them; now she was able to appreciate all the time they'd had together. She felt blessed to have had him. She tried to think of his life as completed, rather than tearing herself to pieces with the thought that it was unfinished. Only very recently had she begun to believe that just as much happiness as she'd once had would come her way again.

There was something else Svetlana wanted to ask: 'Are you going to come back to The Store, Annah? Or are you staying here in your lovely office where we have to come to you?'

In all honesty, Annie hadn't decided.

Paula was the one who had phoned first to announce Donna's demise with the words: 'Ding, dong, the wicked witch is dead!'

'Maybe two or three days a week,' Annie told Svetlana. 'Maybe something like that can be arranged, but I don't know yet . . . I like working for myself. I like taking clients to whatever shop I think will suit them best. And I love bossing them about in my office!'

When Svetlana had left (by taxi – getting her driver back was one of her top settlement priorities), it was time to see what Dinah and Billie were doing in the kitchen upstairs.

The former dining room had been transformed into a modern, glamorous kitchen (but by using only the finest discount suppliers, Annie had come in under Ed's careful budget).

'How's the cake? Oh Billie, what a brilliant idea! Is it a boat?' Annie asked looking at the grey, knobbly sausage of mauled icing Billie had plonked into the middle of the iced 'welcome home' cake.

'No, stupid!' came the insulted reply. 'It's a plane.'

'Aren't you changing, Annie? You know . . . to look your most fabulous?' Dinah asked, expecting Annie to have a whole top-to-toe outfit planned for this big reunion moment.

'Something from your New York trip,' Connor urged.

'It was three weeks ago and you've not shown off a single thing.'

'Ah, New York!' Annie gave a sigh. 'I told you, Connor, it was a total shopping disaster. There I was in the shopping capital of the Western world with three empty credit cards and I never got round to shopping! I never even got up the Empire State Building! I . . . we . . .' and all of a sudden she felt slightly shy in front of her two best friends in the world.

'Shall we take that to mean that you and Ed were a little bit too busy to go shopping?' Connor asked.

'Errm . . . maybe,' was all the answer she made.

'Is that the sound of a taxi engine outside?' Annie ran over to look out of the window. 'Bloody hell!' she shrieked. 'It is! It's him! He must have landed early.'

As Annie flew out of the room and down the stairs, Dinah and Connor looked at each other and grinned. Connor winked and added, 'I don't think she's really very keen on him, is she?!'

They stayed in the kitchen with Billie and listened to the sound of Annie pulling open the heavy front door. The grand, newly painted one with the polished brass handle and letterbox, which was once again the entrance to the house.

They heard the excited greetings and Ed's gasps of admiration as he saw his transformed home for the first time.

'My God, this looks incredible!' he told her. 'Absolutely incredible.'

'So do you,' she told him, arms tight round his waist.

'Cashmere!' she noticed immediately. 'You bought

421

yourself cashmere? The sales assistants over there must be even better than me.'

'Yeah, they are,' he teased. 'But you're the one I wanted to rush back to.'

'Come and see the kitchen. Connor and Dinah and Billie are up there waiting to see you. They've baked a cake – and it's a plane on top,' she warned him quietly. 'Just so you know!'

Later that evening, Annie curled up with Ed on the sofa. There was still an endless amount to talk about but it was difficult trying to have a conversation while Owen and Lana seemed to be trampolining to something loud and blasting in their attic bedrooms upstairs.

'Shall I go and tell them to keep it down?' Annie asked.

'No, no,' Ed insisted. 'I like it! They've picked a good song,' he said approvingly. 'And anyway, it makes this old place feel alive again. Like a proper home. I hated it when upstairs was all shut off and empty.'

'Yeah, well, there's alive and then there's trashed,' Annie warned.

'You really do like this house, don't you?'

'I love it,' Ed admitted. 'It's going to be such a wrench to sell it, especially now that you've made it so beautiful.'

'And what if you didn't have to sell?' Annie wondered. 'What if someone bought a third of the house, so that you could buy your sister out?'

'Sell off the basement and maybe the garden as a separate flat, you mean?' Ed asked. 'Do you think that would raise enough?'

Annie shook her head and waved a rectangular piece of paper in front of Ed's face.

'I have a plan,' she told him mischievously, as he took the paper from her hand and saw that it was a cheque for a hefty six-figure sum.

'I've sold my flat – to the tenants,' she began. 'And with that money and a mortgage, that's how much I could offer you for a third of your house, which I think is generous,' she added, 'and then all four of us could live here . . . together.'

She realized her heart was beating very fast as she waited for the enormity of this offer and all its implications to settle on Ed.

She felt as if she was proposing to him – and in a way she was: 'What do you think?' she finally had to ask when he still hadn't made an answer.

'Oh . . . goodness!' he managed at last, with the hand-in-hair rummage which she knew meant he was nervous. 'Are you sure, Annie? I mean, are you really, really sure? What about the children? This might be too fast for them.'

Holding his hands tightly, she took the time to explain to him that she was making the offer because of the children. She'd talked it through with them at length. They were the ones who didn't want to leave, who loved their rooms, who felt at home here and, most importantly, who deeply approved of Ed. (Provided he acted like their teacher and absolutely nothing else at school . . . in fact if he could practically ignore Lana at school if possible . . .)

'They are very, very into the idea,' she assured him. 'Owen told me the other day that Roddy would have really liked you. Lana and I agree.'

There was a pause while Ed took this, their ultimate compliment, on board.

'So you all want to live here with me?' he asked and when Annie nodded at him, she saw that he was moved to tears.

'And definitely you?' he asked, just to make sure.

Annie nodded: 'Definitely, babes.'

'That's great . . .' he said, blinking hard. 'I really love your children. I mean . . . Owen is great, I find him really easy to understand and get along with . . . I'll need your help to get a much better handle on Lana.'

'Good grief, Ed!' Annie smiled at him. 'We all need help to get a handle on Lana. She's a fifteen-year-old, now. No-one understands her, not even Lana! And what about you?' she asked him. 'Is this what you want?'

Ed pulled her in close. Although he'd wanted to say something, he now found he was too choked to do anything other than nod.

'Excellent! That's all decided then,' Annie said gently against his ear. 'Now, apparently if I make you the children's legal guardian, they get a fifty per cent discount at St Vincent's.'

When he laughed at this, she told him, 'Hey, babes, I never, ever joke about discounts, you should know that about me,' in such a serious voice, he couldn't tell if she was joking or not.

His grip on her grew very tight as he asked her: 'So you're going to stay with me then?'

She nodded slowly in response to this, then told him gently, 'Babes, you are in need of serious modernization and upgrading, but I think you're an excellent investment with long-term potential.'

'I am so glad you spotted that,' Ed said as he squeezed his arms tightly around her.

'You're the real thing, a unique, one-off and no-one else had spotted you, so I got you for a snip,' she added.

'I'm very, very glad you got me,' he said.

'Yes, well . . . I've always, always had an eye for a bargain, babes.'

THE END

Acknowledgements

I am so grateful to my agent, Darley Anderson, and his star team for looking after me, working me hard and always giving great advice. Many thanks to you all for 'lurving' the idea of this book and helping the earliest chapters along.

Very, very special thanks and love to Diana Beaumont, who has been my editor for five books and is now leaving for adventures new. What would I have done without all your tender, loving perfectionism?! You've cared about every book almost as much as me.

I am ever thankful for the fabulous people at Transworld. I know perfectly well I would not have my enviable day (and sometimes all night) job without you. Especially, interim editor Kate Marshall: thank you, thank you! And new ed. Sarah Turner: hello!

Big kiss to the little people, Sam and Claudie, who regularly drag me from my desk and into the daylight. Also to the girlfriends, both old and new, who've made sure I got out of the house at least once in a while!

Now, to the eternal exasperation of my continentally chic mama, I'm hardly a fashion or grooming expert (let's just say I have my own unique style which involves many, many pairs of extra long jeans, woolly socks and bi-annual haircuts) so I am deeply indebted to her and to the fantastic advice books of the US style writer and personal shopper Brenda Kinsel.

Obviously I have been forced to read countless copies of *Vogue*, trawl the floors of Edinburgh's Harvey Nichols and spend endless hours of research on www.net-a-porter.com. A tough job, I know, but somebody had to do it.

My biggest thanks go to my husband, Thomas Quinn, who inspires, bribes or just plain nags me to keep going every day! I couldn't do without you.

THREE IN A BED
by Carmen Reid

Bella Browning is attractive, successful and **ambitious**. She works hard, plays hard and adores her journalist husband Don (even though she doesn't always behave that way). And yet deep down she knows there's something missing . . . a baby.

Don is terrified by the prospect, but Bella's a top Management Consultant turning around multi-million pound corporations . . . she can handle this! **Can't she?**

In between bouts of morning sickness, **raging hormones** and a few indiscretions at the office, Bella quickly discovers how very hard it is to be the perfect, working modern mother with the sex appeal of a Grecian goddess.

'Probably the best book of the year!'
B Magazine

'An entertaining and insightful tale of a 21st century working motherhood with a bittersweet edge'
Cosmopolitan

A fabulous read. A sexy read. A Carmen Reid.

9780552155816

CORGI BOOKS

DID THE EARTH MOVE?
by Carmen Reid

Meet Eve: 4 kids, 1 hectic job, 2 complicated exes and a lot on her mind.

Like, is sex with **the vet** better than no sex at all?

Is she too old to shop at **Topshop** or dye her hair pink?

Are **violets** the new geraniums?

What the hell is in the **fridge** for supper?

And, most important of all, has she let the **love of her life** get away too easily?

Did the Earth Move? is a sexy, thought-provoking and wildly entertaining novel from the bestselling author of *Three in a Bed*.

'Full of love, hope and a dash of sadness.
A great summer read'
Sunday Mirror

A fabulous read. A sexy read. A Carmen Reid.

9780552155809

CORGI BOOKS

HOW WAS IT FOR YOU?
by Carmen Reid

Five years of gruelling IVF still haven't brought **Pamela and Dave** the baby they long for. Their marriage is now so rocky, they need hiking boots and crampons just to negotiate dinner.

So they probably shouldn't be moving out of London for office-bound softie Dave to follow his dream of running an organic strawberry farm. Especially as out there in the countryside is **devastatingly handsome** farmer, Lachlan Murray.

While Dave takes up weeding and becomes obsessed with manure, Pamela wonders if she should escape to Lachlan's **4x4**. Her London friends think she's gone insane, but they don't know just how far Pamela is prepared to go for a baby.

'Carmen Reid's previous bestsellers were only a delicious taste of how brilliantly she can tell a story'
Daily Record

A fabulous read. A sexy read. A Carmen Reid.

9780552155830

CORGI BOOKS

UP ALL NIGHT
by Carmen Reid

**Welcome to a week in the life of Jo Randall – but this
is no *ordinary* week.**

There aren't enough **hours in the day** for Jo, overworked
newspaper reporter, mother of two, and newly
divorced after ten years of marriage.

She's close to cracking the biggest scoop of her career – a
cover-up with serious implications for her own family. If she
knocks on the right doors and asks the right questions (with a
little help from her **outrageously** smart friend, Bella
Browning) then a real exclusive could be hers . . .

But how will Jo meet her deadlines when her distractions
include two needy daughters, a Barbie birthday
party to organize, a pompous ex-husband, his new
'girlfriend' and the romantic intentions of a scruffy
but **delicious** young **super-chef**?

'Cleverer than the average and much
more entertaining too'
Heat

A fabulous read. A sexy read. A Carmen Reid.

9780552155823

CORGI BOOKS